Around the Way Girls 7

Around the Way Girls 7

Chunichi

Karen Williams

B.L.U.N.T.

www.urbanbooks.net

Urban Books, LLC
78 East Industry Court
Deer Park, NY 11729

ISBN 13: 978-1-60162-274-7
ISBN 10: 1-60162-274-0

First Printing July 2010
Printed in the United States of America

10 9 8 7 6 5 4 3 2 1

Distributed by Kensington Publishing Corp.
Submit Wholesale Orders to:
Kensington Publishing Corp.
C/O Penguin Group (USA) Inc.
Attention: Order Processing
405 Murray Hill Parkway
East Rutherford, NJ 07073-2316
Phone: 1-800-526-0275
Fax: 1-800-227-9604

My Best Frenemy

By Chunichi

"When a Woman's Fed Up"

Nina slid the extended clip into the Glock .45 with the intention of emptying all seventeen shots.

Click!

Click-click!

In one motion she cocked the gun, putting one in the head. Pausing only long enough to wipe the burning tears from her eyes, she then headed up the three flights of stairs to the master bedroom. Not making the slightest sound, she walked into the room to find a sleeping Mercedes and Mouse tightly cuddled in bed together. With gun in hand, Nina took a deep breath and pointed it directly at them, wondering what it was about Mercedes that had Mouse so into to her. All she had to offer was a long stripper history with a criminal background just as long, while Nina was a beautiful, intelligent, classy woman, a definite catch for any man.

Nina had to wonder why she even cared; after all, she was doing her thing on the side. But even with that relationship Mercedes seemed to be a small interference. Like with dandruff, no matter how many times Nina scratched, she just couldn't get rid of Mercedes.

She directed the gun at Mouse's head and prepared to fire.

Boom! Boom! Boom! Boom!

Before Nina even realized what she was doing, the loud,

deafening sounds of gun blasts rang out like cannons, sending her instantly into shock, causing everything to go blank.

When she finally came to, she found herself sitting in the corner of her bedroom, looking at Mouse's and Mercedes' lifeless bodies filled with bullet holes.

Nina almost had the urge to spit on Mercedes ass; she didn't give a fuck about that bitch. In fact the sight of her dead body almost put a smile on Nina's face.

Nina looked at her husband and found it very difficult to crack even the slightest smile. Her heart pounding, she couldn't believe she'd pulled the trigger. She was filled with fear as she thought about what would happen if she got caught. Shaking her head, still halfway in a trance, it was almost as if she had just realized what just happened.

Nina quickly snapped out of her spell as she heard the sound of two car doors slamming shut followed by the sound of tires screeching and peeling off on the wet concrete outside. With her gun still in her hand, Nina slowly cracked open the window's blinds and saw a black, tinted-out Range Rover and a BMW X5 speed off. It was obvious that the people behind those wheels were getting the fuck out of dodge.

"Girl Power"

Weeks Earlier-August 2008

What a morning! Nina thought to herself as she sat down on the couch to relax a minute from straightening up her house.

She grabbed the cordless phone to see what calls she'd missed. *Mariah, Rochelle, and my loving husband, Mouse.* Then she flipped through her cell phone. *Awww! My new boo, Jamal.* Nina smiled and decided to start with him. After all he was the one that consumed her thoughts on a daily basis.

Jamal was an NBA star that stole Nina's heart one night while she was working on a nursing assignment in Philadelphia. As a traveling registered nurse she often traveled to different states for assignments. That particular night she was graced with Jamal's presence in the emergency room. Like a magnet they were instantly attracted to each other. Her vagina went off like a radar at the sight of his perfect smile and flawless chocolate frame.

That night in the ER ended up in a night of exotic sex in a secluded section of the hospital's parking deck in the back of Nina's Porsche Cayenne S truck. Nina knew her pussy was like crack, and just as she'd expected, after only one night, Jamal was hooked. She had to admit though; he had it going on, and not only on the court.

Since that day Jamal was constantly on Nina's mind, and she was on his. They'd spoken on the phone every day since then but hadn't seen each other. He was busy playing basketball but had promised to come to Virginia the first opportunity he got. Like a kid waiting for Christmas, Nina counted down the days until she would see her boo.

Jamal answered Nina's call right away, "Hey, sexy."

"Hi, baby. You miss me like I miss you?" Nina said, not interested in holding her feelings back, having already been through that stage of their relationship.

"Of course, I do," Jamal answered sincerely.

"So when am I going to see you?" Nina asked, eager to see her man.

"Well, actually me and a few of the boys are planning to come through this weekend."

Nina noticed the lack of enthusiasm in Jamal's voice. "For real? So why didn't you tell me? And why aren't you excited?"

"Ma, it's something I gotta tell you."

"Oh my God. What is it, Jamal? You're bringing a bitch with you or something?"

"Not exactly."

"So what is it, baby?"

"A'ight. Let me just come with it." Jamal exhaled. "Well, you know a nigga had a life before you, right? I mean, you ain't the first chick I ever hollered at."

"Okay, I know that. We've already had this conversation, Jamal. I'm fuckin' married," Nina said, now practically yelling. "And I'm not the only female in your life. So what? As long as we respect each other, it's all good."

"I know, ma. But it's a little deeper than that. This chick lives in VA."

"What? So you were planning to come to see that bitch?"

"I was trying to see both of y'all, on the real though."

"Well, you're definitely seeing me. You'll just have to make time for that bitch after me."

Jamal was relieved Nina took things so well. "You got it, baby. That's why I fuck with you so hard. You know what you want, and as long as a nigga deliver, everybody's happy."

"Yeah, whatever. And while you at it, you better be delivering my matching Louis Vuitton heels and bag."

"You know I got you, baby girl. How could a nigga ever tell you no?"

"So tell me, Jamal, who is this chick?" Nina said, wondering if it was someone she knew. As a Virginia native, and her husband being the owner of a popular local strip club, she practically knew everyone who was anyone in the mix.

"This chick from Portsmouth name Mercedes."

"Mercedes?" Nina was hoping she'd heard incorrectly. There was no way he could be talking about the backstabbing bitch she knew in this area by that name.

"Yeah. You know her or something?" Jamal said nonchalantly.

"Of all fuckin' people!" Nina sighed and shook her head.

Mercedes was like her fucking archenemy. She was a stripper chick that Nina had problems with in the past, with Nina's husband. Nina was hoping her last encounter with Mercedes years ago was the end of her, but now she was back and the tables had turned. She was now getting at Mercedes' man.

"Yeah, I know her. And I know she's a nothing-ass stripper too."

"You can't knock her hustle, ma."

"You know what? This is just too much. I'll talk to you later." Nina hung up without even giving Jamal a chance to respond.

Her initial reaction was to pick the phone right back up and call her girl Rochelle, but she knew that would be the wrong choice. Mercedes was Rochelle's lover and wasn't only love-blind, but Nina had learned from previous experience that any conversation about Mercedes to her would be falling on deaf ears.

It was times like this that bothered Nina the most. The times when she needed to talk and didn't have anyone to talk to. She'd tried to be mature about the situation and not force Rochelle to choose, but that shit was getting harder and harder.

Nina and Rochelle had been friends since high school, and Mercedes was just some horny stripper that preyed on Rochelle at her most vulnerable time and stole her heart.

Nina couldn't understand how it was the least bit feasible for Rochelle to be one hundred percent loyal to their friendship when she knew Nina and Mercedes were virtually enemies. She and Mercedes had been through so much, from Mercedes constantly making threatening phone calls and sending hate e-mails, to her even going as far as vandalizing Nina's vehicle. Nina wasn't the fighting type, but when Mercedes spray-painted obscenities all over her brand-new Escalade EXT a few years back, it took all she had to keep from driving over to the projects out Portsmouth and beating her nothing, stripper ass.

Her girl Mariah helped to bring her to her senses, her words still fresh in Nina's head.

"Why would you go over there and jeopardize what you have? Hello? You're a registered nurse with no criminal record, making six figures. You have everything to lose. She's a project chick, stripper bitch with a book for a criminal record, fucked-up credit, no education, and no future. What does she have to lose? Besides, you're pretty, and the older you get, the harder it is clearing up scars. And you know scars are a definite result of fighting."

Mariah always had a way of connecting beauty and vanity into any conversation. With that conversation on her mind, Nina decided to give Mariah a call.

After several unsuccessful attempts to reach Mariah, Nina became even more frustrated. She looked at the time. It was already eleven o'clock in the morning, and her husband still had not made it home from the club the night before. She wasted no time calling him.

"What's up, *baaaby?*" Mouse sang into the phone like he had no worries in the world.

"Can you explain to me why it's almost noon and you're still out?" Nina snapped.

"Baby, I'm at the club. We're gambling. I'll be home soon."

"You spend more time at the club than you do at home. I think you better find out what's more important, before you lose one. I wouldn't be surprised if you're up there with one of those nasty stripper bitches!" Nina hung up the phone in Mouse's ear.

Her intuition was right once before. Why couldn't it be right this time too? Nina thought about what had transpired between Mouse and Mercedes years before. She had befriended Mercedes during her time of need, got her a job at Mouse's club, and even opened her doors and allowed that trick to stay in her home, only to come in the club late one night and find Mercedes' mouth full with Mouse's dick. Well, the tip that is, because Mouse was packing, and a bitch needed a big-ass mouth to take that entire dick.

Ever since that encounter with Mercedes, Nina had never fully trusted Mouse. Yes, she did forgive him, but one thing for sure was, she never did forget. She vowed that she wouldn't be one of those women who worried themselves to death every time their man left their sight, so she gave Mouse his freedom and a rope. Rope with just enough room for him to hang himself. Nina wasn't stupid. She knew a man was going to do what a man wanted to do, regardless, and there was nothing a woman could do to stop him.

After hanging up the phone and getting lost in her thoughts, she grabbed her jacket and rushed to meet her girls at Logan's Roadhouse to have their weekly girls' dinner.

The second Nina walked through the door, she spotted Rochelle, Mariah, and some mystery woman.

"Hey, girls." She greeted as she approached the table.

Rochelle introduced the mysterious woman as soon as Nina was up on them. She knew Nina didn't like sharing her space with people she didn't know. "Nina, this is Peaches."

"Hi."

Nina rolled her eyes as she positioned herself to take a seat at the table. She and Mariah looked at each other from the corner of their eyes then shot Rochelle a disapproving look.

Rochelle quickly got the picture and wrapped things up with her little friend. "All right, girl, well, I'll see you at the club later."

The second the girl left the table, Nina looked at Rochelle. "Oh my God. Can we please go out one time without having to be introduced to one of your stripper buddies?"

"Yeah! And no new friends, damn it! How many times do I have to say this?" Mariah chimed in. "Don't you know that our circle consist of us three only?"

"Guys, I do work as a bartender at a strip club, so I'm gonna know lots of strippers. Besides, she doesn't count. She's not a friend—That's potential pussy. We flirt every night at the club. It's only a matter of time before she's yamming on my meow mix." Rochelle laughed.

"Rochelle, please." Mariah waved her hand, disgusted by the thought.

Just like Rochelle, Mariah had been friends with Nina since high school. She had a few self-esteem issues that caused her to do some strange things at times, especially when it came to men. Always portraying who she would like to be instead of who she truly was, she was always attempting to be politically correct. Although she pretended to be perfect, deep inside, she didn't truly love herself. She needed the validation of a man to feel good about herself, and it often showed.

"Whatever, Mariah. You kill me." Rochelle knew Mariah was on that fronting shit once again. "You're the biggest freak out of all of us, with your horny ass."

"Well, at least I have standards."

"Whatever," Rochelle said, trying to dismiss the conversation, "I have standards too."

"Yeah, right," Nina said, thinking of Mercedes. "That's not the way I see it, because to me, it looks like all you want is those nothing-ass chicks."

"Dang! I feel a little aggression here. Do you really have to go there? I mean, I know you hate Mercedes and all, but do you have to constantly throw it up in my face? I don't let her sit around and talk about your ass."

"That's because you and her know the deal. Plus, this ain't really about her," Nina lied. "I just wish you would raise your standard, that's all."

"Have you talked to her lately?"

"Nope, not since the argument I told you about. She's out the door. I'm moving on to bigger and better things now."

"Excuse me?" Nina realized she'd had been left out of the loop.

"I'm no longer dealing with Mercedes, but I didn't tell you because I know you'd rather not discuss her." Rochelle nonchalantly rose out of her seat.

"Yeah, yeah, yeah. You're not going anywhere." Nina placed her hand on Rochelle's arm to keep her from leaving the table. She didn't believe a word coming out of Rochelle's mouth and wanted more information.

Nina had a right to doubt Rochelle because she'd said she was done with Mercedes a number of times, and after each declaration, she'd just end up right back with her. In Nina's opinion, Rochelle just was too pussy-whipped and too weak to walk away. Whenever Nina voiced this to Rochelle, she couldn't say a word, because deep down, she knew Nina was telling the truth. She would swing the door wide open as soon as Mercedes' sorry ass came knocking.

On the real, Rochelle probably would go searching for her

before she even had the chance to come knocking. Her love life had always been a rocky road, and she yearned for the companionship of a lover so bad, she virtually opened the doors to any stranger willing to give her that fulfillment.

"May I take your drink orders?" the waitress said, interrupting the ladies' conversation right in the nick of time, because an argument was definitely brewing.

The girls paused their conversation long enough to place their drink and dinner orders.

Mariah then excused herself to the restroom.

"Aaaaaaahhhhhh shit!" Mariah yelled beneath her breath as the urine ran through her insides and out her vagina, burning a path on its way. She felt like was pissing hot coffee. *Please, don't let this be happening,* she thought as her heart raced and her breathing pattern increased.

She could feel an itchy, tingling sensation beneath her armpits, indicating a sure sign of sweat. Was she having an anxiety attack? *My pussy is on fire! Oh my goodness, not again!*

Mariah took caution wiping herself clean. She noticed a small amount of blood on the tissue. She was sure she had a urinary tract infection, which, in her case, was a definite sign of pregnancy.

As Mariah stood looking at herself in the mirror, she knew exactly what to expect. This feeling was way too familiar. With pregnancy occurring at least twice a year, she had to wonder if she was the queen of fertility. But she already knew her next move—straight to the abortion clinic. Unlike most women, whose dilemma would be whether or not to keep the baby, her dilemma was determining which man she would tell of the mishap.

From which would I get the most attention? Who would beg me to have the baby? Who would be upset? Mariah washed her hands then touched up her hair. Her worst fear was her girls finding out, especially Nina.

She headed back to the table with a worried look on her face. Not even her strongest front game was able to hide her anxiety.

"Is everything okay?" Rochelle asked when Mariah returned.

"I think I'm getting a urinary tract infection."

"Oh Lord. You know what that means," Nina said.

Mariah had been pregnant so many times, her friends knew all the signs and could almost predict with certainty when she was pregnant.

"Nina, please. I don't feel like hearing it right now."

"I'm just saying, you always have something going on. You've had everything in the book, from a bacterial infection to a yeast infection to a UTI, STD, PID, PCOS, HBO, CNN, ESPN"—Nina began to laugh so hard, she couldn't finish her sentence.

Feeling the need to protect her perfect image, Mariah quickly interjected, "I'll have you know, when I went to the gynecologist for my annual exam, he said that my vagina was the cleanest vagina he has ever seen. Fuck you very much!"

"Well, you know what that means?" Nina asked.

"You need to get another gynecologist," Rochelle chimed in.

"No, I'm serious. I thought he was joking, so I asked if he was serious, and he said yes. It made me feel really good." Mariah gave a satisfied smiled as though she was giving herself a silent pat on the back.

"Well," Nina said, "when it's vacuumed out every other month, what would you expect?"

Nina and Rochelle laughed until tears came to their eyes.

Mariah gave them a disapproving look. "You know what? Y'all are some insensitive bitches!" She started to gather her things and leave but realized she had no one to blame but herself.

Mariah had had at least twenty abortions in the past ten years.

It wasn't a laughing matter, because she was using abortions as birth control. Nina and Rochelle had been dealing with it for so long, they'd learned to make light of the situation.

"Umph. Who is that?" Rochelle said, interrupting their laugh session. "He is sexy."

"Where?" Nina said.

They all followed Rochelle's eyes.

"Oh, that's um, what's his name, from out Tidewater Park." Nina snapped her finger a few times as she wracked her brain, trying to remember the guy's name.

"Li'l Man. He's one of Jigga's boys." Mariah sipped her White Zinfandel.

"Yeah, that's his name!"

"Oh, that's Li'l Man? I heard of him. I didn't know he was one of Jigga's boys. All them niggas got money. But I thought he was supposed to be locked up. He must have just got out." Rochelle always knew the latest with all the dopeboys on the streets.

"Yeah, I know. What is he doing with Young Boy? Wasn't he fuckin' Li'l Man's baby momma while he was in jail?" Nina said, adding to the gossip.

"Baby momma? Who is his baby momma?" Mariah asked.

"Some young chick from the park name Tee-Tee," Nina said. "And from what I know about her, she don't play."

"Well, it sounds like he has too much drama for me. I'm definitely not trying to have any problems with a project chick." Mariah stated making it very clear in case of an emergency she had nobody's back.

"Suit yourself," Rochelle said. "I'm from the streets, so the bitch don't scare me. I'll take his ass. Y'all think he still got some money?"

"Well, I know he had it before he got locked up. He used to keep that chick Stacey, which he called his sister, laced. And he comes up to the club all the time gambling with Mouse. I'm surprised you've never seen him."

"Well, I'm about to get to know him." Rochelle looked over to the bar and gave Li'l Man the eye.

As they ate their food, Rochelle continuously sent flirtatious gestures over to Li'l Man, from seductively licking the cherries from her drink to sucking the meat off her chicken bones as though she was sucking the last drop of come out of the head of a penis.

Tired of the performance, Nina said, "Damn, girl! If he doesn't come over here after all that, then he's just not interested. And not only that—"

Before Nina could finish her statement, Li'l Man came walking over. "What's up, ladies?" he said as he stood at their table.

Nina and Mariah both had to admit, he was indeed fine.

"Heeeey!" They all sang, giddy-headed.

"You got my attention. So what's good, ma?" he said to Rochelle.

Rochelle gave him her most seductive look. "That's what I'm trying to find out."

"Me and my man are just finishing up a few drinks. I got a little running around to do. When I'm done, can I call you?" He pulled an iPhone out of his pocket.

Mariah noticed he had the same phone as she. *iPhone? That's an odd phone for a dopeboy.*

"A'ight," Rochelle answered with a huge grin, and quickly began rummaging through her red Marc Jacobs bag that Nina had given her for her cell phone for her birthday.

As Rochelle retrieved her phone so they could exchange numbers, Mariah stood up and began to brush crumbs off her clothes. Her way of showing off her newly purchased plump Brazilian booty and breastlift while giving Li'l Man a whiff of her Dolce & Gabbana Sicily perfume.

Knowing her friend all too well, Nina just shook her head at Mariah's desperate attempt for attention.

"Well, you ladies have a good night," Li'l Man said, after saving Rochelle's number.

Before the girls could respond, they noticed a huge commotion at the front of the restaurant. They all tried to see who it was and noticed some chick wave her hands in the air, and push the waitress out the way. Then she and two other girls with her started making their way toward them.

The second she was up on them, Li'l Man said, "Tee-Tee, I ain't got time for your shit."

"Shut the fuck up!" she hissed.

Nina looked over at Mariah and Rochelle. *I know this bitch better not say a word to me.*

Rochelle looked like she was waiting for Tee-Tee to say the wrong word or make the wrong move.

"How the fuck did you even know I was here? You and your stupid-ass crew following me now? You need to be more worried about being a mother and taking care of my son." Li'l Man attempted to walk away.

"So you fuckin' other bitches now?" Tee-Tee grabbed Li'l Man's arm, rolling her eyes at the girls.

"Bitch, who the fuck are you referring to as a bitch?" Rochelle responded without delay.

Tee-Tee diverted her attention back to Li'l Man. "We are going to be a family. What part of that don't you get?" She turned toward Rochelle. "Look, I don't know who you are and don't care to know," she yelled, her long, colorful, acrylic fingernail in Rochelle's face, "but this here is my man."

Rochelle aimed a punch at Tee-Tee's face, barely grazing her as Nina and Mariah held her back. She then tried to take off her five-inch stiletto heel to beat Tee-Tee's head in.

Nina reached behind her for her purse, sure not to take her eyes off the scene, and felt for the Mace bottle. She watched Tee-Tee's friends closely to see what plans they had.

"Let it go," Mariah begged at least eight or nine times in Rochelle's ear.

By this time, everyone was looking at the ladies, trying to figure out what all the commotion was about.

Tee-Tee gathered her composure and headed out the restaurant with her friends. "This ain't over, Li'l Man," she announced while leaving.

Once she was out the door, Li'l Man turned around and said, "Ladies, sorry about all of this. Rochelle, can I still call you?"

"Yeah."

Mariah shook her head. *What woman would want a man after going through so much drama during the initial meeting?*

When Li'l Man walked away, they all stood there and looked at one another.

Rochelle flopped down in her chair. "Order me a drink!" she yelled. "Matter of fact, order us all one," she yelled out again. "Whew! Now that that's over, I can finish my meal."

"You know you're a trip, right?" Nina said.

"No, I just want to eat. Hell, this dinner costs enough. One of y'all rich bitches got my check?"

"Rocky Marriage"

Later that night when Nina arrived home, she was a little relieved to see Mouse's Mercedes Benz CLS550 sitting in the garage. *At least he's not still at the strip club*, she thought as she pulled in beside his car.

As she walked through the door, she yelled out, "Mouse!" There was no response.

"Hellooooo! Mouse!"

Still there was no answer. Nina started walking in the direction of their bedroom. As she walked through the door, she heard the shower running. She stood outside the bathroom door, deciding whether she should walk up and snatch the door open or just leave him be.

She made her decision when she saw his jeans lying on the floor with some cash sticking out each of the pockets. She bent over and picked up the pants, making sure she grabbed the money first.

Nina laid the pants across the bed and proceeded to count. "Two, four, six . . ." She started with the smallest bills, twenties, then continued with the hundreds. She counted close to ten thousand dollars.

Nina found it odd that Mouse would have so much money on him. Mouse was sure to deposit the money he made from the club in the night deposit drop box each night, and never carried so much money in his pockets. She wondered just what the hell went wrong that he didn't make the drop this particular night.

She placed the money on the dresser and sat on the bed. She turned on the television and waited for him to get out the shower. She wanted to know what the hell was going on, and she was soon going to find out, because she heard the water turn off in the shower.

She glanced toward the bathroom door and happened to notice a business card on the floor where the pants was. Just as she stood up to get it, the bathroom door opened.

As soon as Mouse stepped through the door, Nina confronted him, her hands on her hips. "Mouse!" she said, looking him directly in the face.

Startled, Mouse jumped. "Oh shit! You scared the hell out of me, woman."

Nina didn't say a word. She just looked him up and down.

"Why are you looking at me like that?" He gently brushed past her and went to pick up his pants.

"They're on the bed." She moved toward the business card on the floor and stood on it. She watched Mouse as he searched his jeans pockets and then she pointed toward the bundle of money that sat on the nightstand. "Is that what you are looking for?"

"Yeah. And why is it on the dresser?"

"No, honey. I'm asking the questions. Why do you have that money on you? Did you not make the deposit when you left the club this morning?"

"I made the drop, Nina." Mouse coolly headed toward the dresser to gather his money.

Nina was convinced she'd caught Mouse in a lie. "So where the fuck is that money from? And let me see the deposit receipt."

"There is no deposit receipt. I put the money in the night deposit box, genius."

"So why do you have the fuckin' money, Mouse?"

"You know you can ruin a wet dream, right?" Mouse shook

his head. "I was planning to get you something nice. I came across a page you ripped out the *Elle* magazine that had a boot and bag set you circled on the page. I was going to surprise you with it."

For a second a smile almost came across Nina's face. But then she snapped back to reality. Nina wasn't some young-ass girl who fell for any and everything. She didn't believe a word Mouse was saying. He hated shopping, and he'd never done anything like that before. Nina knew that was straight bullshit Mouse was selling, and she wasn't buying. She watched him as he dried off and put on his boxer briefs.

When Mouse opened the closet and pulled out a pair of jeans, she said, "Where do you think you're going?"

"Out," Mouse said as he put his jeans on.

"What the fuck you mean, out? You just got in."

"My job is away from home. I have to leave the house to make money."

"Yeah, but you don't have to be consumed by your job. It's not like you're a fuckin' doctor, Mouse. Come on."

"Look, Nina, I'm taking care of business. Most women would be happy to have a man that does that."

"What? You think you got all the shit you have from me sitting on my ass? Did you forget I am the reason you have that club?"

"Of course, not. No matter how hard I try to forget, you always seem to remind me. It's funny how you can always remember what you've done for me. Do you have an itemized list hidden someplace?" Mouse gave a sarcastic laugh as he put his shirt on.

"I don't need a list. It's pretty simple. I do every fuckin' thing. What have you ever done for me?"

Mouse laughed. "Are you serious?"

"Dead fuckin' serious." Nina stepped in front of Mouse with her arms folded.

"Okay, Nina, I'll entertain you for a moment and play your little game. For starters, that fuckin' Porsche truck in the garage, that ridiculously large diamond on your hand, and this fuckin' oversized-ass house are just a few things I've done, you ungrateful-ass female!" He pushed Nina aside then stormed out the room, slamming the door behind him.

Nina didn't bother following him. Now that he was gone, she could finally take a look at the business card she'd been standing on. The card read, "Ramona LeShay Real Estate," and had a picture of a nice-looking black woman with a cell and office number. She decided to give Miss Ramona a call on her cell.

"Hey, hon," a female voice said after only a single ring. "So what did you decide?"

"Hello?" Nina said, taken by surprise.

"I'm sorry. Who am I speaking with?"

"Well, it's not your hon, for sure, but it is his wife—"

Click!

The woman hung up.

Nina was furious. She didn't know what to do next. She had dealt with Mouse's cheating one time and refused to accept it a second time. One part of her wanted to call the woman back. Another part of her wanted to call Mouse. But where would that get her? *All he would do is tell another lie.* She went against her judgment and called him anyway.

"Money Problems"

Mouse was pissed off; he was getting tired of Nina's shit. True, she'd put the club in her name and even given him the money for closing costs and down payment, but he'd given that back to her threefold by now.

He looked down at his constantly ringing phone. *Nina. I ain't trying to hear shit she got to say.* He sent her to voice mail. He had some things he needed to take care of and talking to Nina would only distract him. That was the last thing he needed when he was meeting with Jigga. He needed to be on guard at all times. Hell, his life depended on him being on guard.

Again the phone rang. Mouse looked at it and thought maybe it was best to speak with her and get it over with. He looked out the window to see if Jigga or his boys were nearby. They weren't, so he answered.

"What up?"

"What up?' You would really walk out of this house and have me call you over and over and then answer the phone, 'What up?' like nothing happened?"

"Listen, Nina, I don't have time for this."

"You don't have time?"

"Let's talk when I get home."

"Let's talk when you get home?"

Mouse hated when Nina repeated after him. "Listen, there's something I need to do. I'll call you back." He hung up before she could say another word.

Mouse knew he was going to have to come clean with Nina about his issue. It was an issue even he wasn't ready to admit. He kept asking himself how he got in this predicament. How the hell did he end up owing someone money over gambling?

He didn't mean for it to get this out of control. On the real, he never was even into gambling. He started having little card tournaments at the club here and there per the request of his boys. From there he started to participate in a game or two. Then he gradually went from card tournaments to having nightly gambling sessions ranging from dice, to blackjack, to poker. Before he knew it, the number of participants was getting larger, and Mouse ended up with a small casino in his club after hours, with him being the biggest player. After a while the small change he was making at the club wasn't enough to satisfy his hunger for winning, so he started hooking up with a local bookie. Now that shit was a whole new ballgame. These cats gambled big, and there were no breaks when it came to them collecting their money. Before he could blink, Mouse was waist-deep in gambling debt.

So consumed in his thoughts, Mouse didn't hear the knock on the window of his car. He looked out and saw Jigga standing a couple of inches from the driver's side window. Not being the type to fear another man, he didn't even flinch at the sight of Jigga. Even though deep inside he knew that this was one man he should fear because Jigga didn't think twice when it came down to hurting someone, especially when his money was involved. Mouse had witnessed Jigga break a nigga's arm. And to think cats always thought that was some old television mobster bullshit.

Mouse rolled his window down. There was no way he was getting out the car. If that shit made him look like a punk, so be it.

"Big Mouse! What up, baby?"

Jigga and Mouse shook hands.

"Ain't shit, man. I got a little something for ya. You know a nigga trying to straighten you."

"A little something?" Jigga leaned his head in the window of the car. "Nigga, you owe me a whole lot, so what the fuck is a little?"

Mouse took a deep swallow before speaking. "Just hold this ten grand and I got you on the rest. I'm working on something as we speak."

"Time is ticking, nigga, time is ticking." Jigga grabbed the Burger King bag that Mouse had filled with money. "Don't let the clock catch you," he said as he stepped away from the car.

Mouse watched as Jigga walked to his car. After he pulled off, Mouse put his head on the steering wheel. He needed a plan. He needed to come up with some way to pay these people, and he needed to do it fast. He looked at his cell phone and noticed that Nina had called again. He'd deal with her when he arrived home, which wouldn't be anytime soon. Hell, he was already in deep shit; he might as well make the most of his time out. He pulled out his phone and dialed his boy Maurice.

"Yo'!" Maurice answered.

Mouse could hear the music in the background and spoke loudly in attempt to overcome the blaring sound. "I'm about to come check you, nigga."

"Cool. I got a few bitches over here. Come join the party."

Maurice's life was a party. As the little brother of a NFL star, bitches, drugs, cars, and money was all that dude knew.

Mouse pulled up to Maurice's house and struggled to find a parking spot amongst the many cars on the street. He was met by Maurice at the door.

"Big Mouse!"

They gave each other five.

A little on edge about his troubles, Mouse wasn't really feeling the whole party scene. He figured the best thing to do was to get a drink to take the edge off and relax a little. His plan was to stay just long enough to figure out what he was going to say to Nina when he finally arrived home. He made his way to the kitchen.

As he made his drink, Mariah walked up on him wearing a deep V-neck shirt that barely covered her double D breasts. "Hey, Mouse," she said, approaching him with what seemed like breasts only.

Although every manly part of Mouse wanted to just pop one of her voluptuous breasts out and suckle it like a baby, the sensible part of him made him raise his head and look her in the face. "What up, Mariah?" He took a swig of his Hennessy straight.

Mariah stood behind Mouse and began to massage his shoulders, pressing her breasts against his back. "Why you look so stressed?"

"Yo', Mariah!" Maurice's call interrupted the moment.

The beast in Mouse wanted her to continue, but he knew better and was a little relieved that it ended.

"Yes, baby?" Mariah said in her most innocent tone.

Baby? Mouse was taken by her response. *What the hell was that about? Mariah calling Maurice baby like he's her man and shit.* Mouse watched as Maurice whispered something in Mariah's ear then Mariah exited the room.

Mouse asked Maurice, "Dat's you?"

"You know me. She something for the minute. Pussy come, pussy go." Maurice made himself a drink.

"A'ight, man. Do your thing. Just watch that broad, dude." Mouse tried to give his friend a small warning the best way he knew how without straight out telling him Mariah was just all over him.

"So what's up, man? You sounded a little stressed earlier."

"I wanted to talk to you about some things, but now isn't

the time. We're gonna have to talk on some one-on-one shit. It's too busy tonight."

"A'ight. So tomorrow it is then." Maurice then went back to join the party.

Mouse stayed in the kitchen a moment as he finished up his drink then decided to cut.

Maurice saw him walking to the door and said, "Damn, man! What the fuck? You were just doing a quick drop-in?"

"I got shit to deal with at home."

Maurice shook his head like he understood.

"Later."

Mouse heard a woman's voice and felt a smack on his ass once he got closer to door. He looked back to find a Mariah smiling seductively. Without saying a word, he just shook his head and kept it moving. *That bitch is something else*, he thought as he hopped in his car and peeled off.

"Life of the Party"

Still at the party Mariah was on the prowl. Sure, she had just taken on Maurice as her current boy toy, but his brother Tyree was who she really wanted. The way she saw it, why settle for the milk when you could own the cow? And that hunk of lean meat was exactly what she was out to get. Tyree was the one with all the money; plus, his body was irresistible. Mariah had never seen a man's body as flawless as his.

So when she saw a drunken Tyree head up the stairs alone, she took that as the perfect opportunity and followed right behind him. She watched him walk into a bedroom, and a few moments later helped herself in. When she walked in, Tyree lay motionless across the bed. He was so drunk, he didn't even notice Mariah standing over him.

"Tyree," she called out softly.

He responded with a groan.

"Let me help you out of these clothes and get you into your pajamas, baby." She gently rolled Tyree on his back then straddled him.

He lay there without even opening his eyes as Mariah pulled his shirt over his head. Once she'd gotten the shirt off, she moved toward his pants. Within moments his pants were off, and Mariah went right to work, stroking his penis to give it the rise she needed to give him the blowjob of a lifetime.

She grabbed his dick and started to lick the tip of the head gently, just enough to get it nice and moist. Then she slowly moved her way down the shaft, licking it up and down a couple of times then continuing to his balls.

"Aaahhh shhittt," Tyree moaned as a tingling sensation filled his body as Mariah engulfed his balls in her warm mouth one at a time.

By this time Tyree's dick was so hard, it felt as though it was gonna explode. Just when he began to feel like he couldn't take any more, Mariah gripped his dick and began deep-throating it.

A sobering Tyree spread his legs, grabbed a handful of Mariah's hair, and pushed her face deep in his lap as he absorbed each second of this goodness. One thing for sure, even though he was drunk as a skunk, there was no denying that he was receiving a hell of a blowjob.

"You like that?" Mariah whispered between sucks.

"Suck that shit, bitch." Tyree grabbed Mariah's hair even tighter, forcing her head down farther onto his rock-hard dick. As he began to reach his peak, he shouted, "Ah shit! Suck that shit, girl!"

Thank God I have my fusion in and not one of my wigs. He would have straight pulled my wig off, Mariah thought as Tyree pulled her weave tight.

Before she knew it, he was sitting up and forcing her head between his legs as he filled her mouth with warm come. She gagged slightly as the last few squirts rushed out the tip of his dick head and hit the back of her throat. Like a champ Mariah swallowed and licked his dick clean like she was eating her favorite ice cream. She felt good. She'd brought a drunk man sober just by oral sex alone.

Now a bit sobered up, Tyree didn't say a word as he looked at her.

Mariah looked up to see a strange look on his face. He looked like he was about to be sick. She didn't know if he was gonna pass out from being drunk, or if the realization that his little brother's girlfriend had just sucked the hell out of his dick was too much to bear.

Blaaauuuggghhh!

Out of nowhere vomit was pouring from his mouth and onto her.

"What the fuck!" Mariah jumped up and looked around, hoping there was a bathroom connected to the bedroom.

There was, and she couldn't get in there fast enough. She turned the water on in the shower and hopped right in, fully clothed. The smell and sight of the vomit made her gag. She peeled her clothes off while in the shower and washed up quickly.

Luckily there were fresh towels and a terry cloth robe in the bathroom. Mariah threw on the robe and wrapped her wet clothes in a bath towel. She had to find a way to get out of there without anyone noticing. Tyree was her only hope.

"Tyree," she shoved him in the arm.

"Yo'," he forced out.

"You got to get me out of here without anyone noticing. Get up, please."

"This way." Tyree struggled to get up.

Mariah assisted him to his feet, and he led her to another room at the end of the hall that had a back staircase that led directly to the garage. From there she snuck out the side door of the garage and hopped in her car unnoticed.

"Chickfight"

Rochelle was lying in the bed when her phone rang. She'd just had her pussy eaten something fierce and was relaxing in the afterglow.

"Don't answer it," Peaches told her.

Rochelle picked up her cell phone to see Li'l Man's name flashed across the screen. She figured she could pass on that call since she'd just talked to him earlier in the day. No sooner did she press the ignore button than the phone began to ring again.

"Don't answer it," Peaches repeated.

Assuming it was Li'l Man calling back, Rochelle didn't even look at the phone. She looked at Peaches and smiled. "If I don't, are you gonna make me feel like you did earlier?"

"I'll do you after you do me."

Rochelle almost rolled her eyes but thought better of it. She wasn't in the mood to service anyone. She wanted to be serviced and thought Peaches understood that when she called earlier begging to come over.

"I'm about to go to bed," Rochelle told Peaches earlier when she'd called asking, can they get together.

"Well, how about I come get in the bed with you?"

Rochelle almost turned her down, but she didn't feel like being by herself anyway and figured a little company wouldn't hurt. "You can come over, but know before you get here, I'm tired."

"So does that mean we can't get down?"

"You can do whatever you want, but me, well, I'm tired, like I said."

Rochelle was about to let her know that wasn't happening, but the phone rang again. This time Rochelle grabbed her cell off the dresser and answered, "Hey, baby," assuming it was Li'l Man.

"Hey, beautiful," the female voice said, surprising Rochelle.

Rochelle began to panic. She wished she could just cross her arms, blink her eyes, and nod her head like Jeannie and make Peaches go away. Mercedes was the closest thing to love she had felt since her ex-boyfriend had left her, and there was no way she was gonna lose her. Mercedes gave her the attention, affection, constant support, and even financial support she'd always wanted in a relationship.

Minutes passed as Rochelle sat and chatted with Mercedes. They hadn't talked in days, and Rochelle was excited to finally hear her voice. There was no way she was gonna rush Mercedes off the phone and arouse a sense of suspicion and possibly start another argument.

Peaches cleared her throat. "*Ahem!*"

Rochelle shot her an evil eye. If looks could kill, she would have certainly been charged with first-degree murder.

"Who's that?" Mercedes asked right away, hearing Peaches in the background.

"Nobody," Rochelle told her.

Peaches wasn't stupid. She knew when Rochelle said, "Nobody," that meant whoever she was on the phone with had asked who was there. So she sat straight up and yelled, "It's Peaches!"

Mercedes' loud voice blared through the phone like she was on speaker. "Did she say *Peaches*? That skank bitch from the club?"

"Yeah, that's me—that skank bitch from the club, eating your bitch's pussy." Peaches yelled from the background in response to Mercedes' statement.

Rochelle hung up the phone. She regretted it immediately because, knowing Mercedes, she was going to either call back or, even worse, come over.

She instantly dug into Peaches' ass. "What the fuck was that?"

"What the fuck you mean? I come over here and sent you to the moon then you hop on the phone with some bitch and ignore the fuck out of me for ten minutes and think it's all good? You got me fucked up."

"You know what? I think it's time for you to leave." Rochelle began to gather Peaches' things.

Not only did Rochelle want her out because she had crossed the line, but she was sure Mercedes was on her way over. That was just her style. Mercedes loved confrontation.

Peaches snatched her things out of Rochelle's hands and headed out the bedroom. As Peaches walked toward the door, she turned and faced Rochelle. "I'm out! And, please, don't call my ass no more."

"You called me!" Rochelle reminded her as she opened the door.

Standing there with her hand raised as though she was about to knock was Nina. "Hey, girl. Who's that? We need to talk," Nina said all at once as she made her way through the door.

"What the fuck? Is my house Grand Central Station? Fuckin' revolving doors, one in one out?"

"So, is this another one of your bitches?" Peaches asked.

Nina wasn't in the mood. "You know what, bitch? This is not the time. The way I feel, I may just end up whipping your ass in here today."

Rochelle knew Nina was serious and pulled her in, pushed Peaches out, and slammed the door.

"*Eeewww!* What a funky attitude! What's your problem?" Nina asked as she made her way to the kitchen to pour herself a glass of wine.

Rochelle rushed to get Nina to talk before Mercedes arrived. "No time to talk about me. What's so important that you felt the need to pop up?"

"It's Mouse. I think he's cheating again."

"What's new? Kick him out and get on with your life. He had his one chance already." Rochelle had never liked Mouse and always felt like he couldn't be trusted.

"Rochelle! Could you be a little more compassionate, please? That is my husband you're talking about."

"You're right. Maybe you should have chosen to speak to Mariah about this. You know I'm a woman scorned. Maybe you should go home to him and talk it out." Rochelle was trying hard to end the conversation and get Nina out the house.

"Now I feel like you're just saying what you think I want to hear. And, no, I will not talk to Mariah. She has way too many issues. Anyway, Mouse is spending more and more time away from home, and I found some chick's business card in his pocket. I called her from the house phone and she answered, 'Hey, hon.' She knew our fuckin' house number, Rochelle!"

Rochelle couldn't believe Nina was tearing up. She always acted like she was the baddest bitch. Now any thoughts she had about kicking her out were out the window. She had to comfort her friend.

She hugged her as she spoke, "Nina, please don't cry. Men will be men. You for one should know that. It's just a matter of what we as women will accept and will not. So you decide, is this something you can deal with?"

Mercedes walked through the front door and toward the kitchen expecting to see Peaches. "You should learn to lock your doors if you're gonna be doing shit you don't want people to know about." As she walked into the kitchen, she noticed Nina and Rochelle hugging. "Nina? What the fuck is really going on?"

"No! It's not what you think?" Rochelle immediately took her arms from around Nina and tried to explain.

"Oh, so this is your Peaches? I knew that bitch wanted you all the time. Y'all all hugged up and shit." Mercedes was convinced it was Nina at the house the entire time, that there was no Peaches.

"You are so fuckin' ignorant," Nina said, no longer able to hold her tongue. "This is my fuckin' friend and nothing more. But you would know nothing about being a friend." She thought back to Mercedes' stabbing her in the back.

"I don't know about being a good friend, but you obviously don't know about being a good wife because, if you did, your husband would have never come at me."

Nina rushed Mercedes and threw a hard blow.

Rochelle intercepted it. "Nina, no!"

Brought to her senses by her friend's yell, Nina stepped back. "He didn't come at you, you trifling bitch! You threw yourself at him, like you do every man and woman, as a matter of fact. You're nothing. You have nothing you can offer anyone other than sex. You're not even worth my conversation." Nina directed her attention toward Rochelle. "I'm out, girl. I'll call you later."

"Don't bother!" Mercedes spat. "She doesn't need a hating bitch like you around her. I'm all the friend she needs."

"You know what? I think it's time I spoke my mind. One, the only reason Rochelle is with you is because she yearns the comfort of companionship so bad that she will accept anything. She stayed in an abusive relationship for five years, and the only reason it ended is because the guy moved out of state and she lost complete contact with him. You just happen to walk in at her most vulnerable time. So what did she do? Transfer those feelings she had for her ex to you.

"Two, I have everything you, along with several other women, could only dream of having, so I doubt the day would ever come when I will have to hate on anyone." Feeling liberated, Nina swallowed the last sip of her wine from the glass and politely let herself out the front door.

"You call that bitch your friend? I don't know about you, but I don't want no friend that would call me out and put me on blast like that, especially in front of other people. I mean, basically, she was calling you weak and needy."

"Mercedes, just leave it alone," Rochelle said, overwhelmed by the entire situation. "This is just too much. I have a headache."

"The bitch thinks she better than you, Rochelle. Can't you see it? She said it herself—She has everything, everyone wants what she has, so she has no reason to hate."

Rochelle yelled, "Augh! Mercedes, please!" and walked out of the kitchen, her hands over her hips.

"Money Madness"

Mouse was surprised yet relieved when he arrived to an empty garage. He was expecting to meet a fiery Nina at the door. He used this to his advantage. He figured if he moved fast enough he could rush and get dressed for the club and get out the house before she arrived. He had a long day, and really wasn't in the mood for an argument with her.

As he got his clothes out of the closet, he noticed the constant buzzing sound of a cell phone. He turned around to see Nina's Blackberry Storm sitting on the dresser. She had three missed calls.

Mouse wondered who'd been calling so many times, so he scrolled through the numbers. *Mariah, that sneaky little bitch,* he thought.

How ironic that she would pull that shit she did earlier at Maurice's crib then be blowing Nina's phone up. He knew Mariah was a jealous, envious, miserable little bitch and was sure she was calling to tell Nina some bullshit. If he'd played into her little flirt game, everything would have been all good, but since he didn't participate, now Mariah was shook. She didn't know if he would tell Nina what happened or not, so to cover her own ass, she was trying to get to Nina and turn shit around. But Mouse had plans to beat her to the punch. There was no way he was gonna give that bitch the opportunity to ruin his marriage.

Just as he was placing the phone back down, it began to vibrate again. "Jamal? Who the fuck is this?" he said to no one in particular.

He decided to answer the phone. "Hello? Hello?"

Then the phone hung up.

Oh, so she got niggas calling her cell phone. I'll just hold on to this for the night. Mouse placed the cell phone next to his clothes then jumped in the shower.

The entire ride to the club Mouse's brain was racing. He kept thinking about his gambling debt, then that shit with Mariah, and that call from Jamal for Nina.

When Mouse arrived at the club, he headed straight to the back of the club where his office was located. None of his usual flirting with the girls, no briefing the bouncers, or checking with the bartenders, just straight to the back to his office. He got to his office and turned on his monitors and watched the happenings of the club from his desk. There he saw the usual, dancers flirting with the few early customers, bartenders setting up their stations, and the bouncers goofing off. The night was early, so things were pretty quiet.

Ten minutes hadn't passed before he decided to give Nina a call at home. More than anything, that Jamal situation was eating him up inside. The phone rang out until the voice mail came on. He looked at his watch. It was after ten. *Nina should have been home by now*, he thought as he watched the monitor closely at a little commotion that was going on at the front door of the club.

Seeing his boy Maurice at the door, Mouse jumped up and rushed to the door to see what was going on.

"Yo', Mouse!" Maurice yelled as soon as Mouse was in sight. "Tell these niggas I'm good."

Mouse gave the security the okay. "Let him in."

Once Maurice was in the door, Mouse directed him to follow him into his office. Secure in his office and free from any curious flies on the wall, Mouse felt it was safe to talk to Maurice.

"Man, I got a real big problem," he said, getting right down to business.

"What's up? Talk to me." Maurice was ready to kill the first thing thinking or moving, assuming it was beef Mouse had.

"Man, I owe niggas some major dough. I've been doing everything I can to get the money up, but shit just not happening. I've been paying these niggas here and there, but my time is running short. Niggas want their money, duke."

"Damn, man! How you let that shit happen?"

"I don't know. All I know is, I have got to come up with some money, and fast."

"What about your houses? Sell one of them," Maurice said, aware of the few high-end houses Mouse had purchased a few years back when the real estate market was booming.

"Man, I tried, but the number the real estate agent gave me is some bullshit. It ain't worth it."

"Well, if you're in that deep, maybe something is better than nothing."

Mouse knew he was right, but he just couldn't give his houses away for nothing. True, he'd gotten a hell of a deal on them, but he'd also put a lot of work in them with upgrades and things. He knew what his houses were worth and wasn't gonna let a fucked-up market force him to give them away. He'd rather sit on them for a while than give them away for a steal.

"Matter of fact, I told her to call me back with some better numbers. Let me call her ass right now." Mouse scanned his contact list until he came to Ramona's number.

Ramona answered right away, "Hello."

"What up, baby girl? I didn't wake you, did I?" Mouse noted the time.

"Oh, you know me. I work around the clock."

"Oh, yeah? Well, since you work so hard, I hope you got some good news for me."

"Yes and no. Bad news, I won't able to come up with any better numbers. The market is terrible right now, so we're lucky to be at the number we are. Now the good news is, I didn't tell your wife anything crazy when she called me earlier today."

Mouse thought about Nina going through his pockets earlier. He was sure she had gotten Ramona's card from his pocket. "My wife?"

"Your wife. She assumed we had something going on. Rather than get into it with her, I just hung up."

This fucking chick never fucking quits. Something else I gotta deal with when I get home. "Damn! I'm sorry about that shit. You know how women do. Well, we may as well fuck now. My marriage already ruined."

Mouse and Ramona both laughed.

"Good-bye, boy!"

"Gone!" Mouse said as they both hung up.

Mouse turned his attention back to Maurice. "Well, that's a done deal. No haps on the crib."

"Fuck that shit. I got a plan for you. You know how you be holding the gambling sessions, right? Just cheat these muthafuckas. It's part of the game. Hell, they do it in Vegas all the time."

"So how am I supposed to do that?"

"Mark the cards, trick dice, have a couple cats work together to team up on a new dude and get him for his money. There's plenty of ways to do it. I can put you on to my boy from the pen. He knows every trick in the book."

"I don't know, man. These niggas be serious about their dough, especially when they lose big. That kind of shit will get you killed."

"Just do that shit for a minute and quit. Niggas will never know. You ain't gotta do that shit every night, just here and there. Build your money up then wean off the shit slowly."

"A'ight. Call your boy up. Get him in here. I'll let him hold something to get this shit popping tonight. We'll see how that shit goes and move from there."

"Nuff said."

Maurice stepped into Mouse's personal bathroom in his office for a little privacy, and got on the phone with his boy.

"What up, nigga?" Maurice said as soon as his boy answered the phone.

"Chilling. What up with you?"

"I got some work for you, nigga. If you can come by my boy strip joint tonight and put your gambling skills to work, you can get some money."

"A'ight, a'ight. So what he trying to do?"

"Well, he keeps a little gambling session at his club after hours, and he trying to rig things so the house comes out on top. You feel me?"

"I gotcha. Say no more. I'll be there."

"Gone."

After Maurice hung up the phone, he reported the news to Mouse.

As the night went on, Mouse stayed in his office, constantly calling his house, trying to reach Nina. All sorts of things were running through his mind each time the phone rang out to voice mail.

Before long, it was time to close the club and start his nightly gambling session. Maurice's boy had come just in time and set things up perfectly.

The night went just as planned. The players were losing money, and the house was gaining money. The feeling of hope alone was enough to get Nina off of Mouse's mind.

After Mouse wrapped things up, he made his deposit in the night deposit drop at the bank as usual and put the money he owed his bookie in a separate bag then headed home. He pulled up to the house and opened the garage and saw Nina's truck parked perfectly on the left side, like it had been there all day.

Flashbacks of Jamal calling from earlier in the day got him heated as he opened the door to the house. This time instead of heading up stairs he stopped in the office on the basement floor. He quietly opened his safe and put the money for his bookie in there. There was no way he would take the chance of getting caught a second time.

The house was silent as Mouse took his time walking to his bedroom. He opened the door and flipped on the light to see Nina sleeping peacefully like a baby.

Oh, hell no! Ain't no way this bitch is asleep after she had me stressing out all fucking night, Mouse thought. He started yelling like a mad man. "Where the fuck you been all night?"

A startled Nina opened her eyes and sat up, not sure if this shit was really happening, or if she was just having a bad dream.

"What happen? That nigga Jamal fucked the shit out of you, so now you drained? He put that ass to sleep?"

"What are you talking about?" Nina's heart was racing at the sound of Jamal's name, but she was trying to stay calm.

"You ain't miss your cell phone today? You left that shit here, and I saw when he called. Who the fuck is he, Nina?"

Think fast. Think fast. Nina tried to gather her thoughts. She was sure Jamal wouldn't have carried on a conversation with Mouse. If anything, he would've hung up on him.

"Jamal. You mean, gay-ass Jamal? My-personal-shopper-from-Bloomingdale's Jamal? Did you even listen to him speak? He flaming gay, Mouse. He'd rather fuck you than me." Nina started to fuck with Mouse about his manhood, to turn the tables. "Umph! He likes big dicks too. Did you save his number in your phone while you were at it?"

"Fuck you, Nina!"

"No, fuck you, Mouse! I spoke to your little bitch Ramona today. You lucky your shit ain't packed up in some box to the left. *To the left, to the left, everything you own is in the box to the left.*" Nina started to sing the lyrics of Beyoncé. "My girls told me to leave your ass a long time ago, but no, I keep giving your sorry ass chance after chance."

"Your girls? Your fuckin' girls? Nina, you ain't got no girls. All those bitches want to see you do bad. Earlier today I was at Maurice's crib, and I ran into your girl Mariah. That trick had her titties all in my face, trying to give a nigga a shoulder massage and every fuckin' thing. And here you are hollering about your girls. You know what? Have your muthafuckin' girls! I'm out!" Mouse threw Nina's cell across the room then walked out the room, slamming the door behind him.

"Something on the Side"

When Nina heard the garage door go up and back down then the sound of his car peeling off, she was confident Mouse was gone. She gave Mariah a call. The story Mariah gave was much different than Mouse's. The way Mariah explained things was, she came in and spoke to him, and the entire time he was staring at her breasts. When she straightened him, he asked why she was so uptight and proceeded to attempt to give her a massage. She then rushed off to find Maurice because she felt so uncomfortable.

The more Nina listened to Mariah, the angrier she got. She didn't know what to believe. She knew Mariah thirsted for the attention of all men, and it was quite possible in her little twisted mind the idea of getting Mouse to succumb to her would be the ultimate boost, but at the same time Nina couldn't put anything past a man.

Confused and frustrated, she called her only savior, Jamal.

Jamal didn't say anything when he picked up the phone.

"It's me, baby," she said right away, knowing exactly why he didn't say anything.

"Oh, what up, ma? Your boy called me earlier—"

Nina cut Jamal off. "I don't want to hear about that. Are you here? I want to come see you right now."

After Jamal told Nina where he was staying, Nina wasted no time jumping in the shower and getting dressed. She threw on her clothes, grabbed her cell, and headed out the door, never looking back.

***

Knock! Knock!

Nina straightened her clothes and ran her fingers through her hair as she anxiously waited for Jamal to open the door.

Jamal slowly cracked the door open, and she pushed on it, forcing it to open wide. She didn't say a word; she just jumped into his oversized arms and began to kiss him passionately. He kissed Nina back and carried her straight to the bed, allowing the door to close and lock on its own.

Just like the very first night they met, they attacked each other, ripping each other's clothes off. Sex with Jamal was like no other sex Nina had ever experienced before. He sent her to another place, giving her a high like no other.

"Damn, baby! You don't know how bad I want you," Jamal said, ripping each piece of Nina's clothes right off.

Nina moaned as Jamal's hands gently went from her ass to her breasts and then to her midsection. Her vagina was drenched in wetness by his simplest touch. He reached for Nina's lips, and she engulfed his tongue, kissing him passionately. From her mouth, Jamal's tongue found its way to her nipples, while his finger found its way to her clit.

Nina looked up at the ceiling, wanting this moment to last forever. Her pussy quivered at the simple sound of Jamal ripping open the condom wrapper with his teeth.

After unbuckling his belt, Jamal's jeans fell around his ankles, and the condom was on in one quick motion. He pressed his manhood into her.

"Ahh, fuck!" Nina yelled.

"Damn! I love this tight pussy," Jamal said, making sure she felt every stroke.

"Oh shit! What are you doing to me?" Nina thought she was going to faint from pure ecstasy.

"Giving you what you want, baby girl. You love this dick?" Jamal asked between strokes.

Nina knew she loved his dick, but she wouldn't answer, because she didn't want to tell him the truth. She thought she'd married the best dick she'd had in her life, but now she was thinking twice. At this point, Jamal's sex was the best she'd ever had. She wanted to scream it out but Nina couldn't answer because she was so overwhelmed with his dick.

Jamal started sucking on her left breast and literally pounding her head against the headboard with each stroke.

No longer able to fight it, Nina came all over his dick, and the only word she managed to get out was "Jamal!"

"I want to fuck all night." He turned her over. "This may hurt a little, baby girl, but I promise, you will like it."

Nina assumed the position and got on all fours. "Baby, please take your time with me," she whispered as she arched her back and pulled one butt cheek open. Although this wasn't a sexual position Nina normally assumed, she'd attempted it before. In hopes to do all she could to please her man, she rolled with the punches. "Spit in my ass, baby," she said, thinking she needed lubrication.

Jamal spat as she requested then began to press the head of his penis in her ass.

Nina dug her hands into the sheets and buried her face into the pillow. "Aaaaaahhhh!" She closed her eyes and tried not to tense up.

From what her girls told her, within moments her ass would be just as wet as her pussy, and it would be nothing but pleasure. She longed for the pleasure because, at the time, it was pure pain.

After Jamal got his penis in, Nina started massaging her clitoris in hopes of finally getting some pleasure to ease the constant pain. Moments later, the both of them released.

Then ten minutes later, they were at it again.

Nina lay her head on Jamal's chest as she recovered from an hour of lovemaking.

"So what's up with the home front?"

"Who knows? We had a huge argument right before I came over here."

"Damn, baby. I didn't mean to cause such a ruckus."

"Trust me, this didn't stem from you. We've had a lot going on these past couple of days. Mouse has been acting strange, and I believe he's cheating. On top of that, my girl told me he made a pass at her."

"Aw, man. I'm sorry to hear that shit, baby girl. Some niggas just don't know how to appreciate what they have."

"It's all good. What goes around comes around." Nina winked her eye then kissed Jamal softly on his lips.

"Fo' sho! So what you gon' do, boo?"

"To be honest, Jamal, I don't even know."

"Well, you know I got your back, regardless. You need anything? I can throw you a few dollars."

Not the one to turn down a dollar or a dime, Nina quickly accepted. "A chick could always use a few dollars." She laughed. "As a matter of fact, where is my Louis Vuitton bag and shoes?"

"You know I got you."

Jamal stood up and headed toward the safe in his room. He counted out a thousand dollars and closed the safe. Then he went over to the closet and pulled out not only the Louis Vuitton bag and shoes, but a matching belt, and brought it over to Nina.

Nina smiled as she adored her Louis set. *Is this genuine, or am I just another piece of ass?* Every girl dreamt of being the NBA wife or the NFL wife. Nina wondered if she could break Jamal and find herself in such a position.

Buzz! Buzz! Buzz!

The constant vibrating of Jamal's cell phone interrupted Nina's thinking. It actually had been buzzing the entire time they were having sex, but they were so consumed, neither of them acknowledged it. Nina had planned to mention it after sex, but that Louis set had distracted her.

"Who keeps calling you?" she asked, her face screwed up.

Jamal answered without even looking at his phone's caller ID. "Nobody important."

"Jamal, that doesn't answer my question. Who keeps calling?"

"One of my boys," he lied.

"Yeah, right. You don't have to lie to me. I know I'm not the only chick."

"We gon' leave that alone, a'ight, boo? We havin' a good time. Let's not turn things sour." Jamal put his arm around Nina and squeezed her tight.

Nina let it go, and they lay down together and fell asleep.

"On the Verge of Breakup"

Mouse pulled into the garage and saw Nina's truck. After leaving the crib earlier, he'd gone back to the club and slept on the couch in his office. After a few hours of tossing and turning, he figured he'd just have to face the music and go back home.

He walked in the house with the intention of going straight to the guest bedroom and going to sleep, but to his surprise, Nina walked right past him in the hall without saying a word. Relieved that he'd gotten away without an argument, he headed into the kitchen to grab a bite to eat.

As he searched the refrigerator, his cell phone rang. "Yo," he answered.

"What up, duke?" Maurice noticed Mouse's tone of voice. "You a'ight?"

"Problems, nigga, problems."

"After my nigga hooked shit up for you last night, you should be a'ight."

"Nah, man, it ain't that. That shit was gravy. I was loving that shit."

"So what's up, man? Wait. Don't tell me—woman problems."

"You know it. I don't know what's up with Nina. She been on some real bullshit lately, man."

Nina's voice sounded from around the corner. "I been on some bullshit? No, *you* been on some bullshit."

"Man, I'll call you back." Mouse quickly ended his phone call then directed his attention back toward Nina, who was now staring him in his face. "That's what the fuck I said. You been on some bullshilt lately, Nina."

"Nah, I'm just sick and tired of you and your bullshit."

"So, if you so miserable, Nina, then find somebody else." Mouse walked away from Nina. He was tired as hell, tired of arguing, and had more pressing issues on his mind.

"Please don't provoke me, honey, because I'm halfway there. As a matter of fact"—Nina stopped midsentence. She started to let him have it and tell him about the good loving she'd had with Jamal, but she knew a real woman never tells.

"As a matter of fact what, Nina?" Mouse said as he walked up the stairs. "You got fucked last night? This morning? What?"

Once at the top of the stairs, Mouse's phone rang again. He looked down to see it was Jigga calling. He walked into the bathroom of the master bedroom and closed the door behind him.

Mouse answered like he and Jigga were big friends. "What's up, Jigga?"

"My muthafuckin' money, nigga."

"I got you, Jigga. All I need is a few more days, and I'll have that shit in full."

"I hope you really sure about that, nigga, because that's all you got left. Don't make a nigga have to snatch your pretty little wifey up when she sneaking out early in the morning."

Mouse was distracted by a subtle thump on the bathroom door. He was sure it was Nina listening. He could even see the shadow from her feet through the crack at the bottom of the door.

Not even giving a fuck anymore, he pulled the door open, and Nina nearly fell through. Mouse didn't say anything. He just stepped around her and continued his conversation. "A'ight, man. Just give me those few days. I got you." He hung up the phone.

"What the fuck is going on?" Like a gnat that won't go away, Nina was right up in Mouse's face.

"Nothing. I just owe niggas a few dollars, and they're tripping, so just watch your back when you're creeping in the early-morning hours," Mouse said, full of sarcasm.

"Watch my back? Mouse, what is going on? Am I in danger or something?"

Mouse totally ignored Nina as he walked back into the bathroom and locked the door behind him.

Minutes later, Nina heard the shower going, so she gave up on the argument. For the time being, anyway.

"A Night Out"

"Rain, rain, go away," Rochelle chanted in the mirror while applying her makeup in the bathroom. The thunderstorm outside was definitely putting a damper on her plans for the evening. Wet clothes, wet hair, wet shoes and washed-up makeup wasn't the look she was trying to step into the club with. Rochelle preferred for bitches heads to turn and for all eyes to be on her when walked in. The weatherman had predicted that the thunderstorm watch should end by eleven o'clock in the night, but Rochelle had a huge, trusty umbrella to protect her from each raindrop that threatened to melt her sugary-sweet body.

Mercedes peeped inside the bathroom door. "You sure you want to go out tonight?"

"I go out every Saturday night. Unless someone has died, plans won't ever change." Rochelle smiled. She knew Mercedes thought she would be too exhausted to do anything after eating her pussy good and a few rounds with a dildo, but boy, was she wrong.

"How much longer is it going to take you to get ready?" Mercedes asked, disappointed.

"About thirty minutes," Rochelle responded, although she knew thirty minutes really meant an hour. *Hopefully, Peaches won't show up tonight. I want to enjoy myself minus the drama. It doesn't help that Mercedes got an attitude.* She looked at Mercedes. She could tell something was bothering her.

Since Rochelle had gotten out of the shower, Mercedes had

left the bedroom three times to use the phone. She wondered who the hell she was calling, but decided not to even mention it.

Instead, she rushed to finish getting dressed. And, just like she'd figured, an hour later she was dressed, and she and Mercedes were on their way out the door, headed to the club.

"Forty dollars each to get in the club," the bouncer yelled as Mercedes and Rochelle walked up and stood in line for the club.

"What the hell is in that club, other than a few naked bitches, that I need to pay forty dollars to get in there?" Rochelle frowned her face up, shaking her head. She grabbed Mercedes and turned around and started walking back to the car. "Bad enough, we were charged five dollars to park. I fuckin' work here. I should get in free."

After being robbed blind by his own employees a few times, Mouse declared to his staff, "If you're not working you're treated like a customer—You pay to get in, you pay to play, and you pay for drinks."

"Rochelle, you didn't get dressed up all sexy for nothing." Mercedes stopped in her tracks then reached in her purse and pulled out four twenties.

"You got me, baby?" Rochelle cooed in her ear.

"Yeah," she nodded, grinning.

Mercedes always had Rochelle. If she couldn't pay to get her nails, she paid, weave done, she paid. There was even one time, on the brink of eviction, Mercedes stripped at the club to gather the money to pay for two months of back rent she owed. Whenever and however Rochelle needed her, she was always there.

For Rochelle, having a personal ATM and free pussy wasn't so bad, and was better than what she was able to get out of most niggas. "Baby, can you get me a drink?" she inquired as soon as they walked into the club.

"I sure will."

"You know what I like. While you go to the bar, I'm going to the bathroom."

Rochelle stood in front of the full-sized mirror and gave herself a quick glance, confirming she looked like the shit.

She came out of the bathroom and walked up behind Mercedes without her even noticing. She listened as Mercedes screamed into her cell phone, leaving a voice mail for a nigga named Jamal, talking about, they were supposed to be together for the weekend. She gathered that Mercedes was pissed because she thought the guy was with the next bitch.

As she listened, it dawned on her. *That's probably why she seemed so uneasy all night.*

"Rochelle, baby, what's good?" Li'l Man put his arm around Rochelle's waist. "I've been calling, but you've been sending me straight to your voice mail."

"Hey, hon. I've just been busy." Rochelle was lying through her teeth. Between Peaches and Mercedes gunning for her attention and Nina's drama, she hadn't had a free moment to get up with him.

"Who the fuck is this nigga?" Mercedes demanded before throwing their drinks on the floor. She acted as if she was ready to fight.

"Low tones," Li'l Man suggested.

"Don't fuckin' tell me how to talk," Mercedes yelled, getting even louder.

"He's a friend. Calm the noise down." Rochelle's head was starting to pound, and the last thing she needed was to hear Mercedes' never-ending mouth.

"Rochelle, call me when you're free, so I can show you what a real ten-inch chocolate dick feels like in your pussy walls." Li'l Man walked off.

"So you fuckin' that nigga too?"

"Maybe I should say the same for you. Who the hell is Jamal? You couldn't be with him, so you settled for me?" Rochelle walked away, leaving Mercedes speechless.

As Rochelle walked past, Mariah called out, "Chelly Poo!"

"Oh! Hey, hon." Rochelle greeted Mariah with a hug. She was so irritated by Mercedes' statement, she didn't even see Mariah.

"What's wrong?" Mariah asked, noticing the frustration in Rochelle's face.

"Girl, Mercedes. She always is saying some shit to piss me off."

"Oh, lordie."

Mariah shook her head. The drama with Rochelle and Mercedes was so common, she didn't even care to hear about it.

Just then Mouse caught her eye. "Excuse me," she said then walked away before Rochelle could even respond.

Mouse motioned his boys to come into his office and talk business. He wanted to talk with them about gambling, to see what they could set up for the night. Once in the office, he went straight to his personal bar, and made sure everyone had a drink in hand.

As Maurice was introducing everyone, the door opens, and Mariah appears. Her eyes on Mouse, she sees no one in the room and heads directly toward him. Finally realizing there were a group of men amongst her, she scanned them quickly then stopped dead in her tracks after noticing Maurice among the group.

Then she acted like she'd made a wrong turn. "I'm sorry. I was looking for the bathroom."

"Back out the door and on the right," Mouse said nonchalantly. He directed his attention toward the group.

"Okay, thanks. Sorry to interrupt." Mariah gathered herself and walked out the room. From the looks of things, everyone believed she was truly lost. She made her way back toward Rochelle, who sat at the bar alone.

"I'm about to get the hell out of here," Rochelle said as soon as Mariah walked up.

Rochelle was pissed off about being second best, so she hooked up with Li'l Man and convinced him to take her home. She left Mercedes at the club by herself without even saying good-bye.

Lucky for Mercedes, she had driven her own car this night. It didn't take long for her to realize Rochelle was nowhere in sight. And it took even less time to realize Li'l Man was gone as well. When she saw that the both of them were gone, she already knew the deal. Normally, she would have been on her way to Rochelle's house, but this time she decided to cut her losses and stay.

Mercedes spotted Mariah in the corner. "What's up, Mariah?"

"Hey. You know Rochelle is gone, right?" Mariah spat with a slight attitude.

"Yeah, I know. She's tripping because a friend of mine, Jamal, is in town."

Jamal? The sound of that name caught Mouse's attention as he walked past the girls unnoticed. He was headed to the bar to handle a situation with his bartenders.

Bored, with Jamal nowhere in sight, and not wanting to go home to an empty apartment, Mercedes decided to flirt with a few of the girls she knew from the club. Within a few minutes, she spotted Mouse in the corner by the bar talking to a couple of his bartenders. *Finally something to hold my attention.* She headed in his direction.

She gently tapped him on the shoulder and whispered in his ear, "It's been a long time."

Mouse turned around to face her. "Not now, Mercedes.

I'm busy. Besides, I overheard you saying Jamal is in town."
He turned back around to continue talking to his bar staff.

After Mouse finished his business with the bartenders, he
began to think. He sat at the bar trying to put two and two
together, his brain racing. He wondered if it was a coincidence
a nigga named Jamal called Nina's phone and then he hears
Mercedes saying Jamal is in town. *I bet this nigga is the same
person. They probably both fucking him and don't know it.*

Years ago, Mouse had found himself in the same predicament.
This shit was like déjà vu. Nina had made the mistake of letting
Mercedes' trick ass come and stay with them. It only left the
door open to Mouse getting his dick sucked, and not by his
wife.

"Licky or Sticky?"

Rochelle quickly hopped in Li'l Man's truck and shut the door, and Li'l Man sped out of the parking lot, blasting the latest Lil Wayne CD.

As if being known as one of Jigga's main soldiers on the streets wasn't enough, Li'l Man loved being noticed, especially by bitches wishing they were in the passenger side of his ride. Since their encounter at the restaurant he'd done a little research on Rochelle. He hadn't heard much about her, except she worked at the strip club and that she definitely knew how to ride that stick, both of those a plus in his book.

Jigga had sent him out to watch Mouse so anybody that was close to Mouse was an asset to Li'l Man, and to have that asset to be a bitch that rides the hell out of dick was a hell of a deal. Anxious to get into Rochelle's head and panties, he started kicking his best game to her.

"Mmm, you look good and smell just as nice. I like a woman who takes pride in her appearance. The rare times I have caught a glimpse, you always have your shit together. What perfume do you have on?"

Rochelle grinned. "Coco Chanel."

"That's kind of pricey. Back in the day, my mother wore the same thing."

"Well, if I save my pennies, it's definitely worth the price tag."

"Speaking of pennies, besides the club, do you work anywhere else?"

"Nah, not right now. Eventually, I would like to go back to school for interior design. Give me a budget under five hundred dollars and I can fix up a whole house. "

"Ma, your face lights up when talking about that subject. You must really be into it."

"Yeah, I am. Give me an empty room and I can bring it to life. I have to confess, I am a female who loves going to Lowe's to pick out new home décor and giving my walls a new splash of color."

"So when I get my house, you'll help me design it?"

"Not for free. I'm sure we can work something out though." Rochelle giggled.

The late night brought a cool breeze. Rochelle's arms were folded. She was beginning to get goose bumps. Plus, it didn't help any that Li'l Man had all of his windows down, so everyone could see it was him driving the Range Rover.

She was starting to get slightly irritated but wasn't sure if it was because Li'l Man was acting more like a little boy, showing off his new Jordan's, or if it was Mercedes crossing her mind every few minutes.

Li'l Man noticed she was uptight. "Come on, ma. Don't tell me you upset by that lipstick broad?"

"No, I'm good." Rochelle nodded.

"So tell me, are you gay, bi, or what?"

"I'm experimenting." Rochelle smiled.

"Rochelle, the first thing I want you to know is that you can confide in me. Now, I'm going to ask one more time. What's really going on between you and Ms. Lipstick?"

"Her name is *Mercedes*, not Lipstick. I don't appreciate you disrespecting her."

"I stand corrected. You hungry? I'm trying to get IHOP takeout."

"Sure."

"Continue, please." Li'l Man nodded, making a left turn into the IHOP parking lot.

"Mercedes and I go way back. I had my first girl-on-girl experience with her. No matter what the fuck you think, what we have goes deeper than pussy licking. She's more like my rock. Whenever I'm in trouble, need something or someone to confide in, that girl has always been there for me. More than I can say for any sorry-ass nigga." Rochelle confessed.

"Wow! I didn't know it could get that deep between females. And don't knock every man for one man's fuckup."

"Yes, things can get deep between females. As far as that don't-blame-one-for-all statement, I'll just ignore that." Rochelle rolled her eyes.

"Cool. I'll dead the convo about your feelings against guys, but only if you promise not to judge me based on the next cat."

"Okay. I can do that."

"Now back to you. The way I see it, maybe you need to let Loudmouth cool off a bit and talk to her later."

"Maybe, you're right. But do me a favor."

"What's that?"

"Stop disrespecting my friend. You wouldn't like it if someone called you li'l dick."

"Actually, I wouldn't give a fuck. One day, you never know, when I'm holding your titties in my hand, fuckin' you from the back and making you moan, you'll know if I got a li'l dick or not."

"Whatever!" Rochelle giggled, finding Li'l Man's comment amusing.

"So, you like working at the club versus a nine-to-five gig?"

"Yes, I love working at night. For one thing, the money is double what I would make sitting behind a desk. Mouse runs a tight ship, but he's a decent boss. I know his ass make a killing at the club. As the bartender, my little scraps can add to up to three fifty a night."

After getting their takeout and taking Rochelle home, Li'l

Man walked her all the way to the front door to make sure she got there safe and sound. He ended up with a kiss on the lips. He took it a little further and nibbled on her ear before breaking out. He didn't want to fuck her yet, figuring the best pussy was one that was marinating for him.

"Caught Red-Handed"

Annoyed by Mouse's bullshit, Nina had got dressed and headed to pay Jamal another visit.

After hours of lovemaking, she said to Jamal, "Baby, I've gotta go. Mouse said some crazy shit to me earlier about watching my back. So I don't want to be out too late, just in case there is some truth to what he's saying." She searched for her panties and bra.

"You sure everything all right, baby girl? You shouldn't take threats like that so lightly."

"I'll be fine, baby. Don't you worry your little sexy self." Nina put on her clothes then kissed Jamal on the cheek before heading to the hotel room door.

"Be safe, baby girl. Call me or text me when you get in the crib, so I know you made it home safe." Jamal smacked Nina on the ass as she walked through the door.

Once home Nina texted Jamal to let him know she'd made it home safely. Although Mouse was nowhere in sight, the mere idea of being home brought the aggravation she felt earlier. Plagued by the unfinished argument she'd had with Mouse earlier, Nina couldn't think of anything else. There was only one thing left to do. Call him up. Nina knew she wouldn't be able to rest until she got the feeling of frustration off her chest.

She dialed Mouse's number, and the phone rang out to voice mail. Knowing that the club was loud and maybe he couldn't hear his phone, she called his office phone. Again, she got no answer. She decided to give him a little time to call her back, so she hopped in the shower.

After a fifteen-minute shower Nina still hadn't received a call back from Mouse, so she tried again but still couldn't reach him. Feeling helpless, she put on her clothes and headed for the club.

"What the fuck is this?" Nina said to herself as soon as she walked through the doors of the club. Her heart began to race. It was pounding so hard, it felt like it was gonna jump out her chest.

Once again she'd caught Mouse and Mercedes in the act. No, they weren't in the midst of a sexual act. In fact, it seemed like it was only an innocent conversation, but Nina knew, when it came to Mercedes, nothing was ever innocent, especially when her man was involved.

She forced her way past Mercedes and jumped in Mouse's face. "What is going on?"

"Nothing. We're having a conversation. What does it look like, Nina?"

Nina pointed her finger in Mercedes' face. "I don't even want you talking to this bitch."

"Bitch?" Mercedes smacked Nina's hand out her face.

"Bitch, have you lost your fuckin' mind?"

Mouse grabbed Mercedes by her neck before Nina could even react, surprising Nina and Mercedes alike. Sure, Mouse and Nina wasn't feeling each other at the time, but Nina was still his wife, and there was no way he was gonna let some bitch disrespect her.

"Yo', yo', yo'! What's going on here?"

A familiar voice caught the attention of Nina and Mercedes both.

Mouse released Mercedes' neck and focused his attention

toward the man that towered over him. "Fuck you mean? Who are you?"

Mouse thought the guy's face looked familiar, but before he could respond to his question, security was already surrounding them and grabbing him.

"Everything good, boss?" the security asked Mouse.

"It's cool, homeboy," Jamal said, realizing this man before him was probably Nina's husband. "I don't mean no disrespect. I just wanted to make sure my girl was okay."

"Your girl? Oh, you mean this bitch?" Nina darted her eyes toward Mercedes. "Yeah, she's all right, for now anyway, but she better stay away from my man." Nina shot Jamal an eye.

He knew exactly what that meant too. Although Mercedes and Mouse may have thought she was referring to Mouse, it was actually Jamal she was referring to.

"Okay, well, if you all don't mind, we're just gonna take a seat in VIP and enjoy our night." Jamal threw his arms around Mercedes and walked away, shooting Nina and Mouse a taunting smile.

"Yo', don't ever pull another stunt like that again," Mouse said to Nina. He then walked to his office and shut his door.

Minutes later, Maurice came in. He always had Mouse's back.

"Yo', you okay, duke?"

"Yeah, man. I was just in the middle of a little mix-up between Nina and Mercedes." Mouse sipped his Hennessy on the rocks.

"So what the fuck was that nigga Jamal Smith from the Philadelphia Seventy-Sixers talking about?"

"Oh, that's who the fuck that was?"

It was like a light had just gone off in Mouse's head. It all made sense now. This had to be that mysterious Jamal.

Not wanting to move too quickly, he decided to act oblivious to the situation and just monitor what was going on from his office.

While Mouse monitored Nina from his office, she was monitoring Jamal from a bar seat in the corner. She was burning up inside as she watched him shower Mercedes with lots of love and attention. It killed her to see her constantly smiling and laughing while wrapped up in his arms.

"Charge It to the Game"

Li'l Man left Rochelle to dream about him and headed back to the club. He was sure to make it back in time to enter the gambling game he'd heard so much about.

Maurice spotted Li'l Man as he entered and pulled Mouse by the side to point him out. "This is one of the niggas my boys sent over for us to set up tonight."

"A'ight, a'ight," Mouse said, looking forward to the profits he was sure to make from the game later in the night.

After the club closed, Li'l Man stuck around for the classic game of blackjack, where the goal was to get a higher score than the dealer but not exceeding twenty-one.

Maurice and Mouse came up with the plan of counting cards. They knew exactly how many Aces, Queens, Kings, Jacks, and Tens they had, and where they were. Not one time did Li'l Man become suspicious or want to shuffle up the cards himself.

Game number one led to game number two, and before you knew it, Li'l Man was on game number ten and losing big. He finally folded up his cards and gave up on attempting to win some money from these niggas, his losing streak costing him one thousand per game.

He stuck around to watch some more games. As he watched closely, he couldn't believe what he saw. "These niggas cheating," he said to himself.

His first instinct was to go to his truck and shoot the whole place up. Then he thought about it. *That wouldn't get me my money back, but it will definitely get me back in the penitentiary.*

Not wanting to ever see the inside of another cell another day in his life, he decided to be a man about the situation.

He grabbed Mouse and asked to speak to him on the side. "Yo', man, I know y'all niggas cheating on the card games. I ain't trying to blow up your spot or nothing. All I ask is that you just give me back my dough I lost."

"I don't know what you talking about, duke." Mouse began to walk away.

Li'l Man jumped in his face. "I'm trying to settle shit on a cool tip, my man, but if you want to diss, we can take shit to another level."

Not in the mood for Li'l Man's bullshit, Mouse signaled for security. Within moments, they were at his feet. "Escort this nigga out of my club." He pointed at Li'l Man, and minutes later, Li'l Man was out the door.

Pissed off, Li'l Man decided to make a phone call as he sat in his truck, attempting to cool off a bit before driving.

"What's up?" Jigga responded.

"Yo', Jigga, that nigga Mouse lying about what he don't got. This club brings in at least thirty grand a month. Shit, bartenders alone make three fifty in tips on a bad night, and the strippers be bringing in at least fifteen hundred on a bad night. Not to mention, this nigga be hustling cats out their loot on some gambling shit. I peeped all that shit out tonight. Meanwhile, you've been sitting patiently for your money."

"Appreciate the update," Jigga replied before hanging up the phone.

Right after hanging up the phone with Li'l Man, Jigga dialed Mouse's number. Mouse only had a few measly thousands to give to him, which wasn't good enough. Jigga wanted all of his money up front, and to be done with Mouse once and for all. The next nigga wouldn't be so lucky. Trying to give niggas time to pay only gets your ass laughed at on the streets. Mouse needed to be taught a golden lesson—If you don't have money to play with, don't fucking borrow it on credit.

***

The next day, Li'l Man showed up on Rochelle's doorstep with flowers, candy, and a Fendi bag. He ate her pussy, and they fucked in six different positions.

After a hot shower, cuddling, and a massage, Rochelle was putty in Li'l Man's hands. He fed into her weakness of being needy. Rochelle was like most chicks, but what she craved most was someone to be constantly by her side.

They were now lying in bed after they'd smoked two blunts.

"I didn't tell you what happened last night." Li'l Man shook his head.

"What happened?"

"Mouse got me for ten grand. He wasn't playing fair with those cards."

"With all the money he makes, playing you was being fuckin' greedy." Rochelle rubbed the top of Li'l Man's head.

"Yep." He nodded.

"I'm sorry, baby."

"Rochelle, I could really use that money back. All I need to know from you is where he lives, and if he makes any drops to a bank.

"I can't do that." Rochelle got up from the bed.

"No one will get hurt. If you're willing to get that little bit of information, ten grand plus a shopping spree will be waiting for you. It's only fair. That nigga is taking from my kids' mouth. Back to school is right around the fuckin' corner. My baby mom's ain't trying to hear no bullshit."

"I don't want anyone to get hurt. He's married to my best friend."

"No one will get hurt, baby girl. You got my word. I'm just trying to let that nigga know, you rob, you get robbed. He gotta learn to play fair."

"Okay. But you gotta promise me no one will get hurt."

Times were hard, so ten grand sounded like music to

Rochelle's ears. After all, he did promise no one would get hurt.

"Thanks, baby. Rochelle, this really means a lot to me. It lets me know you got a nigga's back." Li'l Man caressed Rochelle's arms. "I'll always have your back in return."

"I'll write his address on a piece of paper. Mouse usually makes the deposits as soon as he leaves the club in the night drop box at Bank Star on Military Highway. Also he has a safe in his office in the bottom floor of his house." Rochelle grabbed a pen and a piece of scrap paper and jotted down the address.

"Deadly Consequences"

Quite tipsy and dog-tired, Nina refused to leave until the very last person walked out the club. There was no way she was gonna take the chance of letting Mercedes get another taste of her man. Who cares if she was occupied with Jamal at the time? All that stank bitch needed was a good ten minutes to give a little head, on the sneak tip.

"What's your problem?" Nina walked up to an angry Mouse.

"Nina, I pay every motherfuckin' bill in that damn house, and you chose to fuck another nigga! Another nigga who already got somebody at that! All you are is the chick on the side. This is the gratitude that I get? I'm not even touching on the damn nagging and complaining I put up with on a consistent basis."

"I don't know what you're talking about." Nina figured the less emotion she showed, the more innocent it made her appear.

Mouse struck a nerve with Nina about being the chick on the side. Despite everything, she was a far better selection than broke-down, pussy-popping Mercedes. You would think most niggas would rather have a T-bone steak over two-day-old bologna.

"That's cool. Act like you don't know what the fuck I'm talking about. Keep on." Mouse nodded and walked away.

"And what? Mouse, you are the first to know my work schedule. In fact, I'm scheduled to leave for Atlanta in a matter of hours. You would think, with the little time I have off, I could get a little time with my husband, but we both know it's never possible. You worship this damn club, and I'm sick of it." Nina held her hands up.

"I got a fuckin' business to run. Everything costs, from the light bill to employee payroll. Every month, I got to make that. I'm carrying the weight of the world, and you have the luxury of working when the fuck you get ready." Mouse cut off the lights in the club and began to head out.

"Mouse, you never listen to me and could care less about my feelings. I'm outta here." Nina headed out of the door before him.

She hopped in her car and sped out of the parking lot, never looking back. Tears dripped off Nina's face as she drove through many lights. She was tired of bickering with Mouse.

She really needed Jamal now, but she was sure he was with Mercedes. She hit her steering wheel many times, just thinking about them together. She still couldn't help but wonder what the fuck niggas saw in Mercedes.

After hours of driving and looking at her phone for the thirty-second time to see if Mouse bothered to call, she pulled into the La Quinta Hotel to try to get some rest. With her mind racing, she didn't close her eyes until five in the morning.

The alarm clock awoke Nina two hours later, at seven thirty. Not knowing how to turn it off, she ended up ripping the cord from the wall and throwing it across the room.

After a hot shower and a bite to eat from the complimentary continental breakfast, Nina headed to the Norfolk International Airport to board a flight to Atlanta for a two-week work assignment. She didn't even bother to go home and pack, or say good-bye to Mouse. She figured she could buy a few uniforms and underclothes when she arrived at her destination.

After spending hours at the airport due to delay from heavy rain and thunderstorms, her flight was eventually cancelled.

She decided to go home and face Mouse. Since she had cooled off, she figured they could have a decent conversation. Despite the fling she'd had with Jamal, she still loved Mouse and wanted their marriage to work. At the time, divorce wasn't an option.

Feeling hopeful of the future and with a positive attitude, she pulled into her driveway, only to see Mercedes' car parked in her spot.

Immediately Nina's blood began to boil. She felt like she was gonna burst a blood vessel. *What the fuck is the bitch doing at my house?* As far as Nina was concerned, Mercedes was supposed to have been with Jamal. Her head was spinning, and her heart was filled with rage. For the second time, she had been fucked over by Mercedes.

Without thinking, Nina found herself holding Mouse's Glock .45 in her hand. Quietly and slowly, she crept into the house. No one was on the first level. She began to move up the staircase, quiet as a mouse.

Once she reached the top floor, she crept into the master bedroom, only to discover Mercedes and Mouse butt-naked in her king-size bed. Her body was numb, and her mind went blank.

Minutes later, when Nina came to, she was cowering in the corner with the gun by her side. She stood up to see Mercedes and Mouse covered in blood.

When she heard tyres screech, she rushed to the window and peeped through the blinds in time enough to catch a glimpse of a black, tinted-out Range Rover and a BMW X5 speeding off.

Frantic, she quickly cleaned her fingerprints off the gun. Then she emptied the clip and whipped each bullet out, counting the bullets as she popped them out the clip.

In total, Nina counted seventeen bullets. "Seventeen? How could there be seventeen?" she said out loud. She knew the extended clip carried sixteen bullets; plus, the one in the head would account for seventeen. There was no way she could have shot Mouse and Mercedes.

As the reality began to set in, Nina began to examine the room then the house. She noticed Mouse's safe had been tampered with. That's when it hit her. Someone had come to rob Mouse. That would explain the trucks she saw speeding off.

Sure, Mouse had a few enemies, but Nina never expected somebody would kill him. She thought back to the conversation she'd overheard Mouse have on his cell phone, and what he'd said to her about watching her back because he owed someone some money.

She rushed back downstairs and replaced Mouse's gun then dialed 9-1-1, and within minutes, police cars were scattered on her lawn.

After the forensic team came to collect bullet casings and gather other evidence, a detective questioned Nina.

Tears dripped down her face again as they carried Mouse's lifeless body out of their dream house in a body bag.

Once everyone was gone, she dialed Rochelle and Mariah on a three-way call. Both of them answered.

"Mouse is dead," she said.

"What?"

"Mercedes is dead too. They were both shot in the head."

"What?" Rochelle cried out. "Nnnnnooooo!"

Mariah said over Rochelle's sobs. "Oh my God, Nina! Are you okay?"

"It was a robbery."

"I'm coming over."

"On the way," Rochelle replied before hanging up the phone.

***

What seemed like only minutes later, Rochelle and Mariah both were at Nina's house.

"I'm so sorry," Rochelle said as soon as she walked into the house. She hugged Nina tight and wouldn't let go.

Mariah joined in on the group hug as they all wept.

"This is my fault," Rochelle whispered.

"What do you mean?" Mariah asked between sobs.

"Li'l Man begged me to tell him where Mouse lived. He said Mouse got him for thousands in a card game. He just wanted his money back and promised no one would get hurt."

Smack!

Nina smacked Rochelle so hard, her hand started to sting. "How could you? I trusted you! If I hadn't of left last night, I would be dead too, bitch!" she said, screaming at the top of her lungs.

"Nina . . ."

"Get the fuck out of my house!"

Mariah didn't know what to say. All she could do was shake her head. She knew the friendship between the three of them would never be the same again.

Diamond in the Sky

By Karen Williams

Chapter 1

"Like a Diamond in the Sky"

On this day, I should have known my life as my young ass knew it was doomed. But I was far too young to know what life meant, or the word *doomed*, for that matter.

"Come on, Diamond."

I was seven years old, staring at my dad's girlfriend after she took her time bathing me up, careful not to wet my hair she had just pressed out 'til it was bone-straight and hung down my back in a ponytail. She couldn't stop staring at it. After my bath, she held out the towel for me, and I stepped into it, pulling my feet out of the tub one at a time. Then she took her time drying me off.

"Twinkle, twinkle, little star, how I wonder what you are," I sang.

For as long as I could remember I had sung that song. For some reason the song always seemed to ring out in my head. It was always a soft voice I heard singing it, but only in my head. Rhonda only yelled and cursed at me. She never sang.

"Shut up and lay on the bed!" she ordered sharply.

I did it quickly, shivering from the cold air.

She took some lotion out of her favorite bottle and rubbed my body down with it, so I smelled like her when she would leave daddy and me at night and not come back until the morning. Once she worked down to my feet, she told me to stand again.

"Them not mine," I said, staring at her underwear in her hand.

She smacked me quickly. "Shut the fuck up and put these on! Ain't asked you shit!"

I started crying because my face started hurting. But I was scared she would hit me again, so I let her push my feet into the pair of purple panties, whimpering all the while.

"I said, 'Shut the fuck up!'"

I bit my lip and squirmed in the panties 'cause they stuck in my butt. Then she pulled my prettiest dress over my head. The one the church down the street gave me for Sunday school. Once she buttoned the back, she pulled my hair from my ponytail.

I sniffled, and she grabbed some tissue to wipe my snot away. Then she grabbed her purse and yanked me by my hand. "Come on, goddamit!"

I knew my daddy's girlfriend hated me, so I was surprised she took all the time to get me pretty. I wondered where she was going to take me. I was hoping it was to the park so I could play.

She marched to the door and held it open. "Come on!"

I ran through the door. But we weren't going far, just upstairs from our place. She gave me a shove so I would go up the stairs. She continued to shove me, so I went faster and ended up falling.

She yanked me to my feet. "Come the fuck on!"

"Mama." I had slipped up and called her that again. Every time I did, I either got slammed against a wall, knocked in the mouth, or spat on.

"I'm not your mama, bitch!"

I followed after her down the corridor. We stopped in front of a closed door. My heart sped up in my chest as she knocked.

"Who the fuck is it?"

"Rhonda."

"The door open."

Rhonda turned the knob, pushed the door open, and shoved me inside.

When I stayed planted in the spot she shoved me in, she pushed me in the center of the room. Fearfully I watched the man seated on a suede couch across from where I stood. He was leaning over a table with something that looked like pieces of soap and a razor.

"Well, here she is."

He took one look at me, shook his head and sliced the soap with the razor.

Why was he cutting his soap? I wondered.

"What the fuck you bring her over here for?"

She shoved me. "Go up to him," she whispered in my ear.

I looked at her confused. When she punched me in my back, I screeched in pain and did as she requested.

"She pretty, ain't she?"

He nodded without looking at me again.

"Well, have a go with her."

He stopped what he was doing and looked at Rhonda. "What the fuck I supposed to do with her?"

"Whatever the fuck you want, D. You can have her for about thirty minutes. Just give me a five-dollar rock and we good."

He studied me for a moment.

My left leg wouldn't stop shaking, and my bottom lip was trembling.

"I'm not doing that shit. Get the fuck out my pad!"

Rhonda lips snarled, and she stomped. "Fuck you, muthafucka! Give me a hit!"

"Get out my place, bitch!" he said calmly, his focus still on the soap.

"What? You need some help?" She snatched me up and ripped the top of my dress.

I started crying.

"She ain't too young. She already got titties and hair on her pussy." She raised the skirt on my dress. "Look!"

I closed my eyes in shame, and I prayed he wasn't looking.

He wasn't. He jumped from the couch and, in a flash, had his hands around Rhonda's throat. He slammed her head against the wall. "I'm gonna say this one more time, you sick bitch! Get out my house!"

She slid her body down the wall, and he released his hands from her neck. She rushed out the door and slammed it, yelling out, "Fuck you!" leaving me behind.

Once it slammed behind her, the man stared at me, and I stared back at him. Even offered him a smile through my sniffles.

He reached in his pocket and pulled out a twenty-dollar bill, which I grabbed quickly, thinking of all the candy I could buy with it. Then he held his door open for me to slip out.

As soon as my feet hit the stairs, I ran for my life. My heart was thumping in my chest. But I didn't stop running until I made it to my apartment. I went straight into my room and hid in the closet.

No sooner that I did, Rhonda storm into my room. "Diamond, where the fuck you at, you little bitch?"

I placed a hand over my mouth, fearful that if I came out she was going to beat me, even though I didn't do anything wrong. I had did what she asked. I let her do my hair and bathe me. I even went into the house like she asked.

I crouched down and could hear her stomp around my room.

"I'm gonna fuck you up for making me look for you in this damn room, like I ain't got better shit to go do!"

How much looking could she have done? All I had in my room was a box spring and a thinning out blanket. My daddy and Rhonda had the soft mattress in their room. My friend at school said her room had a canopy bed, plenty of drawers for her clothes, a desk and chair to do her homework, and a doll house so big, it had to sit on the floor. She said it was filled with dolls and furniture and looked like a real house. And everything in her room was pink, my favorite color. I'd always wondered what it would be like to have a room like that.

Oh no! My nose started itching, and I needed to sneeze. I was going to hold it in, but my teacher at school said to never hold a sneeze in. So I went ahead and sneezed. It was a loud one too.

That's when Rhonda heard me and rushed toward the closet.

I grabbed the knob and held onto it.

"Let it go!" she yelled.

She had managed to twist it, but I used all the force of my body to keep it shut, begging her, "Please don't whip me." But she was way more powerful than me, and managed to get it open.

I stood to my feet quickly, and before I could run out of the closet, she punched me in my nose so hard, blood streamed from it. I screamed.

Then I got a punch in my stomach. "I can't stand your muthafuckin' ass!" She kicked me in my stomach, and I fell on the floor out of breath.

Chapter 2

Eight Years Later

It was Big Homie's birthday, and he was having a party. Me and Danada were going. I really didn't have anything special to wear but a pair of skinny jeans and a black wifebeater. But since my body was banging, I made anything, and I mean anything, look good.

I knew they were going to have some drinks, some bomb-ass weed, and some fine niggas there. Thinking of it made my pussy wet. I tossed my feet in some flip-flops and went in the bathroom to make sure I looked okay. I winked at myself in the mirror.

What I lacked in parents and family I made up in looks. I had caramel skin, light brown eyes, full lips, and a beauty mark that sat at the corner of my mouth. My body was bananas. I had bit titties and a big ass. My waist was tiny, and I had calves like I ran track. While my hair wasn't all extra long, it sure as fuck wasn't short as a lot of these baldheaded bitches me and Danada be clowning. Plus, it was thick.

I turned around in the mirror and eyed my behind. I popped it a couple times and left the bathroom.

As I walked up the hallway I could hear snoring. I knew it was my father. When the rest of the world was up and working, his lazy punk ass was asleep. And his ho of a girl was working all right—on the fucking corner. I couldn't stand that ugly bitch. But I wasn't about to get upset over two fucking lowlifes. I had some fun to get into.

***

Danada was waiting for me outside my apartment. We were going to Eastside Crip territory at the Poly Apartments.

"Hey." She eyed me up and down.

"H—"

"Girl, your ass is getting huge!"

I chuckled to myself 'cause I knew deep down Danada low-key hated me even though she was pretty too. She was high yellow with the kind of hair that all you had to do was put water in it and it got curly. And she had a cute shape like me too, but not as much ass. But that's how it was. The prettiest girls were insecure.

But not me. If it's one thing I knew for a fact, I had that good looks. And I was going to trick the fuck out of them.

"You know how I do it. The niggas like it nice and round."

"Don't get it twisted. Yeah, niggas like ass, but they go crazy over a redbone wit' real long good hair."

"True dat. But ain't no nigga going to be focusing on your face with your feet looking the way they do."

"Well, did you still want to do that?" she asked me.

"Shit, if you down then, you know I down."

"Come on."

We walked over to the nail shop next door to the Mark Twain Library and MacArthur Park. It was busy like we expected, which made it better for us.

"Hello?" the Korean lady said as soon as we walked in.

"Hi," we both chimed at the same time.

"Wha u nee tuday?"

"Two full sets and two pedicures."

"This vayyyy," she sang.

We followed after her, and as soon as we sat down, I slipped off my flip-flops and passed them to Danada, who put mine along with hers in her backpack that she placed back on her back.

"Hi, whata size?" a lady said. She had the brownest teeth I had ever seen. She placed a plastic hand on the table I was sitting in front of.

I picked the longest nails they offered. I turned to Danada. "What are you getting?"

She pointed to the same size I was getting.

Two ladies wheeled their pedicure carts our way, and while we got our nails done, they worked on our feet.

I stared at the booth across from me and wondered what the girl sitting there was even doing there, 'cause if I had feet like hers, I would never show them. Them dogs would be in socks all year round. Even in the summer in one hundred-degree weather. In a heat wave! Her feet looked bigger than Shaq's; my guess was, they were a size twelve, and her feet had corns the size of quarters on every damn toe.

I almost gagged at the bloody cut across her foot. *Damn! The bitch got stabbed in the foot?*

"Yen, make sure you sterilize that razor. I got a open wound, baby," the lady informed her.

The manicurist smiled and mumbled something like, "*Ji ral yhun byung*," to the lady doing my feet without looking up. And she scraped and scraped and scraped; it looked like the customer had psoriasis.

I turned my head and forced myself not to look her way again. When I looked Danada's way, she had her hand over her mouth. "What's wrong?" I whispered.

She gestured with her head toward the lady's feet and whispered, "I just threw up in my fuckin' mouth."

I giggled to myself and made sure the fucked-up feet lady didn't hear me.

When the lady finished my nails, she had a huge smile. "Design?"

"Yeah. What you got?" I asked, knowing she was gonna try to squeeze as much money out of me as she could.

Now I guess I couldn't say all Koreans were bad. Only the ones that owned businesses in inner cities. To me, they exploited the fuck out of black people. A lot of mothers in the hood didn't having cars, so when they ran out of milk or needed some eggs or a loaf of bread, they jacked up the fucking prices 'cause they know it was either, go to a big grocery store which was further away, or go down the street to them. You end up spending fucking eight dollars for a block of cheese!

Then when you spend money in their stores, they wanna treat you like you ain't shit. Like we were so uncivilized. I lost count of how many times I went into their stores and ended up getting kicked out or banned because I cursed they ass out or threatened to burn their shit down. And I knew when they spoke in their native tongue, they were cursing our black asses out.

But what I didn't understand was, if they hated us so much, then why the fuck did they move into our neighborhoods and open up shop? Why the fuck are their beauty supplies for black people? And why are they able to get away with that shit? Answer that for me, Mr. President.

I asked the lady doing my nails, "Which one you think?"

"Pink with diamonds. Dry fast too."

"Okay."

The one doing my feet said, "Same for feet too? Look pretty."

"Okay."

I watched the lady doing my hands place a shiny diamond on each on my fingers that were painted a pink French manicure. The lady doing my pedicure did the same to my toes. Meanwhile, Danada was over at the air brush table.

As the lady who did my pedicure placed a diamond on my last toe to be done, the lady doing my hands asked, "Facial?"

"Huh?"

"Facial." She moved a hand over her face in a circular motion.

"Naw. Maybe next time. I don't have time for that." *Money-hungry bitch!* She probably didn't know how to do a fucking facial anyway. Bitch was probably going to put some mud on my face and rinse it off. I could do that shit myself.

"Yeah, yeah, next time. Your feet and hands beatiful. Your face ugly." Her eyes got wide when she said *ugly.*

My eyes got wide too. I know this bitch did not just call me ugly. I almost flipped a table over on her ass, but I thought better.

The pedicure lady placed the plastic sandals on my feet, and the manicurist placed the last coat of the clear polish on my pinky before saying, "Done. You sit here."

"How long?"

"You wait five minutes."

The pedicure lady wheeled her cart away.

I walked over to the table in the back, where you can place your feet at the bottom and your hands in the middle to dry.

Danada joined me. I was closest to the door. We eyed each other and then looked at the clock.

"Three ten," she whispered.

I nodded.

As more people crowded into the salon, my eyes watched the clock. I kept my hands flat to make sure they dried properly and none of my nails smeared.

"Saw my corns some more, Yen," the lady with the fucked-up feet said, her pedicure still not done.

"*Dak chuh ra!*" The Asian manicurist doing her toes stood and threw her nail file on the floor.

Which was the distraction me and Danada needed. I hopped up from my seat and ran out the salon, and Danada followed after me.

The owner ran out after us and was yelling, "*Nigimi ship e dah! Bul sang han nyun!*"

We just ran toward the park, all the way down, until we tired the lady out.

She stopped running and held a fist in the air. "*Yumago. Bitch!*"

Chapter 3

We kept going until we made it a few streets down. We busted up laughing once we got to Martin Luther King Street.

"Girl, did you hear her ass?"

"She said every word in Korean, except for the word *bitch*," Danada said, doubled over in laughter.

"I know, girl."

I looked at Danada's toes. There were green and had a dollar sign on each one of her hands and feet.

"But it was worth it. We got the complete package," she said.

"Let me get my shoes. Our feet are probably dry enough."

She pulled off her backpack and slid out our shoes. We both put our flip-flops back on.

"I hope it's some cuties at Murder's house," I told Danada. "'Cause I need a boyfriend to take me out and buy me clothes and shit."

See, when you a little kid in elementary school, you don't care how you look, and mostly, name brands don't mean shit to you. As long as you can go outside and play, you cool. But when you move on to junior high school and high school, it's a whole new ball game, where image is everything. You can't wear the same outfit every day and the same shoes my daddy purchased from fucking Salvation Army without getting made fun of. It was social suicide, and there was no way I was going to be a fucking laughingstock at school.

It was bad enough that I didn't know who or where the fuck my crackhead mama was, and that my daddy was a fucking loser drunk. I refused to look tacky at school or in my neighborhood. No way. I made fun of people who wore shoes from Payless and secondhand clothes. And I talked about them so bad, they cried. So there way no way I was going to let somebody be able to talk about me in the same way.

I was a popular girl at school, and all the guys liked me, including those on the football and basketball team. But I didn't care for them. I wanted a thug to take care of me, not some nigga running around with lunch money in his pocket. Let them other hoes date them.

I was considered one of the pretty girls, but I didn't hang with them hating, sew-ditty bitches. In my opinion, bitches were trifling and would do you in a minute, no matter how close you were to them. My thing was, why bother with all of that? I didn't need to be around a bunch of bitches anyway, having fucking slumber parties, painting each other's nails and styling each other's hair. To me, that was some lesbo shit.

I only hung wit' Danada and, occasionally, her friend Tameka. And we did hood shit them Poly girls didn't know nothing about. They were too busy cheerleading, chasing them dumb-ass jocks.

I was too busy hustling for the shit I needed. And I did a decent job at it too. I had a couple of ways of getting clothes. Once a week, I would go to this mom-and-pop store on Long Beach Boulevard, near the Metro station, and grab a bunch of clothes to try on. My trick was to always go in the store in a sweat suit. Then I would sneak on a pair of pants and put my sweats over them.

I also dealt with this sixty-year-old "pisa" dude who owned a store on the East Side, on Pacific Coast Highway that had cute name-brand clothes. Whenever I went to him, he would give me a five-dollar disposable camera. I would go home and take nude pictures of myself and give the camera back to him, and he would get them developed. For every camera I brought him, he would give me a whole outfit.

And as far as tennis shoes, the security guard at the Shoe Warehouse on Long Beach Boulevard wanted to fuck me, so I used to blow his dick when he got off work in the parking lot, and he'd steal a pair of the latest tennis shoes in my size. And that's how the fuck I survived.

But the shit was starting to get old. How many ways could I hold my titties and snap it? Or crouch, so my pussy showed? Or pose with my tongue out?

But his old ass never got tired of receiving pictures. He would get me Ed Hardy, True Religion, Ecko, and Baby Phat. The kids at school thought my family was straight balling. Shit, if they only knew. I'd been sleeping on the same box spring since I was five, and hardly ever had tissue to wipe my ass, or soap to wash it. And the house was roach-and-crackhead infested.

Yes, we had food, only because Rhonda was addicted to food as much as she was to crack. There was hardly anything balling about my household. My dad was a loser lush, and his woman was a fucking crack whore. And that EBT card never went on me.

I never invited them to come to open house. The day they ever stepped foot on my campus was the day they'd have found me floating in a river because I jumped in that bitch.

The thought of going to Murder's house excited me. I had never met him before, but Danada told me he was serious out here in these streets. He lived in the Poly Apartments and ran them muthafuckas. He had the whole management company shook. I lived on Mahanna Street by all the longos.

As we walked to the bus stop, I said, "Speaking of niggas, you know I hope Li'l Murder is there."

"Supposedly, he got a girl who pregnant, but I don't care," Danada said. "He can get it."

Crazy part was, Danada was a year younger than me, and I was fifteen.

I laughed. "How many niggas you fucked?"

She plopped down on the bench at the bus stop. She laughed. "Too many to fuckin' count, girl. What about you? I know you got a long list too."

I sat down next to her and laughed. "No comment."

"I'm sure, ho. Who was your first?"

The last thing I wanted to think about was how I lost my virginity. Because it wasn't anything my young ass imagined. Instead of it being in the back of some nigga's car, or in a bedroom of a hood party, after smoking some sticky-icky and having some drink, it was at home in my bedroom, while I was trying to get some sleep. And it wasn't by some cutie from my neighborhood that I had a crush on.

It was damn near three in the morning, and I was trying to get some sleep, which was pretty fucking hard, 'cause my daddy and his girlfriend was having a fucking get-high party in the living room. Or so I thought. I had just managed to doze off when, suddenly, I felt someone sit on my bed. I couldn't make out their face in the dark, but when a flame came from a lighter, I saw it was a friend of my daddy's, Otis.

I sat up in the bed. He'd volunteered to be my God-daddy but never did shit for me. What the fuck was his fat ass doing in my room? I gasped when I saw him take a long drag from a crack pipe.

"What the fuck you doin' in here?" I looked at his fat, greasy, black ass with disgust. I was only twelve, but I knew how to curse like any adult, 'cause I was always cursed at.

"I came to see how my favorite girl is doing. You want some?"

"Hell no! Get the fuck out!"

"Now, is that anyway to speak to your God-daddy, Diamond?"

"Yeah—when his dope fiend ass is offering me some crack, and when his fat ass won't get off my bed."

He laughed and lifted the covers, exposing my legs. His dirty-ass hands crawled up my thigh.

"Stop!" I screamed for my daddy.

But all that made him do was slam me down on the bed, and that pipe he had in his mouth was now in mine. He was scaring the fuck out of my twelve-year-old ass.

"Take a toke, baby. It's okay. God-daddy said so."

I shook my head and tried to pull it out of my mouth, but he held my hands down with one hand and pinched my nose with the other.

I held on as long as I could. I didn't want that shit, and I didn't want to become no crack ho either.

He laughed as I held my breath. "You so stubborn, baby. Stubborn and fine. *Ummmmm.*"

I shook my head and tried to knock his hand away from my nose by pressing my head into my pillow, which made me more desperates for air, until I had no choice but to inhale that shit.

"That's a good girl, baby.

I froze at the impact of that shit. The feeling was good as hell and paralyzed my whole body and made my mouth completely numb.

Next thing I know, he pushed up my tee shirt and was flicking his tongue all over my body, and ended up licking my pussy.

I called for my daddy to come in the room over and over again despite feeling high out of my mind, but he never came.

Otis had me on my knees and was shoving his dick in my booty. I started screaming my daddy's name at the top of my lungs.

That made Otis stab me harder.

I screamed and bawled at what he was doing to me. I begged him to stop. "Otis, please."

He bucked against me. "That's it, baby. Call my name. Say it again."

I sobbed and tried to pull away, but he had secured my thighs in his hands.

"Oh, baby, I'm coming. Get ready."

Then I felt all this fluid fill up my bootyhole and gush down my booty and thighs. Then he left my room.

I got up and went to the door, prepared to tell my daddy. I rushed in the living room. The house was crowded with people, dirty-looking and half-dead-looking women and half-dead, dirty-looking men. They were all hitting pipes. In the whole group of people, my daddy was nowhere to be seen.

I walked past them toward the kitchen. I felt a hand on my arm and snatched my arms away from this crackhead. His eyes were so red and wide, I thought they were gonna fall out of his head.

He shrugged at me and shoved a pipe in his mouth before walking away.

When I made it to the kitchen, I still didn't see my daddy. But I did see my bitch-ass God-daddy. He strolled up to Rhonda, whose eyes looked red and wide, just like the man who had grabbed my arm.

Before I could call her name and tell her what that fat fucker did to me, I saw him reach in his pockets, pull out a five-dollar bill, and hand it to her.

"Muthafucka, I said ten if you wanted to fuck her!"

A few months later, one day I was coming home from school, and there he was sitting right in the living room with Rhonda, who had a smirk on her face when she saw the horrified look on mine.

I tried to brush past her.

"Now, Diamond, where are your manners, honey? Ain't you gonna give your God-daddy a hug and a kiss?"

He smiled at me and patted one of his fat thighs. "Yeah, baby. Give your God-daddy a kiss."

He looked even worse in the daylight in the soiled-up blue jeans that hung off his fat ass. They looked so old and stained, he probably didn't bother to wash them 'cause the stains probably wouldn't come out. His white top was just as dingy and wrinkled and had a tear in the neck area. Not to mention, there was dirt in his fingernails, and a foul odor was coming from his ass—a mixture of shit, sweat, and musk.

I tried to walk away.

"Diamond! What the fuck is wrong with you? Get your ass over there and kiss him!"

Just being in the same room with him was giving me the flashbacks from that night he brutally raped me.

I leaned over and attempted to kiss his cheek, all the while feeling my stomach knot up, and a nauseous feeling sweep over me. As soon as my lips got close to his cheek, he turned his face quickly so his lips were on mine. Then he slipped his tongue inside.

I gagged and tried to pull away, but a hand stayed on my rump to hold me there. His mouth tasted like a combination of liquor, nicotine, and spoiled food.

When he got the kiss he was after, he loosened his hold on me and patted my rump. "Go do your homework, baby. And be a good girl for God-daddy."

I could hear Rhonda chuckling as I rushed to my room.

"Diamond, did you hear me?"

"No. What?"

Danada applied gloss to her lips until they were shiny. She then handed it to me to use.

"I said you should try to get put on Eastside Crips too. Girl, the shit is fun. We get to hang at all the parties, get free weed and drank. And don't nobody fuck with me either."

"I'm not trying to get jumped by nobody."

She laughed at me and slapped one of her thighs. "I didn't get jumped to get put on, girl."

"Well, what did you have to do?"

She laughed. And before she could reply, the blue 46 bus came.

We hopped on the bus, paid our fare, and mobbed straight to the back

"Damn! Hi, hater," Danada said to no one in particular.

I laughed because bitches were staring nonstop.

"Okay," I said, mean-mugging anyone who made eye contact with me.

We sat in the back row; that way we could see everybody getting on the bus.

As the bus started to roll, I looked out the window, trapped in my own thoughts. I could hear the lady singing in my head again, her soft voice singing, *"Twinkle, twinkle, little star."*

I started humming it.

"Girl, I know you is not humming 'Twinkle, Twinkle, Little Star.'"

I put my head down, embarrassed.

"Hum this, Diamond—*I wish I could fuck every nigga in the world.*" Danada was singing the song by Drake and Lil Wayne, changing the word *girl* to *nigga*.

I laughed and started singing it with her as the bus made its rounds through the neighborhood.

When the bus made a stop for more people to get on, Danada nudged my elbow. "Girl, look at this baldheaded bitch."

My eyes flashed to the front of the bus, to a black girl coming in our direction. She was dark-skinned and ashy as hell. "What the fuck is she wearing, D?"

I had to admit the girl wasn't the best dressed. She had on some jeans that had probably seen better years. They were black but so faded, they looked gray. The knees were worn out and the bottoms flared. Those were out. All we wore in high school was skinny jeans. And she had some tennis shoes called Air. And her black top had a bleach stain on it. Her hair was in a ponytail, but it was so short, the sides and the back had escaped the ponytail and crowned her face in nappy patches. Her baby hair was also full of naps, but still the girl was prettier than me and Danada.

When she saw us, she flashed a smile, revealing white teeth, and sat across from us.

Danada smirked at her. I smirked too.

"Black and nappy," Danada chanted. "Black and nappy."

I burst into laughter and eyed the girl, who looked in our direction and quickly put her head down.

"Ain't no way in hell I would walk out the house if I looked like her ugly ass," Danada said loudly.

My laughter got louder, and people in the front of the bus turned around and looked at us.

The girl kept her head down, but from her profile, I could see tears dropping from her eyes. It made me feel a little bad. I was hoping Danada would stop.

"Some people need to learn how to wash they stank pussy. Three words: Water and soap."

I laughed again.

Danada continued to chant, "Black and nappy. Bitch, you must be unhappy." Then she laughed to herself. "Awww shit! I just rhymed without even trying. I got some serious skills."

Me and her banged fists.

The girl turned her body in a different direction, but I could see her shoulders shaking.

"That bitch look like a black version of the Loch Ness Monster. I bet she got the same panties on that she wore yesterday."

"Probably do."

She endured five more minutes before she pulled the chime telling the bus driver to stop at the next available bus stop. As soon as the bus stopped, she stood and walked to the back exit. She stood in front of the double doors, and just as soon as they opened, I heard her mumble, "Ignorant."

Danada heard it too, and in a flash, she snatched me by my arm, and we rushed off the bus after the girl.

"Come on, D."

I chased after Danada as she followed after the girl, who was rushing down the street.

Danada stopped her, yelling, "Aye!"

The girl turned around and faced us.

"Now, what the fuck was you saying on the bus, bitch? 'Cause this Eastside Crip."

"You can call me out my name, but when I call you out your name you get in my face?" she said, her voice shaky.

"Yeah, bitch!" Danada got further in her face.

"But that doesn't make sense. It's not right." Her voice stayed calm.

"Yes, it is, bitch!"

The girl's eyes widened. She looked from me to Danada and swallowed hard. "Well, it's over. Why don't—"

"Why don't I what, bitch?"

The girl put her hand up in peace. "Why don't you leave the issue alone?"

"Oh, so now you telling me what the fuck to do?"

"No, I—"

Before the girl could finish her sentence, Danada hit her square in her mouth. I watched her eyes instantly tear up, but she didn't fight back.

"Come on, D. Help me fuck this ugly bitch up."

The girl's eyes pleaded with me to stop this, but I didn't. I grabbed her by the back of her short ponytail and slammed her on the ground.

Danada busted up laughing.

I then dropped to my knees and pummeled the girl in the face, while Danada kicked her in the chest and stomach.

The girl screamed.

"Bitch, shut the fuck up! This Eastside." Danada shoved me out the way and punched the girl again in her face.

That's when I heard something pop, and blood flew from the girl's nose.

"Come on, D."

Me and Danada stomped the girl in her head over and over again, which kept slapping the concrete beneath her.

"Move, D!"

I slipped out of the way and watched Danada give the girl a series of blows until her whole face was knotted up, and her lips were as bloody as her nose.

"This Crip, bitch!" Then she slammed her head on the concrete.

The girl was cold knocked out.

I stared at her as long my guilt allowed me to. Then Danada yanked me by my arm, and we were running the other way.

Chapter 4

We didn't stop running until we were two blocks past the girl we had beat up. Once we got to a red light, Danada fell on me and busted up laughing.

"Damn!" she said. "We fucked that bitch up!"

I laughed alongside her.

"Do you think she gonna call the police on us?"

"Who gives a fuck!" I said, even though I had never been arrested before, and the thought of going to jail did scare me.

We continued to walk until we made it to the Poly Apartments. When we got to Murder's door, I could smell the bomb-ass weed and hear them bumping Snoop Dogg. And I was in heaven. Once we got inside, we saw that there weren't a lot of people in there. There were three guys in the room.

What caught my attention was how fly his crib was, with leather couches, a glass table resting on top of a black cougar, and matching rug on the floor. I saw pictures on the wall of Murder holding guns, and one with him in a suit. Then, of course, he had to have big pictures of pretty, naked bitches. His flat-screen TV was so huge, it took the whole side of the wall, and you know he had to have a big-ass stereo with big speakers to bump that gangsta rap.

"Girl, come on," Danada said.

I walked in the room and stood next to Danada, who did the introductions, standing there like she was a boss bitch.

"Hey, y'all," I said to everybody.

I glanced at the dudes. Brown skin, with a goatee, and a

teardrop under his right eye, Murder had to be six foot four. His hair was braided back in cornrows. He was so muscular, like two of me put together. He was the one rolling up the weed.

Danada said, "Diamond, this the Big Homie. Murder."

When I held my hand out to shake his hand, he looked at me like I was crazy and blew smoke in my face. I blinked and took a step back.

The dude to his right looked exactly like Murder. He had to be Li'l Murder, his son. And, yes, he was fine as fuck. He was a younger version of Murder, with the same braids and teardrop. The other dude was named Gutter. He was fine too, light skin with green eyes, baldheaded, and had a muscular body too. They all had on wifebeaters and Chucks, different from the guys I went to school with, and they all wore skinny jeans. To me, skinny jeans should be for bitches only. These niggas were more my "steelo."

That was Gutter who greeted us, "'S up, ladies."

Suddenly a lady walked into the living room, an older dark-skinned woman with long hair in a ponytail. She wore some booty shorts that had her huge ass hanging out of them, and a tank top with no shoes on.

"Murder," she said, eyeballing me and Danada.

Murder yelled, "Bitch, go back in the room!"

She quickly left the room.

My eyes got wide. I whispered to Danada, "Who is that?"

"Trina. Murder woman." Danada plopped down next to Li'l Murder.

"Oh." I sat down next to the dad, even though I wanted to sit by Gutter. *Damn! He's fucking fine!*

The next thing I know, they were passing weed around to us like it was free, and I was getting straight faded. And that shit felt good. I went from being shy and quiet in that room with them niggas to bouncing my booty on the floor to the song, "Gin and Juice."

Then they pulled out some Grey Goose, and I downed that shit too. Me and Danada were on the floor popping our asses for all of them. I wanted to impress Gutter, so I popped as hard as I could, until I could feel my booty slapping against my back.

Weed smoke flowed from his mouth, and he bopped his head to the music, but he wasn't paying me no mind.

But I can tell you whose eyes were on me, both Murder and Li'l Murder, despite the fact that Danada was going in for Li'l Murder and trying her damnedest to get his attention in that house.

"So y'all just gonna tease us?" Li'l Murder asked.

We both continued to dance.

"When y'all gonna stop bullshitting and really dance for us? Or do we have to kick y'all hoes out and go to a real strip club?"

I looked at Murder, whose eyes bore into mine. Nervous, I put my head down.

Danada shook her head. "Hell no. Y'all aint gotta go to no strip club. Right, D?"

I nodded and continued to twist my body.

"Just say what y'all want us to do, and we down," Danada told them.

"Take them muthafuckin' clothes off, for one thang . . . if y'all really trying to impress a nigga," Li'l Murder said.

Danada stripped down to her bra and panties, and I followed suit. Then she stood on a couch and continued dancing.

I took another puff of the weed and stood on the couch next to her. *Fuck that!* She wasn't going to outdo me. I didn't have on a pair of thongs like Danada, but I worked my ass to the song "Some Bomb Azz (Pussy)" by Tha Dogg Pound, so that my panties disappeared in the crack of my ass.

Meanwhile, Danada was crouched down, and her booty was popping.

I stood and bent my upper body entirely over, so my ass was poking out. I even pulled down my panties. *Fuck it!* What I was doing felt good, so why not go with it?

Just then I felt fingers prodding my pussy. Then a tongue. And the shit felt so good, unlike that shit Otis did to me. I glanced up and saw Danada standing with her hands on her hips, staring at me angrily, because all the niggas were crowded around me.

I shrugged and chuckled, enjoying that shit. I split my thighs apart farther and felt a finger plunge deeper into me. Then I felt a tongue flicker into my clit again, and a hand smacked my behind.

Suddenly, a glass of water was tossed in my face. At first, I thought it was Danada, hating. But when I shook my face, wiped it away, and opened my eyes, I saw the dark-skinned lady from earlier. Trina was standing in front of me, an angry look on her face, like she was going to fuck me up.

She shouldn't have done that, or maybe after she tossed that water on me, she should have broke, because Murder came after her and swung a closed fist, catching her in her jaw. She grabbed her faced and fell to the floor.

"Naw. Get up, bitch! You wanna disrespect my company. Now you gonna get disrespected." Murder snatched her up by her hair.

She yelled out, "But she up in here disrespecting my house. I pay the bills in here."

"Bitch, I don't give a fuck!" He punched her in her stomach.

From the corner of my eye, I saw Danada putting her clothes on, all the while mean-mugging me.

Reluctantly, I started putting mine on too, while Li'l Murder and Gutter were laughing at Trina getting her ass whipped. Murder was so into fucking her up, he didn't notice us about to slip through the door.

"Say something else, bitch!"

Eveb though she didn't, he hit her anyway.

I followed after Danada.

"Where y'all going?" Murder said. "Y'all ain't gotta leave."

We sat back on the couch, and I blew some more trees.

When we left Murder's house, Danada didn't speak a single word to me. I didn't give a fuck, though. I simply got on the bus and went to the back like we usually did. But she didn't sit nowhere near me. I giggled to myself and kept singing, "*Bitch, you got some bomb-ass pussy.*"

Chapter 5

When I made it home, I was disappointed as hell to see my punk-ass daddy and his ho. The house stank, as usual, of beer and piss. My daddy would get so drunk, he would forget that the living room wasn't a bathroom and would piss right on the couch, or his ho of a girlfriend would bring her johns home to service them. And my daddy always tried to tell me she was a fucking bartender at The Alibi, a bar on the North Side of Long Beach. Shit, that bitch was a ho-tender.

"Where the fuck you been?" Rhonda demanded.

I wanted to say, "None of your muthafuckin' business," but I told her, "I was at my friend's house. Why?" I sat down on the carpet. Wasn't no way I was going to sit on the couch, which was infested with roaches, piss, and pussy.

"The dishes needed to be done, that's why!"

"Well, why didn't you do them?"

Rhonda was a fucking lie. She probably wanted to slip somebody else in my room to make some quick money.

It didn't make no sense telling my daddy, because he didn't care. After what Otis did to me, I had told him as soon as I saw him, and he said, trying to stand his drunk ass up without falling, "If you looking for some muthafuckin' attention, you coming to the wrong fuckin' person, so go on with your lies, girl."

"But, Daddy, I'm not lying. She even got money for it."

"*Mm-mm.* If she got some muthafuckin' money, then why the fuck didn't she share it with me?"

After that, I left the shit alone. I could have chalked his response up to him being drunk, and maybe, just maybe, if he was sober, the thought of his homeboy raping his daughter might have incited him to go postal. Truth was, I was scared that if I did approach him when he was sober that the response would be the same. What kid wanted to feel like their own daddy didn't care if a grown-ass man violated them?

Rhonda's loud voice snapped me back to the present. "Little bitch, you better stop getting smart with me. You don't pay no bills in this muthafucka."

I rolled my eyes at her.

She looked at my daddy. "You see this little ho?"

He ignored her and me both.

"Without me, y'all wouldn't have that EBT card, and you wouldn't have Section 8."

She gave me an angry look. What the fuck did my daddy see in her ass? She was fucking six feet, towering over him, and damn near bald. And I don't mean bald where you had short hair. Literally ninety percent of her head was shiny bald, with a patch of bleach fuzz here and there. She said she had alopecia. To me, it was a combination of crack and trying to be something her black ass wasn't—a blonde. And all her teeth were rotted out and loose. I was just waiting for the day she would eat a sandwich or take a bite of an apple and they all gave way.

And she had a combination of scars and brown blotches all over her face. Her eyes were always bloodshot red and so huge, the bitch should have invested in some stunna shades. She was rocking the Bobby Brown "lip thing," where your mouth can't keep still from all the crack you smoked, and her lips were always outstretched or twisted to one side, like they had a life of their own.

Her body was even sadder than her face. Her breasts sat on her stomach, her ass sagged down to her thighs, and her legs were covered with all kinds of bruises. Let's not even discuss her kneecaps. Her way of keeping herself up was using nail polish on her manly feet and hands, and putting on lipstick.

But these men out here liked something about her. I'll bet her pussy was so loose, you could put about ten dicks in her at one time.

But my dad wasn't much better, wearing the same dirty, dingy clothes every day. They say he used to be a handsome man, but he had a set of naps that sat on his head, never shaved, and always smelled like liquor. In fact, I didn't see any resemblance between me and him.

"I need to go to work, and when I come home the fuckin' dishes better be done." She flung her ratty purse over her shoulder and slammed the door on her way out.

I turned to my daddy. "Daddy, you know she's not going to no bar to work, right?"

He shrugged.

"I seen her on Pacific Coast Highway the other day." Pacific Coast Highway, by Long Beach City College, was a ho stroll. "She was getting in some man's car. That don't bother you? To know that she has sex with other men for money, Daddy?"

He turned his bloodshot red eyes on me. "Shit! Diamond, a woman like that is the best to have."

"What?"

"A crackhead is the best woman to have. When she on that shit, whew! You can get her to do whatever you wants. You never miss a meal in your life, and you always get the best head." He angled his head and winked at me when he said that part about the head.

***

Rhonda was dirty on all levels. Shortly after Otis had raped me, I came home from school to find her getting high on the living room couch. When she saw me, she smiled and said, "Sit down."

I did, with an attitude.

"Here, Diamond, try some of this."

"Some of what?" I asked, knowing she wasn't offering me some crack.

"Do I need to spell it out for your ass? I know Otis gave you some that night."

She knew?

She saw my eyes and smiled. "Your secret is okay with me." She held the pipe out to me.

To be honest, just looking at it reminded me of that night when Otis forced it in my mouth. I wanted that high feeling again. My lips were watering, and my fingers were aching to snatch it out of her hand and bring it to my lips.

Instead, I slapped that shit out of her hand, and the pipe fell to the floor. I refused to become a fucking crackhead.

"What the fuck! You little bitch!"

I jumped up, and she chased after me.

"You made me drop my shit. Diamond, I'm going to fuck you up!"

I ran straight for the kitchen, where we kept out knives. I should say *knife*, 'cause we only had one. I snatched it up and aimed it straight for her heart like it was a steak. "Get the fuck away from me, or I will stab your ass!"

She rocked back and forth, and her eyes were rolling back in her head. How much higher did she need to get? Her crackhead ass backed away. She went behind the couch, dropped to her knees, and started looking for the rocks that fell out of the pipe.

I left her ass there and walked to my room. But I heard her say, "Your mama is a fuckin' crackhead too!"

***

I came back to the present and shook my head at his nutty ass. "I don't know what's wrong with you, Daddy. I don't get why you would want to be with somebody like her."

"You act like you so much better than her. You traveling down her same path. At the rate you going, you and her going to be servicing the same car in no time. You ain't gonna be no different from your mama."

Why does he have to bring that bitch up? But still I wanted to hear. "What you mean?"

He placed both hands behind his head. "She was a fucking crackhead ho, man, willing to do anything for a set of them chemicals."

"Where she at?"

"How the fuck I know?"

"Come on, Daddy. How you not gonna know where my mama is? If she ain't nothing but a crackhead ho like you always say. You don't make a bit of sense. Yeah, I hate her ass for leaving me here with you. And if I ever run across her ass, I'm gonna send that bitch through it. I'm gonna exact some serious vengance on her ass. But I mean, let's face it. You don't do shit for me. And you let Rhonda do whatever she wants to me. And you don't care. My mama have to care about me some. If she didn't, why the fuck didn't she abort me?"

"'Cause she was too far pregnant with you. That's why. She didn't want you, and that's why she stuck me with your ass. Now get the fuck out of my face! You fuckin' up my high."

I shook my head and went into my room.

The next day when I went to school, I noticed Danada didn't meet me at our usual spot, so I ended up by myself. *Oh, well . . . if she want to be that way, fuck that bitch!*

As I was walking to the bus stop, she saw me and approached me. "What's up, girl?" I said.

"Li'l Murder wanted me to tell you that they havin' a hood party, and they want you to come on Friday."

"Aww shit!" She didn't share my excitement. "What the fuck is your problem?" I demanded.

"You know what my problem is."

"If I knew, why the fuck I ask?"

"You know I liked Li'l Murder, and you was letting him touch all over you."

"Girl, I didn't know who that was. I was high, and I can't see behind me. I like Gutter anyway, not Li'l Murder."

Her face softened. "I don't hang with hoes I can't trust. If you down with me, you down with me." She studied me before asking, "So you down with me?"

"Girl, yes. I would never betray you. Now, are we going to the party or not?"

She smiled. "Yeah, I got this fly-ass dress I'm wearing. What about you?"

"Girl, you know I ain't got shit," I said in a disappointed tone. It was too short notice to go get a camera. I had already worn my new outfit for the week on Monday."

She laughed as we continued our walk home.

Chapter 6

I was surprised to see that Danada didn't show up at school the next day and even more surprised she wasn't at the bus stop to go to the East Side. But the bottom line was, I was going with or without her. I instead saw her friend Tameka, tall and skinny, with a wide gap between her thighs. No titties, no ass, but she had a thick-ass ponytail and some light brown eyes.

She plopped down next to me. "Where Danada?"

"I don't know, girl."

She sucked her teeth. "We suppose to go over to Murder's house."

"Oh. I didn't know you were going."

"You goin'?"

"Yep."

"Well, can I roll with you?"

I didn't feel like I needed her or Danada to go with me. I was a big girl. "That's cool."

The bus pulled up, and me and Tameka hopped on. We mobbed to the back, like me and Danada normally would, and as usual, chicks were staring.

"Hi, haters." I waved like I was a beauty pageant winner.

Tameka laughed loudly, as we both settled in the back of the bus.

I started singing that Snoop Dogg song, "Some Bomb Azz (Pussy)" and Tameka started singing it with me.

When the bus made another stop, who else could get on

but the girl me and Danada had beat up. She quickly put her head down when she spied me, and took a seat in the front of the bus. One of her eyes was closed shut, she had a bandage over her nose, and both of her lips were swollen.

I covered my mouth and laughed loudly. "Damn, Tameka! Did you see that bitch?'

"Girl, who didn't? Somebody fucked her up."

"*We* whipped that bitch ass, me and Danada!"

People on the bus turned around and looked at us.

Tameka laughed.

"Bitch got what she deserved." I swallowed the lump in my throat.

Tameka clapped her hands together. "You cold for that, girl."

"We stomped that bitch. You see her eye?"

That's when some old lady had to take sympathy on the girl because she started crying. The old-ass lady looked like she could barely stand without her cane. "Why don't you leave that girl alone?" she asked me.

My eyes shot to her. *Why did she have to go there?* Now every fucking body on the bus was staring my way, waiting for my comeback. I stood to my feet and yelled, "What the fuck your old ass getting in this for anyway?"

"Because that girl ain't said nothing to you. That's why, now. You think you so damn tough. I want you to do something to me. I was on the bus that day you and your friend was picking with her." The old lady was on her feet too.

"You know what . . . Fuck you! You old raggedy bitch! You ain't too old to get your ass whipped too!"

"I wish you would, honey. I'm from the old school. It may take a village to raise you, but it only take one of my fists to knock your ass cold out!" she said, swinging her cane on every word of the phrase, "knock your ass cold out."

I looked at Tameka's ass. She didn't say shit.

The bus driver said, "Both of you need to either sit down or exit the bus."

"I paid my fare. Ain't no fast-ass, disrespectful gal gonna make me waste my money.

I sucked my teeth and plopped down in my seat, my arms crossed. Although I was embarrassed, I didn't want anybody to see that the old lady had checked me, so I started singing the line from one of Tha Dogg Pound's songs, *"Bitch, you got some bomb azz pussy."*

Tameka's punk ass started talking to me again. She was a big disappointment. At least Danada talked shit and was down to ride. This ho was scareder than a mouse.

"I wonder why Danada didn't come today. All she talked about was going to this party when I talked to her on the phone yesterday," she said.

"Who knows? Who fuckin' cares?"

Her eyes got wide. "You don't like Danada, Diamond?"

I shrugged. "She all right. But she be straight hatin'."

"Why you say that?"

"Because! She be low-key hatin' on me. We suppose to be friends, but some things you just see. She pretty, and she is insecure. And I ain't got no time to play Dr. Phil to any random ho. If you got issues, you need to take a fuckin' self-esteem class, or just end it. Fuck it!"

"You think Danada is pretty?"

"I mean, she all right. She ain't ugly, but, truth be told, if she didn't have that light skin and long hair, she would be average. And the rest of the world wouldn't be calling her pretty."

Tameka giggled

"But the bottom line is this—You don't look better than me, and her body ain't better than mine." I was slapping one hand into the other when I said that. "And that is why she is jealous of me. I got the beauty and the confidence. I can walk into a room, and it could have twenty Beyoncé's in there, and the niggas would still want me. That's why that bitch actin' funny. When we was at Murder's house, all the niggas were on me." I started moving in my seat excitedly as I talked.

"Murder was licking my clit in front of his girl, Gutter was drooling, and Li'l Murder was sticking his finger all up in my pussy." I didn't really know who was doing what, to tell the truth, but you know I had to put extras on it.

"What, girl?"

"Really, girl."

"Oh shit. We almost passing up our stop." Tameka pressed the button.

After we hopped off the bus, I continued to talk shit about Danada, about her bumpy-ass skin, how she's behind a lot of lip-gloss, probably got a loose pussy.

All Tameka kept saying was, "Yep!" and giggling.

I was so happy we made it to Murder's house. Niggas and females were outside. The living room was packed too. Niggas were grinding on women.

But the real fun was in the bedroom. That's where Gutter and Li'l Murder were, and they were blowing serious trees.

"What's up, y'all?" I said, walking in the room and snapping my finger to Mack 10's "Backyard Boogie."

Li'l Murder said, "Hey."

"Shit, this where the real party is!" I exclaimed.

Li'l Murder passed a blunt to me. "Go slow with that, li'l girl."

"I ain't no little fuckin' girl!" I was eyeing Gutter to make sure he hadn't heard what Li'l Murder had said. His eyes were so hooded, he didn't respond.

"Who your friend?" Li'l Murder asked.

"Tameka."

"Hey, y'all," she said, acting shy.

I took a long puff, waving one of my hands in the air to the music.

"You like to have a good time, huh, shorty?" Li'l Murder said to me.

"Yep." I wanted Gutter to say that shit, but that nigga was on the floor doing "the Crip walk."

I passed the weed to Tameka, and she took a long drag before handing it back to me. Then I handed it back to Li'l Murder. There was some Hennessy in the room, so I sipped on some of that.

From the corner of my eye, I saw Trina, Murder's woman, slip past the bed. Her eyes bored into me again like the other day, and she left the room. I smirked.

Murder walked in the room. He was faded and grooved through the door.

As the minutes flew, I became so faded, I was doing the "stankin' leg" like I was in one of them videos.

Gutter said to me, "Aye, I always wanted to know how to do that. How it go?"

I tried not to blush and showed him. "It's easy, see." I did it slowly, so he got it.

Then after he tried, I speeded my leg up to the rhythm. "You drop and push your legs out."

He was too fucking high to get it, and we ended up falling on the floor, laughing.

Then they had the nerve to play "T Shirt and Panties" by Adina Howard.

I screamed, "Awww!" and stood up from the floor. "This my shit, y'all. Tameka, you heard this before? My daddy's girl gets up every Sunday and blasts that song, but the bitch tee shirt be having holes in it, and her drawers be having shit stains on them."

They all laughed.

Tameka said, "This my mama song."

I started singing it and twisting my body. *"T-shirt and my panties on, waiting for you,"* I sang. I grinded up and down and did a come-hither finger to Gutter, who fell back on the couch, seriously faded.

The more I moved, the more Li'l Murder's eyes were on me, as were Gutter's.

"Come on, girl." I motioned to Tameka. But I guess she was satisfied standing in the background.

My hands went up and down my thighs, and I crouched over, so my butt leaned out. "Waiting for you." I winked at Gutter, my hands on my sides and rocking my hips up and down.

Gutter licked his lips at me.

That's when I felt it. My stomach started suddenly doing spasms, and salty saliva filled my mouth. I placed my hands over my mouth and ran out the room in search of the bathroom. Once I found it, I dropped to my knees and hurled the Hennessy and bits of food I had earlier for lunch into the toilet.

As I sat there with my head hung over the toilet, all I was thinking about was how childish Gutter was gonna think I was that I couldn't hold some fucking drink down.

After a few minutes, I started to feel better. I flushed the toilet and stood to my feet. I rinsed my mouth out and splashed some water on my face. Then I dried it with the towel they had hanging up on the door. I looked okay though. I was still fly.

I went back inside the bedroom, expecting to go back to the party, the music, the weed and drank—although I wasn't gonna drink no more—and the dancing. But gone was the music, gone was the weed and drink, and nobody was dancing anymore. Instead, I found Gutter, Li'l Murder, and Murder seated around the room, holding their dicks in their hands.

Tameka was still in the room too, looking at her cell phone, like she was distracted.

How you distracted with three big dicks in the room? "What happened to the party?" I asked nervously.

"Shit! The party right here," Li'l Murder said.

Both Gutter and Li'l Murder were putting on condoms, while Murder just sat there staring at me.

"Huh?" I looked around, confused.

My heart was thudding in my chest.

Li'l Murder said, "Well, Danada told me you wanted to be put on Eastside Crip."

I'd never told Danada that, but I said, "I do." I glanced over at Tameka's ass, now hiding in the corner.

"Well, you ready to be jumped on?" Li'l Murder asked.

"You can party like this all the time," Gutter said. "We always gonna have your back. If you need a place to crash for however long, we got you. If you need us to slice or pop somebody, we got you. We even got a name for you."

"What is it?"

"Naw," Gutter said. "We can't tell you that until you agree to be put on. We ain't gotta waste our time doing this shit either." He stroked his dick. "We doin' you a favor."

"So how 'bout it?" Lil Murder asked. "You wit' it?"

"Yeah, okay." I wanted to impress Gutter with my ability to make quick decisions, but I was really scared as fuck.

I was wondering if I had to have sex with Murder as well. And, if I didn't, why did he have his horse dick out? And why didn't he put on a condom?

"Well, let's go, baby," Li'l Murder yelled. "Get them clothes off and get that pussy in the air."

Tameka gasped as I stripped to my bra and panties.

"Everything," Murder commanded.

I took it all off until I was standing in front of them ass buck-naked. I hoped the other people partying outside and in the living room didn't slip into the room.

"Go 'head, Big Homie. You get it first." Li'l Murder held out his hand for Murder.

Murder slapped it away, mumbling, "I don't fuck with those."

Before I could move, Murder grabbed me by my neck and swung me to the ground, all the while his hands on my neck, and I hit the floor with a thud. He yanked me up until I was on my knees, and my hands rested on the floor, to stop myself from falling on my face.

I screamed out in pain as his dick penetrated my pussy, busting my cherry.

Yes. Aside from the butt-fucking Otis had given me when I was twelve, I was still a virgin. And I didn't envision losing my virginity this way. I wanted it to be Gutter and me kissing, and then him sucking my titties, going slowly and gently, while we listened to Keyshia Cole.

Murder grabbed my hair and yanked me back all the way so his dick had full entry into me each time he pulled in.

All of a sudden, Tha Dogg Pound blasted the room with "If We All Fuc." Only, this time I wasn't so hyped to dance.

"I love young-ass pussy!" Murder grunted.

I glanced up and saw Gutter and Li'l Murder standing over me. Gutter threw up the Eastside Crip gang sign, and Li'l Murder was blowing smoke out of his mouth.

I whimpered.

Murder jammed into me. "Shut up, bitch! You wanted to be put on, take this big dick!"

I shut up, mashing my fist into the floor, 'cause he was hurting me like no other. He kept pumping and pumping. I wondered if Tameka was still in the room.

I closed my eyes as I felt him bite the side of my neck. His pumping got even harder, if you can imagine. He slammed into me so hard, I slipped out from under him and fell forward.

"Come here, bitch!" He snatched me by my hair and put

his dick back into me. Then he slapped the back of my head. "You gonna fuck around and make a nigga lose his nut. A bitch that gives Murder blue balls is a bitch with her muthafuckin' head blown off. Now back that pussy up."

I did as he said. Then his legs started to shake. Then a hot fluid shot into my pussy.

He struggled against me, holding on for a second, breathing heavily. Then he shoved me away and yelled, "Trina!"

I kept my head down, embarrassed when she walked in the room. I could feel her eyes bore into me.

Murder told her, "Go get me a towel."

That's when Li'l Murder came behind me.

Murder wiped his dick then handed the towel back to Trina. He yelled out, "Man, you hittin' that pussy like you a bitch. What the fuck you makin' love to that ho for, boy?" He added, "Get back, bitch!"

That made Li'l Murder get rougher with me than his father was. He gripped my neck as he stroked me from the same position his father had placed me in.

"Get that pussy, boy!" Murder yelled.

Nothing about this felt good. Because I wasn't getting no enjoyment from it. Is that what sex was about? Were men always this brutal to a woman? Why did women like sex then?

Even when Gutter sat down in a chair and pulled me on his lap so that my back was to him and he was gripping my shoulders so that I was bouncing up and down his dick, I was too ashamed to look at anybody in the room. I didn't even know if Tameka ass was even in there.

Then Li'l Murder shoved his dick in my face, and thick, yellow fluid splashed in my eyes and all over my face. I kept my mouth closed for fear some of it would go inside.

"Move, nigga!" Gutter yelled. "You had your turn."

Li'l Murder laughed and moved away.

A few moments later, Gutter bent me over and was humping me.

I grimaced at the force of his thrust and prayed that this would soon be over and I would officially be a part of Eastside Crips. I would be one bad bitch. More powerful than Danada, that's for sure. And I would party so much that when it would be time for school, I would be 'sleep.

Abruptly, Gutter shoved me to the floor. He then snatched me up to my knees, so I was facing his dick. He slid off his condom and flung it to the floor then he took one hand and jerked his dick while holding the back of my head.

I tried not to gag as fluid shot directly into my face, and then they were done.

Chapter 7

The bus ride home was a little rough for me. For starters, the experience I had wasn't something to treasure. I had heard of what I did before. I let them run a train on me. I remember being in school and hearing about girls who had let niggas do stuff like that to them. Or even some dumb girls who took naked pics of themselves and had it sent from phone to phone. Or even up on some Web sites like ConcreteLoop, Necole Bitchie, or MediaTakeOut. I was glad that shit didn't happen to me, and this was as far as it went.

My legs were completely sore. I knew blood had to be still leaking from out my vagina. When I went into the bathroom to change, I stuffed some tissue in my panties. Before I even got the chance to throw my clothes back on, Tameka had split, leaving me to catch the bus alone. Oh well. The bitch was probably hating because they chose me and not her to be put on Eastside.

When I made it to my house, I saw Rhonda and her drunk, ghetto-ass friend sitting on the couch. She gave me a dirty look and put one of her fingers to her lips when I walked through the door. Her friend was on the phone. I hoped she didn't think I was going to say hi to her bitch ass.

I turned my mouth to one side and went into the kitchen. I poured myself a glass of cherry Kool-Aid Rhonda had drowned in sugar. I sipped it while listening to her friend talk.

"Hi. Yes, this is Lyneta Carlton. My son Remy Carlton is detained there." She paused. "Well, I was calling to make sure that my son didn't get his hair cut. See, it is tied to his religion. Mm-hmm."

My eyes narrowed as she talked.

"See, Remy, made a vow to God that he would always keep his hair and never cut it off. Mm-hmm."

Whatever the person said made Lyneta smile. "Oh in the name of Jesus, thank you. My whole church prayed about this. It was his vow to God, and we needed him to keep it. Well, God bless you. Bye."

I shook my head because as soon as she ended the call, she guzzled down some Thunderbird she had sitting in her lap. Her broke ass couldn't afford anything else. And the last time I checked, the bitch didn't go to church.

She high-fived Rhonda. "My son is a gangsta. They ain't cutting them braids. I been growing them since he was a baby."

I walked back in the living room.

"Why you walking so funny? You look like you just finished getting gang-banged." Rhonda's no-teeth-having ass busted up laughing, almost spilling her drink.

"Don't fucking worry about it, you fucking crackhead!"

She just laughed. "Yep. She got gang-banged. I can tell. I don't give a fuck, 'cause all you gonna be is a little ho anyway. So don't think you gonna come to me for the birds-and-the-bees talk, or for some fuckin' sympathy. And I sure as hell ain't taking you to the abortion clinic *when* you get knocked up. County will give us more money and food stamps if you have it."

I stalked up to her with my hands on my hips. "Don't get it twisted, bitch! I'm not gonna ruin my life like you ruined yours."

"Your life already ruined. The moment the nut was busted to make you."

Rhonda took a pull from her pipe before speaking again. She was the most functional crackhead I had ever seen. She never lost weight, and the bitch was always hungry. She had smoked so much crack, it seemed like it didn't get her high anymore. Her face always stayed the same. It was like she was smoking a cigarette.

"Just like your crackhead mama. Nobody."

"Yeah, whatever. Fuck you! 'Cause this Eastside Crip!"

Rhonda and her friend took one look at each other and cracked up at me like I was doing standup comedy.

"Oh, you gang-banging now?"

"What if the fuck I am?"

Rhonda looked at how serious my face was.

"You are one fuckin' dumb-ass kid. Y'all go out in the line of fire, and your ass will be the first one to be shot. And, to be honest, I really wouldn't give a fuck, except we gotta pay these bills some way." She pressed her palms together. "So tell me something, Diamond. How many niggas did you have to screw?"

"What the fuck you talking about?"

She lifted up her shirt. "I'm from Eastside, dumb-ass. I'm an O.G. And you don't look like you got down. Oh wait. You don't look like you fought, so you probably did get down— down on your knees!"

Lyneta snickered.

My eyes widened at the tat on her saggy left titty. I had never heard of Rhonda being a gang-banger. Never. And in all my years of growing up, the only people I seen her congregate with were crackheads.

"And I been claiming that hood since I was seventeen. I get so sick of little pretty hoes like you, sleeping your way into my hood, thinking that putting in work for the hood is fuckin' every damn nigga from the hood."

"Fuck both of y'all," I mumbled, walking toward my room.

Lyneta said, "Yeah, you may of got jumped in, but you slept with most of the niggas from the hood, Rhonda."

"Bitch, shut the fuck up!"

***

The funny part about being put on Eastside was the fact that nothing felt any different to me. Well, except the fact that wherever I went, people kept staring at me. Then I figured out why. And it had nothing to do with being from Eastside Crip.

I was sitting in my computer class when I noticed half the students in the class had out their cell phones, and they wouldn't stop looking from me to their phones. People that normally spoke to me wouldn't. What the fuck was going on?

I continued working on my assignment, although the teacher was half-'sleep.

Then I heard one dude who sat across from me yell, "Aye, send that shit to me!"

A few moments later, I heard him laugh and sing, "And if he fuck, then we all gon' fuck."

I ran over to his desk and snatched his iPhone out of his hand. That's when my heart stopped. It was a video of me last night at Murder's house. And they had that shit, me fucking Murder, Li'l Murder, and Gutter, all on their cell phones.

Chapter 8

I tried to get out of staying at school by going to the nurse and saying I needed to go home, but without a parent picking me up, I was stuck there. So I lay in the nurse's office for two periods. Then I spent the rest of the school day in the bathroom. But everywhere I went, someone was either staring, winking, or snickering at me.

I was relieved when school was over. I rushed out of the gates. I wondered who did that shit to me, set me up like that. It had to be Tameka. That was one trifling-ass bitch. I sure wanted to whip her jealous ass.

I didn't know how I was going to show my face at school again. I figured I could ask my dad to put me in Poly High School because there was no way I was going back there. And if he didn't let me go to another school, I wasn't going back. Fuck that shit.

It was so humiliating too for everybody to see me, ass buck-naked, sleeping with three fucking guys. Just thinking about it again made me want to cry. *Fuck! Why do bitches have to be so damn scandalous? I never did nothing to Tameka. All I did was do me.* When I see her ass, I'm gonna fuck her up like me and Danada fucked up that girl on the bus.

I rushed to the bus stop. Part of me wanted to walk because the walk wasn't real long, but I didn't want people to see me walking. I was probably safer getting on the bus and hiding in a corner. I walked down the street with my head down.

One dude said, "Here she go, y'all. *Skeet, skeet, skeet!*"

Yes, I heard the laughs, but I ignored it.

I heard a girl say, "She a straight ho!"

Disregard, I told myself.

When they started following me and chanting shit, I turned around on they ass. "Aye, y'all better leave me the fuck alone. Don't worry about what the fuck I do. Y'all fuckin' hoes just jealous 'cause they chose me and y'all niggas just mad cause I won't give y'all any pussy!"

Just as I stopped right outside of Poly's Burgers, a car skidded up the street and parked on the curb alongside me and the mob that was fucking with me.

Danada hopped out with Tameka and two other broads I didn't recognize, and they all came running toward me with bats.

The crowd around me rushed away, and somebody yelled, "Aww shit! Somebody gonna get fucked up!"

My heart started thudding in my chest. There was no way for me to escape as Tameka and the other two girls surrounded me and Danada was all up in my face.

"Talk some of that shit now, bitch!" Danada yelled.

"What?" My heart started thudding in my chest.

"Bitch, you heard what the fuck I just said. Talk your shit now."

"Why I wanna talk shit about you, Danada?" I knew my voice sounded shaky, and tears were starting to form in the corners of my eyes.

"I know. Tell me why you been talking shit about me!"

I shrugged nervously, not really wanting to move.

"I mean, you said I be hatin' on you. What the fuck I gotta hate on a ho like you for?"

I nodded, figuring it out. Tameka had told her all the shit I said.

"Talk your shit now, bitch!" she yelled. "Say it now. If I wasn't light skin, what? What?" Spit flew in my face as she was all in my grill.

I put my hands up in surrender.

"And, bitch, you knew I liked Li'l Murder, and you go and fuck him. I can't stand your triflin' ass, Diamond. I was your friend, but I warned you not to fuck with me!"

My lips trembled, and I wanted to cry. A crowd was now forming around us.

Danada laughed. "Y'all, look at this scary bitch, always woofin' shit, but you ain't nothin' but a fuckin' punk."

"I'm coo—"

"Bitch, shut the fuck up!" She swung the bat at me and connected with the side of my face.

I dropped to the ground instantly, and all four of them proceeded to give me the ass-whipping of a lifetime. The bats hit me on almost every part of my body. In my face, head, arms, chest, stomach, and legs. I crawled into a ball and hid my face inside of my forearms, but that didn't stop the assault.

Danada dropped to her knees and punched me over and over again in my face. I was screaming for my life, but that didn't stop them from fucking my ass right up. The other three chicks kept hitting me with those bats. My mouth filled up with blood. Blood also poured from my nose, and I knew that knots were forming on my face. I received a couple more kicks before the shit was over.

"You punk-ass bitch!"

"Come on, Danada," Tameka said.

I could feel their feet slamming against the pavement as they ran away from me, leaving me lying on the ground. Their car doors slammed, and they skidded away.

"Damn!" a dude said. "They fucked her up!"

Then some squeaky-voice bitch said, "I wonder who nigga she fucked? You know it gotta be about a nigga, the way they did her in."

"Bitch shit, no doubt," another said.

I gritted my teeth and picked my ass up off the concrete.

Then in all the pain I was in, I proceeded to walk to the bus stop to go home.

When I got to the bus stop, I heard more people comment about my ass-kicking. I blocked it out by singing, "Twinkle, Twinkle, Little Star," in my head. I don't know why the fuck it was in my head any damn way, at a time like that.

I got on the bus and didn't bother sitting in the back. I sat on the side near the bus driver. And, sure enough, that old bitch that was on the bus the last time with me and Tameka was on the bus again. She took one look at me and cracked up. I wanted to tell her ass to go eat some fucking prunes but thought against it. Her hands were clasped together like this was really a treat to see me all battered and bruised.

What made it worse was when the girl who me and Danada had jumped got on the bus. I didn't even look her way.

The old bitch said, "Damn! Somebody *DT*'ed her ass!"

The passengers roared with laughter.

"I see that heiffa ain't got nothing to say now, do she?" she said. "'Cause somebody clobbered your ass. I told you, God don't like ugly, girl."

That was it! I stood to my feet and ran to the door. "Let me out!" I yelled.

"I ain't got to the stop yet," the driver yelled.

"Let me the fuck out!"

The doors opened, and I ran out into the intersection, hoping a car would run my embarrassed ass over.

When I got home, and once I got past Rhonda, who laughed at all the marks on my face, and my daddy, who didn't bother to look my way, I went to my room, threw myself on my box spring, and cried until I fell asleep.

Chapter 9

I stayed out of school for a week. My daddy knew, but he didn't really care, except until when the school started calling about my absences.

I was lying in my bed under my frail blanket. I had been in bed for days, only getting up to eat, which I forced myself to do, and to use the bathroom. For some reason Danada kept calling for me, but I never answered it. But I did wonder what her ass could possibly want. I now hated her for ruining my reputation. I would be a laughing stock and labeled a ho for the rest of my life. Long Beach was a small city where everybody knew everybody. And the East Side of Long Beach was even worse. They always said, if you were fucking somebody, chances are, either your sister, cousin, or best friend had already fucked them.

My dad asked me, "Why you ain't been going to school, Diamond?" He didn't even mention the bruises on my face.

"Why you care?"

"I don't. I just don't want these white folks to keep calling here, threatening to call Social Services."

"Daddy, I don't ask you for much, so can you please take me out of Poly and put me in Cabrillo?"

My daddy had to have some type of love for me. And when you loved someone, you cared about their happiness, right? And if you could fix it, you would, right?

I started bawling.

"Daddy, I don't want to go back to Poly. Danada hate me

and she passed some ugly rumors about me at school. Then her and three other girls jumped me, Daddy."

"That's why you came back all fucked up?"

I nodded. "I can't go back there. The thought of going back there makes me want to kill myself. Daddy, please take me out of that school."

He stared at me for a long time, taking in the tears, the snot running down my face, and my sobbing. And it wasn't a joke. It was sincere. I really wanted to die before having to step foot on that campus after what went down.

"Okay." He stretched. "Shit. I guess I'll go down there first thing in the morning."

"Thank you, Daddy."

He froze when I said that. I didn't know why at first. But then I figured it was a tender moment for him. I never felt tender toward him. He never represented what I felt a father should represent. He was just there. And he allowed Rhonda to subject me to so much. I guess I wanted to feel fatherly love and he never gave it to me. It wasn't that I didn't love him. I always felt that he didn't love me. And I didn't get it. I would think that my daddy would give me a double dose of love because he knew my mother had abandoned me. But it seemed like he missed his dose as well.

I pushed that shit out of my head and went to sleep. My sleep was a whole lot better too. I wasn't tossing and turning, because I knew I wasn't going back to that fucking school.

The next morning, I felt a sharp pain in my butt. I spun onto my back and found Rhonda in my room with a shoe.

"Get your fuckin' ass up and go to school, Diamond!"

"But—"

Wham!

She swatted me again across the face. "Don't fucking talk back to me. Take your ass to school."

I froze at the pain that spread throughout my face. Although my mouth was open, no sound was coming out, and I could barely breathe. I held my face and sobbed into my arm.

She stood and stared at me. "You tried to play your daddy because you knew he was drunk. Well, it ain't gonna happen. Get your ass up."

Once she walked out of the room, I stood to my feet.

When my daddy walked into my room, I didn't bother telling him what Rhonda did. He wouldn't do shit. I shook my head as he stood in the corner of my room, pulled out his dick, and pissed. Then he fell to the floor and crawled out my room.

I pulled something out of my stack of folded clothes on the floor. Then I went in the bathroom and brushed my teeth. In the mirror I could see the shoe had left an imprint on my face. But I didn't care. It just went well with my busted lip, black eye, and the knot on my forehead from getting my ass beat.

I put on some deodorant and walked out to the bus stop. I ended up dozing off on the bus.

And I almost pissed on myself when I saw the old lady on the bus. *Shit!* I wondered how I hadn't spotted her. And to make matters worse, I had missed my stop. *Damn!* I pressed the buzzer, prepared to get off on Long Beach Boulevard, instead of Atlantic Avenue, and now she was getting off on this stop as well. I didn't even look at her. I knew if I did, she would let me have it.

I simply put my head down and walked the two extra blocks to my school. I knew if I ditched, the school would call home, and it would be another beating for me.

I crossed the street toward Atlantic, and she was walking with her cane, right behind me. *What's the purpose of getting off on Long Beach Boulevard if she's going to walk toward Atlantic?*

"You want a donut?" she asked me.

I looked at her surprised.

"You want one or not, girl?"

"O-okay," I stuttered.

"Then come on."

I followed after her into the donut shop that used to be Winchell's, but some Koreans took it over and called it 24/7 Donuts.

"What kind do you want?" she asked me once we made it inside.

I shrugged.

"Girl, what kind of goddamn donut do you want?"

"A twist," I said in a nervous voice.

She ordered that and an orange juice for me. She handed it to me, and she took her cream cheese muffin and coffee and sat down. "Sit down. You got time, girl."

I tried to keep the frown off my face.

Before I could even take a bite out of my donut, she asked, "Why you so angry, girl?"

"Lady, you don't know shit about my life."

"I know it won't get good at the rate you going, beating people up and whatnot. You always reap what you sow."

I hated to be preached to. Especially when those who preached didn't know shit about shit and wasn't prepared to do nothing to help me. That's why I stayed the fuck out of church. Wasn't nobody there when Rhonda was trying to pass me to drug dealers for dope. Wasn't nobody there when she beat me. Wasn't nobody there when I was raped at twelve. And, most of all, wasn't nobody there to stop my fucking mama from leaving me. So, now that I'm all fucked up, people got so much to say.

I laughed at her comment. "You know what, ma'am? I may be young, but I listen a lot when an older person talks. The problem is that people around me that are older often don't have anything important to say. You talk about how it takes a village and shit, but y'all see. All of y'all see the shit us girls around the way go through, even if you pretend you don't. We get used up like a fucking Kleenex, and in the end, like a fuckin' Kleenex, when there is no use for us 'cause we all tainted up, we better off in the trash. Y'all wanna come around and ask why we are the way we are. Tell me this—How can a fucked-up person make good choices?"

She was silent.

"Then y'all sit back and talk that reaping-what-you-sow shit."

She couldn't say shit. I had her old ass. My appetite was gone. I stood from the table and walked out of the donut joint.

Amazingly, when I got to school, everybody was off my shit and on to somebody else. Some other chick was caught sucking dick, and they had that on their phones. I still tried to keep a low profile.

I was surprised as hell when Danada came to me during computer class. "What's up, Diamond?"

I shrugged. "Nothing."

She gritted her teeth. "Murder want us to meet him at King Park after school."

That got my heart beating. What the fuck did he want with me? Aside from getting my ass whipped, I didn't do anything to anybody. Unless Danada told some lies on me. I prayed she didn't. I didn't want to go toe to toe with Murder. That man scared the hell out of me.

She met me right after school at the back gate.

"Kings Park ain't that far, so we can walk," she told me without looking my way.

"Okay," I mumbled.

And, boy, was that an uncomfortable walk. When me and Danada used to hang out together, we talked nonstop about clothes, boys, and shit. Now it was nothing but a long, uncomfortable silence, other than an occasional sneeze, cough, or one of us clearing our throat.

She didn't offer any apology, and neither did I. I wondered if either one of us would get over this shit and be friends again. The way I looked at it, we were even. I had fucked the guy she liked, and she had fucked me up. Sounds like a fair exchange to me.

As we approached the playground and walked farther into the park past the statue of Martin Luther King and toward the picnic tables, my heartbeat speeded up when I saw chicks over there. I didn't recognize most of them, with the exception of the three that had jumped me. Murder was there, and Li'l Murder, Gutter, and two other dudes were standing near him. I prayed I didn't get jumped again. With all them bitches that were there, I just knew, if they did it this time, I would probably end up paralyzed or dead.

"Why are so many people up here?" I asked Danada.

"It's a meeting," she said.

Before we even got a chance to say anything, Murder exploded on Danada. "Bitch! Who in the fuck gave you authorization to jump on somebody in my muthafuckin' hood?"

"I—"

"Bitch, shut the fuck up! I let Diamond get put on. You got a fuckin' problem with that?"

"No," she whispered.

"'Cause it's one thing that I can't stand, it's a hatin'-ass bitch!"

She pulled her bottom lip in.

"Apologize to that bitch now!"

She turned to me quickly. "I'm sorry, Diamond." She then turned back to Murder.

I kept my head down and didn't speak.

"You ain't runnin' shit. And, since you wanna be so fuckin' ambitious, you about to take a muthafuckin' beating!"

Her eyes got wide, and her lips started to tremble. She looked from me to Murder and nodded.

As soon as Murder and the dudes walked away, all of them bitches rushed Danada. She went up in the air at the impact and quickly fell to the ground. Then I could no longer see her. All I saw were bitches crowded around her, throwing punches and kicks to her little body. But she didn't cry; she took the ass-beating like a woman.

When they were finished, Danada looked three times worse than I looked. Her face was all red, she had black eyes, a busted mouth, and patches of her long hair lay on the ground near her. The whole nine yards. I almost felt sorry for her. Almost.

Chapter 10

"You ready, D?"

I shrugged. "Shit, I guess as ready as I will ever be."

Danada just looked at me and laughed. "Who can ever be ready for the shit we about to do?"

We both hopped out the car. We rushed to the door and knocked.

"Boy, don't answer that door without asking who it is first!" a lady said.

But it was too late. Danada had put her gun to the side of the little boy's head and pushed herself in the house. I followed behind her, my gun also drawn, pointing to whatever I thought moved in the house.

"Don't say shit, bitch! Just get all your little bastards and have a seat on the couch!"

The lady nodded and gathered up all of three of her kids. The boy who answered the door looked to be the oldest, about five. The other kid, a very prettly little girl, with two Afro puffs in her hair looked to be about three, and the youngest was still in a diaper. The sight of me and Danada rushing in their house with guns terrified the fuck out of them kids. But Murder made us do this home invasion to prove we could put in work.

"Diamond, you watch them, and I'll find the shit."

What shit? One look around the house and I knew that lady didn't have no dope or money. It seemed all the shit she had was under her Christmas tree.

The oldest boy buried his head in his mother's lap, while the three-year-old girl wouldn't take her eyes off me, and her lips wouldn't stop trembling. Her trembling matched the trembling in my fingers as they clutched the gun, as I continued to aim it at them.

"It's okay, babies," their mama told them.

I kept quiet, while Danada rambled through the rooms in the house.

A few minutes later, she came back into the living room and said, "The bitch ain't got shit." Then she glanced over at the Christmas tree.

"No, Danada."

"No, what? Murder said to clear her crib out. It's her fault. She shouldn't have shit up so damn soon. It's still November. I didn't know they sell trees this early anyway."

I started to tell her that the tree was fake, but didn't bother. As fucked-up as I was, I couldn't take the lady's shit she had for her kids.

"Leave that shit. Murder don't"—

She shot me an evil look. "I wonder how Murder would like you going against what he told us to do, Diamond?"

I took a deep breath and watched her go to the kitchen and run back out with a huge garbage bag.

The children and the mother cried as Danada filled the bag up with the gifts she had under the tree.

And I wanted to cry too. Really, I did. They were fucking kids. They didn't do nothing wrong. They were just victims of circumstance, like I was. I wanted to punch Danada in her face, empty that bag out, and place that stuff right back under the tree, but I didn't wanna face Murder's wrath.

I sat back and let her do what she was doing. I could imagine how horrible those kids were gonna feel when they woke up on Christmas morning with no shit under the tree.

It's how I felt all those times I didn't get shit. Rhonda would always laugh at me and say, "You dumb little bitch. You might as well take your ass back to bed. Santa ain't brought you jack." Then she would drop her pipe back in her mouth.

I would look at my daddy, and he would be passed out on the couch in a pool of vomit. I would always run back to my room, get in my bed, and pretend I was a part of another family. One that loved me. We would all sit around a big-ass white tree and open our gifts, while sipping on hot apple cider. Then we would sit at a big-ass table and stuff ourselves with tender turkey, dressing, yams, and mac and cheese—

"Diamond!"

I looked at Danada, who was at the front door with the trash bag.

"I called your fuckin' name three times. Quit fuckin' day-dreaming and come on!" She turned back to the lady. "Bitch, I know where the fuck you live."

Duh. We were in her house, so of course we knew where she lived. Danada wasn't too bright.

"Don't even think about calling the cops."

With that, we rushed out of the house. Crazy part was, we robbed somebody who lived in the Poly Apartments. We lugged the big-ass bag over to Murder's house.

"Man, that shit was so fuckin' cool!" Danada kept saying, obviously pleased with herself, when I felt like shit.

When we got to Murder's house, we banged on his door.

Trina quickly opened it. She had the ugliest look reserved for me.

I smirked. I guess she was never gonna get over me fucking her dude. I guess I couldn't blame her.

Murder was seated on the couch with the TV remote in his hand. "What y'all got, Diamond?"

"Um, some Christmas toys."

"Christmas toys?"

The smile on Danada's face vanished.

"Ho, you think you did something?" he asked Danada.
She shrugged. "I mean—"
He waved a hand at her, which shut her up quickly. He
turned and studied me for a moment. "How many kids?"
"Three."
"How old were the kids, Diamond?"
"They looked like they were five, three, and one, because
one of them was still in diapers."
He turned to Danada. "Ho, go get your ass on the track!"
Danada rushed out the house.
"Diamond, get rid of that shit! What the fuck I need with
some kid toys? Danada is a fuckin' dingbat!"
I thought it was just a test, I wanted to say, but I thought
better and lugged the bag out the door before closing the
door.
After I got a few yards from Murder's apartment, I went
back into the direction of the lady's apartment. I knocked on
her door and when her knucklehead son opened the door
again without asking who it was, I shoved my way in the door
with the bag of toys. Without saying anything, I dumped the
bag on the living room floor and walked back out.
"Thank you!" the lady yelled.

Chapter 11

That shit between me and Danada was long over. We went back to being BFF. And we were so deep in that gang shit, it was crazy. Over the next four months, we went from the sweet, innocent girls we were (well, you know what I mean), to some cold bitches.

She ended up telling me that the same initiation to Eastside Crips that I did, she had to do as well. Only, she said it was Murder and four other guys. She also said, when they were done, Murder humiliated her by peeing in her face. So I guess they went kind of easy on me. She said she knew I didn't purposely sleep with Li'l Murder to spite or hurt her. He just so happened to be one of the dudes there. So we were as thick as thieves again.

And we were thieves. Murder taught us how to carjack. And that's mainly what we did. I knew how to break into a car four different ways—with a butter knife, a flat-end screwdriver, or a grinded piece of crowbar. Then the wires were always under the steering, under this flat piece. The crazy part was, jacking the car was the easy part for me. What I had a difficult time learning was driving that bitch after stealing it. After crashing a few good times, I got the hang of it.

And there was no sound better than when you rubbed the wires together and that muthafucka started. I had gotten so good at the shit, I could have taught a class on how to carjack. We had stolen Impalas, Camrys, Saturns, Camaros, and of course, Honda Civics. While my favorite car to take were the Honda Civics, Danada loved her some Impalas.

I was even able to steal a Tahoe one day. You have to know what works for each particular car. For example, to get into a Camry, you need a pair of scissors, which works like a regular key. For a Saturn or Honda Accord, you need a grinded butter knife. You slip in the top window of the car under the black flap. And for a Tahoe, you need a screwdriver.

But Danada would go a little deeper. A lot of times, she would carjack with a gun. That wasn't for me. So when she used a burner, she did those excursions on her own. Fuck the bullshit. Money or a car wasn't worth me losing my life. But she wasn't tripping.

Murder had taught us so much. He had the hookup with someone who worked for the DMV, so we never got caught. I didn't have to go boost no more clothes or take any more naked pictures or suck no dick. Murder would also kick us down with ends too, and we always went shopping, and more importantly, he was proud as fuck of us. He gave me my hood name, Li'l Deadly. And best believe, Danada was my crime partner for sure.

I now had a Sidekick cell phone, countless pairs of tennis shoes. Pastry, Jordan's, Ed Hardy's, what! And, yes, all the skinny jeans I wanted. So I said bye to the pisa homie and the whole naked pictures deal, and the security guard at the shoe warehouse.

I was also rarely home. Some days we stayed up all night, or others, I crashed at Danada's, which I was sure pissed Rhonda off because she had nobody to talk down to, to bring her pathetic ass up. She also couldn't sneak nobody in my room to make a quick buck 'cause all they would get was an empty box spring. Ha! And what could she do?

My daddy didn't give a fuck that I was never there. His program didn't change. Either he wasn't home, or if he was there, he was passed out on the fucking couch. And the vomit. Can't forget the vomit. Passed out in a pool of his own vomit.

For me life was good. And Gutter's ass was on me in a major fucking way. And I was enjoying the hell out of him chasing me. It made me feel like I was worth being with. And the more I resisted, the more he was after me.

When I wanted to be bothered, we would go to the movies and sometimes out to eat to real simple spots because we were still teenagers. We went to Chili's, El Torito, places like that. I only went to first base with him, though. I really wasn't into sex. Maybe if the shit that happened to me hadn't happened, my attitude would've been different. So I only answered his calls or text when I felt like it.

But, hey, he wasn't tripping. He probably had several different broads.

I guess I wasn't the relationship type.

And my girl Danada had managed to snag Li'l Murder, so you know her ass was in straight love. We were living good.

I pondered over how good my life was as I slipped on my True Religion jeans and a black turtleneck, since it was chilly, and some black Air Force One's. I decided to skip school and go to the mall.

I grabbed my Sidekick and sent Danada a text. *Hey, ho. Skip school and roll with me to the Lakewood mall.*

Negative ho. I'm chilling wit Lil Murder - in bed.

I chuckled and texted, *Alright, lil hookah.*

So I boned out on the 112 bus by myself. I needed to get a new pair of boots. They had this new style where you wear them over your knees now, all the way to your thighs. Shit was always changing, but hey, anything for fashion. And I was now "that bitch," so I had to keep up with all the trends.

After I tossed the money for the boots on the counter, I went and got a Dooney and Bourke bag. I got the pink one with all the pretty hearts on it. It was from the money me and Danada had made doing a carjacking. And although I really enjoyed spending this money, I would have done all the shit I was doing for Murder for free. I was gonna be down for that big nigga for life. But, at the same time, it felt good to have money to spend.

I had fifty bucks left, so I went to get a pair of skinny jeans. I had pretty much every color in skinny jeans, but I could've used a yellow pair, just because. I snatched up a size six . Well, really, I was a size five, but my booty was so big, I always had to get my pants one size bigger.

I put the size six on and had a hard time buttoning them bitches. It was the first time I noticed the little bulge my ass was developing in my stomach area. What the hell? I guess my fat ass had been eating out way too much. Stuffing catfish and hush puppies with hot sauce and them big-ass burgers with the hot link on top from Big Mike's joint.

I guess I needed to stop shopping and take my fat ass to a gym. The last thing I needed was to lose my figure. It wasn't like I had anything else going for myself. I wasn't very smart, I could barely read. I didn't have a lively personality and could barely hold a conversation unless it was about clothes or niggas. I was just another pretty face with a killer body. That's all.

I sighed and yanked another pair off the rack, a size seven. I didn't bother trying them on, I just purchased them and was on my way out of the mall. But I couldn't help but smell muthafucking cinnabun.

I resisted the urge to buy one. Instead, I made a bee-line toward an exit, so I could get on the bus and go home. The mere thought of being fat like Rhonda made me put more pep in my step.

Once I was able to get outside, I took a deep breath and was on my way to the bus stop when something caught my eye, a bomb-ass silver Caprice in the parking lot sitting on some serious twinkies. I knew I could hot-wire that shit. And since it was a weekday, the parking lot was almost empty.

I did the normal routine, fired that muthafucka up, and

drove it out of the mall parking lot. I took the streets, so I didn't draw attention to myself, even though Murder had taught me how to use the 710, 405, and the 91 freeways. But the mall wasn't but fifteen minutes away from Murder's crib.

I knew seeing the Caprice was going to make him happy. He had been saying he wanted a Caprice and that he didn't care what condition it was in because he wanted to fix it up.

Once I got it to the Poly Apartments, I parked it in the back of Murder's crib like he always instructed. The security never tripped about it because he was afraid of Murder. Everybody was afraid of Murder. He ran the Poly Apartments. I jogged up to his crib, anxious for him to see what I had managed to do all by myself. I rushed up the steps and was out of breath, which was why I didn't immediately yell his name.

I placed my hand to my chest and took a few deep breaths. The living room door was slightly ajar, and just as I was about to raise my fist to knock on the door—Murder didn't like nodody just barging in—the image I saw in the space of the open door had me frozen.

I had to be seeing things. I held my breath, closed my eyes, opened them again, and I steadied my eyes to peer past the open frame of the door into the living room. Yep. I wasn't seeing things. I placed a hand over my mouth to keep from screaming. There was Gutter and Murder. Gutter was leaning over the coffee table, and Murder was behind him, thrashing into Gutter's body.

I tried to tell myself that Murder was just giving Gutter the Heimlich maneuver. But I heard Gutter whimpering like a girl, and Murder yelled, "Shut the fuck up and take this dick!" He gripped Gutter's neck and kept jabbing his body into his.

They were fucking! No doubt about that shit. They were breathing heavily and making grunting sounds.

Murder bit Gutter on his neck. Then Gutter turned his face toward Murder, and they started kissing.

Murder slapped him upside his head. "Stop that kissing shit, nigga!"

I backed away from the door as quietly as I possibly could and ran the hell down the stairs and out of the Poly Apartments, leaving them two and the stolen car behind me.

And as soon as I made it away without being seen, I vomited the contents in my stomach onto the ground.

Chapter 12

Okay, I needed to do something to confirm the suspicion that was growing in me. So I put that shit I saw between Gutter and Murder to rest and worried about myself. In all the dust that I was kicking up with Danada, my dumb ass overlooked the fact that I had missed my period again! I was irregular, but the size of my titties and my stomach was unnatural to me. *I could be pregnant.* The thought of having a baby inside of me was a scary feeling. I had been drinking and smoking weed, and if I was pregnant, I was going to put a stop to that shit. No baby deserved to be unhealthy. Shit, the way I looked at it, a baby didn't ask to be brought into this world. So if I was pregnant, I was going to stop all of that shit. The weed, the drank, wilding out, and robbing folks, all of it would have to stop.

I'd always wanted a baby. It was someone to love and love me back. And I knew that if God blessed me to have a baby, I would be the best mom ever.

Me and Danada were at St. Mary's Hospital, waiting for me to take a free pregnancy test. Thank God, you could get free medical help. I kept biting my nails.

"Damn, girl! Are you hungry or nervous?" Danada asked.

"Nervous."

"Well, that foster home over on New York Street called God's Children pays cash for babies. The only problem is, you have to sign a paper saying you won't ever try to get it back, and they say that shit is null and void."

I stopped biting my nails. "Selling babies? Ain't that shit illegal?"

"Yeah, girl. Tameka little sister, Jamilah, sold her baby boy over there. Then about a month later she changed her mind. But that white bitch would not give that baby back to her and it was nothing Jamilah could do."

"Well, best believe, if I am pregnant, I am not giving my baby away or selling her for no amount of money. Fuck that! I would keep mine."

"As you should." Danada put her earphones to her iPod in her ears.

After a pregnant pause, I asked, "Hey, Danada?"

She turned off her iPod and turned to me. "What's up, D?"

"You ever been pregnant?"

"Girl, hell yes. I done been pregnant like six times already."

Damn! She was only fourteen. Guess you don't share everything with your friend, because I sure didn't tell Danada my deep dark secrets. I didn't even tell her about Gutter and Murder. Good thing I didn't fuck Gutter. Wait! I did fuck his ass. Well, at least it was only once.

"The first time I got pregnant was by my mama's boyfriend. But that bitch didn't believe me and couldn't be without her precious boyfriend, who really wasn't shit. When I told her I was pregnant, she simply sent me to the abortion clinic. But I said after that experience that I wasn't killing no more babies. Then my older brother call himself trying to rape me. And I knew for sure that I wasn't having that muthafuckin' baby!"

"Why?"

"Girl, that was my brother. I would be the baby's mom and aunt at the same fuckin' time. And you know what they say about incest, mixing blood. That baby was going to come out possessed. Probably have a spinning head with four eyes and shit."

I laughed and slapped my hands into my thighs.

"He probably would have killed me and my brother for bringing his fucked up ass into the world."

"Yep."

She got silent.

"What about the third baby?"

"Oh. I met this one guy, when I was twelve, and he was twenty-five. So you know I thought I was doing big things. When I would get out of school, he would pick me up. Girl, that man did everything you can imagine a man doing to a woman. He made me a woman. He turned my young ass out for sure. I was definitely in love with his ass. And I don't care what nobody say. I may have been young back then, but his ass loved me too. And I could go toe to toe with just about any other woman. I could do everything they could and maybe more. I knew how to cook for him, keep his house clean, wait on him hand and foot, give him good head, and could take his dick."

"Damn!" I wondered if I would ever be in love with some-body.

She took one look at me and cracked up laughing. "You should see your face, girl."

"'Cause your story got me interested. So what happened?"

"The baby ended up in my tubes or some shit like that. And, plus, the doc said I had them abortions too close together. I was half-listening to his ass. Anyway, to make a long story short, he said I would never be able to carry a baby to full term. And once the dude's wife found out about me, she beat me like I stole something, and then he blamed me for her finding out about me, and he beat me like I stole something, and I didn't see him again."

Damn! I wanted to cry for her. I don't know what I would do if a doctor told me that shit. I would probably jump off a cliff. I wanted to have at least three kids.

"That's just what he said he probably don't know what the

fuck he doing anyway. It's up to God, girl. Fuck what that doctor said. You can—"

"I did. I tried at least three more times. Every one of them died." She smiled. "But it's okay. Maybe I just wasn't meant to have no kids. I'm cool with it. I'll adopt some fuckin' kids." Her voice got squeaky. "Or maybe, maybe if you really are preggers, I can be the baby's godmother."

I squealed and hugged. "Of course, you can be the godmother. I love you, Danada."

She got all teary-eyed and hugged me right back.

So we sat there and thought of names for the baby and shit.

"So if you have a girl, what are you going to name it—I mean her?"

"I know I want a different name. And I don't want no ghetto shit like Bomquisha. Or that shit white people name their baby after, forests and shit."

Danada cracked up.

"And if it's a boy?"

Shit! That was the first time I realized since we were talking about this baby shit that I didn't even consider who the father was. I had only had sex with Gutter, Li'l Murder, and Murder. But it could only be Murder, 'cause he was the only one to hit it raw. *Awww fuck!* He was the last person I wanted my baby to be by.

"So who is the daddy?" Danada questioned like she read my thoughts.

"Oh, girl, when me and you wasn't talking, I hooked up with this dude," I lied.

"Damn, girl! You work fast! We only stopped talking for a week. Was he cute? 'Cause you can't be having no ugly baby," she joked.

"Naw. He was fine. Brown, creamy-ass skin, girl. White, straight teeth, and some curly hair."

"Not the nappy shit?"

"Naw, girl, not the nappy shit."

"So what happened with you and him?"

"Girl, he had a teeny-weeny dick. I'm surprised his sperm was able to shoot into me."

Danada stomped her feet and burst into loud laughter. "Girl, I done had a few fools like that!"

I was just glad she believed my lie. So I laughed too. I was never ever going to tell Murder it was his kid. Ever!

"I'm gonna have to steal a lot of cars to get this money up for my godchild."

I looked at her and smiled. "Twinkle, Twinkle, Little Star" started ringing in my head again. Then it hit me. "Danada!"

"What?"

"Star. That's what the baby's name will be."

"Even if it's a boy?"

"I ain't having no boy, you'll see."

"Diamond Grey."

I stood, took a deep breath, and followed a short Hispanic lady who looked like she barely made it to four feet. I followed her into one of the rooms, where they had one of them beds with some silver stems hanging from its sides. *What the fuck is that?*

She told me quickly, "Strip naked." Then she slipped out of the door.

I did as she ordered and slipped the paper gown over my shoulders that sat on the bed. I lay back on the bed and rubbed my hands up and down my protruding stomach. The possibility of being pregnant made me happier and happier by the minute. And now that I knew I had Danada there to support me, I was at ease.

I knew my daddy and that bitch of a woman, Rhonda, wouldn't be any help. And, to tell the truth, I didn't need to take no test to tell me I was pregnant either. I could feel it.

But, still, when the white Dr. Issac came into the room with the nurse that was there earlier and told me, "Well, young lady, it appears you are pregnant. Your test came back positive," I couldn't stop cheesing like I had just won a billion dollars.

He gave me a weird look and said dryly, "Well, it appears that you're happy about this."

His comment made me drop my ear-to-ear grin. "Why the fuck shouldn't I be?" I wanted to demand of his bitch ass. But since he was going to be my doctor, I couldn't have him giving me bullshit checkups and examining me with an attitude. I was now carrying some precious cargo.

I kept a smile on my face and said, "Yes, sir, I am. I'm very happy. I shouldn't be?"

"Well, you're only fifteen. What are you going to do with a baby?"

"Everything that wasn't done to me. I'm going to love her, protect her, make sure no harm comes her way. Make sure she goes to school, gets good grades, eats all her vegetables. Make sure she stays away from drugs, and make sure no one abuses her in any way. Check to see if she is warm at night, teach her what a period is, and how to put on a pad or a tampon. Make sure she always has clean clothes. And kiss and hug her every single day."

He stared at me like he thought I was crazy. He shrugged and said, "Why don't you relax, lie down, and put your feet in the stirrups."

I lay down and did as he told me to, placing my feet in the stirrups. "This will feel a little uncomfortable."

I watched him put some cream on a device. "What is that?"

"I said, relax. It's just to open you up, that's all."

"Well, what is it? You not just gonna stick some shit up in me and I don't know what it is."

"It's called a speculum," he said impatiently.

"Okay."

He barely slid it inside of me, and it started making a sound like a tool, before it snapped me open. I screamed out in pain, but he ignored me. It felt cold as hell.

"Now I'm going to collect some fluid from you to be tested in the laboratory."

My eyes widened as I watched him snatch up a long swab, and before he could stick it in me, I yelled, "Wait!"

He froze and popped his head from between my legs.

"What is it?" he asked with a frown.

"You can't stick that into me. You gonna hurt my baby. You may stab her in the eye."

"Relax."

The nurse said, "Calm down."

I ignored her and lay back down. "Don't stick that in me." I peeked up again and noticed that he ignored me and tried to dip it into me anyway. I pulled myself up quickly and snatched it out of his hand. At this point, tears were in my eyes at the possibility of the doctor harming my baby. "I said don't stick that shit into me, muthafucka!"

"Calm down," the nurse told me again.

"Shut up!" I fired at her.

"You need to keep your legs closed because you certainly don't need to bring any more babies in the world. And at the event that you do manage to bring this baby into the world, I feel sorry for it"

"Fuck you! I'm gonna be a good mother, you punk-ass doctor!"

The nurse rushed out of the room, and came back with a black doctor, while Dr. Isaac stared down at me.

Through my tears, I saw the black doctor looked really young and was fine. He took one look at me then at the red-faced doctor. "I got it, Ted."

"Say no more." Dr. Isaac had his hands up like he was in surrender. He offered me a smile.

I frowned.

"What's your name, sweetie?"

"Why you asking?"

"Because I would like to know your name, so I can properly introduce myself."

"My name is Diamond. You look kind of young, you sure you know what you doing?"

"My name is Dr. Sojl, and thus far, I have delivered exactly forty-seven babies."

"You sure it wasn't four?"

He chuckled. He had some white-ass teeth. "Why don't you let me show you?"

"I don't want nobody hurting my baby. Please."

He nodded. "Diamond, I swear to you, I'm not going to hurt your baby. All I am going to do is swab you so I can I collect some of your fluids. That way, if you have anything that could *hurt* the baby, we can treat you now so the baby is out of harm's way. Do you understand?"

I nodded, feeling tears run down my face. I lay back down and allowed him to swab me. Just as quickly as he slipped it in, he slipped it out and put it into a container that he put a top on.

"Okay, now I'm just going to feel the head. You may feel a little pressure." He pressed down on my stomach, while sliding fingers inside of me. "Okay. Feels fine," he said.

Then he went to the sink and pulled off the gloves. He washed his hands and came back to my stomach with some device. He placed it on my stomach, and my breath caught in my chest.

I could hear my baby's heartbeat. More tears streamed down my face. And as I looked at the doctor, it seemed like his eyes got watery too. And I just couldn't stop smiling.

"Okay, why don't you go on and get dressed. The baby is fine. Right now, it looks to be almost five months, so I'll be seeing you back in another month."

I stopped listening after he said five months. That meant in four more months I would have a baby. I had no idea I was that far along.

"Is it a girl?"

"Now, that I don't know."

"I know it is."

He gave me a smile before he said, "See you in another month." And he and the nurse left the room.

Chapter 13

"I don't even know why I'm bothering to tell y'all, but I am. I'm four and half months pregnant. I'm keeping the baby, and I don't give a fuck what y'all say or even think. I'm not getting an abortion!"

I was on the couch in the living room, facing Rhonda and facing my daddy, who were both seated on the couch across from me. He didn't so much as open his eyes at what I said, so who knows if he even heard the shit. I hated his ass.

But Rhonda sure had a lot to say. "Well, shit, you act like this the first time you been pregnant!"

"I ain't never been pregnant before."

"Girl, go on with that bullshit. As fast and hoish as you are, it ain't no telling how many bastards you aborted."

"Don't get me confused with you."

"Don't get confused. Say the wrong thing and get fucked up!" She waved one fist in the air.

"Daddy, why you let her talk to me like that? She ain't my fucking mama."

He ignored me. It was always like that, so I don't even know why I complained to him.

And Rhonda was too big a bitch for me to take down. So it wasn't any use in fighting her, although I wanted to.

Once when I was eight, with the fear of a lion, I made a move on her and tried to take her down. I got tired of her slapping me upside my head and calling me out my name. So I went into my room and did about fifty push-ups and exactly seventy jumping jacks. Then I jogged from our apartment to down the street.

I then went into the living room and sat across from her and calmly stared at her while she watched TV. And, sure enough, she said, "Bitch, what the fuck you looking at?"

I lunged from the couch and leaped on her, so my little body was straddling hers. My hands went straight for her neck. My little fingers were determined to choke the life out of her. It was the only way for me and my daddy to get rid of her. I was making snarling sounds, and I continued to choke her.

The choking only lasted for about a good ten seconds before she took one of her arms and elbowed me right in my neck. I flew to the floor and couldn't breathe right for a good ten minutes.

"Who the daddy?" Rhonda demanded, snapping me back into the present.

"Don't worry about it. It's not like you give a fuck about me."

"You right, I don't. I mean, I'm just glad that my assumptions about you was correct. I always knew you weren't gonna be shit, Diamond. But, damn! You could have at least waited until you were sixteen to get knocked up."

"Yeah, whatever."

"And you need to stop faking the funk, saying none of my business. You don't know who the fucking daddy is."

"Yes, I do!"

"Yeah," she sneered at me. "You know all right. How you know when you servicing all them men, girl?"

"What men?"

"Look at you, trying to play innocent. I know what you and Danada do."

I took a deep breath.

Yeah, Danada had told me that a couple times she had to visit the track and work. But it was how Murder punished her. She was down like me in the carjacking game. We made more money jacking cars. And I never worked the track, and didn't plan on doing that. It was enough what I did with Murder, Li'l Murder, and Gutter. I didn't really like sex anyhow, so I couldn't imagine selling my body for money, unless it was to feed my baby.

"Diamond, please. You be out there trickin' and hoin'. Stop with the lies."

"I ain't lyin'."

"Okay. Then how were you able to buy all of that shit? Huh? You got a fuckin' three-hundred-dollar phone. I saw that commercial, bitch. I know how much it cos'."

She couldn't say *cost*. Illiterate bitch.

"And you got all those expensive tennis shoes too."

"Why the fuck you all up in my business?" I jumped to my feet and got up in her face.

"You better sit the fuck down, for you not be carryin' shit."

I sat back in the seat I had abandoned, not taking my eyes from hers.

"And to answer your question, bitch, because I can be. And I knew your time would come where you would let somebody knock you on up. You betta kiss them clothes and shoes good-bye, 'cause another little bitch or little bastard ain't living in here for free."

"Don't talk about my baby."

"Fuck your baby!"

I wanted to kick her in the mouth for already disrespecting my unborn child. I could care less what she thought about me, but my baby, that was different.

"I really hate you, Rhonda. You just an ugly, miserable bitch."

"Keep talking, bitch. I'll kick you right in your stomach and make you throw that fuckin' baby up on this living room floor."

I knew she would, so I bit my bottom lip to refrain from commenting again.

"You ain't gonna be no better mother than your mama was to you. You probably gonna abandon her like your mammy abandoned your ass."

"I'm gonna be a good mother. You watch and see. And I couldn't imagine giving up my baby. I could never do that shit to my own flesh and blood. And, truth be told, I don't know how my mama did it neither. So when you calling her out her name and saying how trifling she is, as much as I don't like you either, you right. And that shit don't hurt me."

For some reason, instead of her being satisfied that I was agreeing with her, it seemed like my comments made her upset. Her lips trembled. Then she rose and walked out of the room.

Chapter 14

Over the next few months I eased back from going to Murder's house, although he kept asking Danada where I was. I knew I had no business going over there. I had a baby in my stomach. And I didn't have any intention of telling him that I was carrying his baby. Hell, no! My child didn't need to have a father like him anyway.

I also didn't need to be around people smoking weed and shit. And I didn't need to be out in the streets. I wanted my baby to be healthy. So my only companion during my pregnancy was Danada. Every week, she was tossing money my way to put up for the baby. She was stealing two cars a week now. The shit was crazy. She told me she tried to take a brand-new Impala and almost got pulled over by the cops.

"Girl, you better be careful. I'm gonna need your help raising this baby girl."

To that, she just cracked up laughing. "Don't worry. It's gonna be like the baby got two moms."

And I believed her. She was now like a sister to me.

I stopped going to school and filled my days with eating, going for walks, and resting.

I got into a school called Reed, where I went and got work packets, did them, and dropped them back off. I made sure I put the freshest fruits and vegetables in my body. Every Friday, me and Danada would catch the bus downtown and go to the Farmers Market and get all kinds of shit. I stuffed myself with strawberries, watermelon, papaya, and mangoes.

I ate the mangoes like them muthafuckas were going out of style.

See, the thing was, I never had a problem eating vegetables. I just didn't ever remember Rhonda making them. So Danada had to teach me how to cook them. I learned how to make everything, from cabbage made with sausage, bacon, hammocks and onion, to fried okra, spinach, and collard greens.

I could finish a pot of greens on my own. I had a greedy fucking baby. I was huge as well. I couldn't see my feet anymore, and my ass was sticking out as much as my tummy. My breasts felt like I was carrying jugs of water around, so my back was always killing me. But nothing else seemed to get big on me.

Once I turned seven months, Rhonda dragged me down to the County Office and signed me up for county. It was funny. We had got there at eight a.m. sharp but had waited over seven hours. It was no wonder Rhonda had made herself a lunch. And she didn't offer me any of it, even though she knew I was carrying a baby.

She smacked on a bologna and hot sauce sandwich right in front of me. Then she pulled out a bag of Doritos and demolished it. Then she guzzled a soda.

And I could have sworn her crackhead ass went into the bathroom and got high. Because she was gone for fifteen minutes and came back with bulging eyes and an expression on her face that looked like she just got fucked. And I knew the security noticed her high ass. But he looked the other way.

Once her high went down and the monkey returned to her back, she stepped back in her bitch mode. "I would tell you to lie about your knowing your baby daddy's whereabouts, but you probably wouldn't be lying."

"Don't start that shit."

"Yeah. You betta just sit there and follow my lead when we go in there and talk to the man."

I ignored her and pressed my hands to my stomach and squealed as the baby kicked me. The doctor said I would be able to start to feel her move any day now, and I was waiting for this moment. Only, I would have preferred to have shared it with Danada, or alone.

"What the fuck is wrong with you?"

I smiled and kept rubbing my tummy. "My baby just kicked me."

"You could have kept that shit to yourself. I don't wanna hear anything about your bastard."

"Yeah, but you asked."

When they finally called me, I was relieved. The lady didn't ask me shit, just made sure I filled out everything correctly. She said I would receive my Independence Card in the mail.

When we left the county office, Rhonda went her way, and I went mine. But we ended up on the same bus. Only, we didn't sit together. You wouldn't have known that we lived in the same house or even knew each other. And that was fine by me. I hated her, and she hated me.

I ended up getting off on Alamitos, so I could go to Church's Chicken. I wanted some serious fried chicken and jalapeño peppers. I got my order to go. I waddled my behind home as I ate the jalapeño peppers and prayed that I wouldn't pay for eating them later with heartburn. It seemed like everything gave me heartburn. But Danada said her mama told her that when a woman has a lot of heartburn, it meant her baby gonna have a lot of hair.

I opened the door and walked up my steps. I knew Rhonda was already there, so I was gonna go straight to my room, eat, and go straight to sleep. I walked in the living room and saw Otis lounging in the house.

"What's up, goddaughter?"

Rhoda was in the kitchen frying up something. I wondered where my daddy was. *It didn't matter cause he didn't give a shit,* I told myself

I gritted my teeth and clenched my fist as I watched his ass take a deep bite out of one of my mangoes. The juices ran down his double chin.

"Put down my fucking mango!"

He laughed. "Come get it."

I didn't have time to stare at his ass another second, so I placed a hand over my belly, kept a tight grip on my chicken, and went into my room and slammed the door. I hoped nobody thought of fucking with me. And if his fat ass even so much as thought of coming in my room, I had something for him. That was for sure. And I wasn't about to go easy on him if he didn't respect my personal space. My body was private property. It didn't belong to his fat ass or his dick.

I ate my food and lay down to take a nap.

Later that night, I woke up to the sound of someone fiddling with my bedroom door. Shit. My heart sped up as I saw a shadow step into my room.

"Goddaughter, where you at?" Otis bumped into the wall.

"Get out of my room, you fat bitch!"

"Baby, why you coming at me that way? I'm your goddaddy. Remember, if something were to happen to your pops, I would have to take care of you. I know you don't like—"

"I wouldn't piss on my daddy if he was on fire. That alcoholic bastard could drop dead today for all I care. I know one thing— I'd kill you or myself before I'd go live with you."

I reached under my pillow and prayed that I had something there. And sure I had a flathead screwdriver and some scissors. *He better not think of coming my way.*

But he did. He even had the nerve to sit his fat, stinky ass on my bed.

"I'm pregnant. What the fuck you trying to do, you sick bastard?" I gripped the scissors in my hand.

"I won't get in the baby way, if he won't get in mine."

"You need to lift your obese ass off my bed and get up out of my room. Bitch, you gonna get stabbed if you don't!"

His dirty dick wasn't going anywhere near my baby.

"You already knocked up baby. And, to be honest, god-daddy kind of disappointed you been giving my pussy away to someone else. I wanted to be the one to take your virginity, teach you about making love." He lowered his voice. "How to suck dick."

Why is he trying to sound sexy? He was disgusting the hell out of me. "Get out!"

"I ain't going nowhere, but up in you."

As soon as he laid his fat ass on top of me, I jabbed his ass in his stomach as hard as I could and felt blood splash against my hand.

He howled out in pain and hopped off me. "You stabbed me!" He fell to the floor.

I got up from the bed and waddled over to my light switch. I flipped on the light and saw blood soaking up his shirt. Did I have sympathy for him? Hell muthafucking no! I kinda hoped I had hit a fatal organ.

When he looked like he was going to get up again and come after me, I grabbed the flathead screwdriver and cracked his ass upside his head with it.

He screamed again.

I busted him in his head again and again. And then I prepared to stab him again, until he dragged his fat ass from my room.

"You little bitch!" he said, hustling to get out of harm's way even as he talked shit.

"Touch me again! You fat fuckin' bitch!" I yelled as he ran out of my room. I closed my door. Then I heard a loud thud that must have been him falling again in the living room.

I heard Rhonda cracking up laughing in the living room.

He told her, "Give me my twenty dollars back."

"Hell no. That's already been spent, Otis."

"Well, call the fuckin' cops! Shit, I'm bleeding. She stabbed me."

"Muthafucka, you high, I'm high. Ain't no way I'm letting the po-pos up in my crib. You betta put some alcohol and a Band-Aid on that shit, Otis."

I lay back on my box spring and texted Danada: *Maybe I need to get a fucking gun.*

Chapter 15

I had managed to get to my eighth month without being raped or getting into a fight with anyone. I was still taking my prenatal pills every day, along with my fruits and vegetables. Little by little, me and Danada were buying everything I needed for the baby. So far, I had a beautiful cherrywood crib, a stroller, bouncer, and a swing. Everything was Winnie the Pooh.

I just needed to stock up on diapers, and I planned on breast-feeding. We kept everything at Danada's house, because I just knew that if I brought it home, Rhonda would sell it. Not just to buy crack, which was what people would assume, but also to hurt me. Although it would have been fun to set the room up nice and pretty for the baby, I figured it wasn't worth the risk.

"You got about another month and a half to go, Diamond."

"I know," I said excitedly.

"How is school going for you?"

"I don't go to regular school anymore, Dr. Sojl. I can't waddle my big behind to class. I was taking classes at the continuation school, but I got tired of that, so I stopped going there too." Dr. Sojl was the only adult I felt uncomfortable cursing in front of, for some reason.

"Everybody needs an education, even mothers, Diamond. How do you expect to take care of your baby, if you don't even have a high school diploma? Diapers and formula cost money, and I do hope you don't plan on staying on welfare for the rest of your life. Welfare is a means to an end. And with all these budget cuts going on, who's to say that welfare will still be given in abundance like it is now?" He dropped his paper towel in the trash. "Young lady, these are all things that you should consider. I am sure you want more for your child, right?"

I nodded. I did, there was no way I wanted my baby girl to endure what I had to endure. I was all she had, and I had to be a role model for her. That meant that I couldn't do drugs or even drink when she came into the world. And since I hadn't been doing that during my pregnancy, it wouldn't be so hard to control. I didn't even crave weed anymore.

There was no way a muthafucka was going to be able to touch my baby and live to talk about it. No way would Otis get the chance to rape my daughter. No way was Rhonda going to beat my daughter or call her out of her name. I would kill the bitch first.

"We should always strive to give our kids more than what we had, Diamond. It's our duty as parents."

"I'm going to, doctor. What do you think I should do?"

"Go see Nisa in the Resource and Referral Department and see what assistance she can offer you. I'll see you in another two weeks. Don't have that baby before seeing me."

I laughed. "How can I control when she wants to come out, Dr. Sojl?"

He winked. "I'm sure you will find a way, Diamond. You're strong-willed."

"I am?"

"Yep. You got strength you haven't even tapped into yet."

When he and the nurse left, I got dressed and went to the lady named Nisa. For him. Hey, if he felt like that was something I needed to do, I was going to do it because I know he had my interest at heart. I couldn't say that about any other grown muthafuckas in my life.

"Hi. What can I do for you, young lady?" she asked once I approached her desk. She was a plain-looking, light-skinned woman with a Halle Berry haircut.

"Dr. Sojl told me to come here. My name is Diamond."

She chuckled. "Okay. How—"

"Have you ever met Dr. Sojl's wife?" I asked her before she could get another word off. He wore his wedding band faithfully, and I had to know how his wife was.

"As a matter a fact, I have."

"Well, how is she? 'Cause Dr Sojl is not only fine, but he is a good man. Next to Big Homie, he's the only other black man I have ever respected."

I thought about Murder fucking Gutter. I didn't respect his sick ass no more. He was faking the funk like he was a thug and was fucking dudes and women. That was some down-low shit. It was too many innocent women catching shit from men like him.

"So if that bitch ain't treating him right, I have no problem calling the homegirl and beating her ass."

"Yes, I treat Dr. Sojl very well." Her voice got deeper, and she winked at me.

My eyes widened. "Oh shit! I'm sorry. I didn't mean to disrespect you, ma'am. It's just that Dr. Sojl has always been nice to me. And he shows more concern for me than my own daddy does."

She smiled. "I understand, sweetie."

Next to Dr. Sojl she was a plain Jane. She must have had a good personality.

I continued to smile at her.

"Now what can I do for you?"

I shrugged. "Dr. Sojl told me to come see you because I dropped out of school."

"Okay. I see." She studied me carefully. "What are your goals?"

"If you had asked me that about seven months ago, I would have said, 'to smoke as much weed as I could and wear cute clothes.' But now all I want is to be able to take care of my baby. I want to watch her grow up, and I want her to be proud of me."

"Are you having a girl?"

"Dr. Sojl said he doesn't know, but I know it's a girl."

She chuckled. "Well, the first step would be an education. And I'm not just talking about a high school diploma. I'm talking about a college degree. We are in the middle of a recession now, so you have to be able to compete for a job nowadays. What sets you apart from others is a degree. With you being a single parent, there are a lot of programs out there to help you. You could qualify for financial aid and even get money to pay for your books. But the first step is to get your GED. Long Beach City College assists students with taking the GED test. You know where the campus on Pacific Coast Highway is?"

I nodded. I didn't think I was smart enough to go to college. Hell, I doubted I could even finish high school, but still, I listened to her.

"Read some of these pamphlets. And here is some more information on the GED. You are having a child now, and once you bring that baby into the world, you are going to have to be responsible for her."

I nodded.

"But don't think just because you're having a baby that you are putting your life on hold. If anything, having a baby at such a young age can be hard, but it does not have to stop anything. Now while everyone is not fit to be a parent at a young age, you just might be. Dr. Sojl has told me how well you eat and exercise."

I blushed. *He talked about me?*

She saw the blush and chuckled at my girlish crush, I guess.

"So go ahead and read over this information, and I hope that you enroll back in school. It would be a sad thing to see another bright, pretty girl let her life go to waste."

She thinks I'm bright? I wondered if Dr. Sojl felt that way too. "Thank you, miss." I grabbed the pamphlets from her and went home.

Chapter 16

By the time I reached my eighth month, I was on bed rest. I had to rely on Danada to help me. But when she was out carjacking, I had no choice but to bite the bullet and either ask Daddy, who often ignored me, and sometimes when I had no other alternative, I asked Rhonda for help. But she always ignored me. So, really, asking for their help was a waste of time.

That why she surprised me one day when she started beating on the bathroom door. I was trying to shit, but them damn iron pills often gave me constipation. I didn't want to strain, but I felt so bloated, I thought I was gonna explode.

Every morning I would take some prune juice, and by the evening, I would have a bowel movement. But today I ran out, and Danada wasn't answering her cell phone. So I was suffering big time. "Will you get the fuck out of the bathroom?" she demanded.

"I can't shit," I whined.

"Oh, fuckin' well!"

"Leave me alone!"

"Get out the bathroom!" Rhonda yelled, not caring about my pain.

"I ain't getting off this seat until I drop some turds!"

"Damn! I hate your needy bitch ass!"

A few minutes later, I was still straining, and she jammed her way into the tiny bathroom holding a cup of something. "Here."

I turned my nose up to her. "What is that?"

"Castor Oil."

I had never heard of it. "What is that for?"

"It's minerals. It works like prune juice does, to help you take a shit."

"Will it hurt my baby?"

"No. It's fucking minerals. Women been taking this shit for years. Take the shit."

"Why you trying to help me when you hate me?"

"I'm not. I gotta shit, so I need your ass off the toilet."

So without giving it any more thought, I took the cup from her and drank the fluid, trying not to throw up. It tasted so nasty, like I was drinking cooking oil.

"Give it a few minutes to set in."

She shoved me out of the bathroom, and I waddled to my room.

About an hour later, I wished I hadn't touched that shit. I felt a sharp cramp in my stomach, and before I could even stand up, I ended up shitting on myself. The shit was watery, all over my ass, and covered the bed. I stood to walk to the bathroom, but more shot out of me, leaving a fowl smell in the room.

I dropped to my knees from the pain. I was hit with another cramp. More shit flowed from my ass. Right after it stopped, I got hit with another cramp, and more shit followed, until my ass was raw, and my maternity dress was soaked.

Then when the cramps subsided, a salty liquid filled up in my mouth, and I vomited over and over again, until snot was hanging from my nose. My body felt so weak, I thought I was going to pass out. And since I couldn't get up off the floor, I was lying in a pool of shit and vomit. The odor was making me more nauseous, but I had nothing left to throw up.

I screamed Rhonda's name, praying she would help me.

"Why the fuck you calling my name?" she yelled, storming into my room.

"Help me," I moaned. I was too weak to lift my head, so my face was in the vomit and shit. I was able to open one eye and peek at her.

She doubled over in laughter. "Damn! You look like a fucking pig!" she exclaimed. Then she walked away.

Then I was hit with another cramp. At first, I thought I had to shit again. But when it lasted longer than the previous cramps and no shit came out, I panicked. It was a contraction.

A few minutes later, I was hit with another one. The pain was so intense, I screamed. I called Rhonda's name again. I knew she wasn't gonna be so dirty as to let me have my baby on my bedroom floor that was covered with shit and vomit. But she didn't respond.

Another contraction hit me. I closed my eyes, clenched my fist, and breathed through it. Then, when it faded, I took all the strength I had and crawled over to the outlet in the wall where my Sidekick was charging. I snatched it and dialed 9-1-1.

When the woman said, "Nine, one, one. What's your emergency?"

I yelled, "Eleven hundred Mahanna Street, Apartment four. I am in labor. Please get here now before I lose my baby!" I kept my phone near me, in case they called me back.

Those contractions were killing me. About ten minutes later, I heard the sirens outside. I was praying Rhonda didn't send them away.

When they arrived, they got straight down to business by putting me on their stretcher. Then they wheeled me out, despite the fact that I was covered in the shit and vomit. I knew I smelled bad. But they wheeled me out past my daddy, who was on the couch, watching TV, unconcerned with me, and past Rhoda, who smirked at me.

Bitch! I continued breathing through the contractions and prayed they got me to the hospital in time to have my baby.

They shot me to St. Mary's. Once I got there, they changed

me into a gown and placed me on the hospital bed. The contractions kept hitting me, each time getting worse.

"What happened to you?" The nurse put the IV into my wrist.

"I don't know." I squeezed my eyes shut. "I was constipated and drank some Castor Oil."

Her eyes got wide, and she yelled, "Castor Oil?"

It was in that moment that I realized Rhonda had meant to do harm to my baby. I closed my eyes briefly. I wanted to kick my ass for being so fucking naïve. But who could be so dirty to want to hurt an unborn child?

She put on some gloves and spread my legs wide. "I need to check to see how dilated you are because you are indeed having contractions."

Another contraction hit me, and I gripped the rails on the bed.

When it was over, she placed two fingers inside of me. "Page Dr. Sojl!" she yelled to another nurse standing by. "She's crowning!"

Chapter 17

I was going in and out. The pain was so severe, I was barely listening to Dr. Sojl, who kept telling me, "Push," every time I felt a contraction. The shit was killing me.

I almost passed out when I saw Dr. Sojl take a long needle and shoot it into my vagina. Then he took a scalpel and sliced me between my vagina and my anus. "Diamond, we're gonna count down from ten, sweetie, then you need to push."

"Okay."

"Ready? Ten, nine, eight, seven, six, five, four, three, two, one. Now push."

I nodded, but really I wasn't doing shit but making faces and pretending to push.

They caught on. Dr. Sojl, whose face was covered with a mask, took out something that looked like a plunger, put in on my pussy, and started pulling

I started screaming at the top of my lungs and started swinging on all the nurses that surrounded me.

They backed up quickly, and one of them said, "Not the noise, dear."

"Shut the fuck up! What you mean, not the noise? You ain't the one feeling this shit." I felt like I had to take the biggest shit in my life.

"Dr. Sojl took off his mask and looked at me. "Diamond, do you wanna have this baby?"

"Yes," I sobbed. "But it hurts too bad."

"I know it does, sweetheart. But because you drank castor

oil, your baby inhaled meconium, so we have to get her out before she stops breathing. So I'm going to need you to push, really push, so we get Star out. That's her name, right?"

I didn't know nothing about what he was talking about, but it got me scared that any further harm would come to my baby. I sobbed as another contraction hit me. I nodded at Dr. Sojl. The nurses went back to the bed and coached me through every contraction.

I bore down like I was taking a poop, and they held my legs back.

"Ready? Push down, honey!" Dr. Sojl yelled.

Each time I did, the pain was more severe, like my insides were ripping. But I had to get her out. There was no way to get around it. I wished Danada was here with me.

"Ready, push!"

I pushed again.

"Push down as long as you can, Diamond," Dr. Sojl said.

So I did. This time, I held it for a good ten seconds.

"Okay, one more time."

And I did. I threw my head back, closed my eyes, and pushed while screaming, "Awwwwww!"

I heard a *pop* sound, like somebody had opened a jar of jelly or a jar of pickles. Then blood gushed from between my legs. That's when I saw the head.

Dr. Sojl yanked the rest of her body out of me, and I heard her cry. It was the most beautiful sound to hear. Once Dr. Sojl was done with her, a nurse whisked her away.

I closed my eyes, trying to catch my breath, while they did whatever they were doing. A few moments later, they had her wrapped in receiving blankets and sat her in my arms. God, she was beautiful! Her hair was thick and silky and hung around her face like a wrap.

She had these little pink lips that poked out, and she kept trying to open her eyes. When she adjusted to the light in the room, I saw they were so shimmery. I could tell off the bat that she had my features, and thank God, she looked nothing like Murder. Her ten fingers and toes were so delicate and so soft. I laughed as she kept looking at the ceiling. Then she tried to look at me. And she had this sweet smell to her.

Dr. Sojl sat in his chair and watched me hold her with a smile on his face. That's when I felt tears start pouring from my eyes, and I started sobbing.

"Thank you, Dr. Sojl."

He nodded. "I'm proud of you, Diamond." Then he left the room.

As soon as he did, the nurse whisked her out of my arms.

"What you doing?"

"We have to take her to run some tests. While we do that, you can get some sleep."

I was up bright and early the next day, and was breast-feeding Star when Danada came.

Knock, knock. She walked in the room with a gang of pink and white balloons that said, "It's a Girl." She also had some flowers and a bag with some things I needed.

I smiled. "Hey, girl."

She sat the balloons and flowers down. "Can I hold her?"

I nodded.

She went to the sink, washed her hands, and dried them. Then she sat next to me on the bed.

I gently placed the baby in her arms. "Make sure you cradle her head good."

"Okay. Look at you, so protective of your little angel."

"Yep." I chuckled.

Danada took one look at Star and squealed. "She is so pretty! Look at all that hair she got."

"Hey, little Star. You picked the perfect name for her, D."

I yawned.

"What's her middle name?"

"What you think? Danada, fool!"

My friend gasped. Then her eyes got watery. "You named her after me?"

"Yeah. You my best friend. The only person in my corner. I owed you at least that."

"I'm not ever gonna let her down, D. I promise. If anything happens to you, you don't ever have to worry about Star. I would die for her."

"I know you will, girl. And I know she gonna be a handful. That little heiffa almost killed me. I was swinging on the nurses and everything. I thought that was gonna be my last day."

She busted up laughing. "I don't understand how she came so early. Didn't you have another month to go?"

I nodded. "I was having some more problems taking a dump. And I was out of prune juice so that bitch Rhonda gave me some fuckin' castor oil. I didn't know it could hurt the baby. The next thing I know, I'm shitting and throwing up all over the place. Then I started having contractions."

"What? That is one dirty bitch."

"And she left me there in that shit, even though she knew I was going into labor. I don't get how anyone can be so dirty."

"She got a black heart, yo."

"Yeah, she does. And I don't trust her around my baby. At first, I thought she had limits, but after she tried to harm my unborn child, I now know there is nothing she wouldn't do when it comes to harming me. And my daddy just sits back and allows it. It had always been like that. And, girl, that ain't the worst thing. The other night, my so-called godfather came into my room and tried to rape me again."

Danada narrowed her eyes at me. "What do you mean, again?"

I took a deep breath. "He raped me when I was fucking twelve. And he tried to get me strung out on crack. The cold part about it is, he paid Rhonda five dollars after he raped me, so I know her evil ass set the whole thing up."

Danada shook her head at me. "Damn! She worse than my mama. Diamond, you got to get out of that house. You can't take Star back there. Who's to say they won't try to do something to her? If you can force a fucking twelve-year-old to have sex with you, then you one sick bastard, and I don't put nothing past you."

"I know, but where am I gonna go, Danada?"

She bit her bottom lip. "I don't know yet. I'm gonna figure something out. But you ain't going back there. In the meantime, you just rest and take care of the baby, and don't stress, 'cause it will get in the breast milk, and that can affect the baby. I learned about it in my health class." She pecked Star's cheek and handed her back to me.

"I'm 'bout to get on the grind. At least, I will have some more dough we can work with."

"All right, girl."

"Oh, by the way, Gutter asked about you."

I grimaced before I could catch myself. I tried to play it off. "Girl, I ain't got no time for no man with a newborn baby. Tell him I'm cool."

She chuckled. "I heard that, girl. I don't know why he trippin'. He messin' with Tameka's triflin' ass now."

"Oh. Well, more power to them." *Better her than me to be with his bisexual ass.*

She hugged my free side and, in a flash, was out the door.

Chapter 18

I stayed at the hospital for about five days. The doctors told me that normally premature babies usually stay for two weeks, unless the baby was eating and breathing on its own. Star might have come a month early, but her greedy ass was eating on her own, and thank God, her breathing was fine. But, to tell the truth, I didn't mind staying at the hospital for two weeks because it would give Danada some more time. I hadn't seen her since her last visit. But every day, she sent me texts, asking how the baby was, and telling me to let her know when I was getting released.

My girl was on a serious grind. A grind I was gonna get on too as soon as I was better, so there was no way I'd have to go back to Rhonda's house. It wasn't like I got any of that welfare money, anyway. She kept it all for herself. She even kept my WIC. She would go to the grocery store and find somebody buying the items she was selling and give it to them for a crackhead price. But I wasn't tripping. I knew my baby was going to be okay.

The Filipino nurse came to my room six A.M. sharp and told me I was going to be able to go home at about twelve. I texted Danada and told her that they were releasing me at twelve so she could bring the stroller and Star's first outfit.

She texted me back and told me to sit tight, she would be there.

They had taken Star for another damn blood test. If they asked to take any more of my baby's blood, I was gonna curse them out.

I shoved the nasty-ass breakfast they had given me for the fourth day in a row away from me. It was a damn boiled egg, two hard-ass pieces of bacon, and some damn toast. With these little-ass juices they gave me, I could only get a swallow out of each carton. I knew the nurses were getting tired of my ass asking them to bringing me more of them. Oh, well, if they didn't like it, then they should bring bigger fucking cartons of juice.

The nurse wheeled Star into the room. I smiled and glanced at her. She was knocked out. "Y'all not getting any more of her blood," I told the nurse.

She ignored the comment and said, "What time will your ride be coming?"

"I ain't got no ride. My friend will be here with the stroller after twelve. That's the time I'm getting released, right?"

She nodded. "Well, I will be back a little before twelve to go over any last instructions and to answer any further questions you have. And give you your discharge papers."

"All right." She tried to rush her ass out of the room.

"Aye!"

She turned and looked at me with an aggravated expression on her face.

"Why I gotta get the same damn thing to eat every day?"

"Aren't you on medical?"

"Excuse me? What the fuck you mean by medical? For all you know I could have Kaiser, or Blue Cross, or Cigna. Why I gotta automatically be on welfare? Huh? Because I'm black?"

Her eyes got wide.

"What? A cat got your tongue now? Not every person that's black is on welfare."

" I didn't mean that, ma'am."

"Well, I feel offended."

"I'm sorry. But are you on medical?"

"Yes!" I crossed my arms into my chest. "The fuck that got to do with anything?"

"Then you have to have the same thing. You only get to pick if you have private insurance."

"Well, you can take this shit 'cause I'm not eating it."

She collected the tray and, with a quick pace, left the room. Since Star was 'sleep, I lay back in the bed and used the remote to turn on the television. I was hoping to catch Jerry Springer's or Maury Povich's talk show. Or even some *Married with Children* reruns. But, instead, there was news on every fucking channel.

I almost turned the TV off, but then I saw there was a high-speed chase. *Damn! I thought. Whoever is in that car doesn't have a chance.* There were four police cars coming after them. Whoever they were, they were flying on the freeway, 710 North, and the cops were on that ass. I hoped they didn't get out, 'cause they was gonna get fucked up for sending them po-pos through all that trouble. *Damn! I'm glad that's not me.* But it was cool to see a high-speed chase in my neck of the woods.

I half-listened as the newscaster gave a description, saying, *"While we can't really get a good glimpse of the driver, the victim told police that the driver is an African-American female in her mid-teens. And this was a carjacking at gunpoint."*

That's when my heart almost stopped. No, it couldn't be. I scanned the make and the model of the car, and my mouth dropped. It was an Impala. The driver had to be Danada.

With shaking hands, I reached for the phone and dialed her cell phone number. There was no answer. I watched as her speed increased and she crossed over into north Long Beach near the 91 West. *Danada, pull the car over!*

I dialed her number again. "Danada!" I yelled, when her voice mail picked up. "Pull the fucking car over before these muthafuckas kill your ass!"

I dialed her number again, but she didn't respond. If I was driving ninety miles per hour, I probably wouldn't have either.

She hopped onto the 91, damn near crashing into a car as she did. I screamed so loud, a nurse walking by came to my door. "What's wrong?"

I ignored her and watched Danada go around a car in the farthest lane. She almost hit the wall of the freeway. She popped in front of the car and increased her speed, but the police were still on her fucking heels.

Scared to look, I closed my eyes, my heart thudding in my chest. Then I forced myself to look again.

The newscaster said, "*I wonder how much farther the suspect is planning on going. Why doesn't she give herself up?*"

I was wondering the same thing. She could only go so fast on that freeway and only get so many near misses from the other cars. She passed another curve too fast, and her tires screeched. Smoked clouded the freeway, but she kept on going like she was a racecar driver.

There was a big rig truck in front of her that was gradually slowing her down. That's when I thought my friend was going to stop and turn herself in to the cops, but she didn't.

Please don't do it, Danada.

I watched as she tried to go around the rig truck by slipping into the right lane. But I guess she didn't see that more cars were merging onto the freeway, and before she could brake, she collided head-on with a Navigator truck.

I screamed as the Impala flew, and then it flipped over about three times before her car broke out in a fire that enveloped the whole car. And, within an instant, I knew my friend was dead.

Chapter 19

I was numb when the nurse came to my room to go over some things and have me sign my discharge papers. I wasn't listening. I couldn't. I was too busy seeing that Impala flip over and over in my head and seeing it go up in flames.

Shortly after the incident, the girl was in fact identified as Danada Stewart. The security camera in the parking lot caught her taking the car at gunpoint. And that was the face they flashed on all the channels.

I felt nothing but misery. She'd jacked that car for me, to help me with Star, her goddaughter. And now, because of me and my bullshit situation, she was dead. We had our problems in the beginning with that Li'l Murder bullshit, but she was my friend. She was all I had, and I loved her. Now she was gone.

Tears wouldn't stop falling from my eyes. My heart felt like something was tugging it, and every time I swallowed, it seemed like a lump was stopping my saliva from going down. *What am I going to do without her?*

When it was my checkout time, I knew I couldn't go back to Rhonda's house, so I told the nurse that my legs were feeling numb, that I felt like I was going to pass out. So they ran some more tests.

Luckily, they found out that my blood was low, which was enough for them to keep me for two more days. And when I was able to put Star to sleep, or they took her for a test, I would just sit and cry over my friend.

Sure enough, after the second day, the nurse was up bright and early to discharge me. I was already dressed in clothes Danada had brought me.

"Okay, miss, you are all ready to go."

I ignored the nurse and stayed where I was.

"I'll go get the wheelchair."

She came back to the room with the chair.

"I don't need that."

"Well, you can't stay another day. The doctor already extended you by two days."

"I didn't say I was staying. All I said was, I don't need that wheelchair."

"Okay." She looked around. "Where is your ride and your car seat? Your mom and dad aren't coming to get you?"

I ignored her and grabbed all the baby items in the room—the bottles of formula, the nipples, the receiving blankets, diapers, and all the burping pads—and put them in a pillowcase while she watched.

"Wait!"

I rolled my eyes. "Man, what?"

She jumped at the volume of my voice and put a hand to her chest. "How are you going to get the baby home?

"I'm going to fuckin' walk!" I was tired of her questioning me, and I was still upset about my friend dying. The nurse was the only person I could unleash my anger and hurt on.

"I can't let you leave without knowing who is taking you."

"Okay. Damn! Wheel me out. My ride will be here shortly."

I know she wanted to question me, but to get me out of her hair, she accepted this.

The walk back wasn't so bad, because little Star was a petite baby. But the stitches were killing me. From St. Mary's to my house was about a twenty-minute walk.

***

When I got in the door, I saw that Rhonda had guests over, and they were having a get-high party. The stench of cigarettes, weed, and crack was strong in the air. I covered my baby's face and walked to my room as fast as I could, to avoid my baby inhaling that shit.

I sat the pillowcase down so I had a free hand to open the door. I turned my back and pushed it open so I could use both hands to hold my baby. When I turned around, I froze at what I saw. Although I couldn't see her face, I knew it was Rhonda on my bed, on her knees, ass buck-naked, while some random fucking dude was jabbing her doggie-style. Based on her horse-like body, I knew it was her.

Then I heard somebody coughing. I looked to the corner, near my closet, and saw another random dude slurping on a crack pipe so hard, it must have made him choke. Still, he kept slurping.

When Rhonda felt my presence she turned her wide eyes on me and said, "Get the fuck out and close the muthafuckin' door!"

I shook my head in disgust and walked out the room. The only safe place to go was outside, or the bathroom, and since the baby couldn't be out in the open air, I picked up the pillowcase and was on my way to the bathroom.

A crackhead was on her way too, but I took one look at her and said, "Get the fuck away, crackhead bitch!"

And she made off like she was Road Runner, so it was safe to go into the bathroom with Star.

I closed and locked the door, sat the pillowcase down, and sat on the toilet. I held Star in my arms as long as I could, before my arms started aching. I ignored the ache.

When she started crying, I pulled out one of my breasts and fed her. I chuckled at how greedy she was. It seemed like she was never gonna get tired of the titty. She would suck, take a break, and go right back to it.

I watched her toes flex while she drank. Then I started thinking, *Even if Rhonda decided to get the fuck out of my room, I couldn't take the baby in there because the smell would stay in the room.* I didn't want my baby inhaling that.

After I burped her, I cradled her in one arm safely and spread two receiving blankets in the tub. Then I laid her down in there to sleep. It really was the best I could do.

Chapter 20

It turned out that the party lasted all day and into the damn night. The next day, I opened the windows in my bedroom to air it out, and I bundled up my baby the best I could with the flimsy receiving blankets and walked over to Danada's house. I needed to get the baby stuff. Everything was still in the boxes, and with the little change I still had left, I figured I could take a cab back home with the stuff and set it up in my room.

Danada lived on Gundry Street, so the walk wasn't that far. Her home was a lot more decent than mine. There were no crackheads there, just a stupid-ass mama, a punk-ass brother, and a fucked-up stepdad. I almost hated Danada's mom as much as I hated mine, for letting that shit happen to her. Now that she was dead, I wondered how that made her feel.

Danada's mom opened the door quickly, almost like she was expecting it to be Danada. Was she in denial about her being dead?

Every time I saw her, I couldn't help but think to myself how much they looked alike. Danada was the spitting image of her mother, slender, with the same complexion and hair. Then why in the fuck did her boyfriend need to rape Danada when her mom looked just like her? Men were sick.

"Hi, Ms. Stewart."

"Hello, Diamond. I see you had your baby." She stared at Star cradled in my arms.

"Yeah." I shifted Star in my arms.

"Can I see her?"

I twisted my lips to the side. *What the fuck for?* You and my daddy and mama are all alike, fucked-up, selfish parents, whose life is so fucked up, you want to get revenge by fucking up your kid's life.

I peeled back the blanket from Star's face and showed her.

"Awww, she is so pretty. And look at all that hair." Her eyes watered. "You know Danada had hair like that when she was born." She took a long, ragged breath.

"Yeah? Well, I was coming to get the stuff for the baby." I wasn't trying to get into no long-ass conversation with her. If she'd made different choices as a parent, Danada would have been still alive.

She looked at me confused. "We took that stuff over there a few days ago."

"What?"

"Yeah. When Danada left that morning, she told me, not 'I love you, Mama. I'll miss you,' but, 'If anything was to happen to me, make sure Diamond gets the stuff for the baby.' We dropped off the envelope too."

I started to ask her why she thought something was going to happen to her.

Her voice cracked. "She left your address. It was easy to remember, eleven hundred Mahanna Street. I have a girlfriend that lives over there."

I shook my head and closed my eyes. I was praying I hadn't heard her right. "To who? Who did you drop my baby's stuff off to?" My heart started speeding up, and my body felt clammy all over.

"To a nice lady named Rhonda. I thought that was your mama. She said it would be in good hands with her."

I walked off holding my baby. I knew that bitch had "cracked off" my baby's things. Where else in the fuck could they be? If only I hadn't stayed those two extra days in the hospital. *That's probably how she was able to have that all-day-*

and-night crack party. And if she didn't refund me my shit, this was the day I was going to fuck her ass up anyway I could, with or without a weapon. There was no way my baby would be without her things. And all I had to my name was twenty bucks. *I'm not playing with Rhonda this time.*

I held the baby close to me as I crossed the street, past the library and MacArthur Park, to Mahanna Street. It seemed like I got there in a matter of seconds. I walked up the three steps to the porch and opened the door to the living room, yelling, "Bitch! I know you cracked off my shit. You either gonna give me the money back, or you gonna replace everything that's gone! And I'm not playing, Rhonda!"

It wasn't until I was done with my rant that I saw a white woman in the room. She was seated across from Rhonda and my daddy, and looking at me like I was shit on the back of her shoe.

I pulled Star closer to me and looked right back at her in the same way. I wondered if she was a social worker. My heart started pounding in my chest, and there was a serious pain there. I'd been having those pains since Danada death.

"Oh. Diamond, you just in time, honey. I want you to meet Tammy."

Why is Rhonda being nice to me? She never ever in her life called me honey.

"Tabitha," the white lady corrected. "Tabitha Black."

"Who the fuck are you?" I demanded.

"Sit down," Rhonda said.

I tossed a hand to Rhonda. "Who the fuck are you?"

"I work for God's Children. You met with Melissa, I believe, back in January."

"I met with who? Yo', what the fuck is going on? 'Cause I don't know you or no damn Melissa."

"We are an adoption agency. You signed these papers months ago for your daughter to be legally adopted by Shawn and Kari Cruz."

I gasped and felt a sick feeling in my stomach. I looked at Rhonda.

"Diamond, why are you sitting here acting silly? You remember we had that talk, and I explained to you what your options were when you first found out you were pregnant? And you decided, *against my urging*, that it was best to give little—the baby up for adoption."

"You know what, bitch? It's enough that you sold all my baby's shit, now you gonna sit here and lie and say I gave my baby away? I will fuckin' kill you!"

An evil glint came over Rhonda's eyes. "Calm down, honey. This is why I tell you not to take drugs."

The white lady looked at me like she wanted to put me across her knee.

Star moaned in her sleep.

"I ain't signed no papers, and I have no intention of giving my baby away. I love her, and I want to keep her."

"It's too late," Rhonda said. "You already signed them."

"Why the fuck are you lying? Am I in the twilight zone?" I turned and looked at my father. "Daddy, you just gonna sit here and let them take my fuckin' baby?"

"You don't need no baby. You tried to kill her the other day."

"What! No, that was your bitch who gave me the castor oil!"

The white lady exploded on me like she was holding it in all the time. "You know, you blame everyone else for your mistakes, young lady. Your aunt told me all about you. You don't deserve to be a mom to a rattlesnake, let alone a baby. Your aunt told me about all the awful things you were doing during your pregnancy. I see little black girls like you all the time, taking drugs, drinking, and prostituting themselves. I have no problem at all taking this precious baby away even through illegal means, if necessary. But I don't have to, because you signed the papers. And we have a legal clause. Once you sign your baby over to a family, you cannot come back and reclaim her. You signed her away."

"Look, bitch, you not taking my baby!"

"It's already been done." Tabitha showed me some papers with my name on them and my signature, saying I gave the baby to her.

I slapped them out of her hand and hauled a free fist back to punch her. That's when my dad grabbed me, and I grasped onto my baby so she wouldn't fall.

"Give me that bit- give me the baby, Diamond," Rhonda said.

"No!" I held my baby as tight as I could without hurting her.

"Do something before she hurts the baby," Tabitha said.

"Shut up, bitch! You not getting my baby!"

Then my father did the unthinkable. He hooked his arm like a V around my neck. "Let the baby go, Diamond."

I refused, even as he applied pressure to my neck. He gripped tighter and tighter until I felt weak, like I was going to pass out. As soon as my hold on my baby loosened, Rhonda scooped my baby in her arms and passed her to Tabitha.

Star started 'larming up the place, and I started crying as the lady tightened her hold on my daughter. My father still had his arm wrapped around my neck, so I couldn't do too much moving.

"Daddy, you ain't never done nothing for me in my life. So for once I am begging you, don't do this. Don't let them take my baby away, please."

"You don't need no baby, so shut up."

I fought him though. I scratched at his arms and tried to slip out of his arm by sliding to the floor. But he grabbed me by my hair and yanked me back up. I reached a leg out and tried to kick Rhonda.

She stepped back and shook her head at me. "You really shouldn't act so uncivilized, Diamond. "

"Fuck you! You crackhead bitch!"

The white bitch shook her head at me. "Might I suggest you get her tubes tied."

"Bitch, I'm gonna kill you!"

She shook her head at me and walked out the house with my baby in her arms.

Chapter 21

Maybe that lady was right. Maybe I didn't deserve to have Star. Yes, I wanted to keep her. Yes, I loved her. But maybe I wasn't the best thing for her. Maybe she would end up fucked up like me or have to go through the shit I went through.

But I missed her and wanted her back. Damn! It hurt. I cried every day. I didn't sleep. I would hear her cry, feel her on my breast sucking my milk. My breasts were so swollen with milk, I couldn't lay down comfortably.

I couldn't stop thinking about her. I hid myself in my room. I didn't eat shit. I only sipped water from the bathroom when I had to pee then I went back to my room and back to sleep.

And Rhonda was partying it up while my daddy continued to consume his liquor. I didn't care about much of nothing, so when Otis came into my room one night, I didn't fight him when he slipped the pipe in my mouth and didn't care to stop him when his dick found its way into my mouth.

I got up the next morning and I went to the last place I expected to go. Back to Murder's house. I didn't want nothing from him, except for help getting high. And I was willing to take whatever he was willing to give me, to get the image of Otis panting above me with his sweat pouring off his face on mine, the image of that car Danada was in flipping over and over, and most of all, the sound of my baby's cry and her little face. These are the things I was running away from.

I wondered if my daughter would grow up to hate me like I hated my mother. And I swear, as sure as the sun is shining that if I ever found out who and where my mother was, I was going to go after her ass with vengance. She was gonna seriously pay for abandoning me. All I ever wanted was for someone to love me, that's it. Fuck a big house, fancy clothes. Just my mama's love. That's all I ever dreamed of since I was little. And I never got it.

I knocked on Murder's door, and he let me in. I sat down not really giving a fuck that he had fucked Gutter because, truthfully, I didn't want to fuck either of them. Their little secret was safe with me. All I wanted was some bud.

But I wondered if his girl knew. She wasn't there at the moment, so it was just me and him.

"What it do, Li'l Deadly?" he asked when I plopped down on his couch.

"Everything's good."

"Yeah? You ain't been around in a minute, girl." He puffed on his cigarette.

I shrugged. "I just been busy and shit. You heard about what happened to Danada?"

"Yeah, man. That was my best worker." Then he shrugged. "But I see I got you back now."

Damn! That's how he saw Danada, just as a way to make him money? "You got some bud?" I asked.

"Damn, nigga! You just arrived on the scene after a minute and want some seed?"

I nodded and watched him open a fresh blunt, split it open, and add some weed to it. He rolled it back up and licked it. Once he lit it and took a long puff, he passed it to me.

That shit made me feel good. Cool, relaxed, not a worry. Those demons that had been chasing me were out of sight and out of mind.

"Damn! This some good-ass weed," I told him.

I kept taking long drags from it. Then I lay back on the couch. Next thing I knew, Murder was peeling my clothes away. And, yeah, I was high, but not so high that I forgot the nigga liked fucking niggas.

I tried to push him away. "Stop!"

Out of nowhere, he gripped his hands around my neck. "Bitch, you think you gonna smoke my weed and hold out on the pussy?"

As I struggled against him, he tightened his hold on my neck. "Relax!"

I closed my eyes briefly and bit my lip as he lifted my shirt and started licking my nipples. Breast milk started dripping out of them, and he asked no questions, just slurped it up like he was an infant.

His other hand dropped to my crotch, and he slipped it in there. I was still bleeding, but I wondered if he even noticed. "Damn, baby, you already wet," he said against my breast.

The thought of sleeping with him made me sick, but I knew I had to, for the weed I had smoked.

Just as he started pulling my pants down, the living room door flew open and his girl stalked in the living room and stood in front of us.

"Muthafucka, how long do you expect me to put up with you fuckin' other bitches in front of me?"

"Bitch, shut the fuck up!"

"No, you shut the fuck up!"

He ignored her and went back to sucking on my titties.

"Oh, you gonna keep disrespecting me?" She rushed out the room, and in a flash, came back with a gun. First, she pointed it at me, and then at Murder.

I jumped and yanked myself away from Murder, putting my hands up in peace.

"Tell me something, Murder," she said in a cold voice. "Is she how your muthafuckin' ass got AIDS and gave it to me?"

She had AIDS? One thing was for sure. I didn't have it. They tested me when I was pregnant with Star. So somebody else gave him that.

I looked at Murder. He looked unfazed.

"Bitch, I ain't got no damn AIDS."

She took a balled up paper out of her purse and tossed it at him. "Read it if you don't believe me."

When he ignored her, she aimed the gun at me again. "Pick that shit up."

I did. I then unballed it and scanned the paper. It was a copy of blood work results.

"Read it."

I read the results to her that said she had full-blown AIDS. Not HIV, but AIDS.

"Man, you tripping," Murder said.

In a shaky voice, she asked me, "Now, bitch, did you do this to me?"

"I just had a baby. I ain't got AIDS."

"Who the daddy of your baby?" she asked in a low tone.

Damn! "This g-guy named—"

"Bitch, don't lie! Is it Murder's baby? You better answer, 'fore I blow your fuckin' head off!"

I closed my eyes.

"Is it?"

I nodded.

She tossed her head back and started looking at the ceiling and moaned.

I looked at Murder, who seemed still unfazed by the chick. He grabbed the TV remote and flicked through the channels.

Trina started slapping herself in the head with the gun. "Why did I let you send me through this? Why did I let you do this to me?"

Murder cleared his throat as he settled on BET.

"I love you. Why you had to dog me out, Murder? You can't answer me?"

"You talking that bull—"

Trina fired the gun, sending the bullet right through his

forehead. Murder's body fell on mine, and blood shot from his forehead.

I opened my mouth to scream, but nothing came out. That's when she turned to gun on me. I started crying, begging her at the same time not to shoot me.

"I'm sorry." As I pleaded with her, for the first time in my sad life, I prayed to God that she didn't kill me.

She looked at Murder's dead body and started sobbing like she all of a sudden realized that he was dead. She sat down on the couch across from me.

"A baby. How old are you?"

"Fifteen, almost sixteen, ma'am."

"Oh, now I'm *ma'am*. I wasn't *ma'am* when you was fuckin' my man, was I?"

I looked away.

"Was I?"

"No."

"A baby." She sat the gun in her lap.

For a moment I contemplated getting up and running out the apartment, but I didn't because I was scared she would shoot me in the back.

"I guess you gave him something I never could. I have been with him since I was fourteen. He was my first. He kept fuckin' around on me and gave me chlamydia. I didn't catch it in time to cure it, so it fucked me up to the point where I couldn't have kids. But I didn't trip because I still had my health, and when he was sticking his dick in those other hoes, I thought it could have always been worse. I could have had AIDS."

Tears cascaded down her face.

"Shit! Now I got it. My mama always told me not to fuck with thugs, but I chose not to listen. And she knew. She knew he was no damn good for me."

"I wish I had a mom to tell me something."

There was a brief silence.

She stood and took the gun and aimed it at me.

I dropped completely to my knees, but I didn't say anything. *If it's my time–Fuck it!–It's my time.*

"I wish I had all those hoes he fucked the whole time he was with me lined up here so I could blow all of their heads off."

I nodded and started sobbing as quietly as I could. My bladder exploded in my pants, and pee ran down my legs.

Suddenly she took the gun off me and shook her head. "Naw, this ain't your fault. It's mine."

I watched horrified as she placed the gun deep in her mouth and pulled the trigger. The shot blew out the back of her head, and blood and brains splattered everywhere, including on me. And her body wasn't moving.

I stood to my feet quickly, screaming all the way, and ran out of the house. I ran for my dear life like that gun was still pointed at me.

So many questions were in my head. Why was my life so fucked up? Why did my baby have to be taken away? And why did my mama have to leave me to a life like this?

The house was empty when I got home. I stood in the living room looking around. Enough was enough. I knocked the only TV we had over. Then I lifted it with all my strength and threw it into the wall, shattering the screen instantly and leaving a big hole in the wall. I grabbed Rhonda's boom box and swung it into the wall over and over again, smashing it into pieces. Then I took her collection of ten bootleg CDs and broke all of them into pieces.

I stalked into the kitchen for the knife and went into the living room and stabbed both couches as many times as my energy would allow. Then I took the knife and destroyed all the pillows, until feathers were all in the air and covered the dirty carpet.

I went back into the kitchen and removed every article

of food from the refrigerator and tossed meat, bread, eggs, ketchup, and mustard, whatever my hands came into contact with, all over the walls, until I could see no more walls. I broke every dish we had in the house, which wasn't a lot, but now we had none.

Then I went in the bedroom that Rhonda and my daddy shared. I pulled out every single shoe Rhonda and my daddy had and put them in the tub with all her and my dad's clothes. I grabbed a bottle of bleach from underneath the bathroom cabinet and poured it over all of the clothes until they were drenched and the strong smell filled the air.

I went back into the room to see what else I could destroy. But there was pretty much nothing left, except for the dirty mattress they slept on, and rails that threatened to collapse any minute. I grabbed the butcher knife and flipped over the mattress, prepared to stab up the mattress like I had did both the couches, but something resting on the floor between the rails caught my eye. It was a big yellow manila envelope.

I dropped the butcher's knife and grabbed it. I tore it open and emptied the contents onto the space on the floor in front of me. Inside were letters and cards. I saw a pretty birthday card with pink balloons on it that read, *"For a very special girl."*

I flipped open the card and read it. *"This is for Diamond's birthday. I am sending two hundred dollars. Please buy her something special with it."*

There was a total of sixteen cards, and the stamp was always for the month of March. My birthday was in March, and they were all addressed to me. And they were always from a lady named Deidra Grey. It had to be my mother. It had to be.

I flipped through the rest of the cards, and a folded piece of thick paper fell into my lap. With shaking hands, I peeled it. It was a birth certificate. I took a deep breath and scanned it. It had my name Diamond Deshanae Grey, born March 24, 1993.

I searched for the name Deidra Grey under mother's name, but my world was when I saw Rhonda Lashawn Grey, Mother. The paper dropped, and my hand holding it slipped over my mouth. My heart thudded in my chest like a drum, and it seemed like the room started spinning. Rhonda was my mother.

I took a deep breath 'cause, for a second, I had stopped breathing. Tears slipped from my eyes. The whole time I been hating my mother and wondering where she was and she was right in front of me.

I shifted through the stack of cards, hoping to discover something else. There was also a letter addressed to Rhonda. It read:

I'm not going to debate with you over this again. You have made your decision to keep Diamond, and I have no choice but to accept it. I only hope you get past whatever issues you have so that you can raise her the right way. Diamond is a blessing, despite how you see it. And what love you may not be willing to give to her, trust me, sister, I am willing. So again, if you do not want her, I will gladly take her and give her the love that she needs.

I have opened up a home for young girls in Los Angeles. It is a non-profit where we use Christ to help young girls turn their lives around. We offer drug counseling, job training, parenting classes, and we help them get their GED. Feel free to visit some time. Here is the address: 1515 Normandy Ave, Los Angeles CA 90061.

Take care,
Deidra.

I also found a copy of a money order. It was addressed to Rhonda Grey, and the purchaser's name was Tabitha Black. What tripped me out more than seeing that white bitch's name on the money order was the amount: Three hundred dollars. Rhonda had sold my baby for three hundred dollars. I could get more for a stolen car. *They sold my baby.* I couldn't get it out of my head. I wasn't stupid. I knew they did. *But who the fuck is gonna believe me?*

Still I grabbed all the cards, papers, and the money order and stuffed them back in the manila envelope. Then I went into my room and changed my clothes. I took the now empty pillowcase that I had brought home the day I had brought Star home. I stuffed it with some of my clothes. Then I stuffed the manila envelope in there as well. One of Star's receiving blankets was on the floor. I grabbed it and put it to my nose.

I broke down crying again, as her sweet smell was still on there. There I was trying to have my baby, to take care of her, love her, make sure she was clean safe, and she was snatched away from me.

I stuffed it in there too.

And all these years Rhonda had me and never loved or wanted me, why did she lie to me all these years, saying my mother had abandoned me? And why couldn't she she ever show me any type of love or affection?

I figured I could get the answers to my question from the lady Deidra, and that was where I was off to. I walked out of my room, went into the living room, glanced around, and took in how fucked up it was, as fucked up as I felt.

Chapter 22

I got off the bus, on the corner, and searched for the address. There was a small business located next to a liquor store and a Laundromat. It had a sign that said, Distinguished Ladies Inc. I knew this was the place that Deidra owned. I didn't know anything about Rhonda's family. It was hard as hell to think of her as my mother. I didn't know if I would ever be able to call her that or accept it.

I urgently pressed the buzzer on the iron gate. An older woman walked out and came to the gate. I wondered if she was Deidra. I scanned her face to see if she had any features similar to Rhonda. She didn't.

She offered a friendly smile once she made it to the gate. "Hello. May I help you?"

"Yes. I'm here to see Deidra Grey."

"Is she expecting you?"

"Yes," I lied

She opened the gate, and let me in. "Follow after me."

I did as she requested, catching a glimpse of young girls hanging out by a swimming pool. Some of them had small children with them that they were playing with in the shallow end of the pool. It made me think about Star and what she was doing.

They all offered me smiles. I tried to smile back, but it was too tight to be called a smile.

"Well, I don't know if she is here yet, but I didn't want to leave you outside those gates. This is not the best neighborhood, you know."

I nodded as we walked into a waiting room.

"Go ahead and have a seat, honey. I will check with her secretary to see if she is here."

I watched her slip back into another room. I sat down and rubbed both of my hands together.

In a flash, the old woman came back out. "Deidra won't be here for a few hours. Would you care to come back?"

Damn! I have to see her today. "I'll wait."

"Okay. But it will be a few hours."

"Fine."

She stared at me for a moment before walking away going back to the secretary.

I ended up there for the next three hours, but one thing was for sure, I wasn't leaving until I spoke to her and she answered some questions for me.

Two hours later, when I couldn't hold my pee any longer, I slipped away to use the bathroom.

When I came back, the secretary, a slender Hispanic woman, walked up to me and said, "Oh, there you are. I had hoped you hadn't waited all this time and left. Deidra is here. You can go ahead and go into her office. It is to your right. You don't have to knock, just go right in."

I nodded and did as she said. I entered the room. Directly in the center was a big oval desk, and I saw a woman I would never even consider having any type of relation to Rhonda sitting behind the desk

The woman was beautiful. She had bronze-colored skin, the same complexion as me. Long silky black hair covered her head and hung around her shoulders. Her cheeks were round and plump, and when she smiled, dimples popped out. Her nose was long and dipped down long in the front. Her eyes were the only thing I could see that were similar to Rhonda's, and as she sat I could see she wasn't holding all the weight Rhonda held. But she was also tall like Rhonda.

She smiled at me, and placed one index finger in the air, telling me to wait a moment while she wrapped up her phone call. "Yes, we have a bed for you. Know we are always here to help, should you change your mind. Okay. God bless. Bye."

She turned to me with a bright look in her eyes. "How can I help you, young lady? Were you interested in becoming a part of our program?"

"No. I'll get right to the point. My name is Diamond Grey. You are in some way related to my, my *mother*, Rhonda Grey."

A hand went over her mouth like my hand went over mine when I read the birth certificate.

My eyes brushed over her long, slender, manicured fingers. "Diamond?"

I nodded.

Before I could say another word, she stood, her shoulders shaking. "Can I hug you?"

I shrugged, not really wanting her to, but needing her to. So she walked over to me and wrapped her arms around my shoulders and her sobbing had me crying until I was literally bawling like I was a baby. Over my baby, over Danada, over confusion.

"I'm your aunt, baby. I don't know if things are okay, but if they aren't, they are going to be okay now."

And we stayed that way for what seemed like fifteen minutes.

Snotty-nosed and eyes red, I finally pulled away from her. "Why?"

"Why what, baby?"

That's when I told her, this woman that was pretty much a stranger to me. I told her everything. How my life had been, how Rhonda had treated me since I was little. How she abused me and let Otis sexually abuse me. How I had a baby and how it was taken away from me.

"Diamond, I know that I have not been there, but it wasn't by choice. When your mother had you, I wanted to take you and keep you with me forever. Your mom wasn't in a position to properly take care of you, so that is why she gave you to me."

"Why wasn't she able to take care of me?"

She struggled to get it out.

"Is it 'cause of the drugs? If so, you can say it. She done not only smoked drugs in front of me, but she offered me some."

Her eyes got wide, and she nodded. "Yes. And she gave you to me. But she decided against her decision and came for you."

"Why? I don't get it. She never got off the drugs, so why bring me into a fucked-up life? I thought you were supposed to sacrifice for your child, that it ain't about you anymore. And I'm not just talking about the drugs. Why wasn't my mom willing to love me or give me to someone who was able to love me and want me? Why couldn't"—My voice cracked—"Why couldn't she love me?"

Her eyes were watery, and she said softly, "Oh, Diamond. I think your mother loves you."

"She don't. As sure as I'm black, that woman don't love me."

She nodded and put her head down.

"But I don't get it. Were you guys molested? Beat? Why did she travel down a fucked-up path?"

"We had very good parents who are alive and well to this day, baby."

"What? I had grandparents?"

"Well, where are they?"

"They actually stay in Georgia."

"Then how did you two come out here?"

"Rhonda had always been a problem kid, but with me being out there, I was able to keep track of her, and most of all, she always looked up to me and listened to me. But once I left to come out here for college, she had gotten worse. My parents told me she was running with the wrong crowd, experimenting with drugs, stealing, and disrespecting them. So I told my mother to let Rhonda come out here and stay with me, and maybe I can get her on track. A track she has never ever been on. You understand?"

I nodded.

"But the only change she made was, getting worse. She started indulging in the wrong things out here, and like back home, she was associating with the wrong people. I took what my parents gave me, the love, the lessons, the morals, and I became what I became. Rhonda rejected it and became what she became."

"So there was nothing, no particular reason other than Rhonda just chose to be a fuckup?"

Deidra nodded. "I'm afraid so. I said, if I ever saw you again, I would be honest with you, should you ever want to know."

"On my birth certificate, it listed my father as unknown. All my life she told me that my father was Frederick, the guy that lives with us, and she always told me that my mother had abandoned me."

Her eyes got wide again. "In her own way, Diamond, she did abandon you. And I am sorry, I don't know who your father is. I never met him, and she never disclosed who he was to me. "

I sure hope my daddy wasn't Frederick.

"You know what? I had a fucked-up life, so I felt it was okay to have a fucked-up attitude. I have done some dumb stuff to people and to myself. I guess ever since I got pregnant with Star, I felt I needed to make some changes in my life because it's not just about me anymore. Then that was snatched away from me. So then my attitude was like, fuck it, again."

She placed my hands in hers. "You have had it hard. And I swear to you I wish I could have saved you, baby. You were always so precious to me. I remember I used to dress you in all this pink, and you loved it when I sang "Twinkle, Twinkle, Little Star" to you."

That's why that song is always in my head. It's her voice I keep hearing.

"I feel as though I have failed you as well. I backed away because I could not stand to see the life my sister had chosen for herself. But I would have never ever thought she would do those horrible things to her child." She sniffled.

"But, baby, there is gonna have to be a moment where you step back, look at yourself and take personal responsibility for the choices you are making. There are people who have gone through some of the same things you have gone through, and they are still able to be good to people, they are still able to be right. They are also able to be successful. Diamond, that can be you too. And I can help you."

I thought about the girl me and Danada had beat up on the bus, the house we robbed, all the cars I had stolen, sleeping with Murder, knowing he had a girl, the many grown people I had disrespected, and it made me feel so ashamed to be me. So ashamed, I didn't want to hold my head up. It made me cry more.

"Diamond, with all that has been said and all that has been done to you, what do you want?"

No one had ever asked me that before, what I wanted. And I didn't even have to think about it. "I want my baby. Can you help me get my baby back?"

Without blinking, she said, "Yes. Anything else you want?"

"Yes."

"Okay. What is it?"

"Justice. For all the Diamonds and Danadas walking around."

Chapter 23

"Okay. Miss Grey, can you tell me who that lady seating directly across from you is?"

I took a deep breath and looked at the district attorney. "Yes. Her name is Tabitha Black. She is the one who took my baby away from me."

"And what was her reason?"

"She said I signed some papers, allowing her to give my baby away."

The DA held up the same papers that the lady had held up to me the day they took Star from me. "Are these those papers?"

"Yes, sir."

There were murmurs in the courtroom. This time testifying against someone was not as bad as when I'd testified against my mother and Otis. In front of the jurors, judge, lawyers, and people in the courtroom, I had to recount in detail the times Otis had forced me to have sex with him and gave me the drugs. I had to also testify how he paid Rhonda to be able to do it. I was afraid to do it, but Deidra said this was my way of getting what I requested: Justice for the Diamonds and Danadas in the world.

Because of my testimony, they put both Rhonda and Otis behind bars, and they were going to be there for a long, long time. Rhonda was also going to get prosecuted for the case, for selling my baby. And this lady Tabitha was going to be in jail right along with them, where she deserved to be. And I would be happy when this was over 'cause all I wanted was to be able to hold my baby girl again.

The DA said to me, "Ms. Grey, do you mind signing your signature on this piece of paper?"

"No, sir." I signed my first and last name like I normally did.

The DA showed the jurors the paper I signed and the signature on the adoption papers. Then he showed the paper to the judge.

"As you can see, both these signatures are completely different."

The judge nodded.

"Your Honor, I would also like to enter into evidence a money order receipt in the amount of three hundred dollars. This is the amount that Ms. Black pays young girls for their babies."

It was the same amount that Jamilah's sister testified before me that she was paid for her son. She was here in the courtroom too. Rhonda was brought in from her cell for this case as well. She looked miserable in all orange sitting in that room next to Tabitha.

"No further questions, Your Honor," the DA said.

Without looking up, the judge said, "Defense."

"Defense does not wish to cross-examine, Your Honor."

"Fine. We will deliberate and be back at twelve."

I took a deep breath and was able to step down. Once I did, I slipped out of the courtroom and sat down on a bench near the courtroom.

"Diamond."

I looked up quickly to find Deidra in front of me with a drink and sandwich in her hand.

"I brought you something to eat." She handed it to me.

"Thanks."

I had been staying with Deidra ever since that day I'd showed up at her business. She had opened her arms to me like I always wanted my mother to. I had become a part of her program, was getting counseling, taking parenting classes, and studying for my GED.

"It's almost over, baby," she sang.

"I know." I took a deep breath.

My worries were that they would be unable to find my baby girl. The dread probably wouldn't go away until she was back in my arms.

I forced myself to eat the sandwich and swallow down the soda.

"You have to be positive. Everything will fall into place for you."

I sighed, wishing she had been my mother.

She handed me my GED book, and in that three hours we waited, I studied. When it was almost noon, she told me, "Okay, it's three minutes to twelve you better get in there."

Deidra said she couldn't be in the same room with Rhonda, so she waited outside for me.

I understood. I nodded, closed my book, stood and walked back to the courtroom. I sat down and waited for the judge to come back into the room.

He took his time sitting down, put on his glasses. "Does the jury have a verdict?"

A female juror stood, cleared her throat, and said, "We, the jury, find the defendant, Rhonda Grey guilty and sentenced to ten years in state prison."

I jumped because she was also sentenced to nine years for the case with Otis.

"We, the jury, find the defendant, Tabitha Black, guilty and sentenced to ten years in state prison."

The people in the courtroom clapped.

I glanced at my mother. She wouldn't look at me.

The judge told the DA, "Prepare the paperwork to release the infant back to her mother."

***

Fifteen minutes later, me and Deidra were standing outside the home of some white couple who Tabitha had sold my baby to. The cops were inside the house, and were supposed to retrieve Star for me.

I kept pacing around Deidra's car. "Damn! What's taking so long?"

"Be patient," Deidra said.

"Yeah, but what if she is not here, or dead?" My lips trembled as I talked. I continued to pace like a mad woman.

Finally, after ten minutes, I said, "Fuck this." I walked toward the door.

Deidra grabbed me, and that's when the door opened. I saw the two police officers exiting the house, one with a baby in his arms.

A white woman chased after them as they walked down the porch steps, screaming at the top of her lungs. Then a man came out and grabbed her before she could get any closer to the cops.

She sobbed in his arms and kept screaming, "No! Don't take my baby." But the officers ignored her and continued down the steps.

The officer holding the baby made his way toward me. He uncovered the blanket off her face to show her to me. And it was Star.

With hungry eyes, I stared at my daughter. My lips trembled as the distance between us closed and he placed Star in my arms. God, no feeling felt better than this.

I pressed her body into my chest, inhaled the sweet smell of her hair, and couldn't help but sob as hard as the woman on the porch was sobbing.

Deidra watched me with tears in her eyes. Jokingly, she asked, "Anything else you need help with?"

There was one more thing I needed to do, but I knew I had to do it alone. "Yes. Tomorrow I need you to babysit."

Deidra gently pulled Star out of my arms. "No problem."

So the next day, a Saturday, before they had a chance to ship her out, I went to Twin Towers to visit Rhonda, my mother. I waited in that line forever before they had me sitting across from her with a glass between us.

I picked up the phone. She just stared at me for a moment before picking up her phone. This confrontation had my stomach in some serious knots. But I came here for a reason, so I had to get it over with.

"So I guess you wanna know why, right? That's what you here for, answers?"

"Yeah."

She licked her dry lips. "Everyone got their reasons for what they are, the way they are. Maybe they were abused and shit. Made to feel like they were nothing, not loved adequately and then they didn't know how to give their kid what wasn't given to them. Or maybe they turned to drugs to deal with their demons, and maybe the drugs made them make fucked-up choices when it came to their kids. But the truth is, I don't have one."

She had me confused. "You don't have a one what?"

"I don't have a reason for why I treated you the way I treated you, other than I never wanted you. And I never loved you, Diamond. I never bonded with you even when you were a baby. And it wasn't because you were bad, or anything you did. You were a good baby, and started off being a good kid. You turned bad as a result of the household I brought you up in. But there is no rocket science to this shit, no deep, hidden meaning. I just plain out didn't want you, Diamond. That's what it is."

Some tears ran down my face at what she was telling me, but she was unfazed by them.

"I don't understand why you lied to me all these years about not being my mama."

She slid the phone to her other ear. "Because, look, I didn't want you to expect me to be motherly to you. All I felt I was liable to do was provide a roof over your head. And I always did that, didn't I?"

What about food? Clothes? Love? Checking on me when I didn't feel good? Kissing my boo-boos away, or tucking me in bed? Teaching me about why women have periods, talking about the birds and the bees? Making sure I ate, making sure men didn't come in my room at night and rape me? Making sure I didn't experiment with drugs? Not giving me drugs? Seeing if my room was warm at night?

I didn't ask her this 'cause I didn't want her to hurt my feelings further.

"But if you didn't want me, why did you take me back from your sister?"

"'Cause at that time they were giving out Section 8 vouchers, if you had kids."

More tears dropped, and my heart felt like somebody was crushing it with a boulder. "Who is my daddy?"

She shrugged. "Some crackhead. I don't remember his name. We got high and fucked one night. I don't recall ever seeing him again."

I closed my eyes and opened them quickly. "Why did you pass Frederick off as my daddy all this time?"

"Shit. 'Cause you was calling him daddy. He never had a problem with it, so I rolled with it. And, plus, if I wasn't your mama, what other reason did I have to say why you were there? You had to be related to someone, just as long as you wasn't related to me."

"Yeah, but for sixteen years I thought he was my daddy."

"Well, he ain't your fuckin' daddy. Live with it!"

"Why you sell my baby?"

"Gotdamn! You like torturing yourself? I sold your baby for

two reasons. I didn't want no fuckin' baby running around thinking I was gonna be a grandma to it."

"And the other reason?"

"I didn't want you giving someone something I couldn't give you."

"What's that?"

"Love. Shit! Now you happy? You feel good?"

I shook my head. My shoulders were shaking so hard, I couldn't talk.

"The thing you gonna learn about life is that people are who they are because that's who they are. I'm not shit because I chose to not be shit, and that's before drugs ever entered my body. I made a choice to be who I was. And once I became that person, I embraced it."

I stared at her for as long as I could, tears running down my face and my whole body trembling. I didn't cry because of what she said. I cried because I knew. I knew deep down in the core of her that she was telling me the truth. She wasn't lying to me.

And knowing that killed me, but I knew I had to get past it. Before I could ask another question, she sucked her teeth at me, rose from her chair, and walked away from me. That was the last time I ever saw her.

Epilogue

"Twinkle, twinkle, little star, how I wonder what you are."

Star was cracking up as I sang to her while I was giving her a bath. And unlike most babies, she loved getting in the water. She just cracked up.

So much had happened in the past year, finding out my mama, the woman I craved to meet, was right in my face all my life, and the man I thought was my father was not. I wondered if I'd ever know who my father was. Yes, I wanted to know. But if I never found out, I would count the other blessings I have: Star, my baby girl. I don't care how down and out I get, how lonely or depressed I felt, I would never, ever let any type of harm come my baby girl's way. And if a nigga so much as unsnapped my baby's diaper, I was gonna kill his ass!

I was also blessed to discover and meet Deidra. She has brought so much direction in my life. I am emancipated from my mother.

I have my own place, a small one-bedroom, but mine nonetheless, and it was decorated so fly. I got some bright red couches with a gang of pillows in different colors in the living room, a bomb stereo system, and a flat-screen. I sleep in the living room, and the bedroom is for Star. It is decorated in pink, from the comforter in her crib to the pink hearts and angels I hand-painted myself on her walls.

She even had something I always dreamed about having when I was a kid: Her very own doll house. It was so big, it had to sit on the floor.

When I'm not busy, we sit on the floor, and I play with her like I am a little girl all over again.

I ended up passing my GED, and I'm taking classes at Long Beach City College, to be a registered nurse. Who would have thought my ass would be in college? But I have to provide a stable future for my baby girl.

And if that ain't crazy enough, I also go to church. I also decided to be a born-again virgin and not have sex until I was married. Sometimes, I think about my past and laugh at the foolish girl I used to be and the dumb things I used to do. I realized they were all my way of acting out and crying out for attention. I buried her, the old me, with all that drama and all them monkeys on my back, the anger of never having my mother's love and the anger over being sexually abused.

Since I buried the old Diamond, I have changed so much. I rarely curse, I am more respectful to adults, and I live a regular life. No weed or drank or wild partying. My life is about my daughter and being something she can look up to. I wanted her to be able to say I'm her mother with pride.

But don't get me wrong, I still have a little attitude. But the baggage is so gone. Whenever I feel myself about to go there with someone, I think back to what it was like sleeping on a box spring. That always humbles me.

In my own way, I was even able to forgive my mother for the role she played in my life. I mean, I had to understand the whole purpose of forgiving to get to that point, and it wasn't easy. Forgiving wasn't something I did for my mom, but it was more for myself 'cause, once I did forgive her, I was able to let go and move foward.

I also had to look in the mirror and take accountability for the bad decisions I was making, despite what I had gone through in my life. I couldn't blame everything on her.

Yeah, my life had come full circle. I may not have a father and probably never would, I may not have had my mother's love and probably never would, but I had a daughter who was so special, so sweet, and she loved me. Finally, I knew what it felt like to be loved.

Paper Chase

By B.L.U.N.T.

MISHA

"Give me that pussy! Aaah, uhm, aww yeah, girl! You got some sweet-ass pussy."

Misha knew damn well her pussy was sweet. She didn't need this half-ass-dick-having motherfucker to tell her that. She was ready for him to be done. And with Pete, she knew that it wouldn't be much longer. Lucky for him, he was good at eating pussy, or Misha would have already gotten rid of him.

Misha was so tired of the same old thing—niggas getting their shit off and leaving a few measly dollars behind. Yeah, she may have gotten a few outfits here and there. Some of the dudes took her out to dinner to some all right places, but she knew she was just as good as those bitches who niggas tricked on heavily. Her cousins who lived in Harlem had ballin'-ass niggas buying them furs, renting them whips, and paying their rent. Shit, she looked just as good as they did, if not better. She wondered why she kept winding up with the wack niggas with little to no money.

"Misha, girl, I'm tellin' you, you da bomb!" Pete lifted his heavy sweat-filled body up from off of her.

The bomb? Who in the world uses that word anymore? Misha wanted to laugh out loud at this pudgy cornball now standing at the edge of her full-sized bed, putting his clothes back on, but she knew it was time to ask for what she needed, and that was no laughing matter.

Misha needed three hundred dollars to add to her Section

8 voucher. She had to make an appearance in housing court in the morning. Financially, it had been a rocky month, and she was facing eviction from her apartment in Webster Projects for the fourth time this year.

"Pete, I need a favor."

"Uh, huh, sure, Misha, anything for you."

She really hoped that he had meant what he had just said because she desperately needed him to come through with some real scrilla, not just the hundred dollars that he usually left her.

"I need more than your regular drop, baby. I need three hundred dollars."

"Uh, um, well, wow!"

"Uh, um, well? You wasn't at a loss for words when your dick was all up in me, so what the fuck is the problem now?" Misha asked, switching her tone up completely. Fuck the nice-girl approach. Nice girls finished last.

"I mean, damn, Misha, I don't have no three hundred dollars. A brother got a lot on his back. I had some shit to take care of. You know my situation."

"Well, a sista got a lot on her back too, and I have some shit that I need to take care of, Pete, my muthafuckin' rent. That's my muthafuckin' situation!"

Pete stood in her bedroom looking lost. He didn't want Misha to kick his ass to the curb, but he didn't have what she was asking him for. Pete had a wife and three teenagers at home, and with the recession that had kicked in, he was having a hard time supporting them all. Misha was just someone he loved to fuck, not to mention, she was really nice to look at.

He knew that Misha was looking for a sugar daddy when they had met one another two months ago at Lucky Strikes, the bowling alley on Forty-second Street and Twelfth Avenue. Pete had played the role like he could handle what Misha was dishing out to him that night. The way she stretched her fat

ass across the pool table to slide her eight ball in the corner
pocket had him wanting to put his balls in her corner pocket,
but the truth was he simply wasn't financially qualified to deal
with her. He should have known that once he had fucked her,
he was signing his name on the dotted line of Misha's very
own employment application.

Misha caught herself and slipped back into her original
mood. She needed this man's money and she wasn't going to
get it by turning him off, so she figured that she had better get
on her job and turn him back on.

"So wha's really good, Pete? Are you finished with this sweet
pussy that you love to fuck?" Misha took her finger, licked it,
and began to finger her clit. She slipped her finger inside of
her wetness and then pulled it out. She seductively looked up
at Pete, put her moist finger in his mouth, and said, "Or are
you gon' find a way to get me what I need?"

Pete slowly pulled her finger out of his mouth. He had
never tasted anything so sweet. He then frantically began
pulling every dollar and dime he had out of his pocket. When
he had finished counting, he had come up with a little over
one hundred and fifty dollars. He handed the money over to
Misha.

She happily took it. It wasn't the whole kit and caboodle,
but she was halfway where she needed to be on her rent. It
was still early in the afternoon. Misha was sure that she could
go through her black book and find someone to come to her
crib later on in the evening to secure the balance. She wasn't
due in housing court until nine o'clock. Shit, by then she
could fit in two niggas if she had to.

As soon as Pete left, Misha got into the shower. She lathered
up her golden skin with Suave Cocoa Butter Body Wash. She
made sure she cleaned herself thoroughly and let the water
wash over her body. She didn't want Pete's scent or his juices
lingering in her pussy for her next victim to smell or taste.

Misha began to add up all of the bills that she had due. Her rent was just the tip of the iceberg. Her home phone had been cut off two weeks prior, and now her cell phone was about to be cut off if she didn't pay what she owed. She had two rooms of furniture that she was still paying on. She didn't know who was stupid enough to give her broke ass three credit cards, but they did, and now after maxing them all out, she owed them too.

She stepped her naked body out of the shower to a ringing cell phone. The display said unknown, but she decided to take a chance and answered anyway, even though she didn't know who was calling. Misha had given her number to so many niggas, she didn't know if one of them was trying to get at her, and she didn't want to miss out on any monetary opportunities.

Once she realized who was on the other end, she wished she hadn't bothered to answer.

"I don't have it!"

"Well, when do you think you will have the payment, Miss Stokes."

"When I get it!"

"And just when do you think that will be?"

"When I know, you'll know!"

"Are you still employed as a special services consultant?"

"Yes, but business has been slow. Don't you know that we're currently in a recession?"

"Yes, I know that, Miss Stokes. Uh, I see your account has been delinquent for some time now. Is there any specific reason for this?"

"Are y'all muthafuckas stuck on stupid or what? What part of 'I'm broke' don't you understand? Are all of your fuckin' bills paid?"

The representative that was questioning Misha didn't answer her question.

"Yeah, uh huh, that's just what I thought. Yo' ass is probably broke too. Now hear this—Don't call me, I'll call you!" Misha hit the end button on her cell phone.

Damn, there they were, calling again. She knew she shouldn't have accepted that stupid-ass credit card offer, but once she had accepted one, more kept coming, and she wanted to start building up her credit. She knew how important it was to have good credit. And if she ever planned to have the life that she dreamed of, which was the life of a celebrity video vixen, she needed to start somewhere. However, her start ended quickly once she couldn't keep up with the payments. Now she was receiving a ton of bills in her mailbox and annoying phone calls at all times of the day and night. Had she known the company would harass her in such a manner, she would have thought twice about accepting their offers.

Misha now wanted to change her cell phone number, but she didn't want the headache that came along with losing some of her contacts, so she quickly decided against the idea. With everything that Misha had on her plate, she was beginning to get stressed out. Something had to give.

Misha prepared herself to make the call she needed to make in order to secure the balance of her rent money. With all of the bills that she had stacked against her, she now wondered why she didn't make this call before she hollered at Pete's broke ass. She needed more than just one hundred and fifty dollars. She needed some serious stacks.

She called one of her clients who went by the name of Clutch, an OG from Brooklyn, who was still hustling to make his cake. She'd known him for a few years. He was always a reliable source for some funds. The only thing was, Clutch had a fetish for phone sex, and Misha wasn't in the mood. She just needed some cash, but she really had no choice, so she went to work. After all, this was her job.

"Hey."

"Well, if it isn't my pretty girl. What's good wit' you tonight?"

Misha looked at her cell phone in disbelief. Usually, Clutch came straight out the gate with the sex talk. He managed to get out a statement and a question without talking to her like the pervert he was. She figured he must have been in front of someone and was unable to get himself into freak mode, because he was one of the freakiest niggas she had ever known.

"I need to see you."

"Oh, hell yeah, I need to see you too. My wood is gettin' hard an' stiff just listenin' to your sexy-ass voice. How's my kitty kat? You strokin' that twat for me? I'ma pull out my wood and stroke it for you. I know you like that. Aaah, yes, I'm strokin' my dick for you. Aaahh!"

Damn! It was just too good to be true. Misha knew this nigga was about to get his jones on, so she just spat it back at him. She thought that maybe if she talked the right shit, she wouldn't have to fuck him.

"Yeah, baby," she whispered, "you know my hands is all up in this wet-ass kitty kat."

"Oh, yes, my pretty girl, is it wet? Is it real wet?"

"Yeah, baby, it's drippin' wet, and so am I. I just got out of a nice hot shower. My fingers and toys just weren't enough. I need you. *Mmmm!* I'm gonna taste my juicy pussy for you until you can get here and taste it for yourself. *Slurp! Mmmm!*"

"Oh, yes, I gotta have me some of that wet twat. I'ma stick my dick down your throat and make you choke on this big dick."

"Well, come on and get this wet pussy, baby. I want your hot-ass tongue on my shit. She need that. And, um, I'm low on funds, baby, real low. I need some money, a'ight, some real money, so bring that for your pretty girl, okay, baby?"

"Yes, oh yes! Aw shit! I'm on my way to you. Oooh, oooh, my pretty girl! Ahhh! Aaahhh! Aaahhh!"

Misha knew that Clutch was jerking his dick off. He always

jerked his dick off to the point of ejaculation while they were on the phone. She just wanted to make sure she slipped the money request in. She didn't want him getting all the way to the Bronx without the dollars she needed, because she would then have to send his ass right back to Brooklyn without the pussy he needed.

Knowing it would take him at least an hour to get to her apartment, she decided to slip the next nigga in before Clutch arrived. Why not make valuable use of her time? She was already dressed for work. Misha was determined to make as much money as she could, as fast as she could. Then she could have her entire evening to herself. It was Sunday night, and she really just wanted to chill and kick it with her two homegirls, Whakelah and LaShawn.

Flipping through the numbers in her phone, she landed on June, a local nigga. Misha was at least attracted to June, which was a switch from any of the other niggas she was fucking, so she pushed the talk button her phone. She was truly in telemarketer mode. Whatever it took to get her bills paid.

"Yo', yo'."

"Yo', June, this Misha. You busy?"

"Never too busy for you, Miss Misha."

"I like that. I like that a lot. Look, June, I know shit is rough for everybody right about now, but I really need some paper to get a few of my bills straight around here."

"I got a few dollars for you, baby love. What's in it for me?"

"Whatever you need, but I need to wrap things up quick. Can you get here in the next half-hour?"

"I can do better than that. Open your door."

Misha ran to her apartment door and looked through the peephole. Sure enough, June was on the other side of the door with his cell phone still plastered to his ear. Misha wondered what the hell he was doing so close to her apartment, when he had just become a thought in her mind, but she needed his money and she was pressed for time, so she dismissed any foul thoughts and opened the door.

"What? You got ESP, nigga? How did you know I was going to call you?"

Normally, she wasn't even interested in her clients' appearance. It didn't matter what they were wearing, as long as their pockets were wearing a couple of dollars. Oddly, she found herself appreciating June's smooth chocolate skin inside of the beige fleece sweat suit he had on, and the depth of his brown eyes.

June stepped inside of her apartment extremely pleased to see her in her birthday suit. "Nah, I was just in the neighborhood. You always open the door butt naked?" He wasted no time slipping his fingers into her pussy.

"Sometimes I do, sometimes I don't," Misha answered, loving the location of his fingers.

After the door closed behind him, Misha grabbed his belt and loosened it. She tugged at the button on his jeans and zipped his zipper down. She slid his pants down and got on her knees. She took June's hard dick into her hands and slid it in and out of her wet mouth.

He grabbed her hair, which was styled in a short bob, and slid his fingers to the back of her neck, where he held on firmly.

Misha sucked the shit out of his dick and swallowed all of his cum, leaving not a drip of it behind. She then stood up and put her hand out.

"So what? That's all a nigga gets?"

"What you talkin' about? You got your shit off, right? That was the purpose of your visit."

"Oh, okay, I get it. You real cold wit' your shit, huh, Misha?"

"Ain't nobody being cold, June. I just hit you off. You came crazy. It's going to take you a while to get your dick back up. I already told you that I was pressed for time. It's all good, though. We can definitely make your visit longer next time."

June couldn't believe this young bitch just took his cum so

quickly and was now ready to send him on his way. But there she was, standing in front of him with her hand out, waiting for him to give her his money. He also couldn't believe how much her little ass was turning him on.

He peeped how Misha talked to him like he was just a piece of dick. Bitches from all the five boroughs were dying to get some of his time and would kill for some of his dick. To Misha, however, that was exactly all he was, a piece of dick.

Misha Stokes was a very pretty young woman. Thinly slit dark amber eyes flickered through her golden honey complexion. Her five foot five and a half stature was matched with the shape of an hourglass. Her thick hips were a highlight to her frame, and her thin waist was every woman's envy. She made a living by doing one of the oldest professions known to man and woman, but she didn't call it prostitution. In her words, she was simply making niggas pay for her special services. Therefore, she labeled herself a "special services consultant."

Most of her clients were considerably older than she was. She found that young dudes wanted to fuck for free, and that just wasn't happening. A few of her clients were married with full-fledged families.

Misha didn't care that some of her men were other women's husbands. She didn't want them, she just wanted their money. She didn't have true feelings for any of them; it was strictly business. They fully understood that they were getting some prime ass and had better be glad to be a part of her clientele. The least they could do was give her money to pay her bills. But it seemed as though times were really getting tight, and she couldn't even get her bill money lately without doing a song and dance. Misha was fed up with listening to grown men bitch and moan about not being able to handle their business in order to take care of her financial needs.

Misha thought that she had to be living someone else's life.

As a little girl growing up, she never imagined that as an adult, she would be still living in the projects, unable to escape from the hood.

Misha had tried looking for jobs, but she wasn't a nine-to-five type of chick. She wanted to be in music videos. She had the face, and the body, but she didn't have a contact in the world. And at her age, she was running out of time. She felt deep down in her heart that she was meant to be in the video industry. She thought that if she could just get discovered, she could make enough money to pay her own bills. Then she could stop sleeping with men for money. She wanted out of Webster Projects and would give anything to be a part of the rich and famous. She knew one thing. She was tired of crying broke.

"So what you got for me, June?"

"Here. I got you. I told you I had you," he said, as he handed her two fifty-dollar bills.

"Now that's what's up. I appreciate your business, June." Misha took the money to her bedroom and put it in her stash. That was going to help her cause. Every little bit helped.

She took the opportunity to go to the bathroom and brush her teeth. She wanted her mouth to be fresh and clean for Clutch. She returned to find June still standing her living room.

"You still here?"

If it were any other night, Misha wouldn't mind having June hang around. She actually wanted to fuck him, which was a rarity, but she was about to have Clutch come through, and he had some major paper for her. Plus, she didn't like for her dudes to see one another in passing. The less anyone knew about her, the better.

"Yeah, man, I'm still here. I wanna know when you gon' stop all this crazy shit and be my girl."

Misha looked at June and laughed. "Your girl?"

"Yeah, you doin' too much, Misha. You too pretty to be goin' out like this."

"Goin' out like what?"

"Come on, man. Don't make me say it."

"This is what I do, June. I work for mines."

"You call this work?"

"You paid for it, didn't you?"

"Yeah, I paid you, Misha, but you don't have to fuck me to get my money. I wanna do a whole lot more for you than just that."

Misha didn't know what to say. Yeah, June looked good as hell, but she wasn't expecting him to be coming at her like he was. To her knowledge, he wasn't doing all that good for himself, so even with the small-time dudes she had on her roster, he wasn't someone she would consider giving up her clientele for. But, damn, he was standing there looking good as hell.

Always a sucker for a handsome face, Misha shook her head quickly from side to side to snap out of her daze. "You know what, June? Hold that thought. I'll think about the things you said to me tonight, and I'll get back at you."

"Yeah, a'ight, you do that."

June knew Misha was far too young for him. He was pushing forty-five, which made him twenty years her senior, but he wanted her. He wanted her badly. If she said she was going to think about it, he was willing to take that and bounce.

It seemed as if only seconds had passed after June left before Misha heard her doorbell ring. She jetted to the door thinking that June may have forgotten something, but when she opened her door this time, Clutch was standing in her doorway already drooling at her naked body.

She invited him in with the gesture of her hand, and Clutch followed her like a dog being led by a bone.

Misha wanted her money from Clutch up front. She wasn't trying to have him holding out on her, or trying to play her out by making her do all kinds of sick shit for him, and to him to get her bread, as he had done in the past. She needed his money, and she wasn't playing this time around.

She placed her hand on his crotch and stroked his dick through his pants with her fingertips. Her tongue found its way to his ear as she circled her tongue through the tunnels of his right lobe.

"Let's take care of your pretty girl before we start, okay, baby."

"Oh, come on now, pretty girl. I can't pay for the goods until I get the goods."

Misha could tell from his response that he was going to make her earn every dollar he had brought for her. She at least wanted to see the money. As long as she could see it with her own eyes, she didn't have a problem earning it.

"Let me see the money, Clutch, or you'll go home with a stiff dick."

Clutch didn't hesitate. He pulled a wad of bills out of his pocket and fanned them in front of hers face.

Misha's eyes followed the bills back and forth in a hypnotic stance. She couldn't tell how much was actually in the bundle of bills he was waving, but it looked to be over a thousand dollars. "How much you got there, Clutch?" she asked him, visually calculating the money.

"I got enough to pay for what I want. Now come on over here." Clutch reached out for Misha and pulled her close to him.

Misha had counted over fifteen hundred dollars in Clutch's caramel-colored hand, so she was ready to put in work. She got down on her knees, opened Clutch's pants, and served Clutch some of the best head he'd ever had in his life.

But he was determined not to come quickly. He wanted his money's worth.

Misha pulled back from him, grabbed one of her voluptuous breasts, and slid her nipple in her mouth. She sucked it lightly and then looked up at Clutch with innocent eyes.

Clutch couldn't resist her pretty face. *Fuck the money! She could have it.* He threw the money up in the air, and it came down like rain.

He pulled Misha up from off of her knees and placed her back up against her living room wall. He parted her legs with his hands as he guided himself into her.

Clutch went to kiss Misha, but she turned her head. She didn't kiss her clients.

Clutch, however, was determined to kiss Misha. He figured if she allowed his dick in her mouth, what harm could his tongue do? He jammed his dick into Misha as he tried once again to jam his tongue into her mouth.

Misha turned her head to the opposite side. He was upsetting her. "You know I don't kiss, baby," she said politely. "So come on and just handle your business."

"Oh, I'm going to handle my business." Clutch grabbed Misha's face and squeezed her cheeks until her mouth was forced open. He shoved his tongue into her mouth and swirled it around until he found her tongue.

"Ahh! Slurp! Ahh! Slurp! Ahh!" Clutch repeatedly darted his tongue in and out of her mouth, totally disgusting Misha, but she wasn't going to let a little tongue stand in the way of her getting paid.

Clutch continued to pump his shaft into Misha's tight warm flesh. He placed his hands on her plump ass cheeks and began to rub and squeeze. Clutch was nearing climax. The sweat from his face was dampening his black silk shirt, while the muscles in his legs bulged from the adrenaline that flowed through his veins. He clenched his thighs together as he held on to Misha's ass and pounded himself into liquid glory.

"Ohhh! Aaaaahh! Aaaaahh! Oooooh!"

You would have thought that was Misha producing those sounds of joy from her lungs, but it was Clutch singing a song of sixpence, or in this case, sexpence.

"Oh, Misha, you're my pretty, pretty girl," he said melodically, as he proceeded to jerk his dick off in her direction while holding on to her hair. He looked into her pretty eyes and came once again, shooting thick cum all over Misha's stomach. Clutch slid his hand through the slippery substance and placed all five of his fingers into his mouth.

Misha watched as he ate his own cum. Yes, he was most definitely the freakiest motherfucker she had ever encountered.

"I have some things I have to take care of, Clutch. I appreciate you stopping by," she whispered into his ear, trying to keep it nice.

"I'm not done yet. There's a lot of money on that floor."

What's up with everybody wantin' extras tonight? Misha's body was taking a beating on this day.

But her pussy was in prime condition, and Clutch was well aware of that fact. Shit, he was just getting started.

After two more sexual sessions and a role play rendition of "Clutch the Dog chases Misha the Cat," Misha finally convinced Clutch to leave.

Feeling like she had put in three full days of work in just a few hours, Misha collapsed on her sofa and closed her eyes. She hated doing what she was doing, and she wanted out.

After resting for a few moments, she opened her eyes. She looked around her living room at all of the money Clutch had thrown and mustered up enough strength to get her butt up of the sofa and picked it up from the floor. She counted it all up. Her visual calculation was exactly on point. He had tricked fifteen hundred dollars on her.

Now, that's what the fuck I'm talking about. Now we're getting somewhere.

WHAKELAH

"Fuck that! My TV show is going to be the shit! Anybody who ain't feeling my show don't know what talent is!" Whakelah said, her dark-skinned hands resting on her slim waist.

"Girl, there's just too many of them reality shows on the air. They're taking over. Every time I turn on the damn TV, all I see is somebody's reality show. I think it's ridiculous. They're getting rid of all of the good television shows and all of the good movies too." Misha had finally made it to Whakelah's apartment.

"That's 'cause that shit is fake. People are tired of that fake shit. They wanna know the real deal. Shit, I'ma keep it one hun'ed, you know what I'm sayin'."

"Yeah, like when a nigga says he's gonna call you, and the nigga don't call. He ain't gotta lie. I can handle it. Just keep it real and keep it movin', and a bitch won't be waiting to see the number pop up on my phone."

Whakelah didn't know what that comment had to do with what she was saying, but her girl was always talking about niggas in some way or another, so she continued doing what she was doing.

Whakelah had just come from shopping and getting her hair braided from the African braid shop on the Grand Concourse and Fordham Road. She was busy popping on a piece of Doublemint gum and dumping her and her kids' new clothes out of countless shopping bags onto her green faux leather sofa. She couldn't stay out of the boutiques and department stores, though she couldn't afford to be in them. Layaway was her best friend.

Whakelah Brown was collecting a welfare check and receiving food stamps for her and her two kids, and had the nerve to have a shopping fetish. She would give anything to be able to go to Beverly Hills and shop on Rodeo Drive like the true rich bitches of the world. She was also overly caught up in the reality shows that had taken over the cable networks and prime time stations. She had dreams of creating her own reality show and was willing to do whatever it took. But she didn't have a dollar in her pocket.

"Damn, Whakelah! Y'all don't need no more clothes. You be on a mission. You got a bad habit, girl, and you need to fix that shit. You need to stay out of the stores."

"Hmph. And why do I need to stay out of the stores? Rich people get to shop until they drop. And do you see the price tags on their shit? They be buying shoes and bags that cost thousands of dollars, and ain't nobody telling them they need to stop shopping."

"Uh, I don't know if you've looked in a mirror lately, but yo' ass ain't nowhere near rich. Bitch, we live in the projects, and we're on public assistance."

"A bitch can dream, can't she?"

They both laughed.

"And I may not be rich, but I can spend the hell out of a damn dollar, I bet you that."

"Shit, you and me both."

They both laughed again.

"Nah, but really though, you need to slow down with buying all these clothes, and all of these crazy gadgets and toys that you really can't afford." Misha told her.

Misha knew that she had just escaped her financial blues by coming up with the rent money just in the nick of time, and she didn't have any children. Whakelah, on the other hand, had two children, but she seemed not to worry about where her next dollar was coming from. Misha never knew of any man that Whakelah was dating to be providing for her in any substantial type of way, so she wondered how in the hell she was making her situation work. She wanted to know Whakelah's secret. Whatever her secret was, Misha needed to get on the same program, because her ship was sinking, and it was sinking fast.

"You need to stay out of the stores, Whakelah. You're spending too much money, money that you don't have, on shit you don't even need."

"You need to stay out of my business."

"What about your household bills?"

"What about 'em? Shit, they'll get theirs when I decide to give it. I ain't livin' to be paying no damn bills. Those bills are going to always be there, steadily coming in every month. Shit, a lady like me is going to stay fly."

Whakelah continued folding up their new clothes and placing them in their particular piles so that they could easily be deposited into their clothes bank, which was their closets. She gave some thought to what Misha was kicking to her. She knew she had a serious problem; she was a shopaholic. But shopping was the only way she could drown her sorrows.

Whakelah wasn't where she wanted to be in life. She was a twenty-four-year old single mother of two, with no real skills. She'd dropped out of high school to have her daughter when she was fifteen, gave birth to her son two years later, and never bothered to go back to school. She had been on public assistance and found it easier to live off the system than to get a job and have to worry about her kids being safe while she was at work. Sure, she juggled her shit, and robbed Peter to pay Paul, but she thought she was doing pretty well for herself.

Until she became obsessed with wanting her own reality

show. The world of television seemed like it was a million miles away and far out of Whakelah's reach. Without a high school education and financial stability, she had no idea how she was going to make her dream come true, but she was determined to do so.

"I can't be on my reality show looking tore up," she told Misha.

Just then, Whakelah's son, Marvin, came running into the living room. He was seven years old, and a straight A student in second grade. "Mommy, can I have the new Xbox 360?"

Whakelah looked at Misha. She knew Misha was waiting to see what her answer would be to her son.

"See? What I am I supposed to do when my kids ask me for stuff?"

"Tell them no!"

"I can't tell them no. Shit, they didn't ask to come here. I brought them here."

"Hmph. See, your ass is buggin'. I would tell their little asses no in a heartbeat. They'd be like, 'Ma, can I'—NO! See how easy that is?"

Whakelah giggled. It seemed easy enough, but she knew her kids were not having it. They were used to getting what they wanted, when they wanted it, and so was she. In a way, Whakelah felt that she needed to be an excellent mother to her kids so that they wouldn't miss having a father around. And, sure enough, having all of the clothes and toys that they wanted seemed to divert their attention to the fact they didn't have a father figure in their lives. But Whakelah knew that she was burying herself under a financial burden.

Whakelah also had been lying to various caseworkers for the past three years, receiving public assistance and food stamps for herself and five kids, not the two she had. The Department of Social Services had discovered this information and had contacted her, informing her that she was under investigation. They advised her that she could very well receive federal jail time, in addition to having to pay back all the money stolen from the government.

The days of caseworkers coming out to the homes of welfare recipients to perform home inspections had long gone. However, the Social Services Department still had their ways of finding out who was trying to cheat, or beat the system.

Misha saw that she wasn't going to get anywhere trying to convince her best friend to curve her addiction and stop shopping. Misha knew deep down that it was Whakelah's personal way of relieving stress. She really couldn't blame her. After all, isn't shopping every woman's stress reliever?

"I don't care about your ass, but I'm worried about the kids. You're teaching them bad spending habits. And as far as you and your crazy reality show, do you know what stardom and television does to children. It screws them up. Look at Michael Jackson."

"Don't be comparing my kids to Michael Jackson. My kids are nothing like he was when he was a child, God rest his beautiful soul. My kids, they have their childhood. I'm not rushing them to grow up. They want to be on television just as bad as I do."

"Sure, they do, Whakelah."

Whakelah had actually drilled the idea of having their own reality show into her children's heads. She had them watching all of the latest reality shows on television, even the ones that were inappropriate for their age group. Her daughter was a fan of *For the Love of Ray J*, and her son's favorite was Diddy's *Making the Band*, and they both loved *Run's House*.

Whakelah felt that her kids needed to have a deep sense of reality, how people behave and react in real-life situations at a young age. She believed that, when they approached their later years, they would be well informed as to the ways of this unpredictable world and would know how to cope, and handle themselves. She also believed that fewer people would be able to take advantage of them in whatever career path they chose to pursue.

To Whakelah, her life was fairly decent, but she wanted a whole lot more. She regretted not finishing school. She knew that if she had finished school and not taken the easy way out, she would've already had the knowledge she needed to take herself to the next level. She also knew that there were young girls and boys who needed to know what she'd been through coming into adulthood and would benefit from seeing her life portrayed.

Her next purchase was going to be a computer. She had no idea how she was going to afford it, but she knew that both she and her kids would benefit from the purchase of one. A computer would help the kids with their school assignments, and it would also help her branch out into the world of networking.

Whakelah wanted to start making a name for herself on web pages like MySpace, Facebook, and Twitter. Her cousin, Tank, who was a DJ, had blown up just by being popular on these sites on the Internet. Whakelah realized that, for her reality television show to be a success, she had to have a following and a huge fan base. There were a lot of people that utilized the web to make connections, and she desperately needed to get connected.

"You need to stop teaching them how to be the next reality superstar and start teaching them how important it is to get an education," Misha said, not realizing that, in Whakelah's mind, reality shows were educating her kids.

"Didn't I tell you that you need to stay out of my business? What about you? Did you get an education in being a ho? Oh, excuse me, I mean, a special services consultant. Or were you self-taught?"

"I'm self-taught, bitch, and I'm a pro. Film that!" Misha snapped her head from side to side.

"I'll pass on that. I'm not into porn."

"You need to be. That's where the money is."

"Then, bitch, I guess that's where *you* need to be. You the one tricking." Whakelah walked from her living room into her kitchen to begin cooking dinner for her and her kids, leaving Misha behind.

Misha didn't take offense to her best friend riding her about what she was doing to make her ends meet. She knew Whakelah didn't approve of her lifestyle, but they were still best friends, and nothing would ever change that.

"Whateva, Miss Stinkness. Like I said, reality shows are supposed to be real. You shouldn't have to teach them how to act," Misha yelled from the living room.

Whakelah wasn't trying to hear what Misha was saying. She was hell-bent on having her life on television for the entire world to see. She felt that Misha was too caught up with men to have a valid opinion about anything, except for subjects pertaining to men. How could she possibly have advice for her when she was no further in life than Whakelah was? Then, on top of that, having something to say about what was going inside of Whakelah's apartment, when pure sin was going on in her own.

Meatloaf, mashed potatoes, and broccoli was on the menu for the evening. Whakelah washed her chocolate brown hands, gathered the ground beef from out of the refrigerator, her roasting pot from her bottom cupboard, and reached up to grab her seasonings from the cupboards on the top. As she blended the ingredients into the roasting pot, she reflected on her life, and what brought her to the point to which she was currently at, the point of emotional and financial turmoil.

***

Whakelah had been digging a huge hole for herself for quite some time with her bad spending habits. There wasn't a day that she hadn't purchased an item or multiple items for her or her children. Her debt was mounting, and she was making matters truly worse by spending more and more. She thought she was buying things to try to make herself feel better, but in all honesty, she was buying things to cover up her pain.

Whakelah wished she could have the heart her best friend Misha had. Then she could get her a roster of men and start charging by the session as well. But she was a mother of two, and there was no way she was going out like that. She wasn't knocking what her girl was doing, but everything wasn't for everybody, and that lifestyle just wasn't for her.

In Whakelah's mind there was nothing a man could do for her that she couldn't do for herself. All men ever did for her was cause her pain and give her grief. Her father had disappointed her at a young age by leaving her and her mother, and making another woman and her children his focal point, leaving Whakelah and her mother to fend for themselves. This left a bad stain on Whakelah's heart, and she started to dislike and distrust men.

After a few bad relationships, she met her children's father. He had showed her mad love in the beginning of their relationship. She was a tough cookie, but he hung in there with her and knocked down a lot of the walls that she had built up in regards to her feelings toward men. He had treated Whakelah like a queen, and she thought she had finally found the perfect man. Until she had gotten pregnant with their first child.

In her third month of pregnancy, she received a phone call from a woman who claimed to be his wife.

One year and a half after that phone call, he turned up at her apartment to see his daughter, and in that visit, they conceived her son. Her children's father had never seen their son and had seen their daughter that one time. Whakelah had no idea where he was, nor did she care. She had made the decision to lie down with him, so she had no problem raising her children on her own. She knew one thing—She was never going to be anyone's wife. She wasn't interested in women either. She was simply interested in her kids, and her reality television show, of course.

Living on welfare, receiving Section 8, WIC and food stamps helped her to survive and raise her kids all of these years. There was no way she would have been able to pay rent, utilities, and keep food on the table for the three of them without the help from those services.

And what about the other things they needed? Clothes, shoes, day-to-day necessities. She had to provide for her family, and the task was getting harder and harder to do. She felt she had no choice other than to exaggerate a little bit on how many children she had. Now she may have to pay them back money that she had long since spent, not to mention the possibility of prison that was lingering in the air.

Whakelah's head was spinning with all of her thoughts. She suddenly began to cry. She didn't know what she was crying for. She had an idea, but she really wasn't absolutely sure just what it was that made her cry. She had so many different issues that she had been dealing with, that she had been keeping inside.

The thought of her going to prison and leaving her children to her mother was at the top of the list. Her mother had warned her about trying to cheat the system, but she never thought she would get caught. Her cousin, Tank's girl, had been completing all of her paperwork and providing her with social security numbers that she swore were safe to use, but Whakelah knew better.

At that moment, Whakelah's daughter, Kadayja, came running

into the kitchen. She had come in to find out what her mother was cooking because it had the whole apartment lit up with its delicious smell. She stopped in her tracks when she saw her mother's eyes filling up with tears. Whakelah's entire face was soaking wet from tears that been flowing down her dark brown cheeks.

"Mommy, what's wrong?" Kadayja asked her mother. She didn't ever recall seeing her mother cry, ever.

Whakelah grabbed an onion, picked up a knife that rested on the kitchen counter and began chopping the onion without even removing the skin.

"Nothing, Dayja. Mommy's good."

"Then why are you crying?"

Kadayja was nine and was extremely curious about everything, especially her mother. She was the splitting image of her mother, tall, thin, and dark brown. You could tell that she was going to be tall like her mother.

"Mommy's cutting onions, Dayja, and they make my eyes burn."

"I thought I saw you crying before you started cutting the onion."

Whakelah loved and hated the fact that her daughter was so smart and perceptive. She had no idea how to tell her children that they may lose their mother for a while and that they may have to go and live with their grandmother while she went away. But she always kept it real with her kids, and if it came down to it, then they would have that talk, but for now, there was no need in upsetting her daughter and having her worry.

"You know what, I was crying, baby, but for real, Mommy is fine." She wanted to be honest with her daughter. Whakelah always told her kids that the truth would set them free and she didn't want to go against her own values.

Bad spending habits aside, Whakelah had done a good

job raising her children on her own, and their behavior and attitude was a reflection of such. She had a rule, which was instilled in her by her own mother—Do as I say, not as I do. There was to be no cursing whatsoever in her household. And respect must be shown and given to adults at all times. Whakelah felt that just because she lived in the hood didn't mean she had to be hood. Nor did she have to teach her children how to act hood. She wanted her children to be respectful, well-rounded individuals.

Kadayja knew that there was something bothering her mother, but she didn't want to upset her further by being disobedient. If she said she was fine, then Kadayja was going to accept that.

She rolled the roll of paper towels, snatched one free and handed it to her mother. As Whakelah wiped her face, her daughter hugged her waist and squeezed her tight.

"I love you, Mommy."

"I love you too, Dayja."

"Aww, and I love both of y'all. Now can we eat, please!" Misha exclaimed, as she and Marvin stood in the doorway of the kitchen.

"Yeah, we can eat, but nobody said Misha's name was in any of these pots," Whakelah joked.

"God, you actin' stank tonight!"

Whakelah played the previous scene back in her head. She felt that the conversations and thoughts that had just taken place in her home would be great for the ratings of her television show. *A video camera! That's what I need.*

"Y'all know what? With a computer and a video camera we can make our own reality show and just put it on the Internet," Whakelah stated in excitement.

"Yeah, Ma, we can do that," Marvin chimed in. "That's easy."

"And I can ask Tank to film it," Whakelah said. Her cousin

Tank was always down for her and willing to help her with whatever she needed.

She didn't know what took her so long to think of the idea of doing her show on her own, but boy, was she glad that she had come up with the idea. Now she had to come up with the money for the computer and video camera. She was just at a loss trying to figure out how to get a computer; now she added a video camera to the list.

Whakelah was done crying. It wasn't something she was used to doing, and she wasn't fond of how it made her feel. Crying made her feel weak and she was far from weak. This was a woman who raised two kids single-handedly since she herself was a teenager, a woman who depended on no one but herself to provide for her and her children. Nah, she was by no means a weak individual and was going to get all of those skeletons out of her closets and bury them all.

The five of them sat at the table in Whakelah's small kitchen. It was crowded, but there was nothing but love at the table, so it was all good. Whakelah had put her foot in the food by seasoning the meat to perfection. By the way everyone was going at their plate and the pure silence in the room, you could tell that everything tasted just as good as it smelled, if not better. Whakelah had been like a kangaroo in her mother's pouch on those Sundays when dinner was being prepared for just the two of them. Her mother had taught her everything she knew about cooking, and had done a fine job.

"Girl, you don't be playing with them pots and pans. You be gettin' your cook ON! This food is on one thousand!" Misha said, giving her girl props.

"Tha's wha's up! I wanna have some cooking episodes on my show too."

"And just what's the name of this show?" Misha asked.

Whakelah took a moment to think. She had never really thought about that. She wanted the name of her show to be one that people would remember. Whakelah also wanted the name of her television show to be intriguing, so that viewers would want to tune in just by hearing the name alone. She played around with a couple of ideas in her head and began to try them out.

"Livin' with the Browns," Whakelah said.

"No, that sounds too much like Tyler Perry's movie, *Meet the Browns*," her daughter told her.

"The Life and Times of Whakelah Brown," she said, trying again.

"What about us, Mommy?" Marvin asked.

"Baby, Mommy can't have a show called 'Whakelah and her kids!'"

"Why not?" Marvin asked.

"Because that sounds stupid," Kadayja told her little brother.

"Mommy, Dayja called me stupid."

"I did not. I said the name was stupid, not you, dummy."

"Ma, Kadayja called me a dummy!" Marvin whined louder.

"Y'all two cut it out. Go on and finish up your dinner, and Dayja get you and your brother's clothes ready for school tomorrow."

The kids had finished their meals first and went back into the back of the apartment to their bedrooms, to finish off their evening. They both had to be at school in the morning, and it was approaching the ten o'clock hour. It was pretty late for them to be eating dinner at ten o'clock, but Whakelah had gotten back from shopping a little later than she had expected, and she just had to roll with it. She didn't keep them up past their bedtime often, so she saw it as no big deal.

"I know what the name of your show could be," Misha said.

"What? And don't play. Be serious, for once." Whakelah knew Misha clowned around about most matters, but her show was no joke.

"You say you wanna keep it real, right? So how about, 'Keepin' it Real-ah with Whakelah'?"

"Okay, now *you* sound stupid," Whakelah told her.

"I was trying to help."

"Do me a favor, and just stick to helping those sorry-ass niggas you call clients come," Whakelah said.

"Fuck you!" Misha said, meaning no harm at all.

"You heard from LaShawn?" Whakelah asked Misha, changing the subject. LaShawn was their best friend also. Together, they were the three *amigas*, all for one, and one for all.

"Nah, come to think of it, I haven't heard from her all day."

Whakelah and Misha finished their meal and had started clearing the dishes from the kitchen table and placing them in the sink. Whakelah knew that it was time to tell her best friend about her dilemma. She wanted to tell Misha and LaShawn together, but with the mind spell that she had before they all had sat down to eat, Whakelah knew she needed to tell someone else what was going on with her before her head exploded.

"Yo' chick, I got something real serious I'm dealing with right now. I could be in some trouble," Whakelah said.

Misha stopped what she was doing and paid full attention to her best friend. "Wha's up, chick?"

"You know I've been getting over on them muthafuckas for a while now, right?"

"Who? The Social Services people?"

"Yeah, well, they hollered at me and told me that they're investigating me."

"Oh shit!" Misha knew that a lot of people getting over on the system and felt bad that her girl had gotten caught up. "So what they talkin' about?" Misha asked.

"Well, right now, they're just investigating, but if they catch me up for real, then I have to pay back all of the money they ever gave me."

"What? How the hell are you going to be able to do that?"

"I'm *not* going to be able to do it."

"What are you going to do?"

"That's not all. They're threatening jail time."

"What!" Misha shrieked. She immediately thought of Kadayja and Marvin and what would happen to them.

"Chill, Misha. I don't want the kids running back in here."

"That's why I'm buggin'. I'm thinking about the kids."

Whakelah really hadn't thought about the seriousness of her situation until Misha registered her reaction. Whakelah was slowly coming out of her denial and was starting to realize that she could, in fact, go to prison and be taken away from her children. The thought put a sharp pain through her chest. She felt as if someone was killing her.

Misha saw the effect the conversation was having on Whakelah and she wanted to make her best friend feel better. "Yo', fuck that! It's gon' be all good. I know a good lawyer. He knows all of the judges, and I know he would help you."

"Lawyers cost money, Misha. Where am I going to get money for a lawyer? I'm trying to get money to put on my reality show."

Misha didn't have an answer to her best friend's question, and she didn't know about money for no damn reality show. But she knew one thing—If she had to fuck this lawyer to retain him for Whakelah, then that's what she would do, so her girl wouldn't have to stand in front of a judge alone, and have her and her kids' lives destroyed.

Misha now knew why Whakelah was acting so erratic. Why Whakelah had been shopping until she dropped, drowning herself into an endless pool of debt, and why she was obsessing over wanting a reality show that she most likely would never have, especially with all of the current events now brewing with her and the law. Misha recognized the symptoms. She had just read about them in a pamphlet at the free clinic. Her best friend was fighting depression, but she was slipping anyway, and didn't know it.

Damn! Misha thought. *And I thought I had problems.*

That just went to show Misha that you never know what's going on in someone else's life, even if it is your own best friend.

LASHAWN

"Whose pussy is this?"

"It's your pussy."

"You sure?"

"Yeah, I'm sure."

"You'd better be sure, bitch, 'cause if I find out you been fuckin' around on me, I'll kill you, you hear me?"

"Yes, I hear you."

"You better hear me, bitch, 'cause I'll fuck you up!"

LaShawn could feel the spit as it shot from the inside of his hot mouth on to her chilled skin. He had jabbed her in her side with his fists one too many times, and she was in complete pain. She didn't know why she stayed with this poor example of a man. All he did was abuse her emotionally, verbally, physically, and sexually. She had heard many times that if a man hit you once and you stayed with him, nine times out of ten, he would do it again. LaShawn never thought that she would be in a relationship such as the volatile and unsafe relationship she was currently trapped in.

"You know what? You're an ugly bitch! And I'm going through too much for your ugly ass. I get pretty bitches!" He pulled his limp dick out of her and got up out of their bed.

LaShawn, her feelings crushed, couldn't look in his direction. He knew that she knew that she wasn't the prettiest thing that had ever stepped onto the Earth, but the way he said it was simply cruel and unfeeling.

"Yeah, bitch, that's right. I said it, and you heard it, so don't get it fucked up. You's a ugly bitch!"

"I'm ugly? I'm ugly, Larry?"

"Hell fuckin' yeah!"

"That's cool, Larry. Go on and get you a pretty bitch then and leave this ugly bitch alone." LaShawn turned over to go back to sleep. *Does he have someone else?*

"Shut up, bitch! I already left you alone and you don't even know it."

"You shut up. I don't give a fuck about you or your new bitch! Congratulations to the both of you bitches. I hope you're happy together," she said, under her breath. She wouldn't dare say it aloud. That was sure to get her another ass-kicking.

It was evident that her man had been out drinking and clubbing, and now he was going to make her night a living hell. Larry, LaShawn's man, was a small-time drug dealer with a small mind, and a smaller dick. He grew up in a household where there was physical abuse. He had seen his mother get her ass kicked plenty of times, and he himself had been physically abused by his father. So he grew up thinking that hitting women was cool, a way to display his bravado.

To say that LaShawn was simply having issues with her man would be putting it ever so mildly. Insecurities associated with his sexual organ, or shall we say his little dick, coupled with violent tendencies which he had harbored for years were causing him to lash out at her in ways so severe, at times she couldn't bear to be in the same room with him. Then there were other times when he was the sweetest person in the world to her.

LaShawn had tried to tell Larry that the size of his dick didn't matter to her, and that he actually pleased her in bed, but in his world a man needed a big dick to please a woman. In his world, a man's steez was measured by the length of his dick. And since he had a little dick, no matter what she said or did to try to make him feel better, he still thought that he was less of a man. So he tried to make up for the size of his dick by acting like a big dick, so to speak.

There was a time when LaShawn thought it was cute that her man wanted to know her every move. She felt that Larry was showing how much he cared for by wanting to know where she was and who she was with, but then it got to a point where he didn't want her out of his sight. She noticed he was becoming too possessive, and that the matter was getting out of control.

LaShawn's mother had warned her when she'd moved out of her apartment just three floors up to go and live with Larry. The scene of her leaving her mother's apartment, the only place she had ever lived, played back in her mind. She could see her mother standing there yelling at her, as if it were just yesterday.

"Don't move out of here. You'll regret it."

"Ma, Larry and I love each other. Why can't you see that?"

Her mother could see the love, or rather the infatuation, that her daughter had for the man that had turned her daughter's world upside down, but she in no way saw the same affection coming from him.

"What I see is, he is a jealous man. And he bucks at you whenever someone looks in your direction. Now just where do you think that's going to lead?"

"Oh, Ma, please. You'll say anything to keep us apart," LaShawn said, as she continued to throw her clothes into plastic C-Town shopping bags.

"What mother wouldn't want to keep their daughter away from a drug-dealing pimp?"

"Ma, Larry is not a pimp!"

"The shit, he's not! Do you see those clothes and the jewelry that boy wears? If that ain't a pimp, I ain't never seen one a day in my old-ass life."

"I'm leaving, Ma." LaShawn turned to leave her mother's apartment.

"That man got you fooled all the way, huh?"

"Bye, Ma." LaShawn let her mother's apartment door slam behind her.

That was two years ago. Now, here LaShawn was, wishing like hell that she hadn't been so hardheaded and had listened to her mother. She wanted to run out of there and jet up the staircase and knock on her mother's door and beg her to let her come back home. She wanted to tell her mother how right she was about Larry being an asshole, that he didn't give a damn about her. But she didn't want her mother to tell her, "I told you so." She couldn't allow herself to admit to her mother or anyone else that she was a victim of abuse and needed help.

Every time LaShawn got her ass beat bad enough and got bold enough to make a move to break out and leave him, Larry would run out and buy her clothes and teddy bears and take her out to dinner. Once they returned home, he would throw the little dick on her, eat her pussy real good, and tell her repeatedly how sorry he was for hitting her, how much he really loved her, and that he needed her. That he couldn't do what he did without her. This gave LaShawn the tremendous ego boost she constantly needed, and she would be wrapped up in his trifling ass all over again, until the next battle.

LaShawn had to literally fight her man every time she wanted to go out and spend time with her girlfriends. It was amazing that Misha and Whakelah had no clue that her girl was being beat up by her man. So far, he hadn't hit her in an area where anyone could tell what she was going through, but the summer was approaching and LaShawn wasn't going to be able to hide the bruises that graced her arms and back.

Larry wouldn't allow her to get a job because he thought she might cheat on him with someone she worked with. She stayed in their apartment most of the day and night. The only time she really went out of their apartment was to go check out her girls, Misha and Whakelah. And that usually wasn't for long because she had to make sure she had returned by the time Larry had finished hustling. LaShawn stayed in the relationship for several reasons, but the main reason was because she feared Larry.

Larry, being a small-time drug dealer, had access to some of the best weed LaShawn had ever smoked. He supplied her habit, a habit that cost a minimum of one hundred dollars per week. He also paid all of the bills and kept their refrigerator stocked with food, which was more than a lot of other niggas was doing for their women.

Larry wasn't alone in his battle with low self-esteem. LaShawn had her own problems too. She didn't consider herself to be very attractive and actually felt lucky that Larry even wanted to keep her at all, much less keep her all to himself. But now he was telling her that she was ugly, and he had never told her that before. He had always made it a point to make her feel pretty, even though he used to beat her ass. So was he lying to her all of this time by telling her that she was his pretty baldheaded baby? Was he laughing at her looks behind her back? She didn't know what to think. With Larry one could never tell.

LaShawn was short, at five foot three and a half. Her size fourteen jeans gave her the appearance of being considerably thick. Her skin was high yellow, and her hair was cut close to her scalp. She never did well with perms, so she kept her hair naturally short and cut low. To add a little pizzazz, she colored it bright red. There were several things about her appearance that she would have liked to change, but she didn't need this little-dick nigga telling her she was an ugly bitch. His words were really fucking with her.

***

LaShawn sat up in bed, reached blindly for the lamp that was on the small table near their bed, and turned the light on. She ripped the blanket from off of her body and turned to her left to look at herself in the large-mirrored armoire that almost filled up the entire bedroom. She was nowhere near the ugly monster Larry had painted her to be. But there was a part of her that knew deep down inside that she wasn't considered pretty either.

Studying her features in the mirror, she looked at her round head and chubby cheeks. She then concentrated on her nose. In LaShawn's opinion, her nose was way too big for her face. She felt the same way about her lips; they were pink in color and just too big, and her hips, they were way too wide. LaShawn did like her eyes, which were a soft brown and held a hint of mystery.

Although LaShawn wasn't secure with her looks, she didn't think Larry had the right to belittle her and make her feel so unattractive. She made a promise to herself that she would begin to work on herself, to improve areas she could, and the areas she couldn't improve, she was simply going to learn to love. She would be damned if she would ever let someone make her feel so low.

LaShawn knew that if her best friends knew how Larry was flipping on her and that she was getting her ass beat on the regular, they would have told her that she was stupid for staying with him. But her best friends couldn't feed her weed habit, and they couldn't satisfy her sexual needs. And although Larry had a little dick, LaShawn had grown quite fond of it; it worked for her.

Larry had no problem keeping LaShawn high on weed all day and all night. She didn't know it, but that was a part of his plan for keeping her stagnant. He kept the refrigerator stocked with food so that she didn't have to go out to get any food to feed her bouts with the munchies. He would roll a fat blunt in the morning and smoke it with her. Then he would leave her a "dove" a day to smoke all to herself. Once she smoked some weed and ate some food, she would lie down, go to sleep, and get up and do it all over again. That was her life.

Larry didn't think that LaShawn was the best-looking girl he ever had. He was used to fucking with girls with long, pretty hair, and hers was nowhere near long. But she did have the best pussy he'd ever had. He played on her self-esteem because he knew he had low self-esteem. He felt that if LaShawn had experienced a man with a bigger dick, he would be history.

LaShawn turned the lights back off and was trying to go back to sleep. She was very much fed up with Larry and his bullshit. She was hoping that he was asleep in their living room and that his drunkenness was wearing off.

Her hopes were shattered when he came back into their bedroom in a bigger rage than when he had left out.

"Get up, bitch!" he said, as he flipped the light switch back on.

"Larry, please. What's the matter now?"

"I said get the fuck up!"

LaShawn didn't move. She was too scared to move. She had never before seen the look he had in his eyes. He stood over her with her cell phone in his hand. Fear pierced through her as she tried to reach for the phone to get it away from him. She had forgotten to erase her text messages. And there was one text that she didn't want him to see.

"Who the fuck is Calvin?"

"Who?" LaShawn said, trying to play dumb.

"Oh, okay, you don't know who he is? How about I call him and see?"

"No! Larry, please. I swear, he's just a friend of mine."

"Okay, well, since he's a friend, he wouldn't mind confirming that for me, right? Call him."

LaShawn didn't know what to do. Calvin was a dude she was just getting to know and was secretly hoping he would be her next man. He had a real job with benefits..

"Larry, please. Give me the phone."

"Man, fuck that! I'll call him."

Larry attempted to call Calvin, but got his voice mail instead. He took the opportunity to let it be known who he was.

"Look here, muthafucka, don't be calling my bitch! You hear me, dawg? This is *my* bitch. And if I find out who you are, I'm gon' see you, nigga. I'll piss in your mouth, muthafucka! You'd better stay away from my bitch!"

LaShawn was stuck. She didn't know how to react. She knew there was no chance of her ever seeing Calvin again, or him even talking to her again, for that matter.

"Who the fuck is this nigga, LaShawn?"

"I told you, he's just a friend."

Larry smashed her cell phone into the bedroom door, breaking it into pieces and then lunged at LaShawn and started beating her ass. The punches were coming so hard and fast, there was no way she could block them all. He gave her several blows to her head and her face. There would be no way to hide the bruises this time.

That wasn't the end of her beating. He got quite a few body shots in also, after he had damn near twisted her left arm out of its socket.

"Larry, please, stop!" she cried, as her light skin began to discolor.

"What the fuck you mean, he's just a friend?" Calvin asked between punches.

"I swear to you, that's all he is."

"Bitch, you ain't allowed to have no fuckin' male friends! You ain't allowed to have no fuckin' friends at all!"

"I'm sorry, baby."

"Yeah, you're right, you're sorry. You're a sorry-ass bitch!"

LaShawn was in a lot of pain. He had really gone too far this time. She knew she was wrong for trying to get with another man, but she had been at the end of her rope with Larry for quite a while. He had been good to her some of the time, but the bad times had by far outweighed the good times.

One day when she was on her way to Whakelah's apartment, she happened to meet Calvin. He had been installing cable for one of the residents on Whakelah's floor. As he was leaving the apartment, and running for the elevator that LaShawn was stepping off, he bumped into her and apologized to her for his rudeness.

Calvin never made it on to the elevator. He stopped to carry on a conversation with LaShawn; he liked them thick, and thick, she was.

Seeing that she really wasn't allowed to go anywhere or have any outside relationships with anyone, whenever another man showed the slightest bit of interest in her, she jumped on it, not knowing if or when she would ever get the chance again.

She did tell Calvin that she had a man. He then asked her, was she interested in having friends. She said that she was.

She had seen Calvin two times after that day. He had to install cable service in several apartments in her building. He had also installed his cable into LaShawn on the roof of the building in which she lived. They were trying to hook up again, but he was always working, so she had sent the text to him to see when he would be available.

"Get your fuckin' ho ass outta my fuckin' house!"

"What? Where am I supposed to go?"

"I don't give a fuck where you go, bitch. I told yo' ass I fuck wit' pretty bitches, and I'm going through all of this shit for yo' ugly ass. Fuck, no! I don't think so!"

"Larry, baby, please, we can work this out."

"There ain't shit to work out. You fuckin' another nigga!"

"I am not fuckin' him. I didn't fuck him!"

"You lying! You's a lying bitch and I hate a bitch that lies!"

"Larry, I'm not lying to you, baby. Please, just come here."

"Bitch, I don't want your ho' ass! You been hanging with your ho friends. Now you a ho, just like them ho bitches!" Larry stated, referring to Misha and Whakelah.

LaShawn could see that his mind was made up. She got some clothes on and started grabbing whatever she could, so she could get out of there as fast as she could. She had no idea where she was going, looking the way she did, but she was leaving Larry's apartment.

"What the fuck you think you doin'?"

"I'm leaving," she said, looking at him in bewilderment. *Didn't he just tell me to get out?*

"Not with the shit I brought you, you not. You came here with the clothes on your back, bitch, and that's how the fuck you leaving here!"

LaShawn couldn't believe he was doing this to her. She had stuck with him through all kinds of bullshit in the two years they had been together. Bitches were always calling his phone and texting him, but she didn't blow his spot up. She knew he had other women, but she never called anyone or questioned his movement.

All of the times he had hit her, she never called the police on him. She never once tried to get him locked up for abusing her or for selling weed, when she very well could have. Yet, he was throwing her out like spoiled milk.

She didn't realize just how much she didn't have until this very moment, but what she did realize was, she had to get her own place. She didn't like the feeling of someone telling her to leave a home that was never really hers in the first place. She now knew what her mother meant when she kept telling her, "God bless the child that got his own."

It was three in the morning, and LaShawn didn't know where to go. She wasn't going to her mother's apartment. One look at her face and her mother would be sure to call the police to come and lock Larry's sorry ass up.

LaShawn didn't know why she still wasn't trying to call the cops on Larry. Was she just as sick and twisted in the head as he was? Did she simply have a heart and didn't want to inflict the same pain on him as he had inflicted upon her? Or was she just waiting for an opportunity to get his ass back for all the wrong he had done to her?

She thought about going to Misha's place but decided against it. She really didn't want to disturb Whakelah and her kids at this hour. LaShawn couldn't face Misha or Whakelah. She knew they were like her sisters, but she just couldn't let them see her this way.

She hadn't even looked at herself, but from the way her face felt, she was picturing Angela Bassett's face in *What's Love Got to Do with It?* One thing was clear to LaShawn—Love ain't have a damn thing to do with what Larry had done to her.

She didn't have too many choices, so she went to the only other place that her clouded mind could think of.

"Yeah, we got a cot, but I don't know if you gonna want it," the attendant told her, as he pointed to the available cot.

LaShawn looked around the shabby homeless shelter. Her mind was reeling as she tried to figure out how in the hell she went from sleeping in her warm and comfortable bed to standing in the cold, drab, rat- and roach-infested homeless shelter in which she now stood. She knew she wasn't dreaming, that her circumstances were as real as the homeless man on the cot to her right, picking the skin out of his toes and putting it into his mouth.

"I'll take it."

LaShawn just needed a place to sit down and gather her thoughts. She had to map out a game plan. She never had a place to call her very own. All she knew was her mother's apartment and Larry's apartment. It was definitely time that she got up, got out, and got something of her own.

LaShawn didn't dare pull out her wallet or check her pockets to see how much money she had. She would have been beaten up again and possibly robbed for every dime she had. She decided to wait until the sun came up, which was in another hour, and then she would hit the streets and see what was good.

She had learned a little something from Larry in the time that they had been together. All she needed was a thirty-dollar bundle of weed and she could turn that into a hundred dollars in cash in no time. Then she would take the hundred and get an ounce and flip that, and she would work it like that, until she could get up enough money to rent a place.

A homeless woman asked her, "You gonna eat that bread?"

The smell that reeked from the woman's body was almost stifling. She had a pound of dirt caked on to her already black skin. The layers of clothing that adorned her body most likely consisted of every item of clothing that she had ever owned. Her hair was filthy and matted into four huge dreadlocks. And by looking at what was left of her teeth, bread was about all she could eat.

"No. Here, it's all yours." LaShawn handed her the piece of bread from the tray of food they had given her. As the woman began to walk away, LaShawn called her back and gave her the whole tray of food.

She looked around the homeless shelter at all the people who had nowhere to go, no one to love. She didn't have much, but now realized just how much she did have.

Once she secured her a place, she was going down to Social Services and get straight. She could have used her mother's address to apply for emergency funds and food stamps, but LaShawn wanted to handle this situation all on her own.

Two weeks had passed and LaShawn had yet to go back to Webster Projects to check her girls out. She had bought a TracFone, but she hadn't called them either. She hadn't even bothered to holla at her mother. Needing some dollars to set her straight, she was on a straight grind.

GIRLS 4 LIFE

Noticing that LaShawn hadn't reached out and touched them in a minute, Misha went to Larry's apartment looking for LaShawn. She was surprised when another female answered the door. When Misha asked the female to tell Larry to come to the door, she called him, but he wouldn't come to the door. Misha simply put two and two together.

Once she checked with LaShawn's mother and she hadn't seen her either, Misha started putting the word out on the street that she and Whakelah were looking for LaShawn.

Tank, Whakelah's cousin, had run into LaShawn as he was coming out of the barbershop on 145th Street in Harlem. She was selling weed, hand to hand. He called Whakelah as soon as he had copped a bag from her and told her that he had located LaShawn. Tank had informed Whakelah that LaShawn wasn't looking like her usual self, like she was going through some rough shit.

Whakelah got off the phone with Tank and took her kids to her mom's crib, which was only a few blocks away. She then called Misha and told her what Tank had said.

Once Whakelah had gotten back to the projects, she got up with Misha. They jumped in a cab and went downtown to Harlem to find their homegirl. She was in the exact same spot that Tank said she would be.

"Yo', why the fuck you ain't tell us what was going on?" Misha asked LaShawn, once inside the cab they had to force her into.

"I just couldn't."

"Man, we ya girls," Whakelah said. "If you can't tell us, who can you tell?"

LaShawn knew Whakelah was right, but she was just too embarrassed to let them in on what she was experiencing with Larry.

"Where the hell have you been at all of this time?" Misha asked her.

"Trust me, chick, you don't wanna know."

"Oh, but I do, so tell me," Misha said, waiting for an answer.

LaShawn had taken a pause for the cause. Should she tell her girls where she had been, and still was resting her head, or should she lie to them? LaShawn was tired of lying.

"I've been staying in a homeless shelter on Kingsbridge Road."

"A what!" Whakelah yelled.

"Oh shit! Chick, for real?" Misha asked in astonishment.

"Yeah, for real."

As the cab driver drove the three young ladies up Lenox Avenue, and over the George Washington Bridge, Whakelah and Misha caught LaShawn up on things that had been going on in the hood since she had been away.

They arrived back in the Bronx and in front of Webster Projects in no time at all. LaShawn had only been gone a few weeks, but coming from the surroundings in which she had just come from and seeing how the truly poor was living, she was grateful to be walking into her old building. She wanted to go to her mother's first to let her know that she was all right, since Misha had expressed to her how worried her mother was.

Whakelah ran toward their building. "A'ight, y'all, come on and hurry up, 'cause I'm chocolate and I will melt."

Misha went to pay the cab driver, but he declined. The middle-aged Hispanic man had been studying her from his rearview mirror. So he proposed a movie and dinner, and she accepted.

Bam! Just like that, she had another client. Things were looking up.

LaShawn watched her girl do her thing. The crazy thing was, Misha didn't have to do anything. Men simply flocked to her. LaShawn wished she had that effect on men.

Misha and LaShawn got out and followed Whakelah into the building.

Misha pulled the hood of her Rocawear sweat jacket over her head. She had just gotten her hair done, so she wasn't trying to mess it up. It had been an all right week for her in terms of her clients. Nothing special like the paper Clutch had dropped her a few weeks before, but she was able to get her hair freshly permed, cut. and styled, have her nails done, and pay her cell phone bill.

LaShawn's mother was extremely glad to see her daughter. By looking into her eyes, she could tell her daughter had been to hell and back. She wanted to go grab her .38 special and go knock on his apartment door and blast his fucking brains out for hurting her baby. She could see through the cheap makeup that LaShawn had on. That no-good pimp had been putting his grimy hands on her child. Well, LaShawn's mother had brothers, and they had something for niggas like Larry. And she would be giving them a call as soon as her daughter and her friends left her presence.

LaShawn took a hot shower and wiped the days of dirt off her skin. She then went to her old room to get some clothes and came back out with a couple of bags.

"Where are you going this time?"

"It's time for me to do my own thing, Ma," LaShawn told her mother.

Her girls saw that it was about to be a Hallmark moment. Whakelah and Misha said their good-byes to LaShawn's mother and let LaShawn know that they would be waiting for her in the hallway.

Her mother wanted to shake some sense into her daughter. Hadn't she learned anything at all from this whole crazy ordeal? Didn't she know that her mother's home was the best place for her to be? It was her safest option. Her old room was right there waiting for her, and she wouldn't have to worry about where her next meal was coming from.

"Why are you making life so hard for yourself, LaShawn?"

"Ma, I'm not trying to make life hard, it just is."

She wanted to tell her mother that she was grown and that she was going to make decisions that may not always be good, but life was hard anyway. After Larry had put her out with nothing but the clothes she had on her back, she knew she had to take some losses, and it was evident that she had lost this round. But she wasn't going to keep on losing. She had some things to prove to herself, her mother, and that no-good, son-of-a-bitch ex of hers.

"Come back home, LaShawn," her mother pleaded.

"Ma, I can't. I need to do this for me."

Her mother went into her housecoat and pulled a small sack out of the pocket, a handkerchief she had sewn together. She opened the handmade sack and pulled out a roll of ten-dollar bills. She counted ten of them in all, and she broke her daughter off five. Fifty dollars wasn't much, but it was all that she could afford.

LaShawn didn't want to take her mom's money, but she she needed it. She took the money and gave her mother a kiss on her cheek and a long hug. She could feel her mother's tears as she creased her head into LaShawn's neck.

"Come on, Ma, please don't cry," LaShawn said, now on the verge of tears herself.

"Don't you ever let that man, or any man, put their hands on you, LaShawn. You do whatever you have to do—Fight 'em back, kick 'em, stab 'em—I don't give a damn if you have to shoot 'em, but you better not ever let another man touch you again for as long as you live."

"I know, Ma, I won't, I promise you that."

LaShawn left out of her mother's apartment with bags for the second time. This time it was to live on her own, to live her life the way she wanted to live it. She didn't know what life had in store for her, but after staying in the homeless shelter, she was ready for whatever came her way.

LaShawn found Whakelah standing alone in the hallway. "Where did Misha go?"

"She had to go to her place for a little while. One of her clients called for an appointment."

"Hmph! That girl needs to chill. She gon' fuck around and get caught out there. I hope she be screening them niggas she be fuckin'."

"I don't know." Whakelah didn't want to say too much about Misha and her profession to LaShawn.

"I mean, I ain't tryin' to knock her hustle or nothing."

It sounded as if LaShawn was trying to knock Misha's hustle in Whakelah's opinion, but she was going to leave that right there where it was.

Whakelah suggested they go to her apartment, where Misha would be, once she finished with her client. LaShawn didn't want to take a chance on seeing Larry in the building, so they took the staircase up.

Misha had already told LaShawn while they were riding in the cab about Larry having another girl. She mentioned to her that the girl must have been on the scene before now, to be answering his door the way she did. LaShawn figured that the girl must have been the pretty bitch that Larry was taunting her about. She wanted to ask Misha what the girl looked like, but to know would have hurt her feelings. No matter what the girl looked like, her feelings were already hurt just knowing that someone else had taken her spot just like that.

LaShawn couldn't understand why she still had some sort of feelings for Larry after all the foul shit he had done and said to her. She hoped that, in time, her feelings for him would go away. She didn't want to have any love for him. None at all.

Whakelah unlocked the locks on her apartment door, and they went inside. It was quiet without the kids around. Whakelah found pleasure in the awkward silence. She then went straight to her kitchen and started pulling food out of the refrigerator.

LaShawn was right behind her. She didn't want to tell or show her mother just how hungry she was, but she could tell Whakelah. And she did so when they were jetting up the staircase.

Whakelah started running hot water over some chicken wings that hadn't completely thawed out. She then grabbed a bag of potatoes and began to peel them into homemade French fries.

LaShawn knew her girl made the best French fries in the world. Her mouth began to water, and her stomach began to growl.

"Daaamn, LaShawn!" Whakelah said.

"Sorry," LaShawn said.

"Nah, man, I'm just fuckin' wit' you. You good."

Whakelah felt bad for her homegirl. She could tell that the past couple of weeks was rough. She didn't even want to imagine the nights that she went through being in a shelter with a bunch of stinking, dirty people.

"I would have loved to have been able to get some footage of you in that homeless shelter, with me right there, of course," Whakelah said, as she continued to peel potatoes.

"Yeah, trust me, I thought about you and the show when I was in there. It was really real. You would have really gotten some good footage."

Whakelah was so happy that someone besides herself, and her kids, saw her having a reality show. LaShawn was her girl for life, just for making that statement. For, she knew from LaShawn's statement that LaShawn believed in her dream too.

The doorbell rang, and Whakelah asked LaShawn to get the door for her because her hands were now immersed in a bowl of vinegar that included the chicken. She was soaking the wings, rinsing them off one by one, and preparing them for her special seasoning.

LaShawn opened the door for Misha to come inside. She noticed that Misha looked a little disheveled. Her zipper on her Deréon jeans was open, and her button had been popped off her blouse. Her fresh hairdo had been sweated out and had fallen flat. Misha had a strong scent of sex on her, but it didn't smell bad, it just smelled like sex. Good sex.

LaShawn was a little envious, it had been a couple of weeks since she had sex, and the last time for her was too rough to enjoy. "You could have at least closed up the cage, Misha." LaShawn looked down at Misha's open jeans and saw the tuft of pubic hair that rose above her panties.

Misha pulled her zipper up. "What you busy lookin' for?"

"Girl, please. Ain't nobody lookin' at you."

They joined Whakelah in the kitchen.

"You need some help with that?" Misha asked.

"Hell no. You just got finished touching somebody's dick, and probably their balls too, you ain't wash ya stinkin' pussy, so I know you ain't washed ya hands," Whakelah joked.

"Fuck you, bitch!" Misha shot back.

"You do enough fuckin' for all of us," Whakelah said.

"Shit! Somebody gotta hold y'all bitches down." Misha went into Whakelah's refrigerator and grabbed a soda.

Misha noticed that Whakelah's refrigerator had less food than usual. She was sure it had to do with her benefits being cut off, but she wasn't going to put her girl on blast in front of LaShawn. She didn't know if Whakelah had shared the information with LaShawn, so she wasn't going to put it out there. There were certain lines that she simply did not cross. She sat down at the kitchen table along with LaShawn as Whakelah did her thing.

The first batch of chicken had been seasoned with Whakelah's secret ingredients and placed into the frying pan. Her girls watched as she handled the seasonings and the utensils like a professional chef. She cleaned up behind herself as she worked to get their meal prepared as quickly as she could. She knew LaShawn was starving. It was apparent that there had to be some reality shows that focused on cooking and that Whakelah had been avidly watching them. She moved with smooth agility around her small kitchen.

LaShawn noticed some chocolate chip cookies on the kitchen table. She didn't know how she had overlooked them, but now that they were in her sight, she attacked them.

"God! Godzilla, slow down," Misha joked.

LaShawn, cookie crumbs all over her mouth, looked up at Misha. The dark circles under her eyes looked like a football player's face paint. She had tears that were swelling up in her eyes. It was her breaking point. She was tired. She was hungry. She was hurting. She wasn't sad, she was fighting mad.

"Don't cry, LaShawn," Misha told her. "I ain't mean nothing by that shit."

"Nah, it's not that," LaShawn said, sniffling, as her tears mixed into the cookie crumbs.

"What is it then? That bitch-ass Larry? You want to jump his punk-ass? He can't handle all three of us at one time," Whakelah said, demonstrating her karate moves.

Misha sighed. "Whakelah, please."

"Hell, yeah. We can get some baseball bats. Misha, you can get at his dome piece. I'll take his midsection, you know, bust him all up in his gut. And, LaShawn, you get the nigga's legs. Hit that nigga with everything you've got. Shit! Cripple that muthafucka. I bet you he'll never put his hands on you again."

"Girl, you is crazy." Misha shook her head back and forth.

LaShawn was glad to be with her girls. Even through the bad times and through tears, they found a way to make her laugh.

"Nah, for real, I know what it is," Whakelah said in a serious tone.

"What is it?" Misha asked.

"She's tired of the bullshit. I think we all are," Whakelah said.

Misha knew that was right. She was definitely tired of the bullshit. But what were they going to do about it? None of them had any money, or any connections to make their situation better. She grabbed a paper towel from the dispenser over the kitchen sink and handed it to LaShawn.

"Man, fuck all dat. I'ma call Tank. Shit, that nigga deejays all over this fuckin' city. He gotta have somethin' poppin'." Whakelah lifted the crispy, golden brown chicken wings out of the frying pan.

"Tha's wha's up," Misha said.

After the ladies had finished their meals, they all went to chill in Whakelah's living room. LaShawn still had some weed left, and even though she couldn't afford to smoke from her own stash, she needed a blunt badly, so she rolled up.

Misha took twenty dollars out of her back pocket and slid it to LaShawn.

"What's that for?"

"For the blunt."

"See, that's what I don't need—Y'all treatin' me like I'm a charity case." LaShawn tried to hand the money back to Misha, but she wouldn't take it. She grabbed Misha by the waist and put the money back into her back pocket.

Misha took the money out of her back pocket yet again, and

forcefully placed the twenty-dollar bill back into LaShawn's hand. This time she folded LaShawn's hand around the money and folded her arms around her friend.

"We got you, chick," Misha told her. "We ain't got much, but we got you. We girls for life."

Determined to start living her dream even if it meant taking baby steps, Whakelah had her cell phone up on video mode. While she was filming the touching moment between Misha and LaShawn, a call came into her phone, and she answered it.

It was an investigator from the Social Services Department, and the news wasn't good. She was going to have to pay back $12,000, and could still face possible jail time.

"What's the matter, Whakelah?" LaShawn asked her.

"They tellin' me I owe them twelve thousand dollars, and on top of that, I could still get locked up," Whakelah said in disbelief.

"What the hell?"

"Who is *they*?" Misha asked.

"Some man named Mr. Irving, he said he's their investigator," Whakelah said.

"Well, don't tell that nigga nothing until you talk to my dude," Misha said. She had already fucked the lawyer that was going to help Whakelah out. Four more sessions and the bill would be paid in full. "Matter a fact, fuck callin' Tank. You better call my dude and get that shit straight."

Whakelah called the lawyer and put him on speakerphone, so her girls could hear what he had to say also. She knew they would want to know what was said, so rather than have to repeat the conversation, she allowed them to listen in. She explained to the lawyer in detail what the investigator from the Social Services Department had said to her. The lawyer told her not to worry about the criminal charges. He felt that the agency may have been trying to put fear into her by threatening her with possible incarceration. He advised her to concentrate on coming up with the money, and that if she could come up with half of the money, and had no prior criminal record, he could ask for leniency, with no jail time.

He asked Whakelah for the investigator's name and number and advised her not to speak with him directly anymore, saying he would take care of the matter. He also told her to tell Misha that he would be looking forward to seeing her soon, not knowing she was listening to his horny ass.

LaShawn couldn't believe her ears when she had learned what Whakelah was dealing with, especially the charges she was facing, and the two kids who depended upon her solely. *Oh my goodness! What would happen to her kids if she went to jail?* LaShawn now knew that she wasn't the only going through a life crisis. She handed her girl the blunt. She needed it.

Whakelah was cool with what the lawyer was kicking to her. If he could get her some breathing room on the payments and throw that jail time out the window, that would be a good look. She still had no idea where she was going to get the six thousand dollars. She called her cousin, Tank.

"She's handling all of this extremely well, don't you think?" LaShawn said to Misha while Whakelah was talking to Tank.

"She's good. She's handlin' hers. She's a lot better than she was at first, when all of this first came down."

"Oh, so you knew from day one, huh?" LaShawn always felt that Whakelah and Misha kept her out of certain things.

"Yeah, but does it matter who knew first? We just need to be there for her, like we're here for you."

"And what about you, Misha?"

"What about me?"

"You act like you don't have any problems?" LaShawn said, a jealous tone in her voice.

"I got a shitload of problems. A bitch need some money, some real money. I'm up to my neck in credit card debt, and I just came out of housing court a few weeks ago. Ain't no shame in my game. I ain't no pretender."

LaShawn didn't know why she was glad to know that Misha had problems too, but she was. She thought Misha had it made, with all of the men that she had, paying clients or not, and would have loved to have that type of attention showered on her.

Whakelah was very excited when she ended her call with Tank. She still had possession of the blunt as she danced around her living room. "Are y'all bitches ready to come up or what?"

"What you talkin' about? What crazy bullshit has Tank filled your head up with now?" Misha asked.

"I'ma be fillin' my head up at the bar at this party he's gon' get us passes for tonight." Whakelah said.

"I ain't going to no party. I don't have nothing to wear."

While LaShawn was bitching about having nothing to wear, Whakelah went into her bedroom and came back with a Baby Phat jean outfit that LaShawn had left there months ago when they had snuck out to go to the club behind Larry's back.

"Ha! Gotcha now! Here you go." Whakelah handed her the outfit. "Now you do."

Misha immediately ran down to her apartment to grab her black-and-beige snakeskin Rocawear two-piece leather outfit, her flyest. She also grabbed her black leather "fuck me" pumps to strut her stuff in.

The tradition was that they all got dressed in one apartment when they went out. It cut down on time. So once she had her clothes, she returned to Whakelah's to get dressed there.

Whakelah slid her slim thighs into a pair of black leggings. "Yo', this party is gon' be all that. I can't wait to be up in the place. I just know there's going to be a bunch of ballers up in that piece."

"Fuck the ballers! I need a fuckin' shot-caller to get me in some videos. Shit, can't y'all heifers see that a star has been born. Y'all better clap for her!" Misha said, mimicking Jay-Z off *The Blueprint 3*, as she finished applying her makeup.

"Ho, ain't nobody gon' pick you to be in their video. Your behind is over the hill, compared to those little bitches running around with their big fat juicy asses dropping it like it's hot," Whakelah said, messing with her, as she slid on a silver sequined top. She knew her best friend was a five-star chick. "I can drop it like it's hot too." Misha dropped her plump booty to the floor and wiggled her way back up.

"Yeah, okay, now try that four more times," LaShawn said, laughing.

"Fuck you, LaShawn! I could if I felt like it, but I don't feel like messing up my outfit."

"Yeah, one drop too many, and your ass is going to drop out of them damn pants," LaShawn said. "Damn! Them shits is tight!

"Do I detect some haterade in this muthafucka?" Misha asked. "Bitch, don't hate 'cause yo' ass is wide as hell and flat as a pancake. A nigga can't even grip it, much less slap it up, flip it, or rub it down."

"Forget all that small talk. Let's talk business, shall we. Y'all said y'all ready to come up, and wanna get paper. Well, look, I went and had these business cards made while I was on the streets." LaShawn showed the ladies one. It read: Get Your Mind Right Productions—Specializing in natural remedies, exotics, and powders.

"How smart is that?" Misha asked her. "You're advertising weed and coke on a fuckin' business card?"

"Well, I can't go and have Tank shout it out on the mic. Shit! You the stupid one. This is the best possible way for me to touch everybody in that joint."

"Will y'all two cut it out? We have a party to go to; a party with some A-list muthafuckas on it, if I may add, we all about to come up."

Whakelah knew the rivalry between these two ladies and didn't need the drama tonight. They were on a serious mission tonight. That party held the access to all of their dreams coming true, and she was ready to make it happen.

She needed some money to keep her ass out of jail and needed to meet someone who could help her with her television show. She was tired of seeing everyone with a reality show on television, and hers seemed to be going nowhere fast. She could just see her name rolling on the credits.

PARTY OVA HERE

When Whakelah, Misha, and LaShawn stepped into Club Mansion, their eyes bulged, and their mouths fell open when they spotted faces they had seen in many of the popular hip-hop magazines. Everybody who was anybody in the industry was at that party. The three of them looked as if they were stuck together like popsicles that had been in the freezer too long and had to be carefully peeled apart.

The entertainment industry was becoming so saturated with everyone who was really no one, but who really thought that they were someone. But everyone looked like they were someone important at this party, and personas and egos looked to be at an all-time high. Females lined the walls like they were at a casting call for America's Next Top Groupie, waiting to be selected.

The temperature hadn't fully dropped in New York City, but that didn't stop niggas from having their furs on. It seemed as though minks was reigning on this night, as the ladies spotted almost every color fur had ever been dyed into.

Some ballers took it there and had multi-colored minks on. The amount of ice niggas had on their necks was unbelievable. Most of the dudes were rocking colored stones, but for the ones who didn't quite have it like that, and whose paper wasn't long enough, platinum and gold links were still a luxury.

Gators and Wallabees were on the feet of the slickest-looking niggas in the place. There were reserved signs on most of the tables. Some had people at them, but most of them were still empty. It was only one A.M., so it was still early.

***

"All right, ladies, let's act like this is what we do," Whakelah said. "Just act natural."

They went to one of the bars in hopes that there were some real niggas in the place that might buy them all a drink. Sure enough, as soon as they stepped in the area of the bar, they heard some dude throwing back the Goose call them out. It was all good. Shit! He was buying.

As the bartender took their orders, the dude who was buying their drinks came over to holla at them.

"Hey there, pretty ladies," he said. Dude's breath was kicking. He needed a breath mint, some mouthwash, and some more shit to help him out with his condition. Misha, Whakelah, and LaShawn tolerated him for a little while, only because he had been nice and bought them all a drink.

As soon as Whakelah spotted Tank in the DJ booth, she immediately pulled the girls in that direction. Everybody knew, once you were allowed into the DJ booth, you HAD to be somebody worth knowing. And all of the ladies wanted people to think they were indeed worth knowing, and planned to milk it for all it was worth.

"Excuse me. Excuse me," Whakelah said. "Pardon me. Coming through."

The crowd of people lining the steps to the DJ booth was reluctant to let the ladies through, but Whakelah's persistence voice convinced them to let the ladies go through.

LaShawn hit them all up with her business cards.

When Misha saw they were trying to read what she had to offer, she wished she had made some sort of advertisement about herself that she could have passed out. Turned out LaShawn's idea wasn't so stupid, after all.

"Tank, wha's good, cousin? You mixin' the hell out of them CDs, my dude!" Whakelah yelled.

The days of LP's long gone, deejays were using laptops and

computer files. It took the heart out of the art, in some people's opinion, but Tank was just keeping up with the trends. Who wanted to carry a bunch of big old crates filled with records around anyway? Carrying laptops added to a nigga's swag.

While Whakelah was kickin' it with Tank, LaShawn and Misha took the opportunity to look down at all the enticing prospects scattered below. A few people were dancing, but people were mostly schmoozing. The chicks were looking too cute to move, and the dudes were all acting like the next Diddy.

A large portion of the crowd was glued to the DJ booth. Maybe it was because it was up in the air and surrounded by lights. The sounds were hittin' on one thousand, so the crowd was checking to see just who was serving it to them just the way they liked it.

Tank threw on Jay-Z, Kanye, and Rihanna's "Run This Town," and the crowd went wild.

Misha began to dance and soon felt someone dancing behind her. She turned around to see who had taken such liberties with her ass. She was ready to curse a nigga out, but when she looked up, she was halted by the sight of one the sweetest-looking specimens she had seen in a minute.

Misha was speechless, which wasn't something that occurred often. She didn't know what to say to him. She turned her back on the dude and continued dancing. He held her waist and rocked to the beat with her. She could smell his cologne and was already diggin' him. But something told Misha, this was no prospective client. She would be chumping herself if she carried him in that way.

From the quick glance she had taken, he had the look of a thug, but there was something else. He had a very strong aura. She could tell that he smoked weed because she could smell it on him. That was a plus in her book.

He turned Misha around to face him. "Let's go somewhere

where we can talk," he told her in her ear, not wanting to yell over the extremely loud music.

"Nah, I came with my girls. I can't leave," Misha yelled, too short to reach his ear.

"I didn't say you had to leave. Come on, follow me," he said into her ear. He took her by the hand and led her out of the DJ booth.

LaShawn watched her go with him. She knew what her girl was about, so she figured dude was a duck, about to be plucked and sucked. She took note of what the dude looked like and what he had on, just in case she had to report his ass to the police if something had happened to Misha. She then continued handing out her business cards, letting some of the partygoers that looked like they knew what time it was know that she had some trees on her if they were ready to cop.

Tank had taken a moment to stop deejaying. He passed the laptop over to his protégé and let him get some shine for a few while he kicked it with his cousin.

Tank's and Whakelah's mothers were sisters, so they had played together all of their lives. They'd even all lived together in a one-bedroom apartment at one time. Whakelah could remember Tank, when he was about ten years old, getting his ass beat for scratching up all of his mother's records, trying to learn how to mix records.

"Wha's good, cuz?" Tank asked.

"You know you the nigga for being able to get us all into this party, right?"

"Ain't no thing, cuz. I got a few people for you to meet."

"For real?"

"I told you, I got you this time, cousin."

She knew Tank knew a few famous people in some big places, but she never thought he would really introduce her to them. Tank had a habit of saying he was going to do something and then not doing it. So Whakelah was real glad when they got to the door and their names were really on the guest list. There had been invitations to other events where things didn't go so smoothly.

Tank felt bad about all of the times he'd had his cousin and her friends come out and not be able to get in on the strength of his name alone. There were times when he was spinning tunes and his protégé wasn't with him and he couldn't leave to go and validate their entry.

Tank took Whakelah over to one of the tables that had a reserved sign on it. A white man sat, smoking a cigar and drinking a glass of Dom. Whakelah assumed it was Dom, since he had a whole bottle of it chilling in a silver bucket of ice on the table.

Tank sat down, and invited Whakelah to do the same. "Hey, Steve. This is Whakelah, my cousin with the idea for a reality show. Whakelah, this is Steve Smith. He has connections with HBO."

Whakelah extended her hand, but she was the only one who did. Steve simply wanted to know what the concept was for her reality television show, and told her so.

Whakelah immediately explained what she wanted her show to be about. To depict the real life of a hood chick that had been caught abusing the welfare system and was at risk of losing her two kids. She described how heartwrenching it would be for America to go through her trial on television.

She did mention to Steve that she had a lawyer, who was confident she would receive no jail time, thus securing her freedom for future episodes. Then she would prove to the hood chicks of America and everyone else who watched her show that you can't give up when your back is up against a wall.

She also told him that she wanted to have a few episodes showing her shopping sprees, her and girlfriends interacting with her, and of course, her cooking skills.

Whakelah laid it all out for him in less than five minutes.

"Nobody is going to want to see that," Steve said.

"It may not sound good coming out of my mouth, but here, look, I have some video of my friends on my cell phone." Whakelah scrolled through her cell phone in search of the footage she had of Misha and LaShawn.

Steve Smith looked at Whakelah as if she had to be kidding. She wasn't possibly about to show him video on a cellular phone. "I'm not interested."

Tank saw how Steve's comments had affected his cousin. He felt bad for her, but he had been telling her the same thing for a whole year.

"Fuck you, and HBO!" Whakelah got up and walked away.

Whakelah didn't care what anyone said. There were still a lot of other important people at this party. She was still hoping to rub elbows with someone who could land her on MTV, VH1, or any other station interested in the idea. She just knew that her life was worth watching.

The public didn't only want to see who was living large. They also wanted to see families that were struggling just to make it, period. People wanted to see others who were dealing with real-life trials and tribulations. She wanted the world to see how she was still standing strong, after facing civil and criminal charges for receiving illegal welfare and food stamps, but yet she still managed to stay rocking the latest fashions, while her kids wanted for nothing.

She knew she was sitting on a gold mine with her reality show idea. Fuck a Steve Smith, and her cousin Tank too. For all Whakelah knew, Tank could have told Steve what to say. She knew how muthafuckas could hate on peoples' dreams, even family members.

LaShawn adjusted her fake Gucci sunglasses on her round

face. LaShawn didn't want people looking all up into her face. Her bruises weren't so evident, but there was still a hint of discoloration in her light skin. She feared that someone might be able to see the pain in her battered soul, even though it was dark in the club, and she could hardly see through the tinted lenses of the sunglasses.

Nor did she care how the sunglasses looked with one Gucci symbol on the side, instead of the two symbols that they come with. These sunglasses, which she had bought from the Chinese store on Webster Avenue, served as a force field between her and the crowd. They gave her the protection to come out of her shell and get her grind on.

LaShawn didn't know where her homegirls had gone, but she knew what they were there to do, so she knew they were on their grind as well.

She stepped outside of the DJ booth and continued mixing and mingling with the crowd. When it came to selling her weed, her self-esteem was at an all-time high. When she sold weed, she felt like she was in control. She had what people wanted and needed.

A few of the people who had copped a bag or two from her had apparently sampled the goods and was coming back to her, showing her madd love and attention. It made LaShawn feel sort of important.

She had the "crazy tree connect" thanks to her ex. That was the best thing about her breakup with Larry. She was now selling her own weed and making her own money. And she could do what she wanted without Larry's overbearing presence. She could come and go as she pleased. Now, all she needed was a place to live.

LaShawn worked Club Mansion like a hustler on the block, as she worked off the ounce of weed that she had brought in with her. She had broken the ounce down into dime sacks and sold them for twenty so that she could fully capitalize on the small bundle of trees.

Her business cards also said that she had powder available, but when inquiring minds asked her, she told them she was already out of product, but to hit her up later. LaShawn never had powder, but she knew that was a surefire way to get her clients. She planned to cop her first small bundle of cocaine with the money that she had just made.

Wanting to know that she had made the $350 she expected to make for the night, LaShawn headed to the ladies' room. After asking about five people where the bathroom was located and being sent in five different directions, she finally found one of the ladies' rooms.

The line was a mile long, as chicks waited to release their liquor-filled bladders. LaShawn wasn't trying to wait in a long line. She had done exactly what she had come to Club Mansion to do. Get money. Now she needed to count up and find her girls and get out of there, so she could get that bundle of coke and take her hustle to the next level.

"Where the fuck you think you goin', bitch?"

LaShawn turned around to find a female in her personal space.

The female was next in line to use the bathroom and wasn't about to let LaShawn get in front of her. She stood there, drunk as a bitch,

"Check this fake-ass bitch out with her fake-ass Gucci glasses, trying to skip somebody," the female said, staring at LaShawn through the lenses of her authentic pair of Gucci sunglasses.

LaShawn didn't say a word. A warm rush came over her body, and she simply snapped and started beating the brakes off the female.

The girl's friends tried to get LaShawn off her, but LaShawn had a powerful grip on the female's hair, and was pounding into her face like a boxer does his punching bag.

She managed to take the honey's glasses off her face and slide them into her jacket pocket before Club Mansion's bouncers rushed to the scene.

Although they were male bouncers, due to the circumstances, they put gender aside and went into the ladies' bathroom. They grabbed LaShawn and forcefully escorted her to the door. Minutes later, they threw her out of the club without giving her a chance to say anything in her own defense.

"Where are you taking me?" Misha asked, yelling over the music at the dude. She still had yet to even get his name. These days you couldn't go with anyone you really didn't know. People were on too much sheisty shit.

"What? You think I'ma stick you up?" Swag laughed.

"Oh, nah, but you could dick me up," Misha said on the low, not quite loud enough for Swag to hear. "I don't even know your name," she said aloud.

"Swag," he said, turning back to look at her. *Damn, she fine!*

"Swag?" Misha knew everybody was using the word a lot lately, but she thought he had taken it just a tad bit far, using it as a name for himself.

Swag had Misha by the hand and was pulling her through the crowded club. Her fingers incidentally touched on a diamond bracelet he was wearing. Misha looked down in the dark club at his wrist and was almost blinded by the white ice in the piece of jewelry.

That shit can't be real!

Females were standing in a row peering at them as if they were mannequins in Macy's window and they were window-shopping. They were trying to catch Swag's eye, while giving Misha dirty looks. She paid them no attention whatsoever. In fact, she dared anyone of them bitches to get at her live and direct, because she had something for all of their asses, a razor in her mouth on the right side of her cheek.

They went up to an exclusive area of the club, where there was thick red carpet and red velvet drapes surrounded by mirror and glass. Humongous crystal chandeliers glistened like ice glaciers as they hung low from the ceiling. And bartenders with white, collared shirts and black bowties filled glasses with premium labels of all types of alcohol.

In this section the liquor was being given away for free, and there was a long table with a full buffet of various foods, and two large ice sculptures resting at each end of the table.

As Misha walked with Swag through the room she saw the silver plates on the walls that proved her suspicions true. She was in the VIP section of Club Mansion.

Misha knew that he looked like he was on his grind and that he had some paper, but she didn't know dude was rolling with the *real* very important people of the industry. Whoever this dude Swag was, he was the muthafucka to know.

Misha let Swag's hand go. She then used both of her hands to perk up her titties in her black satin bustier, and perked up her attitude as well. She could smell her dream of getting in the door of the video industry, and the scent was overpowering.

Swag led Misha past a few celebrities as they continued down a long corridor toward a private suite in the back of the VIP section. As Rihanna's "Hard" blared through the club, Misha listened to the words of the song and swung her head to the beat. She just knew Rhianna was singing about her.

Misha wasn't sure, but she could have sworn that she had just seen Jadakiss and Styles P coming out of one of the suites with some real hot Puerto Rican chicks. Misha had never been in a club such as this one, and she had never ever seen a VIP section in her life. She felt like Cinderella at the ball, and Swag was her Prince Charming.

Once they were all alone in the private suite, Swag locked the door and was able to relax. He was a bit uptight around large crowds, having been in several shootouts and stampedes in New York City nightclubs. He took his .45 caliber pistol from the harness that rested underneath his burnt orange leather jacket and sat it on a small chrome and glass table near the bar.

"Aw, shit! Please don't tell me you five-O?" Misha asked. She had dislike for police officers and if Swag turned out to be one, she didn't care how fine he was, her ass was out of there.

"Come on now. Nah, baby, I ain't no cop. The truth be told, I don't even like them muthafuckas."

"Tha's wha's up. That's one thing we already have in common." Misha smiled. She liked that Swag kept his heat on him. *That's gangsta.*

"You got a pretty smile."

"So do you." Misha grinned.

Swag was a giant compared to Misha. His six foot three height matched with the weight of two hundred and fifteen solid pounds, making him a nice piece of eye candy for the ladies. His milk chocolate skin was rich and smooth. His eyes were almost the same color as Misha's, a soft brown.

The sensuality of his eyes made you want to stare endlessly into them. His teeth were white and straight, giving him a dazzling smile. Misha noticed the bulge in his dark blue Sean Jean denims. Swag looked to be working with a real nice package. *Looks could be deceiving,* she thought.

Misha could tell that he lifted weights. His abs was damn near protruding through his cream Sean Jean crew neck long-sleeved shirt. Misha just hoped he didn't lift too much, because too much weightlifting was known to lift a nigga's dick off his body.

Swag was already standing next to the bar, so he took the liberty of asking Misha what she would like to drink. She pointed to the Cîroc vodka. That's what she had had earlier. She didn't want to make a bad impression on Swag by throwing up in front of him; that's wasn't sexy.

He placed ice in a rock glass and poured a nice amount of the liquor in her glass. "Did you want to drink it straight. I mean, there's ice in it, but—"

"Oh, nah, I mean, no. Cranberry juice will be good."

Misha tried to bring herself out of the hood and speak with a little bit of class. She could tell Swag was used to refined women, and she didn't want to miss out on her golden opportunity to be with him in whatever way he wanted her to be. Misha was going to go hard, or she was going to go home. She didn't know what her girls were getting into, but she had her mind set on getting in to Swag, or letting Swag get into her, whichever came first.

Swag handed her the drink he had made for her. She tasted it. It was real good and strong, just the way she liked her dick.

"So what do you do?"

Misha almost choked on her drink when the question was posed to her. Should she tell him that she fucked niggas for a living? *Hell, no!* She gave him a seductive look. "Since you brought me all the way up here, I think I should be asking *you* that question."

"I'm a producer."

I knew it! This is the nigga that's gon' make it happen for me. I can feel it! Misha didn't want Swag to see her get too excited. She didn't know what type of producer he was, but it didn't really matter to her.

Sitting down on the red velvet love seat that rested in a corner of the suite, she wished she had worn a skirt. Then she could have really given him something to look at. But Misha was really feeling what she had on. The leather snakeskin outfit showed off her figure. The tightness of her jacket made her waist look extra small, and her pants made her ass look double the size it really was.

"I like that suit. You all up in that shit. Yeah, I like that a lot. It's real fly."

"Thank you very much," she said, blushing. She thought he must have been reading her mind.

Swag reminded Misha of June. She put it in the back of her mind to call June. She still hadn't answered his question on whether she wanted to be his girl or not. Ironically, she had been giving it some thought in the past couple of weeks, but now that she was looking at an upgraded version, she was glad that she hadn't yet answered him.

He came and sat down next to her on the loveseat. She was sure he had a bunch of bitches trying to get with him, but for real, with her walk, talk, and swagger Misha knew them other bitches didn't have nothing on her. But she still wanted to make sure that she set herself apart from all of the rest of the women that were vying for Swag's attention.

"You look like you could be in videos," Swag told her.

"Be careful, Swag. Compliments will get you everywhere." Misha, a sultry smile on her face, stirred her drink with her finger and then placed her finger in her mouth and swirled her tongue around her finger, her glossed lips pouted around her finger. She pretended that her finger was Swag's dick as she sucked lightly on the tip.

Misha knew how the business worked. Females usually fucked their way into the music video industry. So why pretend?

"So, Swag, what kind of producer are you?"

"I'm a music producer. I do beats for a lot of the up-and-coming artists in the industry. Right now, we're working on DiViNCi's project."

"Word? That nigga is hot. He's underground though. I didn't know he was signed." Misha followed the underground hip-hop scene heavily and started naming a bunch of the mix tapes she'd heard him spit on.

"No doubt, no doubt. Yeah, he been doing his thing underground for a minute, but he just got signed and we about to drop his first video."

Swag was impressed that Misha actually knew who DiViNCi was. Not many females did. He had been working with DiViNCi for over two years and was very involved in his project. Swag was

really feeling Misha's style as well as her looks. He could tell
that she was a bit rough around the edges, but with the right
nigga behind her, he thought she had the potential to be a
star.

"So, you wanna be in it?" Swag asked.

Misha definitely had the look that would keep DiViNCi's
fans eyes glued to the television screen. The budget that they
had for the video wasn't as large as Swag was used to working
with, so he couldn't get the chicks in the industry that he
really wanted. But with Misha, he figured he could give her a
few thousand dollars and he would have her gorgeous face in
the video. Swag didn't know about Misha being DiViNCi's
love interest. He wanted that starring role all to himself.

"Who me?" Misha asked, wanting to piss in her pants.

"Yeah, you." Swag smiled his winning smile at her.

"Well, I guess, I mean, if you want me to," Misha said,
trying to play off her utter disbelief. *What? I don't have to fuck
this dude to be in the video? He can't be for real . . . Dreams don't
come true this easily, do they? But, wait, I wanna fuck this dude.*

"Why don't I give you a down payment for the job, so you'll
know that I'm a man of my word, and that I mean business,"
he said, looking intensely into Misha's eyes.

Their eyes locked and her heart melted from the sincere look
in his eyes. Misha felt as though she had to be dreaming. The
whole entire evening was too good to be true. She wanted to
literally pinch herself, but she didn't want Swag to know she
was feeling so out of pocket.

When Swag reached into his pocket and pulled out a wad of
hundred-dollar bills, Misha's pretty brown eyes nearly jumped
out of their sockets. She tried to remain as calm as she could,
but it was getting harder and harder.

Swag counted off one thousand dollars and handed it to her,
and she didn't hesitate to take it. She could pay off a few of her
credit cards with the gwap he had just given her. Fearing he

would change his mind and take the money back, she hurried up and placed the money in her front pocket. She wanted her favorite thing in the world, money, to be close to her favorite part of her body, her pussy.

Misha never wanted this night to end. She was feeling Swag in a major way. He was tricking on her like a true baller. She wanted his attention, and a whole lot more.

"So you'll do it?"

"Is the video all you want me to do?"

Swag wanted Misha bad. He wanted to fuck her as soon as he'd laid eyes on her. He had locked her into the video. Now it was time for him to have her legs in a lock. And her question left the air wide open for him to stake his claim. Normally, he didn't like to mix business with pleasure, but he was more than willing to make an exception in Misha's case.

Misha didn't know how it all had happened so fast. The last thing she remembered was them sitting together on the loveseat. Now they were now on the floor, their naked bodies floating on the plush red carpet.

She opened her legs wider and wider as Swag kept blessing her with solid strokes of his dick. Her hands caressed the softness and hardness of his beautiful dark chocolate skin as she slid her hands up and down his strong back.

Swag touched Misha in places no man had ever touched her before, mainly her heart. Her body began to shudder under his. She climaxed simply from the thought of Swag and he being the cool-ass nigga he was.

He climaxed too, from the feeling of her sweet-ass pussy, and they held each other close after their escapade. Both Misha and Swag were silent. No words needed to be said.

This night was the best night of Misha's life, and she owed it all to her girl Whakelah.

MAKIN' MOVES

"Y'all bitches straight left me in the club!" Whakelah puffed on the blunt that LaShawn had rolled for them. She was seeing her homegirls for the first time since that crazy night two weeks ago.

"Shit, I'm the one who had to set it off in that muthafucka. That bitch thought she was gon' get the best of me. I beat the shit out of that bitch! Y'all missed it," LaShawn told her girls, as she unpacked her new dishes.

Misha took the blunt from Whakelah. "I can't take y'all bitches nowhere!"

The night at Club Mansion had been a wild one. Once LaShawn had gotten thrown out of the club, she ended up taking a cab up to Harlem to cop the bundle of coke she needed. The city never slept, so she had no problem finding what she needed at four in the morning. She rented a hotel room on 145th Street and Amsterdam Avenue and bagged her shit up.

She could have called Misha and asked her to stay at her crib, so she could save some money, but she decided against it. Whakelah's crib wasn't even a thought in LaShawn's mind, with her having the kids there. Plus, LaShawn had meant what she said about doing everything on her own.

The same day that LaShawn had started selling coke, her money had doubled. The day after that, her money had tripled, and she was able to persuade one of the managers of Webster Projects to rent her a studio apartment.

Slowly, she was getting her shit together. It made her feel good to know that she didn't need anybody's help to get her own place.

Misha had left with Swag the night of the party and had pretty much been tied to his hip ever since. She had been chilling with him at his crib in Long Island a lot. He was getting her prepared for her debut in DiViNCi's video.

Misha was going to be the leading lady in the video, and had been bragging about it ever since she had gotten to LaShawn's new apartment.

She was still sneaking in a client here and there. Whakelah's lawyer was a must-do, but Swag was making it almost impossible for her to serve her clients in the manner she was used to. It didn't bother her one bit. She didn't miss fucking those broke-ass niggas she'd been dealing with.

Swag was treating her better than anyone ever had before. She had been shopping twice since she had been dealing with him. He had taken her to Macy's and let her pick out whatever she wanted. He gave her money without her having to ask for it. Swag was holding her down crazy.

Misha was still curious to know what Clutch had been up to. She hadn't been able to reach him lately, and he hadn't called her either. Even with what Swag was peeling off, Clutch's money would always be good with her.

She had been receiving madd calls from June, but was ignoring them.

Whakelah was no closer to her dream of her reality show than she had been before the party at Club Mansion. She had a similar experience with yet another executive producer that Tank had introduced her too, but she didn't bother to curse this one out, she simply threw her drink in his face and walked off.

Whakelah then decided that she was going to enjoy the rest of her time at Club Mansion. After all, it was the first time she had actually made it inside of one of her cousin's A-list parties. So after three more drinks, she let herself go and partied like a rock star.

When it was all over, her cousin Tank, had to literally carry her four blocks to where his car was parked, drive her home, and then carry her up to her apartment. He went through hell trying to find her keys, but he finally did and was able to put her to bed. Whakelah woke up later on that afternoon with her mother and kids standing over her, yelling for her to get up.

Whakelah was still trying to figure out how she was going to come up with the six thousand dollars her lawyer said she needed to make her case go away. Whakelah was very grateful to Misha for getting her a lawyer and paying for him with what she did best. Whakelah had to admit, Misha used what she had, to get what she wanted and she was starting to see that there was nothing really wrong with that. In fact, she was starting to see there had to be something very right about what she was doing because she was getting everything that she wanted. Maybe I have been going about my hustle all wrong.

"So what? You think you Lauren London or somebody now?" LaShawn took a long pull off the blunt.

"Man, please. Why is everybody bugging out so hard 'cause I'm getting this opportunity?"

LaShawn looked at Whakelah, who looked at the floor.

Misha thought they would be happy for her. They both knew how much she always talked about wanting to be in videos. They saw her dancing and watching herself in the mirror for years, wishing she could be on the screen and be seen by millions of hip-hop lovers. The fact that it was really happening was incredible, and she couldn't understand why her girls were reacting this way.

"That's fucked up. I thought y'all was my girls! Y'all know how much we all want to get up out of the hood. Well, we can get out now," Misha told them.

"Nah, seems more like *you* can get out now," LaShawn said.

Misha peeped LaShawn's actions more than her words. LaShawn's eyes had hatred in them. Misha really didn't want to see it, but it couldn't be denied. LaShawn's jealousy was becoming a problem.

LaShawn didn't even realize she was jealous of Misha. These newfound emotions had somehow risen to the brim of her brain. She didn't want to be jealous of her very good friend. She had never been the jealous type, but for some reason she found herself envying Misha. She envied her looks, her perfect shape, and she envied the fact that Misha always seemed to be in a relationship with a man who wanted to be with her all the time. Plus, Misha's size nine was a total contrast to LaShawn's size sixteen. And although the niggas loved to make comments about LaShawn's humongous ass, that was all they seemed to be interested in. Nothing more.

Misha's phone rang. She pulled her new Sprint BlackBerry out of her new brown Gucci signature bag that Swag had paid sixteen hundred dollars for on the day he had taken her shopping at Macy's, and answered it.

LaShawn and Whakelah peeped the bag, and the phone. They then looked their best friend up and down and noticed that everything that she had on was brand-new.

This ho really lucked up this time. She fucked around and got herself a winner, Whakelah was happy for Misha. She had wanted her friend to find one man to settle down with, and maybe Swag was that man.

The only reason she was somewhat hatin' on Misha was because Misha had gone shopping and bought a bunch of new clothes and Whakelah's name was nowhere in any of the bags. She had to silently check herself. She thought about all of the times that she had gone on shopping sprees and had never bought either one of her friends a damn thing. The only difference was, Misha was spending Swag's money, while Whakelah had always been spending her own money.

When Misha got off the phone, she was back to her happy self. She had been invited back out to Swag's house in Long Island. He was sending one his boys to pick her up. Swag didn't care one bit that she lived in Webster Projects.

Misha had asked Whakelah and LaShawn if they wanted to ride out with her. Yeah, they were acting fucked up, but they were her girls, and she wanted them to meet Swag so they could see why she was so crazy about him. She was also hoping that Swag had some friends that could dick her girls down. In Misha's opinion, they both needed some dick so they could take the edge off their attitudes.

"So we finally get to meet the infamous Swag, huh," Whakelah said.

"Yeah, finally," Misha said, blushing.

"Oh, Lord, look at Miss Sensitivity over here, actin' all sappy and shit," LaShawn said, teasing Misha.

"Whatever, LaShawn, when you see him, you'll understand."

"Oh, yes, I must see this nigga that got yo' ass all wound up like one of those cheap-ass toys they be selling on the sidewalk for five dollars."

"Fuck you, LaShawn!"

"That's all you know how to say and do, huh?"

"It works for me!"

Whakelah wasn't paying either one of them any mind. She was too excited. She had heard about some of the phat houses in Long Island, but she had never seen them Whakelah had family in Queens, and to her, they were living large, but she had never been to Long Island before. She had heard that some of the rich and famous people of New York lived out in Long Island.

Whakelah called her Mom to see if she would keep her kids for the evening. After her mother agreed to keep them, she told the girls that she would be right back and jetted to her apartment, which was four floors below LaShawn's new apartment, to get ready. *Misha lucked up. Shit!* Whakelah thought maybe she could very well luck up too if she put on a little makeup and some brand-new clothes of her own, which she had plenty of.

While going through her bedroom closet to find an outfit to wear out to Swag's crib, Whakelah couldn't help but marvel at the abundance of clothes she had accumulated during her shopping sprees. All of the closets in her apartment were filled to capacity with a bunch of designer labels.

Whakelah's hands touched on a host of clothing from Baby Phat, Rocawear, Apple Bottoms, and House of Deréon, all still with the tags on them. It was at that very moment when a light bulb went off in her head. *That's it! I could sell all of my brand-new clothes to get the money I need!*

Whakelah returned to LaShawn's new apartment decked out in a cream Rocawear knit, hooded mini dress trimmed with gold piping. She had on a pair of metallic gold Baby Phat heels with a peek-a-boo toe. And she carried her large gold Rocawear sack bag. She knew she was looking good and couldn't wait for her homegirls to see her.

The unknown man who had opened LaShawn's door had startled Whakelah upon her return. Once he saw her reaction, he quickly introduced himself as Ty, Swag's partner.

Whakelah asked Ty where LaShawn and Misha were, and he quickly pointed toward the bathroom. Whakelah went to join the ladies in the tiny room.

"Oh my God, that nigga is fine!" she said, attempted to squeeze into the small space with Misha and LaShawn.

Whakelah was sure Ty had heard her. LaShawn only had a studio apartment, and there weren't any rooms in it besides the bathroom, which was only two feet from where Ty was standing. She wasn't tripping about him hearing what she had said. He needed to know that she thought so.

As soon as Ty had walked into LaShawn's apartment, and LaShawn saw him, she, too, thought he was fine. Misha was in the process of adding mousse to LaShawn's short red hair. She told LaShawn that if she wanted to attract a man like Ty, she had to get her appearance together. Misha wasn't feeling LaShawn's spiked look and told her that she should style her hair so that it would have a softer effect. She told LaShawn that it made her look hard, like a butch. Misha didn't know that Whakelah was going to go gaga over Ty.

"I saw him first," LaShawn told Whakelah.

"Bitch, whateva!" Whakelah told her, which meant, every bitch for herself, because Whakelah was going for hers.

They left the Bronx and headed to Long Island. Once Misha knew Whakelah wanted to hook up with Ty, there was nothing she wouldn't do to help her girl make it happen. She owed Whakelah. If it wasn't for Whakelah, she would have never gone to Club Mansion, would have never met Swag, and she would still be broke.

Misha let Whakelah take her spot and sit up front with Ty, while her and LaShawn played the back of the black '09 Cadillac Escalade.

LaShawn was heated. She wanted to sit up front with Ty. She felt as if she was being doubly tortured as they drove out to Swag's crib, having to listen to Misha sweet-talk Swag on her cell phone, as well Ty and Whakelah get to know each other.

The deal was sealed when she heard Ty punching his phone number into Whakelah's cell phone. She thought that Misha and Whakelah were pulling their two-against-one tag team on her again.

After cruising through the city for a while, they jumped on the Long Island Expressway and made their way out to Swag's house.

"I thought I was gon' have to send one of my niggas out lookin' for y'all," Swag said.

Swag had been standing there waiting for them in the circular driveway of his grey-stoned mini-mansion. He opened the back door of the Escalade so Misha could exit the vehicle.

LaShawn's heart skipped three beats as she looked into the most beautiful brown eyes she had ever seen. She quickly looked away.

"What took y'all so long to get out here, nigga?" Swag asked Ty. But once he saw Whakelah step out of the truck in that Rocawear mini dress and those heels, he already knew the answer to his question.

After meeting each other, they all went into Swag's house. Once inside, Swag took Whakelah and LaShawn on a tour of his luxurious home.

Misha stayed behind. She had already been on a tour of his home. As a matter of fact, they had already christened just about every one of his sixteen rooms. She wanted the girls to get their fill of Swag on their own so they could see for themselves just how cool he really was.

She also wanted to get the business on Ty and Whakelah's conversation. Her girl was chasing paper too, and Misha knew that Ty had some.

"So, Ty, you feelin' my girl, or what?" Misha asked him as he walked toward the game room of Swag's home.

Ty was a good-looking dude in his own right. He wasn't as fine as Swag, but at six feet even and two hundred and fifty pounds, he held his down. He didn't have a six-pack, but he was tight in the stomach area. And his legs weren't too thin, yet they weren't too thick. His caramel complexion complemented Whakelah's dark brown skin, and Misha thought they looked real good together. Misha knew that Whakelah wasn't into a lot of men, but she could tell that her best friend was very much interested in Ty.

It was Sunday, and there was a football game on. The Dallas Cowboys were playing the Washington Redskins, and Dallas was down. Ty, a Cowboys fan, was so engrossed in the game, he hadn't bothered to answer Misha's question.

Misha knew what would get Ty's attention. She went into the kitchen and grabbed him a bottle of Heineken and came back into the game room with a nice cold beer for him.

"Thanks, Misha," he said, as he took the beer from her.

"No problem. So, um, Ty, you feelin' my girl?"

"She a'ight," he said, nonchalantly.

"What does that mean, she a'ight?" Misha couldn't read his body language.

"I mean, she a'ight, she cool, but, Misha, I really ain't lookin' for no girl."

Misha assumed that if Ty wasn't looking for a girl then just maybe he was looking for a guy. "Ooooh, I'm sorry, I didn't know."

"You ain't know what?" Ty asked, now looking directly at Misha like she was crazy. He saw her facial expressions and knew right away what she was thinking.

Misha slowly reiterated his own statement. "I mean, you sayin' you not lookin' for a girl, so—"

"Yo', get that shit out ya head. I ain't no fuckin' faggot!"

"Oh, okay, cool. I mean, they my peoples too, so, you know, it's all good," Misha explained, laughter in her tone and a smile on her pretty face.

"Yo', you wild," Ty told her, laughing.

Ty liked Misha, especially for his man. Swag needed to settle down. He had been fucking with too many girls, and it was bound to catch up with him sooner or later. Misha was able to keep up with Swag's sexual appetite. At least, that's what Swag had told him, so she was a keeper. He could see why his homeboy was falling for this young vixen. Misha was pretty, she was sexy, she was down-to-earth, and she was funny.

"So what's up?" Misha asked, still pressing the issue. "You already got a girl?"

"Nah."

"So what's your deal?"

"Let me put it this way. I don't have time for a relationship, and women want you to spend time. I'm into my work, Misha."

"What kind of work do you do? I mean, I know Swag is a producer, but what's your role in all of this?"

"I'm the money behind all of this."

Misha's eyes batted extremely hard. Wasn't Ty just full of surprises? All the time she'd been thinking Swag was the money behind it all. She wondered why Ty was acting like he was Swag's flunky, if he was the one with all of the money.

Oh well, she wasn't chasing the paper like that anymore, happy with what Swag was doing for her. With him, it wasn't just the money. She actually had feelings for him, and she had never really had genuine feelings for any man. Misha was feeling June, somewhat, but it was nothing like the feelings she had for Swag.

Misha thought about Whakelah. Shit, her girl needed six thousand dollars, and this nigga was sitting here saying he was the money behind a nigga that had money. She had heard

Whakelah mention on their way to Swag's house that she was about to sell her brand-new clothes, which was a good idea, and may, in fact, get her some of the money, but she really didn't want her girl to have to do that.

Misha didn't know quite yet what she was going to cook up between Ty and Whakelah, but she had just turned the burners on.

"You mean you live in this gigantic house all by yourself?" LaShawn asked, her voice resembling a little girl's.

"Yeah, I do. But it's not as sad as you make it sound," Swag told her.

"I know that's right!" Whakelah chimed in. "You have a beautiful house, Swag. I wish I could film some of the episodes of my reality show here. That would be sweet."

Whakelah rolled her eyes at her LaShawn. She thought her attempt to get Swag's attention was foul and lame. Swag didn't want a damn thing to do with LaShawn, and she was making a complete fool of herself. Whakelah couldn't wait to tell Misha all of the underhanded shit LaShawn was doing.

"Swag, I need to use the ladies' room," Whakelah said.

"Do you remember where it is?"

"Yep, I think I can find it." Whakelah traced her steps back to one of the four bathrooms he had just shown them.

Whakelah wasn't feeling the way LaShawn was acting and didn't trust her sneaky ass with Swag all by herself. She didn't plan to be gone long, but she really needed to go to the bathroom.

Whakelah agreed with Misha. Swag was cool. She liked him a lot and could see why Misha was so shaken by him.

LaShawn knew that niggas like Swag loved bitches with big

fat asses, just like the one she possessed. She was willing to bet all of the money that she had in her pocket that if she was left alone with Swag, she could make him fuck her.

They waited in the hallway upstairs while Whakelah went off to use the bathroom.

"So Whakelah's doing a reality show?"

"It's a dream of hers." LaShawn looked at him with wanting eyes.

"That's what it do," Swag said. "You gotta have a dream."

LaShawn had a dream. Her dream was to be butt naked with Swag fucking her doggie-style and Misha watching in horror as she came endlessly, and raced off into the sunset with Swag as her new man. That was the least she could do after Misha had fucked up her chances with Ty.

LaShawn got closer to him. "You smoke weed, Swag?"

"Yeah, I smoke weed."

"*Mmm!* That's what's good. 'Cause I sell."

"Oh, word? I respect that, mama."

"You buyin'?" she asked, as she stepped into his personal space.

"Nah, I ain't buyin', mama, but thanks for the offer. Let me know if you need some weight, and I got you."

LaShawn was so turned on by Swag's swagger, she couldn't control herself any longer. She moved even closer and was now a breath away from him.

Swag knew exactly what she was trying to do, but he wasn't going for it. This scenario of one girlfriend trying to secretly steal him from the other one, or trying to set him up, to prove that he was a dog, had played out many times before. He couldn't keep count of the amount of chicks and their girlfriends who had gotten into fistfights and had literally declared war over him.

This time he was totally amused. At least all of the other chicks had some sort of looks about them. He wasn't attracted to LaShawn in the slightest.

Out of nowhere, she put both of her hands on his dick.

"Look, Mama, don't embarrass yourself." Swag removed her hands.

"What?" LaShawn asked, playing dumb.

"I ain't the one for all'lat. I'm feelin' ya girl hard, and I don't think she would take kindly to you doin' what you just did."

LaShawn's self-esteem was shattered once again. Her fat ass wasn't even an asset anymore. Niggas just didn't want her at all. Larry's ass kicking was nothing compared to the pain she was now feeling inside.

She wondered if Swag would still be so into Misha if he knew what she really did for a living and just how many niggas she had fucked. She wanted to hurt Swag, just as much as he had hurt her, but in a physical way.

When Whakelah returned from the bathroom, she could tell that something had transpired between Swag and LaShawn. She noticed a complete change in LaShawn's attitude.

The evening was a lovely one for Misha and Whakelah. They enjoyed Swag and Ty to the fullest. Swag had cooked steaks and burgers on his outside grill, and they ate, drank, and chilled.

DiViNCi had slid through Swag's place with his crew and had hung out for a while. He got to meet Misha for the first time. He had heard a lot about her, and from what Swag had told him, it was all good. He felt that she would be perfect for his video. They even went into the recording studio that Swag had built in his home and DiViNCi got in the booth to spit some freestyle lyrics for all of them.

Meanwhile, LaShawn stayed to the side, watching, hating, and plotting.

REAL LOVE

It had been a minute since they were all chilling out at Swag's crib. Whakelah wanted to go back to Long Island again soon. She hadn't heard from Misha in over a week and had tried calling her countless times, but her phone kept going straight to voice mail. She knew her girl was living it up out there at Swag's house, without a care in the world.

Whakelah hadn't heard from Ty either. She thought they'd made a connection the night they were kicking it at Swag's house. She figured that she probably wasn't his type and that he wasn't into her. She realized they were from two different worlds. That wouldn't stop her from searching for someone. Ty woke up the sleeping beast of lust in Whakelah, a beast that she thought she had on lock.

She had heard from her lawyer, who informed her that the date for her hearing with the judge and the Social Services Department had been moved up for the convenience of the court. Whakelah was in a real bind. She now had to come up with that money by next week.

Selling her clothes wasn't going as well as Whakelah had expected. She put up handwritten flyers all around the hood, but she wasn't getting any real call backs with any serious offers. The people calling her back were trying to get something for nothing, and her clothes were worth some money. So far, she had only accumulated nine hundred dollars.

Whakelah had been leaving her kids with her mother every weekend now. She'd been a little short-fused lately and had been yelling at them, something they were not used to. Both she and her moms thought it was a good idea, but Whakelah wasn't so sure now. She was so used to having the kids up under her, she was going crazy in her apartment all alone.

Whakelah hadn't talked to LaShawn in a few days. She was over the drama that went down at Swag's house and wanted her to know that, no matter what they went through as best friends, at the end of the day, and through all of the bullshit, they needed to remain best friends. She called her up. LaShawn wasn't up to anything special, so Whakelah went to her crib.

Whakelah showed up at LaShawn's apartment with a blunt in her hand. She wanted her girl to know she wasn't there to smoke up her weed all the time.

"Aw, shit, that's what I'm talkin' about! Light that shit up," LaShawn told her.

Whakelah explained to LaShawn why she really needed to smoke the blunt. She told LaShawn that she had gotten another call from the lawyer and that she was spazzing out. She was worried that she could lose everything, most importantly, her kids.

"I gotta come up with this money, or my ass is gon' be homeless, and some more shit," Whakelah told LaShawn, while looking out the window at the drab environment in which they lived.

LaShawn was sitting on her very first faux leather sofa that she had purchased on a rent-to-own agreement from the furniture store. It was long and black with thick cushions for seats and a contoured back. It looked like it cost a few dollars. She had a plastic crate with a slab of mirrored glass that she had found one day while taking the garbage to the incinerator. She gladly took the mirrored glass and plastic crate back to her apartment and made treasure out of another's trash. It turned out to be a great coffee table.

Even though she was slinging weed and coke, LaShawn was still moving on a small level, and all of her money was going to grease the hand of the manager that had gotten her the apartment. There was also day-to-day living and travel expenses. She wasn't able to see any real profit. If she had the money, she would have handed it over to Whakelah so she wouldn't be going through the hell she was.

"I feel you. I need to come up with some money, too. This nickel-and-dime hustling ain't hittin' on shit."

"What the hell are we going to do?"

"I don't know, but I know we need a good break." LaShawn then thought to herself, *What the fuck am I talking about, we need a good break? We gotta take our break out this muthafucka. Ain't nobody gonna give you shit! I'ma make my own break!*

"I'm trying to think," Whakelah said, her mind drawing a blank.

"Oh my God! I don't know why I didn't think of this before!"

"What?" Whakelah was willing to consider almost any idea at this point in time.

"Did you see that nigga's crib? We gon' rob that nigga for everything he's got!" La Shawn said, talking about Swag.

"LaShawn, are you fuckin' crazy?"

"Hell no, I ain't crazy. This bitch done struck gold. She ain't breaking no bread over this way. So, shit, we gon' get ours."

"That's her man, LaShawn. She doesn't have to share what he gives her with us. She can if she wants to, but—"

"But, my ass! Misha's caught up. You see that shit. She don't know if she's coming or going. That nigga got her ass sprung. Where she at? You seen her? She ain't even thinking about us no more. We was all supposed to come up, not just her."

"LaShawn, this is a crazy idea. We need to come up with a different plan."

"Ain't no other plan. This is the plan."

Convincing LaShawn not to rob Swag and to let the plan die wasn't going to be an easy task. LaShawn wasn't playing. She was tired of getting the short end of the stick. She had seen for her own eyes how Swag was living, and the nigga told her he was moving weight. If her homegirl wanted to turn into a punk, that was cool. She had other peeps she could get at to execute her plan.

Whakelah didn't know what to do. Should she tell Misha what LaShawn had planned, or should she go along with LaShawn's plan to rob Swag? Maybe they would come away with enough money to set them both straight. Misha had not called her all week, and she had not been answering her calls. Misha knew Whakelah still needed the money for her case. Maybe she was forgetting all about them.

"Aye, B, I got a job for you," LaShawn said, as she spoke on her cell phone.

LaShawn had met Bernard through one of her uncles. B did his the ski mask way, and was known in the hood for running up in a nigga's crib, quickly getting the stash, and being out within minutes, with no one seeing him come or go.

"What you workin' wit'?"

"A nice score, man. I'm over here in the Web. You know where I'm at, apartment 7A. I ain't gon' do too much singing," LaShawn said, letting B know that she wasn't going to be saying too much over the phone.

"On my way."

Whakelah asked LaShawn, "You sure you know what you doing?"

"I know I need some money, don't you?"

LaShawn knew B liked to smoke and lace his nose, so she spread some weed and coke out on the table. She really didn't have the work to give away, but she looked at it as an investment. The payoff from Swag would more than cover the little bit of shit he was about to smoke and sniff.

B was pleased to see his treats on the table and wasted no time indulging in the trees and powder that rested before him on the reflective glass.

LaShawn allowed B to get nice and lit before she mentioned a word of what she wanted him to do for her. She thought he would be easier to persuade. Long Island was a different area than what B was used to. He was used to sticking and moving from apartment to apartment via staircases and elevators. A getaway car was going to be needed for this job, and neither B, nor LaShawn, nor Whakelah had a car, or a driver's license.

"So what you got going on, LaShawn?" B took his burner out and placed it on the table. He wanted the ladies to know that he stayed strapped at all times.

"I got a nigga that got so much fuckin' money and drugs, it'll make your fuckin' head spin."

"Get the fuck outta here! Who this nigga is?"

"This wack-ass nigga out in Long Island."

"LI?"

"Yeah. Now I know you ain't got no ride and, nigga, neither do we, but we gotta make this shit happen. There's a crazy payday at the end of the rainbow."

"Word? How crazy is the payday?" B sniffed a line a coke from the mirrored glass.

"Yo, it's fuckin' crazy!" Whakelah said, out of the blue. She didn't know where the statement had come from, but before she knew it, it was already out of her mouth.

Something about Whakelah made B believe her. Maybe it was her pretty chocolate skin. He then looked at LaShawn. *Damn! That ass got fatter than it was before.* As the drugs began to take effect, B realized his power. He was in an apartment with two females who needed him to do something for them. His mind started to wonder just how far they were willing to go to gain his services.

"You know I really want to help you fine ladies, I really, really do," B said, tugging on his nose. The coke was making it itch.

LaShawn wasn't stupid. She saw the bulge in B's pants. She was horny anyway and hadn't had any dick since Larry's tired ass. There was really nowhere else to go besides the bathroom. LaShawn could have told Whakelah to leave, but she thought it was time Whakelah saw how real shit could get. They both needed money, so they both needed to handle B.

"Whakelah, let me talk to you for a second," LaShawn said, pulling her best friend into the bathroom.

Whakelah closed the bathroom door behind LaShawn. "You think he's gonna do it?"

"Nah. We gonna have to fuck him."

"What!"

"Sshhh! Don't fuck up that nigga's high. We ain't even gotta do much to him, but that's what he wants. If you want in on this money, you better decide what you gonna do."

There was a knock on the door.

LaShawn looked at Whakelah, and Whakelah nodded her head up and down, giving the okay.

B came into the bathroom. He'd overheard everything. The cocaine had his spider senses on high. They were as ready as they were ever going to be for what he had in store for them.

Whakelah was out of her element, but she was going to be out of her kids' lives if she didn't do something about her circumstances.

B led her over to the sofa and laid her down. He pulled her clothes off slowly and played with her small breasts.

Whakelah kept her eyes glued shut. She didn't want to see any of what was happening. She couldn't believe she had let LaShawn talk her into fucking this man that she didn't even know.

B entered Whakelah, and her body made him feel as if he

had died and gone to heaven. He forgot all about what he had gone there for, but whatever it was, they had him, hook, line, and sinker. B got lost in the warmth as she wrapped her inner muscles around his dick like a baby in a blanket.

"Ooh! Oh shit! You got some tight pussy, girl," B said as he rammed himself up into her slim frame.

Whakelah felt disgusting. She knew the next time she let someone penetrate her flesh, it would be someone she had real love for. Just days ago she was saying that she would like to do what Misha had done to get her paper, but she knew now that she would never chase her paper this way. She couldn't imagine how Misha made this a way of life.

LaShawn fucked B for a second time. She didn't realize how much she needed some dick until she hopped her thick ass onto B's thick shaft. He wasn't bad at all. He was working with a little something. She might even have to get her some more of that. She wanted to show her appreciation for the good dick as well as seal the deal on their anticipated caper, so she capped off the evening by sucking his dick.

"Mmm, hmm, yeah, y'all bitches is all right with me," B said as his dick spurted cum down LaShawn's throat.

LaShawn went and got B a wet paper towel so he could clean himself up. She also told him that she wanted him to know what would be expected of him the night of the robbery, so she set up a meeting time for them to get back up the next day when B was in his right mind. She knew he would be there and on time.

Misha and Swag were lying together, cuddled up in his king-sized bed. She had been in Swag's bed for the past week and hadn't bothered to check on her homegirls. Swag had told her that LaShawn had tried to feel his dick, so she had nothing to say to her. She recognized the signs of jealousy and no longer considered LaShawn one of her best friends. She wondered why Whakelah kept calling but never bothered to leave her a message. Misha figured if Whakelah really needed her, she would explain what she needed. She had her phone turned off because she didn't want her clients interrupting her time with Swag, but it was time for her to get back on the map.

June had been leaving her messages back to back. His proposition was still fresh. She was going to call him and tell him she was good, that she'd found a man, but she was just too wrapped up in Swag to take the time out to do so. Misha made a mental note to call June and to holla at Whakelah as soon as she got the chance.

"This video shoot is the most important and positive thing that's ever happened to me," Misha said, as she ran her fingers through the soft, fine hair on Swag's muscular chest.

"Really? What about the nigga who helped you get the video shoot?"

"Oh, baby, you know what I mean."

"No, I don't know what you mean, but I heard what you said."

"Come on, Swag, you know I love you. That's from my heart. I'm just talking in terms of my dreams."

Swag thought about what Misha had just said. He had never heard her say that it was her dream to be in videos. He brought the idea to her, or so he thought. Swag was more than used to females jocking him for his position, but he thought Misha was different. He was hoping she wasn't like all the rest of the females that jiggled their asses in his face to get a shot at fame?

Misha sensed his disdain for her statements and wanted to correct the situation instantly. She didn't want to upset Swag or to make him change his mind about her being his lover or being the lead in DiViNCi's video. He had no idea of how much he had changed her life. She thought about coming clean and telling him that he'd answered her prayers that night, but one of 50's rules was, never let anyone know your intentions.

"Swag, you mean the world to me. You changed my whole life, and I will never forget that. My feelings for you are real. This is not infatuation. I know in my heart that what I have for you is real love."

"You too young to know what real love is, Misha."

"I am not. I'll be twenty-five soon."

Swag was just testing her. He had hoped that Misha did him love him as much as she said she did because he was falling fast for her. He didn't know what it was about her, but he was very much drawn to her. Swag called Misha young, but the truth was, he had never asked her how old she was. She could have been jailbait, it wouldn't have mattered to him.

"You're not ready for me to say that back to you yet."

"Yeah, right, go 'head, make my day. Make my month. Shit, make my year." Misha grinned from ear to ear.

"Nah, you gotta earn my love."

"Okay, I will," Misha said, still grinning. Swag sure had a way of making her smile and blush all over herself.

"You know how it is in this business I'm in, Misha. I have to protect my heart." Swag kissed her on the forehead.

"Swag, baby, what about me? You don't think that I have to protect mine?"

Misha took a second to put herself in Swag's shoes. She knew he had chicks coming from him at every direction, yet he was taking the time to help her, and give her things that no man ever did. He had dropped her dream of being in a music video right in her lap and showed her that she didn't have to sell her body for money. He showed her that she was worthy of someone simply giving it to her. Yes, she loved this man. Misha had fucked hundreds of men and never had as much an inkling of emotion for any of them. She had gained more in one month with Swag than her lifetime of being Misha Stokes, special services consultant."

"Can we start over?"

Swag looked at her with a bit of confusion.

"Swag, me meeting you was the best thing that has ever happened to me. You making this video shoot possible for me is like a dream come true, and I want to say thank you."

Swag knew she was being sincere. Swag knew why he was feeling Misha. Ty had told him about the condition of the projects she lived in and the area of the Bronx she'd come from. He could tell by looking in her eyes that she'd had a hard life. But through it all, her little tough ass was still looking good and going for hers, hard, and Swag could do nothing but admire her for that.

He grabbed Misha and made passionate love to her.

Misha had rolled over after Swag had gotten finished with her. She checked her cell phone and saw several missed calls. Whakelah had been trying to reach her, and June was also calling her again. Misha thought she had better call Whakelah back to see what she wanted and why she hadn't left a message.

"What's up, Whakelah?"

Whakelah screamed into the phone, "Fuck you, Misha! All you care about is you!"

"Bitch, I'm in love!" Misha didn't mean to scream in front of Swag, but she was caught off guard with the verbal blow Whakelah was dealing her.

"Bitch, please. You don't know what love is. You done fucked every nigga in the metropolitan area!"

Misha quickly got up out of Swag's bed and ran into his bathroom and shut the door, her cell phone stuck to her ear. "What the hell is up with you, Whakelah?" Misha asked in a harsh whisper.

"I should be asking you that!" Whakelah shot back. "I been calling yo' ass all week, but you too busy with a dick up in it."

"Chill, bitch! I'm not in the mood for that shit right now."

Misha didn't need Swag overhearing Whakelah blab about her lifestyle, or rather, her old lifestyle. She wasn't going back to turning tricks in the hood to pay her bills. She wished she hadn't bothered to call Whakelah.

"They moved the date up for my hearing," she told Misha, the sadness ringing out in her voice.

"Oh shit!"

Misha had forgotten all about Whakelah needing money. She had been so wrapped up in Swag and her upcoming video, she hadn't bothered to figure out a plan on how to come up with the money. Now she wished she had called her back earlier. Misha felt obligated to help her friend. She had about two thousand dollars that she had stashed from the video shoot money that Swag had given her, and Whakelah was more than welcome to it.

"LaShawn is saying that you out there chillin' and we still out here starving."

"Fuck LaShawn! That bitch tried to feel my man's dick. Did she tell you that?"

"No, but I knew something was up." Whakelah was calming down, and now that she was able to speak to Misha, she was feeling a whole lot better.

"Well, you was supposed to get back at me. I may not have been answering, but I was checking my messages. You could have hit me with at least that much, if you knew something was up." Misha was getting hot about the situation all over again.

"You know how y'all get down. I try to stay out of it. That shit can get sticky sometimes."

"Whateva, Whakelah." Misha recognized that Whakelah was playing both sides, as she always did.

Misha came back into the bedroom to join Swag back in the bed, but she discovered that he wasn't there. She then began to tell Whakelah how Ty had told her that he was the money behind Swag's operation, that she needed to call up Ty and get her ass back out there and work her way into his money, just as she had worked her way into Swag's.

"I got two gees for you but, girl, you need to make that nigga Ty look out!" Misha said, hinting to her girl that she needed to use her feminine wiles.

"Look out? He hasn't even called me. I don't think he's feelin' me."

"Girl, please. That nigga ain't doin' shit. He's all into his work. Give him some real work to do."

Whakelah was relieved to hear Misha say that she would give her two thousand dollars. She knew then that Misha was still her best friend, that she hadn't completely left her side. Along with the nine hundred that she already had, the two thousand dollars Misha had agreed to give her put her almost at the halfway mark of the six thousand dollars she needed.

After her horrible experience with B, Whakelah just wasn't interested in sleeping with a man for his money, so Ty wasn't an option for her.

Misha had told Whakelah that she had shared her vision for her reality show with Swag and Ty and that they were feeling her idea. Whakelah couldn't believe she had told them about it. Misha went on to tell her that Swag and Ty were friends with some big-time producers and directors down in Atlanta, and that she was trying to get a meeting set up for her.

"Why you ain't tell me all of that before?"

"I didn't want you to get all gassed up and then the shit don't come through."

All of a sudden Whakelah wanted to know all of the details of what Misha had told Swag and Ty about her reality show.

Whakelah had her television show concept copyrighted and registered. She may not have finished high school, and she didn't have much book sense, but she knew enough to do that much. She saw what had happened with Damon Dash and his *Ultimate Hustler* reality television series, and wasn't about to go out like he did.

"You didn't tell them *everything* that I'm planning to do on the show, did you?

"Bitch, please! Don't nobody want to steal your show."

Thoughts of the robbery filled Whakelah's mind while she was talking to Misha on the phone. She wanted to tell Misha about the planned robbery, but she really didn't know how Misha would react. She thought it best not to say anything at all. She would just make sure that Misha was nowhere near Swag when it happened.

FLASHING LIGHTS

LaShawn was concluding her second meeting with B. She described the layout of Swag's house and told him about the significant rooms where she thought he might have money and drugs stashed. This time, it was just B and her. Just as in most singing groups, there was always one member who felt it was time to go solo, LaShawn felt that everything that she was planning would go smoother if she did her dirt all by her lonely.

LaShawn had already talked to Whakelah, who had been in touch with Misha. LaShawn could tell that they had been licking each other's ass. At this point Whakelah would just be in the way. Whakelah had been trying to talk LaShawn out of robbing Swag, but that wasn't going to happen. She let Whakelah know that she could tell Misha if she wanted to, she didn't give a fuck, 'cause it was going to go down. And if Misha got in the way, oh well. . . .

B was able to secure the vehicle for their trip out to Long Island. He was looking forward to that big payday LaShawn was bragging about. Whakelah told LaShawn where Swag lived. She didn't know the physical address, but she described it well enough for them to draw a map.

From the information LaShawn had gotten from Whakelah, there was a video shoot going down tonight, and no one would be in the home, so this would be the perfect night for the robbery. There would be no trouble getting in and out for this master lock-pick.

LaShawn didn't hear any type of alarm system when she was at Swag's house. She really wasn't familiar with what they looked like or what they sounded like, but B assured her that he could tell. He had done a few homes out in Queens and in White Plains that had alarms, but to be absolutely sure, all he had to do was cut Swag's telephone wires.

"You ready?" LaShawn asked B.

"To get paid, and you know this," he told her.

LaShawn opened her apartment door for them to leave, but Larry, who was standing in her doorway, stopped her in her tracks. She had to wipe her eyes to make sure she wasn't seeing things.

"Who the fuck is this nigga?" Larry asked, pointing at B. "My opponent?"

LaShawn was bugging. She had been back in the building for a few months now. The hood ain't do shit, but talk, so she knew Larry was well aware that she had been living a few flights up from him. And wasn't this nigga doing him the whole time? Why had he waited until now to come to her door?

Larry was the last person LaShawn wanted to see. Sick thoughts of the way he'd treated her came rushing to her mind. She pictured herself killing him in various ways. She saw herself reaching for B's gun and blowing his brains out. She then thought of squeezing his neck so hard that he would choke to death. She pictured his face with his eyes bulging out his sockets.

Another sick vision came into her mind. She wanted to cut into him with a knife or any sharp object that would give her the satisfaction of seeing blood gush from his body.

B didn't know who Larry was or what had come over LaShawn, but they were both standing in the way of his crazy payday. He pulled his gun out of his waist and grabbed Larry by his throat, pinning him up in the hallway.

"Look, nigga," B told him, "don't let ya ego get ya ass shot. I'll kill you nigga. Send ya ass straight to the Lord. You feelin' me?"

"Y-y-you got it, man," Larry stuttered, piss trickling down his pants leg.

B let Larry go, and he slid down to the hallway floor and slumped over in his piss puddle.

LaShawn watched as B exposed Larry for the bitch he truly was. All of the times he had laid his fists into her, this nigga couldn't stand up to the next nigga. Nigga was straight pissing on himself when faced with the real heat of the street. She knew she would never have to worry about him coming to her apartment ever again.

She kicked him in his dick with force as they stepped around him to get on the elevator.

"Aaahh!"

"Shut up, you bitch-ass muthafucka! Fuck you!" LaShawn had gotten some of his piss on her natural colored Timbs. She gathered a wad of spit in her mouth and shot it in Larry's face before walking away.

DiViNCi's video was being shot in the evening in several locations in Manhattan. For this particular shot, they were in a large warehouse in the downtown section of TriBeCa, where stars such as Jay-Z, Beyoncé, and Robert De Niro resided. Misha was floating on air knowing she was filming close to where Jay-Z lived. She was hoping to somehow run into him while they were in the area. Misha was a huge fan of his and would have loved to have been in one of his videos.

Misha's outfit for this scene was a pair of faded blue skinny jeans, a leather cocoa-colored motorcycle jacket with nothing but bare skin underneath, and a pair of Gucci cocoa-brown leather boots.

She had makeup artists applying the best makeup to her already beautiful face, and wardrobe stylists pulling her clothes for future scenes and holding them up to her body to see how they would look. They were fussing all over her as they worked to get the look the director desired.

The way she was being treated, you would have thought she was the music artist. They had her feeling like a star on a movie set, and she couldn't get enough of it. People were running here and there to make sure she had whatever she needed. They had her favorite foods, drinks, books, magazines. Whatever she wanted, she had it at her disposal. Misha, a no-name video vixen, knew Swag had to pull some serious strings for her to receive the royal treatment she was getting for her first time in front of the camera.

Whakelah stood to the side and watched as her girl was pampered like a queen. *Now this would have made a great episode on my show,* Whakelah thought. She wanted to bring Kadayja and Marvin with her, but no kids were allowed on the set, by DiViNCi request. They would have jumped out of their skin to be there with her. Whakelah thought it was probably best that the kids not be on the set anyway. The robbery was going down tonight, so there was no telling what to expect.

Whakelah had owed Misha her life after Misha arranged for the lawyer to take $3,100 of his own money to put with the $2,900 she had to make her case go away. He resisted a little in the beginning, but when Misha told him about the pictures that she had been taking of their sexual business meetings he decided he would go along with the plan so that he could keep his marriage intact and make her go away. Misha didn't have any pictures of him and her together, but he sure as hell didn't know it.

Whakelah started to feel guilty. Misha had done nothing

but look out for her, and here she was going along with LaShawn, a chick who meant Misha no good, and who had pretty much convinced her to sleep with a stranger.

The music was starting up. DiViNCi's song, "Money Maker," blared through the sound system that they had set up in the warehouse, and people were taking their places on the set. Dancers were still warming up. It wasn't time for them to do their thing yet, but they were making sure they would all be in sync when it was time.

The warehouse had been broken down into three small sets, a bar scene, a bedroom scene, and a scene where the two of them would be in a Jacuzzi. Multiple scenes of DiViNCi and Misha were filmed. On the surface it looked as if they were involved in a romantic love affair, but those on the set knew otherwise. Misha didn't have eyes for anyone except for Swag.

Whakelah wondered where Swag was. He was supposed to be on the set along with Misha; at least that's where Misha had told her he would be. She hadn't seen Ty either. She was looking forward to seeing him again. She wanted to talk to him about the reality show and what he really thought of it. Misha had told her about Swag and Ty being interested in her show, but after the incident at Club Mansion with that asshole, Steve Smith, and the other jerks who weren't feeling her concept, she needed to hear the opinion straight from the horse's mouth.

Whakelah didn't know why she'd waited so long to call Ty. In fact she hadn't used it since putting it in her phone. From all of the things that Misha had told her about him, she had been blocking her own blessings by not calling him.

She scrolled through the contacts in her phone and pushed Ty's name. She was calling to see if he and Swag would be arriving on the video set anytime soon. She didn't get an answer.

***

Ty was smoking a blunt with Swag at the dining room table of Swag's home. "Aye, man, shouldn't we be leaving for the video shoot?"

"Yeah, in a minute. This shit needs to be weighed out." Swag had a bunch of coke on his dining room table and still had quite a few packages to make. He sifted the cocaine around in its container. He was packaging up for some people on the set, plus members of the cast that he had to get straight. That's how he was paying for DiViNCi's video.

Swag and Ty never filled Misha in on how they funded their record company. It seemed as though everyone was building a recording empire off drugs, so Swag fell in love with the idea. It proved to be a wise decision. They obtained a distribution deal through one of the major labels and was granted the opportunity to be able to own the rights to their songs and keep control of their recordings.

"Come on, man, they can't start the video without us there, dawg," Ty told Swag.

Swag was dressed for his cameo appearance in the video. He had on a blue denim LRG suit with beige Timbs and a beige Gucci skullcap on his head.

"Yo', Ty, go up and get the haze that I left on my dresser. I'ma need that shit."

Ty didn't feel like going to get the haze. He had just smoked a blunt and was about to make himself a quick sandwich. Swag's room was upstairs and on the other side of the house. It took almost five whole minutes to get there.

"Nah, man, I ain't tryin' to go all the way up there. That shit is like eight miles away," he joked.

"Nigga, don't you run marathons and shit? Stop bitchin' and go get that shit." "Nigga, you go get that shit. This is your house, it's your shit, and it's in your room." Ty had the munchies, and all he was about to do was make his sandwich.

"A'ight, nigga. Damn. At least make yourself useful and finish baggin' this shit up."

Swag was on his way up the stairs when his cell phone rang. He looked and saw that it was Misha. He figured that she was at the video set and she was probably wondering where he was. He didn't answer his phone, knowing he'd be seeing his baby in a few.

B had the lights out on the burgundy '07 Dodge Charger, as he and LaShawn approached Swag's house. They saw cars outside and a few lights on inside the mini mansion. LaShawn thought Swag was going to be at the video shoot, and were not expecting anyone to be in the house. She figured he had left some of his friends behind at his house. But it didn't matter to her if Swag was there or not. Someone was there, so it wasn't a good time.

"Yo', B, we gon' have to come back and do this shit some other time."

"Fuck some other time! I'm here now, I ain't goin' nowhere, but in that house right there," B said, pointing to Swag's crib.

B had never seen a place like Swag's in his career of burglaries. LaShawn had been on point like a muthafucka, in his eyes. The house was a castle compared to the apartments, one-family houses, and duplexes that he fucked with. The largest score he had ever done was a church he had hit over on 167th Street and the Grand Concourse. Swag's house looked to be twice the size of the church.

B's dick was hard just sitting there waiting to get inside. He knew there was a bunch of goodies inside of Swag's house just waiting for a nigga like him. There wasn't going to be no coming back. He was getting up in there and he was getting his.

"You think you can take on everybody in that house?"

"LaShawn, I get it in for real. I'm that nigga for real." He pulled his Glock out of his waist. "I'll lift a nigga eight feet off the mufuckin' ground with this shit right here."

"Nigga, we ain't came to catch no bodies, we came to get paid. We gon' chill until they break out, then we go in."

"See, you be dealin' with them bum-ass niggas, like that nigga I had to lay out before we got out here. Keep dealing with them bums, you gon' keep comin' up with crumbs."

LaShawn thought about what B was kicking to her. He was right. Wasn't she there to set it on Swag? So what if he was in the house? Didn't she want to hurt him like he had hurt her the night he dissed her? The nigga had money and drugs, two things she needed. And everything she needed was on the other side of Swag's front door.

"A'ight, nigga, I'm wit' you," LaShawn told him.

B handed her a ski mask. She slid the dark wool mask onto her light face. She reached into the pocket of her navy blue South Pole bubble jacket and pulled out a pair of black wool gloves and put them on her hands. B had a pair of leather gloves that was worn in the middle. You could tell he'd used them an awful lot.

Swag did have a security system. He had an ADT sign sitting right in his front yard that LaShawn missed on her initial visit. B led LaShawn around to the back of Swag's house. He saw the network interface device that connected his phone wires. He was able to unscrew the screws on the network interface device, and disconnect the wires for the telephone system that alerted the security system of a break-in.

Once the security system had been disarmed, LaShawn showed B a patio door that would lead them into the house. It was dark inside of the room where they gained entry. They remained in the dark room, in the cut, until they could assess how many people were there with them in the house. It was very quiet, so B thought it couldn't have been that many people there. That was a good thing, less people meant less witnesses. Witnesses that would not be left behind.

Ty had finished bagging up the coke Swag had left on the table. He had packed it away in a camera bag that held one of the video cameras that was needed for the video shoot. He was now making his sandwich, silently cursing at Swag for making them so late to something that was so important to their music company, when he heard something fall in one of the other rooms.

"Aye! Yo', Swag, nigga, you a'ight?' Ty called out.

No sound followed.

Ty put down the piece of turkey he had in his hand. His gut told him something wasn't right. He turned around to the hole of B's Glock staring him in the face.

"My name ain't Swag, nigga!" B said from behind his ski mask. "Run it!"

"Run what? You must have me fucked up with another nigga!"

"Nah, I ain't got you fucked up, money. Run ya shit!"

Ty's neck was iced out with several chains with pendants swinging from them and his wrists and hands were blinging too. He didn't know what move to make. He had been caught totally off guard. His gun was in his car, and his car was in Swag's driveway. He thought about the knives lodged in the wooden block on the kitchen counter.

B eyed the knives also. "Don't even think about it, nigga! You'll be talking to God by the time you reach for it."

"What you here for?" Ty asked.

"We came to get everything y'all got, nigga! Tell him what we here for," B said.

LaShawn acted like she didn't hear him. She wasn't trying to have her voice identified. B just needed to tie Ty up, find

Swag, tie him up, and they could go around the house and get what they needed and they could be out.

Just as she walked over to B and started to whisper this in his ear, Swag came down and walked in on his own robbery. He didn't bother to ask any questions. He simply pulled his gun, and shot at the person who had a gun pointed in his man's face.

"Aw shit, dawg!" Ty yelled, as B fell at his feet.

"Man, fuck that! Who the fuck are these niggas?" Swag ran over to LaShawn and grabbed her up before she could run.

Ty bent down and pulled B's mask off his bleeding face. "I don't know this nigga." He stood up and kicked him to see if he was dead or alive. He wasn't moving.

"Yeah, well, we know this one," Swag said, as he pulled the ski mask from over LaShawn's face.

LaShawn was shook and she was stuck. Her mother was going to have a heart attack behind this. *Oh my God! What the hell am I supposed to do now?*

The flashing lights of the police cars set Swag's normally quiet neighborhood on blast. He explained to the police officers that LaShawn and B had attempted to rob his home and that he used his registered weapon to halt them, mentioning the ski masks and strange vehicle on the scene, to corroborate his story.

But before the cops had arrived, Swag had sent Ty ahead to the video shoot with everybody's pay. He didn't want the entire night to be a disaster.

He would still have to be processed for the murder, but with the connections he had, he more than likely would not see the inside of a jail cell.

Misha spotted Ty. It looked as if he was handing out envelopes to the cast and crewmembers on the set. She ran up to him wanting to know where Swag was. She had done the entire video without Swag being there and was past worried. He had not answered one of her calls, and that wasn't like him.

"Ty, where's Swag?"

"Ask ya girl," he said, looking in Whakelah's direction.

"Whakelah?" Misha asked, looking confused.

"Tell her, or I'll tell her," Ty said.

Whakelah didn't really know what to tell Misha. She didn't know where Swag was. She had been trying to find out just as well as Misha was. "I . . . I don't know where he is, Ty," Whakelah said.

"What were you calling me for earlier? To see if we had left the house, so you could send ya peoples to come and rob your girlfriend's man?" Ty looked at Misha with suspicion. "Or maybe you was in on it too, Misha."

"In on what?" Misha looked from Whakelah to Ty.

"She didn't know anything about it!" Whakelah blurted out.

"Oh, but now I see, you did!"

"Please, somebody tell me where Swag is?" Misha said, now on the verge of tears.

Ty was glad to know Misha didn't have anything to do with setting up his man, Swag really had true feelings for her, and that would have really fucked his man up.

"Swag and ya girl LaShawn is in jail!" Ty screwed his face at Whakelah.

"In jail?"

"Tell Misha what you know, Whakelah," Ty demanded. He didn't know how much Whakelah knew, but he wanted to know. He was considering fucking with her, but if she was on some larceny shit like this, he was leaving her right where she stood.

Whakelah cleansed her soul, telling Misha everything she knew. She even told Misha that LaShawn had her sleep with B.

She told Misha how sorry she was, that she too had a moment of jealousy over all of the goodness coming into Misha's life. She told Misha that she loved her as a best friend, and that she was grateful for all of the things she had done for her, no matter what Misha thought of her afterward.

BEHIND THESE WALLS

The lights from the camera were bright as the cameraman adjusted the power of the glare. The warden had allowed Whakelah and the crew from her reality television show, *Keepin' It Real*, to come in and interview one of their inmates. Whakelah sat face to face with this prisoner in hopes of deterring people who watched her show from suffering the same fate.

As soon as Ty heard Whakelah's explanation for keeping quiet about the robbery, he had to admit, he believed her. He was already interested in expanding his record company into other media outlets, so he thought, Why give the production company in Atlanta the chance at Whakelah's show, when he and Swag could very well do it themselves?

Misha was smiling as she held onto Swag's waist. She was happy to be at his side and planned on being never without him again. Misha was so relieved when Swag had called to tell her that the police had released him after what had gone down at his crib. They had shot the cameo scenes the next day, and he was still able to make it into DiViNCi's music video. Thanks to the video editor, he looked like he was never missing.

Swag was there at the prison because he had to be, he was one of the executive producers of *Keepin' It Real*, and was checking on his investment.

Whakelah was now living her dream, a dream that not many believed in. But she believed, and she never stopped believing. She made it a point to tell all of her viewers in each episode before closing out her show to keep believing in their dreams and to keep striving to accomplish their goals no matter how unattainable they may seem.

Misha, Swag, and Ty stood outside of the cell along with a few prison guards. The prisoner didn't want them inside.

LaShawn had been served with five years in prison for her part in the robbery. When Whakelah reached out to her to do the show, at first, she didn't want to do it. She wasn't trying to see Whakelah or Misha. She no longer considered them her best friends. They had caused her enough trouble. But when Whakelah told her she would make sure her books were good for her whole bid, she didn't hesitate to accept. Whakelah also told her the name of her show and to make sure that she lived up to its title while the cameras were rolling, LaShawn promised that she would.

"Are you happy now?" Whakelah asked.

"In a way, I am. Can't nobody hurt me no more," LaShawn said, meekly.

"So you felt that people were trying to hurt you?"

"Yeah, I mean, I was in an abusive relationship. He hurt me."

"Who else was trying to hurt you, LaShawn?"

"That bitch, Misha, that muthafucka, Swag, and you too! All of y'all!"

"Well, LaShawn, Misha's right there on the other side of the cell door. Is there anything you want to say to her, or me, or both of us?" Whakelah pointed to Misha. She knew she was opening a can of worms, but that's what reality television was all about.

"Hell, yeah! Fuck both of y'all bitches. Y'all didn't want to see a bitch come up. Well, I'ma come up anyway. Five years ain't shit!"

"So you blame us for what you're going through?" Whakelah

was saddened by her homegirl's comments. She was hoping LaShawn had time to think about what she had done and to feel some type of remorse.

"Yeah, I blame y'all. Y'all made me feel like I wasn't good enough. I'm just as good as y'all. Nah, fuck that! I'm better. Yeah, that's right. I said it. I'm better than both of y'all."

LaShawn jumped out of her seat, and the prison guards warned her to stay seated.

"That nigga done beat the brains out that dumb bitch," Misha said, watching LaShawn's actions from in between the openings of the steel cell bars that separated them. Misha didn't understand why LaShawn was still so hateful toward them. She had brought all of this mess on herself.

"No one person is better than anyone else, LaShawn. We all breathe, and we all bleed, and eventually we will all die. I know you're hurting right now, and so you're lashing out at us because we're all you have right now," Whakelah told her. "And that's fine. I'll accept that."

LaShawn could see that Whakelah was putting on a show for her viewers, and she was doing a really good job. But LaShawn wasn't acting, she was hurting for real. Once the cameras stopped rolling, Whakelah and Misha would be going on with their new lives and she'd be going back behind the concrete walls and sliding steel bars. She suddenly felt like an animal trapped in a cage and needed desperately to escape. Whakelah wanted her to keep it real. Well, LaShawn thought it was time she make good on her promise.

"Since we suppose to be keepin' it real, why don't you tell your viewers that you could have been sitting in this chair that I'm sitting in now for welfare fraud?"

"I don't have a thing to hide. Yes, I almost did time for welfare fraud. And I would encourage all who contemplate scamming the system to think again, because they'll catch you up in some mess that you don't want to be in." Whakelah dark brown skin appeared pale in color as she addressed LaShawn's snitchin' ass.

"Tell them how you got out of it, since you keepin' it one hun'ed. Tell them how your girl Misha fucked your case away, with her ho ass. She fucked your lawyer, and fucked Swag, just to get into that music video."

"Don't worry about it, bitch!" Misha yelled, lunging at the steel bars that separated them. "You just mad because he didn't want to fuck your triflin' ass!" She wanted to burst into the cell and beat the life out of LaShawn.

Again, Swag held onto her. He wasn't feeding into LaShawn's performance. After all of the underhanded shit she tried to pull, her words held no weight with him. Once he had Misha calm, he gave her a deep and passionate kiss to let her know everything was still all good between them.

Whakelah didn't appreciate LaShawn putting them out there like that. She told her to keep it real, but she was expecting her to talk about her own fucked-up circumstances, not theirs.

She thought about the night LaShawn convinced her to fuck B, a dude that she didn't even know, violating the love and respect she had for her body. She thought about all of the times LaShawn had eaten food at her house and all of the other ways she had helped her. Before she realized it, she had lost control of her actions, and her slim fists were pounding into LaShawn's face.

"All we did was try to help yo' ass! Who came and got yo' ass off the streets? We did! Who fed yo' ass when you needed something to eat? We did! I didn't have to fuck that nigga. You could have handled that on your own, but I did it, 'cause I thought you was my girl!" Whakelah shouted, as she punched away.

The cameraman zoomed in and made sure he captured every bit of the drama that was unfolding. The prison guards rushed in to stop the pummeling Whakelah was giving LaShawn, while Misha was cheering Whakelah on, wishing she could get a piece of the action.

"Get this little bitch off of me!" LaShawn told the guards. "I'm outta here!" She knew that one punch from her heavy hand would send Whakelah to the other end of the jail cell and she didn't want to get into any more trouble than she was already in.

"We ya girls, LaShawn. We been ya girls, we still ya girls, and we gon' always be ya girls!" Whakelah yelled.

The guards had been ordered to take LaShawn back to her cell. Once the warden had gotten wind of the altercation, it was time to shut the production down.

As LaShawn made her way back to her cell, she took a moment to reflect. She knew she couldn't be mad at no one but herself, but it was much easier to blame everyone else. Her mother was so very disappointed in her, she wouldn't even come to visit her. She didn't have anyone but Whakelah and Misha, and she was turning her back on them, when they were the ones who should have been turning their backs on her.

"Is there anything that you wanna say to the people of New York City and around the world, Whakelah?" Whakelah's cameraman anxiously asked her. If they had more episodes like this one, *Keepin' It Real* was guaranteed to be a success.

Whakelah regained her composure and thought long and hard before she spoke. "Yeah, I got something I wanna say," she said. "LaShawn ended up in prison because we were all on a paper chase. Y'all know what I'm talking about. A serious mission. A chase to get that paper by any means necessary. So I want all of y'all to keep this in mind—Don't chase the paper, let the paper chase you!"

Notes

Notes

Notes